A CHRISTMAS KISS

As William neared the stairs, Melanie came out from her place of concealment. "William," she said timidly, "I wanted to talk to you."

At her voice he started slightly and turned around with a look of surprise. The candle in his hand threw a flickering light over his features.

"I wanted to talk to you," she said again. "To thank you, rather. I don't know how we—how *I* would have managed without you today."

He smiled a little and shook his head. "What I did was a pleasure."

"But I do need to thank you. I haven't been very deserving of your kindness, William. I've treated you abominably these past few days. And yet you've been so good, so generous . . . so forgiving about it all. I wish there was something I could do to make it up to you."

"Do you?" said Sir William. There was a peculiar expression on his face. He glanced upward, and Melanie, following his gaze, saw that they were standing beneath the hall chandelier, among whose branches had been entwined a few sprigs of mistletoe. Sir William put down his coat and candlestick upon the stairs and took a step toward Melanie. She realized what he was going to do an instant before he did it, but somehow her mind failed to act in that instant to prevent it. Putting his hands on her shoulders, he bent down and kissed her gently, a mere brushing of his lips on hers. . . .

—from THE CHRISTMAS BEAU by Joy Reed

A CHRISTMAS COURTSHIP

Carola Dunn
Karla Hocker
Joy Reed

Zebra Books
Kensington Publishing Corp.
http://www.zebrabooks.com

ZEBRA BOOKS are published by

Kensington Publishing Corp.
850 Third Avenue
New York, NY 10022

First Printing: November, 1996
10 9 8 7 6 5 4 3 2 1

Printed in the United States of America

Contents

THE CHRISTMAS PARTY

Carola Dunn

One

Candle in hand, Prudence stood in the middle of the deserted ballroom, head cocked, listening. The thud of booted footsteps crossing the anteroom swiftly approached. She was about to be caught snooping.

Oh, *bother,* she thought, snuffing the candle. Who could have guessed anyone would come to the ballroom at dusk on a winter's afternoon? At the front of the great mansion, Christmas guests were arriving in swarms. What with greeting them, offering refreshments, showing them to their chambers, heating and carrying water, preparing dinner, the entire household from marquis to scullery boy should be fully occupied.

Someone was not. On silent, slippered feet Prudence sped to the nearest French window alcove. The doors were locked. She pulled one crimson velvet curtain across the bay just enough to hide her, at the last moment whisking a corner of the hem of her brown stuff gown out of sight.

The footsteps stopped. She held her breath. The footsteps resumed, rapid now, coming straight toward her.

Resigned, she let out her breath on a sigh. She was about to emerge when a brusque hand flung back the curtain. A tall man in a caped greatcoat stared down at her. The last light entering through the glass behind her showed no more of his face than dark hair and a frown, but he smelled of sandalwood, horse, and fresh air.

"Who the deuce are you?" he demanded, stepping back to look her up and down.

Prudence raised her chin. At eight-and-twenty she was too old to be intimidated by that sort of look. "I am Miss Savage," she said with what dignity she could muster after being discovered skulking behind the arras.

"Savage by name but not by nature, I trust." He sounded odiously mocking. "Are you a guest here?"

"Not precisely."

"A guest's servant?"

"No!"

"Don't tell me I have captured a female burglar! It will be a nine days' wonder in the county."

"I'm not a burglar," Prudence said crossly. "If you must know, I am an actress with the company the Marquis of Easthaven has hired to entertain his guests."

"Ah, I see." Now his tone was enigmatic. She wished she could make out his expression. "Might one enquire, Miss Savage, just what you were doing in his lordship's ballroom in the dark? I hope I've not been so crass as to interrupt an assignation?"

"Certainly not! It wasn't dark when I came, still isn't quite, and besides, I have a candle." She waved it at him. It promptly fell out of the candlestick.

He stooped to pick it up, and courteously replaced it in the holder. "An unlit candle—useful!" he observed.

"For heaven's sake, I blew it out when I heard you coming."

"Too late. I rode cross-country, and I saw the light through the windows when I passed the end of the garden. I came straight here from the stables."

"I wondered how you knew I was here. It didn't seem likely anyone should come in by chance at this hour."

"Most unlikely, ma'am. So I venture to repeat my question: What are you doing in his lordship's ballroom?"

Cornered again, Prudence sighed. "I daresay you will consider me both impertinent and gooseish. I've never been in such a splendid house before, and I simply wanted to see a grand ballroom."

"Now you have seen it, what do you think of it?"

"To tell the truth," she confided, "it's somewhat gaudy. Crimson curtains, royal blue chairs, daffodil-yellow walls, and gilt everywhere. It's like something a stage manager might dream up."

The gentleman laughed. "How would you decorate a ballroom?" he enquired.

"Palest blue walls," said Prudence at once, "the shade of the winter sky on a fine day, with straw-colored chairs and curtains and everything else white. Nothing to clash with the ladies' gowns; nothing to draw attention from their ornaments."

"I can tell you've been pondering the subject. What an unusual actress you are!"

"Not at all," she disclaimed hastily. "I'm really quite ordinary. Oh, dear, it's quite dark now. I must go."

"Take my arm and I'll pledge to navigate us both to a safe harbor."

A hint of warm intimacy in the way he spoke alerted Prudence instantly. She had been an actress long enough to know what *that* meant.

"No, thank you, sir, I believe I can find my own way." She set out tentatively in the direction of the arch to the anteroom. The white pillars on either side provided landmarks even in the gloom. A thought struck her as she reached the threshold, and she turned. His black bulk loomed close behind her. A trifle breathless, she begged, "Pray don't tell any of the marquis's family I stigmatized their ballroom as gaudy."

"Too late again, Miss Savage," the tall gentleman drawled, unmistakably amused. "Permit me to introduce myself: Rusholme at your service. Lord Easthaven is my father."

With a smile, the Earl of Rusholme watched the young woman scurry away. As soon as they reached a lamplit passage, she had put on speed and dashed ahead, leaving him sauntering after.

He still had not seen her face; but her figure was trim enough, even in the sober gown more suited to abigail than actress, and though tall, she moved with a sprightly grace. Her short, curly hair glimmered in a halo not quite red, rather the tawny color of autumn beech leaves.

Delightful—and he was tiring of Yvette, who grew more rapacious every time he visited the small house in Bedford Street.

Though the little Savage would no doubt turn out as avid for expensive gifts as any of the sisterhood, she was, despite her denial, different from any actress he had ever met. For a start, that gown: he'd like to see her in silks and satins, prior, of course, to seeing her in nothing at all.

Then there was her speech. Any moderately good actress could ape the accents of the gentry, but her vocabulary was another matter. "Stigmatized as gaudy," indeed! Rusholme grinned. Mama's taste was notoriously *outré,* though no one would dream of saying so in the marchioness's hearing. He would not betray the girl's candid judgment.

She had refused to take his arm. A little coyness did her no harm in his eyes. Perhaps she had a jealous lover from whom he'd have to woo her, or perhaps she was simply teasing, leading him on. Either suggested a practiced Paphian, which suited him very well. Given that few actresses earned a decent living on the stage, nonetheless he had no stomach for beguiling any female onto the primrose path. Nor had he any desire to teach an inexperienced ladybird the tricks of her trade.

His pleasant ruminations on the joys of a new mistress were cut off when he heard voices in the entrance hall ahead. He was tempted to escape up the back stair to his chamber. However, he had promised his parents he would be on hand to greet their guests and he was already late, due to Salamander's cast shoe. Best make his excuses before removing the travel dirt from his person.

"Confound it!" he swore *sotto voce* as he strode into the spacious, domed vestibule, brightly lit by a huge chandelier, and saw the new arrivals.

Only one possible reason for the Winkworths' presence came

to mind. Rusholme had hoped to have Christmas free of the machinations of match-making mamas. He should have known better. His own mother was as anxious to see him married as any mother of an eligible damsel.

Before he could cut and run, Lady Winkworth spotted him. "Dear Rusholme," she gushed as he reluctantly approached the group. "How obliging of you to take the trouble to be here to welcome us when you have clearly only just arrived yourself."

He bowed. "A fortuitous encounter, ma'am."

She beamed, obviously under the impression that fortuitous was a synonym for fortunate. He found himself wondering whether Miss Savage knew the difference.

Turning to his parents to apologize for his tardiness, he was taken on the blind side by Lady Anne Winkworth, who clamped herself to his arm. "So kind of you to invite us, Lady Easthaven," she cooed, fluttering long, dark eyelashes at Rusholme. "I quite dreaded being parted from so *dear* a friend over the holidays."

"I trust you will enjoy the festivities," said the marquis jovially.

Lady Easthaven's manner was considerably cooler. Beckoning to the nearest puce-liveried footman, she said, "Samuel will show you to your chambers, Lady Winkworth. If your personal servants are not yet arrived, you have only to ring for assistance."

Unwillingly detaching herself from Rusholme's arm, Lady Anne followed her parents and the footman. At the foot of the marble, gilt-banistered stairs she glanced back, smiled, and gave a little wave.

"Have you an understanding with that young woman, Garth?" the marchioness asked austerely, pulling her green and pink Norwich silk shawl closer about her purple-clad shoulders.

"No, Mama," he assured her, kissing her cheek. "I have stood up with her at several balls in Town, but I've never even so much as called on the Winkworths."

"Then her conduct is unbecomingly forward."

"Come, come, my dear," said her husband. "Modern manners

are freer than in our day, and a little flirtation does no harm. A pretty chit, hey, Garth?"

"Lady Anne is considered a dazzler, sir."

"And her family and fortune are irreproachable," Lady Easthaven conceded.

"Otherwise you'd not have invited her, would you, Mama? I believe Lady Anne has refused a number of acceptable offers, but if she's holding out in hopes of becoming a marchioness, I fear she is doomed to disappointment."

His father laughed. "Your mother has more than one string to her bow, my boy," he commiserated. "Come, my dear, let us sit down for a few minutes before the next consignment of feminine pulchritude and good breeding arrives."

"She's here," said Rusholme as the door knocker sounded, "and I'm off."

Taking the stairs two at a time, he was at the top of the first flight when a familiar voice stopped him. After a moment's hesitation, he ran back down. His friend's recent marriage had been a nasty shock, but the Honorable Mrs. Denham was an inoffensive young lady.

Two carriages must have arrived on each other's heels, for another group entered as he greeted the Denhams. "David, my dear chap, good to see you. And Mrs. Denham, welcome to Easthaven."

"Thank you, Lord Rusholme."

"Hello, Garth." David looked oddly guilty. The explanation was not far to seek. "Let me present you to my sister-in-law, Miss Kitty Wallace."

Betrayed! Rusholme flashed his so-called friend a fulminating glance. Gad, a fellow had only to get himself leg-shackled and he wanted the rest of the world to join him in parson's mousetrap!

Miss Wallace, shrinking behind her brother-in-law's broad back, had to be bodily hauled forth by her sister to make her timid curtsy. Rusholme bowed and said everything proper. No doubt the poor little mouse had had dinned into her that she must · endeavor to fix his interest. Already she bored him, but at least she didn't appear at all likely to chase him shamelessly, as did Lady Anne.

For David's sake he'd be kind to her, without giving the slightest excuse for raised hopes.

A footman bore the three away, and Rusholme turned to the latest comers. No marriageable females, thank heaven! The stout, good-natured Lady Adeline had been his mother's crony forever, and her husband was a political colleague of the marquis's.

With them was Lady Adeline's nephew, Henry Ffoliot. Though not an intimate friend, he was one of Rusholme's Corinthian set, a good enough fellow if rather more of a libertine than Rusholme quite cared for. He was rumored to be all to pieces, in fact to be hanging on his aunt's sleeve, desperately in need of a wealthy bride. No doubt he'd be glad to take Lady Anne off Rusholme's hands. Unfortunately, that worldly young lady would never cast a second glance at an untitled wastrel, for all his dashing good looks.

Yet another footman led the trio away. "How many more are you expecting today?" Rusholme asked his mother.

"No more, I believe. Julia and family will not be here till tomorrow. Maria arrived earlier. I understand your nieces and nephews are eagerly awaiting a visit from their uncle."

"I'll go up to the nursery as soon as I've changed. More guests coming tomorrow, too?"

"Yes," said the hospitable marquis with deep gratification, "we'll have a full house, as usual. Did I tell you I've hired a troupe of actors to entertain us? Old-fashioned mummery and carol singing on Christmas Day, and they'll put on *She Stoops to Conquer* on Twelfth Night when the neighbors join us."

"An excellent choice, sir."

Rusholme went up to his chamber at last. He looked forward to seeing Miss Savage as Kate Hardcastle, a lively rôle to suit her lively nature.

He stopped with his greatcoat half off as a horrid notion struck him. He had never seen her face. Suppose she was not to play

Kate but old Mrs. Hardcastle? Suppose she was buck-toothed, pudding-faced, or afflicted with a frightful squint?

It didn't bear thinking of.

Two

"Miss! Miss!"

The urgent whisper in her ear drew Prudence from her dream in which she waltzed around a pale blue ballroom in the arms of a tall man in a greatcoat. All she could see of his face was a pair of dark eyebrows, but she knew he was laughing at her. She just had time to wonder when she had learned to waltz before full awareness returned and she opened her eyes.

"Miss, you said to wake you." By the light of a tallow candle, the kitchen maid looked down at her anxiously. "I brung you tea."

"Thank you, Rosie. But it's still dark out."

"They goes out soon as it begins to get light, miss, acos ev'yone's so busy once the nobs start to wake up. In about twenty minutes, Mr. Samuel said. I got to go. There's scores o' kettles to be filled."

She scampered out. Prudence sat up, filled with a moment's thankfulness. Her own life had not been easy, but compared with that poor child. . . . Somehow she'd spare a sixpence for Rosie when she left Easthaven.

Swinging her legs out of bed, she shivered and reached for her shawl. Behind her Aimée stirred.

"What the devil . . . ?" came her sleepy voice.

"Sorry, I didn't mean to wake you. It's Christmas Eve. I'm going out with the servants to gather holly, remember?" She pattered across to the washstand and doused her face in icy water.

"You're dicked in the nob, Sera, you know? Still, since I'm awake, I suppose I might as well go, too." Aimée sat up, stretched, and yawned.

"We have twenty minutes. Eighteen now. Rosie brought me tea. Do you mind sharing a cup?"

"Share a bed, share a cup, there's . . . Eighteen minutes?" she shrieked. "Dammit, I can barely dress in eighteen minutes; what about my face?"

Prudence laughed. "You don't need powder and paint to cut evergreens. Come on. Hurry."

Half an hour later the two actresses perched beside the carter on a farm wagon pulled by a huge cart horse whose breath formed clouds in the chilly air. As they rolled across a misty park white with frost, Prudence was glad of her new cloak. Though made of cheap duffle, it was thick and warm, and a gay spring green quite unlike the drab browns, grays and navy blues she had always worn before.

Behind them, on piles of sacks among ladders, pruning hooks, and shears, sat Samuel, First Footman and director of the operation, two lesser footmen, and a pair of giggling maids. Several undergardeners trudged alongside.

Aimée shivered in her elegant rose-pink velveteen pelisse. "I can't think why I let you persuade me to come," she grumbled. "I haven't picked holly since I was a child."

"I never have. My father said decorating with holly and evergreens was a pagan custom to be condemned by all good Christians. Oh, look!"

A blood-red sun rose through the mists ahead. The track curved to the left and started up a wooded hillside. On the very edge of the wood stood a luxuriant, glossy-leaved holly with masses of scarlet berries glowing in the ruddy light.

"Do stop," said Prudence as the cart rumbled on. "We shall never find any better berries."

"Can't cut that lot, miss," Samuel told her. "We have to leave the best berries, 'specially them closest to the house. Later on some of the nobs'll come out, the young uns, and they won't want to look far."

"If the ladies and gentlemen go gathering, why must you?"

"They get bored afore there's near enough picked. His lordship likes a good show."

"This afternoon," put in one of his juniors, "they'll stand about giving orders while we run up'n'down ladders, and then they'll say they been putting up decorations."

"Anyways," said a maid tolerantly, "it's fun and we get to decorate the servants' hall. We even hang mistletoe, though her la'ship won't allow it in the rest o' the house."

"Who needs mistletoe?" Samuel leaned over to give her a smacking kiss, and everyone laughed.

The wagon stopped in a clearing. Surrounding it, scattered among the leafless oaks and birches, grew holly, laurel, spruce, and fir.

"Remember," said Samuel, "don't cut the berries on the bushes closest to the clearing. Leastways, only the ones growing round the back."

Laughing again, they spread out between the trees. Heaps of frosted leaves crunched beneath their feet as they filled sacks with greenery, calling to each other when they found a particularly good crop of berries. To Aimée's delight, she was the first to find an oak with mistletoe growing on its branches. She granted a kiss to the gardener who climbed up to pick it. Prudence started singing "The Holly and the Ivy," and they all joined in.

It was when the carol ended that she heard childish voices back in the clearing. Her sack was as heavy as she could manage, so she had an excuse better than mere curiosity to return to the cart.

The man stood with his back to her, a tall figure in a caped greatcoat, bare-headed, dark-haired. She knew at once who he was. He had danced in her dreams.

She stopped, ready to flee. After all, she had sneaked about Lord Rusholme's home and insulted his family's ballroom. He had every right to be affronted, though he had sounded more amused. Then a small girl ran up to him, grabbed his hand, and pointed at Prudence.

"Look, Uncle Garth, there's a wood elf."

Rusholme turned. The wood elf stood poised for flight, her spring-leaf green hood thrown back, revealing her autumn-leaf curls, revealing a faultless face: delicately arched brows, rosy cheeks, mouth made for kissing, chin slightly pointed as befitted an elf.

"She's not an elf," said his ten-year-old nephew scornfully. "She's a lady. And she's got a pair of shears." He dashed up to Miss Savage, skidded to a halt, removed his uncle's beaver from his head and made his bow. "I'm William Braverton, ma'am. Please may we borrow your shears? We came to cut holly for the nursery, but Uncle Garth forgot to bring shears or a knife or anything."

"Perhaps your uncle forgot on purpose, Mr. Braverton. They are very sharp. Ask him whether you may borrow them."

"May I, sir? I swear I'll be careful."

"As long as you don't let your sisters near them."

"Thank you!" The boy took the shears Miss Savage held out to him, then said off-handedly, "As a matter of fact, it's *Lord* Braverton. Are you taking that sack to the cart, ma'am? I'll carry it for you."

She smiled at William—but it was Rusholme's heart that turned over. He moved toward her as if drawn by a magnet.

Maria would have his blood for letting her children consort with an actress. He didn't care. Yet Miss Savage could not possibly be as captivating as he had thought her yesterday, even before he saw her face.

And now that he was closer, he saw even that was not perfect. Her nose was not quite long enough for Classical beauty, her chin was definitely pointed, her mouth a trifle too wide, her brow too broad. And she was older than he'd expected, though he'd had no reason to think her any particular age.

No diamond after all. Had he seen her properly last night, he'd not have been so bewitched by her voice and her disarming candor as actually to judge her intelligent on the basis of a single word!

"A fortuitous meeting, Miss Savage," he said.

Her sparkling eyes were hazel, he noted as she raised her eyebrows. "How can it be anything else, my lord? You could not know I was here, and I was specifically informed that ladies and gentlemen are not expected to rise for several hours."

"Indeed! I'd have you know I generally ride at this hour, only this morning I was captured by these little . . ."

"Savages?"

"Imps. How did you guess I deliberately forgot to bring any cutting implements?"

She laughed. "I beg your pardon for divulging your secret. I believe you may trust your nephew. He has excellent manners."

" 'Manners makyth man'?" he queried.

"That's rather overstating the case, but they certainly smooth the paths in life of both he who possesses them and those he encounters."

Intrigued, he was going to pursue the subject, but Sophie pulled on his sleeve. "I have good manners, Uncle Garth," she said in a loud whisper.

"You certainly do, and I am forgetting mine. Miss Savage, may I present my niece, Lady Sophie Braverton."

"How do you do, Lady Sophie," said the actress gravely as the child curtsied. "Are you enjoying your walk in the woods?"

"Yes, ma'am. Please, are you a wood elf?"

"I'm afraid not, just an ordinary person. I expect the wood elves have all gone to sleep in their trees for the winter."

"Oh, yes, I 'spect so. Do you want to come with me and Uncle Garth to watch William cutting holly?"

Miss Savage looked questioningly at Rusholme. He nodded, knowing he ought not. The contrast between her profession and her cultured speech and manners fascinated him. Perhaps she was no dryad, but she was a mystery he was determined to solve. What was more, the vivacity of her less than perfect features was more alluring than any static beauty.

Sophie took her hand, and he saw it was bare, the slender fingers red with cold. "Have you no gloves?" he said roughly.

"I do indeed, in my pocket. I took them off to keep them from

being stained with sap, which is horridly difficult to wash out."
She pulled on gray woollen mittens.

When she was his mistress, she'd have kid gloves and a fur
muff, and a maid to do her laundry.

He must be mad to let the children talk to the woman he intended to take under his protection! But Sophie was tugging them
both toward the holly tree where William's shears snip-snapped
as little Bella crowed in delight, her tiny hand firmly held by her
big sister. Too late now to change his mind.

Prudence was surprised at Lord Rusholme's tolerance. Young
William had put him in an awkward spot, to be sure, yet most
gentlemen would have no difficulty dismissing a mere actress,
with or without courtesy. Perhaps, overwhelmed by the responsibility for four children not his own, he felt that any female—
even an actress—must be of assistance!

She stole a glance at him. He was about her own age, maybe
a year or two older. Not quite handsome. Though his aristocratic
features were finely carved, his cheekbones were a trifle too
prominent, adding to a somewhat arrogant, cynical air.

Still, the heir to a marquis was entitled to a touch of arrogance
while the toadying he must often meet with accounted for the
cynicism. In contrast to his general air of superiority, his dark
hair was in disarray, although there was no breeze. Prudence
suspected he had given a ride on his shoulders to the moppet
now dancing up and down with excitement ahead of them.

"Sera!" Aimée came through the woods toward them, a doting
gardener at her heels carrying both her sack and his own. "Who's
your friend?"

"Lord Rusholme." Prudence was dismayed to find herself
ashamed to be associated in his mind with her flamboyant colleague. Despite their hurry, Aimée had found time to rouge her
lips and cheeks and darken her lashes. Her pelisse might be in-
adequate against the cold, but it fitted snugly over a generous
bosom and was short enough to display a neat pair of ankles.
"Miss Orlando, my lord."

His lordship nodded curtly.

Unabashed, Aimée batted her eyelashes with a coy smile, then winked at Prudence and said, "Never fear, Sera, I'm no poacher. Come on, Billy boy, let's dump this lot and see if we can find some more mistletoe." She tripped off toward the cart, followed by the scarlet-faced gardener, who ducked his head to the earl as he passed, his hands being full of sacks of greenery.

"Is that lady your friend, Miss Savage?" Sophie enquired.

Lord Rusholme's set mouth and drawn brows proclaimed his displeasure. He had flatteringly ignored Prudence's unsuitability as an acquaintance for his nieces and nephew, but Aimée's brazen vulgarity obviously reminded him of Prudence's background. She started to excuse herself, to say she must go and help fill another sack.

However, at that moment, the littlest girl set up a wail of fright. Instinctively Prudence ran to her and crouched at her side.

"Bella tried to pick up some holly," her sister explained.

"It did *sting* me," sobbed Bella.

"Did it feel like a sting?" Prudence said soothingly. "It was only a prick, my dear. Look, the holly leaves are prickly. Let me see your hands. Goodness, you are wearing mittens just like mine."

" 'Cept mine's blue."

"So they are." Prudence pulled them off and examined the chubby little fingers.

"Is there blood?" asked Sophie hopefully, which set off another wail from Bella.

"Not a drop. All it needs is to be kissed better. There, and there."

Wails and sobs ceased. Prudence glanced up at Lord Rusholme, who stood there looking distinctly harassed. She couldn't resist: "Perhaps Uncle Garth should kiss it better, too."

His expression martyred, he complied with the demand of upreaching arms. "It's time we returned to the house," he announced. "Your nurse will be wondering where you are. William, see if there is a sack to spare in the cart for your spoils. Yes, Miss

Savage," he said as the boy ran off, "I deliberately forgot a sack as well."

"Unnecessary in the circumstances," she agreed with a smile.

The girls went after William, to see the big horse. Once again Prudence was about to make her excuses and leave, but Lord Rusholme seemed to think it incumbent upon him to make polite conversation.

"Your name is Sarah?" he asked.

"No." She felt an irrepressible blush rising. Why had she picked such a ridiculous alias? "Aimée calls me Sera, short for Seraphina."

He grinned. "Seraphina Savage? As likely as Aimée Orlando! A stage name, I take it."

"Yes. I was going to call myself Seraphina Silver, but it sounded too cloyingly sweet."

"Savage is much better, an intriguing contrast. Your taste is impeccable—as I already have reason to know."

Her cheeks grew hotter. "I was too flustered by my *faux pas* last night to apologize for my rudeness about your ballroom."

"I'll forgive you, provided you tell me your real name."

She looked up at his teasing smile, the quizzical gleam in his brown eyes. He was dangerously charming, and she was an actress, fair game to gentlemen of his kind. Perhaps her staid, stodgy, commonplace name would protect her, depress notions romantical and erotic alike.

"Prudence Figg, my lord."

He shouted with laughter. "Prudence! Could anything be less appropriate?"

His reaction was justified, she had to admit; although for twenty-seven years she had been the most prudent of females. But just a few months ago she had rebelled against her name and her upbringing. She had not regretted her choice until now, until she met this infuriating, exciting, alarmingly seductive nobleman who set her nerves a-tingle.

In her new life he took her for a lightskirt, fit to be his *chère amie,* no more. Not that in her previous life he'd ever have regarded her as worthy of his hand, but nor would he have gazed down at her with open desire, making her feel as if her clothes had vanished in a sheet of flame.

She pulled her cloak about her and said reproachfully, "I did not choose my name."

"I beg your pardon; I should not have laughed, particularly as mine is much worse. My surname is Warrender, which is tolerable, but I was christened Valentine Tregarth. As you have heard, my family calls me Garth. So do my most intimate friends," he added in a voice full of meaning.

To her relief, the children were on their way back. "I really must rejoin my party, *my lord*," she said, and bidding the children farewell she fled.

She looked back when she reached the safety of the cart, where the others were beginning to gather. Lord Rusholme was strolling down the hill, Lady Bella on his shoulders, Lady Sophie holding his hand. Young Lord Braverton and his eldest sister lugged their sack between them. An innocent scene.

Yet for the second time Prudence had run away from the earl.

For the next two weeks she'd be living in the same house. Surely the Easthaven mansion was vast enough for her to keep out of his way?

Three

Rusholme, having returned Maria's offspring to the nursery, was cornered at the breakfast table by Lady Anne.

"I am so looking forward to gathering holly this morning," she exclaimed, smiling to display pearly teeth. "Such a delightful, quaint tradition, is it not, Lord Rusholme?"

"Certainly, ma'am. Carriages will be waiting to take into the woods everyone who wishes to join in. The grooms know where to take you."

"I am sure you know the best places."

"No better than they, and I have already taken my sister's children to pick holly this morning."

"La, how excessively amiable of you! But we cannot go without you. The fun will be quite spoilt, I vow."

"Then of course I shall go," he said dryly, and turned to David's mousy sister-in-law. David had explained that her presence was Lady Easthaven's notion, not his or his wife's let alone her own, so Rusholme was feeling slightly more kindly toward her. What the deuce was her name? Ah yes, "Miss Wallace, may I hope for the pleasure of your company?"

She turned bright pink and mumbled acquiescence, while Lady Anne pouted and tossed her golden ringlets.

"Let's all go, shall we, David?" said Mrs. Denham diplomatically.

Between Lady Anne's affected gaiety and Kitty Wallace's tongue-tied bashfulness, Rusholme's second outing was an exercise in acute tedium. At least he easily avoided Lady Anne's attempt to draw him deeper into the woods in search of the best berries. How he wished it was sweet Prudence enticing him onward!

When they returned to the house, Lady Anne needed his advice on directing the footmen where to place the sprigs of holly whose gathering she had personally supervised. Fortunately Henry Ffoliot was more than happy to advise her.

Unfortunately, Lady Estella Redpath, daughter of the Duke of Essex, had just come in from a ride. A robust, jovial young woman, she had apparently decided the way to Rusholme's heart was to admire the hunting country around his home. This involved describing every hedge, ditch, and copse she had observed on her ride, interspersed with tales of her prowess in the hunting field.

"Let's ride together this afternoon," she proposed, "and you shall show me your favorite jumps."

"You must be tired after being on horseback all morning."

Her booming laugh half deafened him. "Tired! I'm no namby-pamby miss, Rusholme. When the scent's high I often ride eight hours at a stretch."

It was a perfect day for a ride, sunny and crisp. No use praying for rain, which doubtless would not give Lady Estella pause anyway. He racked his brains. "Then I . . . ah . . . nothing would please me more, but . . . hm . . . I arrived rather late yesterday, and my mother will be most displeased if I'm not on hand to greet her guests today."

"Pity! Another day, then. Still plenty of time, we're here till after Twelfth Night."

"Another day," he agreed reluctantly, hoping she'd not consult the marchioness, who would certainly want him to ride with the duke's highly eligible daughter.

In the circumstances, Rusholme was delighted when his sister Julia arrived and her children, who had missed the morning's excursion, begged him to take them out.

"No more holly!" he insisted. He never wanted to see another red berry or prickly leaf in his life. "We'll go to see the Yule log brought home. And we'll take your nursemaid with us to look after the little ones."

A combination of factors drove Rusholme out to help bring in the Yule log. It was really an occasion for the servants, those who could be spared after luncheon when family and guests were for the most part repletely inactive. The servants' hall, once the Great Hall of the old house, had the only fireplace wide enough to hold a log large enough to burn throughout Christmas Day.

The ancient country custom, repressed—like mummers and mistletoe—during the Puritan Commonwealth, had never widely revived. Lord Easthaven, an enthusiast for lost traditions, had proposed rebuilding the elegant Adam fireplace in the gold drawing room for the purpose. The marchioness had put her foot down. So much disruption for the sake of burning a Yule log once a year was not to be thought of.

Instead, his lordship encouraged his servants to observe the custom: those, at least, who could be spared for an hour or two

from the duties attendant upon his lavish notions of Christmas
hospitality.

When they reached the spot where a lightning-struck oak had
been felled and trimmed, the first thing Rusholme noticed was
a leaf-green cloak among the spectators. Prudence! He was rewarded for his excessive amiability to his sisters' children.

As the nearest servants greeted them, she glanced round, and
he caught her eye. She smiled, nodded, and turned back to speak
to the man at her side.

Jealousy lanced through him. Who the devil was the fellow?
Of medium height, he wore a capeless topcoat a trifle too tight
in the shoulders and a rather dusty-looking beaver with a curly
brim sagging at the back.

An actor, no doubt, one of her colleagues. Rusholme breathed
again.

Prudence—somehow he couldn't think of her as Seraphina—
would be embarrassed if he sought her out in this crowd, he
realized. In the world of the theater, lovers were an accepted part
of life. Among the respectable servants of a great house, chastity
was the rule, lack of chastity cause for ignominy and dismissal.
He didn't want to make her uncomfortable. His pursuit would
have to be discreet.

He took the children closer to watch a cart horse being har-
nessed to the log. The horse brasses gleaming in the sun fascinated his littlest nephew, and the two older boys had to be
restrained from going to help.

The last buckle was fastened, and the carter cracked his whip.
The horse strained at the yoke. The log quivered.

Rusholme handed over the boys to the two nearest house-
maids. "Hang on to them," he ordered, then cried, "Come on,
fellows, put your shoulders to it!"

Leading the rush of cheering footmen, gardeners, and grooms,
he heaved with all his strength at the stubborn mass. He knew
he was showing off and wondered at it. He hadn't felt a need to
impress a female since he was one-and-twenty, yet here he was

displaying like a peacock, all for an actress whose only interest
was undoubtedly his money.

All the same, when the Yule log at last slithered forward, he
was glad to see her actor companion had not soiled his hands at
a man's task.

Prudence looked amused, but she joined in the applause of the
watchers and even called out, "Bravo, my lord."

He gave her a rueful grin, self-consciously sure she had
guessed at his motives. Nonetheless, a few minutes later he found
himself quite unable to resist temptation.

Once set in motion, the log slid along easily behind the horse.
One of the grooms vaulted on top of it and balanced with wind-
milling arms as it bumped over the rough grass. Maids cheered;
menservants jeered. Losing his balance he sprang clear. Another
took his place.

Rusholme was the fourth up. It was more difficult than he had
thought. The log was slippery as well as in erratic motion. He
had to keep shifting his feet to stay on, and he knew he soon
must jump or ignominiously topple.

He timed his leap with care. As his boots hit the ground he
stumbled forward, reached out for support, and grabbed Prudence's arm.

She steadied him, laughing up at him. Then she was in his
arms.

He held her close, distantly aware of the crowd now shouting
for someone else. Gazing down at her tender mouth, he struggled
against an overwhelming urge to kiss her—but while an embrace
might pass as a continued effort to find his feet, a kiss would
surely damn her.

A spark of anger flashed in her eyes. "I believe you have
recovered your balance, my lord," she said coolly, pulling away.

"Yes," he said with deep regret, which changed to relief as the
boys dashed up. If they had caught him kissing her . . . !

"You were simply splendid, Uncle Garth!"

"A regular Trojan!"

They dashed off again, and Prudence hurried after them. In a few strides he overtook her and walked alongside, careful not to touch her.

"I'm sorry. You're so damnably tempting."

Giving him a speaking look, she increased her pace. They caught up with the slow-moving log.

The man riding it now made it look easy. Lithe in his shirt-sleeves, he stood there barely swaying, arms outstretched with a dancer's grace instead of flailing as Rusholme's had. His audience fell silent, scarce breathing.

"Your friend, Miss . . . Savage?"

"Yes, Ben Dandridge."

Rusholme looked up again just in time to see Dandridge perform a sudden handspring, returning to his feet without visible unsteadiness. A collective "aah" rose from the crowd, followed by a burst of cheers.

"Ben used to be a horseback acrobat in Astley's circus," Prudence said.

"A *particular* friend of yours?"

She frowned at him. "A colleague and a friend."

"What part does he play in *She Stoops to Conquer?*"

"Tony Lumpkin."

An uncouth bumpkin, not a romantic hero—good. Not that he feared competition from a tumbler, however nimble. "And you are Kate Hardcastle, among your other aliases."

"Gracious no!" She shook her head, smiling. "Aimée is Kate. I have nowhere near experience enough to tackle that rôle. I hope I shall do justice to Constance Neville, though I daresay I can manage the maid, Pimple, well enough."

"Pimple!" he exclaimed, revolted. "I wager you never had a pimple in your life."

Laughing, she retorted, "You cannot expect me to admit it if I did. Now here come your nephews, my lord. I must be off."

She slipped away into the crowd. As Rusholme responded to the boys' thrilled comments on the acrobat, he watched for her green cloak.

He had annoyed her, first with his embrace, and then by questioning her relationship with Dandridge. Though she had recovered her humor before she left, she *had* left. He could not flatter himself she desired his company.

Besides, if she was interested in him as a lover, surely she'd not have drawn attention to the maid's repulsive name. Pimple, indeed!

He was disappointed he would not see her as Kate Hardcastle. Still, at least he'd not have to watch her flirting on stage with whoever played Young Marlow. Reflecting upon the play, which he had seen more than once, he recalled the scenes between Constance Neville and her betrothed, Hastings, as few and sedate.

Why he cared he wasn't sure. He had often watched previous mistresses cavort on stage in breeches parts, or kick up their heels in the chorus line, with never a blink. In fact, he had revelled in the envy of his acquaintances. Somehow Prudence was different.

Different enough to be worth taking the trouble of wooing her to his bed.

He observed her as she watched Dandridge dismount from the Yule log with a double somersault ending in a flourishing bow. The actor took his coat and hat from the maid who had carried them for him. To the applause of her fellow servants, he bussed her heartily, while Prudence looked on with a smile. Clearly she had no interest in him.

No one tried to match his feat on the log. As they approached the house, the indoor servants began to hurry ahead to return to their duties.

Gathering the boys and the nursemaid with the two little ones, Rusholme followed. In front of him, Prudence and Dandridge strolled together, chatting but a good yard apart, friends and colleagues, as she said.

So what did it matter that—as he suddenly recalled—Constance Neville and Tony Lumpkin spent a good deal of the play pretending to be in love?

* * *

Prudence dared not set foot outside the house for fear of meeting Lord Rusholme.

Not that she disliked his company. The trouble was she enjoyed talking to him; she did not remember ever feeling so comfortable with anyone, male or female—until the gleam of passion entered his eye.

If only he would stop his pursuit so they could be friends, at least as much friends as was possible between an actress and the heir to a marquisate.

Inside the house their paths had not crossed so far. She was busy with rehearsals. He was busy dodging the three eligible young ladies invited by the marchioness to entice him into marriage, according to a gossipy footman. The footman said none of the three was worthy of his lordship, the only possible reason for Prudence to find herself hoping he'd not be caught.

She certainly had no intention of being caught. She even missed church on Christmas morning because she learned all the family would attend. Rusholme could hardly get up to much mischief in church under the eye of his parents and sisters, but Prudence thought it best to see as little of him as possible.

Yet her eyes sought him out immediately that evening when she entered the gold drawing room. Sought him out and found him in the vast room, almost as big as the ballroom, crowded with ladies in every hue of the rainbow and gentlemen all in stark black and white.

Evening dress suited Rusholme. Orange did not suit the lady at his side, but judging by descriptions circulating below stairs, she was a duke's daughter, Lady Estella something. He didn't appear to be enjoying himself, not until he looked up at the sound of pipe and tabor and saw her.

He obviously recognized her, though the tall, conical hat and veil hid her hair. The white, vaguely medieval gown she wore was skimpy but decent, at least so she had thought until his eyes widened. She wished she had insisted on another two inches of muslin around the neckline.

A space had been cleared for the mummers in the center of the floor. Thither the piper proceeded, followed by a splendid two-man dragon in green with gold spangles. The children, allowed to stay up late and come down for the treat, squealed and clapped. It was not for their benefit that the first of the captive princesses, led in chains by the dragon, swayed her hips and clasped her hands to her ample bosom in an excess of terror. The gentlemen certainly appreciated Aimée's act, thought Prudence, walking behind with more dignified alarm and considerably less exposed bosom.

Spouting bad verse to explain that the princesses were tomorrow's lunch, the dragon arranged a row of Windsor chairs and imprisoned his captives behind them. In worse verse they bemoaned their fate. Then he emptied a heap of gaudy baubles from a sack he carried, crouched down and went to sleep beside his treasure.

Seated on the thick, soft carpet, Prudence peeked between the chairs at the audience. A dazzlingly beautiful young lady with golden curls, elegantly dressed in celestial blue, had joined Lord Rusholme. She must be Lady Anne Winkworth, another of the earl's prospective brides, Prudence guessed. Why on earth should Rusholme look twice at Prudence when he had a diamond of the first water at hand? She must have imagined his interest. Even if she had the bluest blood in the realm, she could not compete with Lady Anne.

The rumor that he was leading her a merry chase must be false, Prudence decided. Then Lady Anne threw a spiteful glance at the plain Lady Estella, gestured dismissively at the performers with a supercilious expression, and laid a possessive hand on Rusholme's arm. No doubt he had seen through the lovely face to the less lovely character within.

Unlike Lady Anne, Lady Estella seemed to be thoroughly enjoying the show, with childlike enthusiasm. "St. George!" she bellowed. "Bring on St. George!"

Rusholme smiled at her, the same sort of indulgent smile he had bestowed upon his excited nephews.

St. George duly appeared. Ben Dandridge, in a papier-mâché helmet and tinfoil armor, came in backward on a hobbyhorse berating the two sheepish varlets who skulked after him. Scurvy knaves they were, afraid to face the dragon with him, he announced, waving his sword.

Before he could turn to face the dragon himself, a stout woman bustled in. The varlets, looking terrified, turned tail and ran.

"Did you remember to sharpen your sword, George?" she demanded.

"Yes, Mother."

"And polish your armor?"

"Yes, Mother."

"And feed your horse?" Hands on hips, she frowned at the hobbyhorse. "He looks a bit thin to me."

The audience loved that part. When St. George's mother made him wait while she went off to fetch his muffler, the gentlemen roared with laughter, and even the most refined ladies tittered. Ben Dandridge's resigned patience made Prudence hide a smile, though she had watched him practice the attitude a dozen times.

Lord Rusholme had deserted his ladies and moved forward to join the children at the front, sitting on the floor. Lady Estella, intent on the show, did not appear to have noticed his defection. Lady Anne glared after him with an angry pout, which quickly changed to a flirtatious smile as his place was taken by a good-looking, fair-haired gentleman. He whispered something in her ear that made her rap his hand with her fan, then spread it before her face as if to conceal a blush.

Watching, fascinated, Prudence almost missed her cue. As St. George, swathed in a red and white muffler, approached, she and Aimée reached out toward him through the bars of the chairs.

"Save us, Sir Knight," they pleaded.

The dragon did not stir. St. George poked it with his sword. "Go away," it grumbled sleepily. "It's not time to get up yet."

"Rise and fight, O baleful beast," cried St. George.

Roused in the end by a threat to steal its treasure, the dragon, roaring horridly, chased the knight around among the audience. Lord Rusholme's older nephews cheered it on, while two of the smaller children turned to him in fright. Prudence saw him put an arm around each and speak to them comfortingly. Perhaps he really was fond of them, she thought, not just using them as an excuse to avoid his own pursuers.

At last the dragon was slain and the maidens released from durance vile. St. George's mother reappeared.

"Well done, my boy," she said, picking through the treasure, "but you needn't think you're bringing any hussies home with you."

"In that case, Mother," cried the hero, "by George, I shall simply have to marry 'em both!"

Amid laughter and applause, the players took their bows, the dragon splitting in the middle for the purpose. Then pipe and tabor struck up again. They gathered in a group facing outward and started to sing "Here we come a-wassailing." When they reached the verse, "We have got a little purse . . . ," the two scurvy knaves passed among the guests collecting tips.

They went on to "Past Three O'Clock," Ben Dandridge nudging Prudence in the ribs at the words "Seraph choir singeth." Next the audience was encouraged to join in "The First Nowell," before the troupe ended with "We wish you a Merry Christmas."

"Now bring us some figgy pudding . . . ," they carolled. "For we all like figgy pudding!"

Prudence met Lord Rusholme's eyes. He grinned and winked. Bother the man! What on earth had possessed her to tell him her real name? She might have guessed he'd consider it a hint of a desire for intimacy.

She was glad to slip out with the others as footmen brought

in platters of hot mince pies and steaming wassail bowls of mulled ale and cider. Supper was laid on for the players below stairs, where they belonged.

Four

The panelled gallery rang with raised voices as the first reading of *She Stoops to Conquer,* on Boxing Day, degenerated into an argument.

"Well, I shall bloody well go," said Kate Hardcastle in Aimée's obstinate tones.

"But a *Servants'* Ball," Mrs. Hardcastle protested. "We're not servants."

"We haven't been invited to the nobs' ball," pointed out Young Marlow, the juvenile lead.

"Nor we won't be," Hastings seconded him.

"It's just a bit of fun and gig," said Tony Lumpkin, "and one or two of the maids are devilish pretty." Ben Dandridge had kissed the girl who carried his coat while he showed off atop the Yule log, Prudence recalled. She herself had had to give him a stiff set-down when she first joined the troupe. Fortunately he was not one to hold a grudge.

"No wenching with the maids," commanded Mr. Hardcastle, owner, manager, and director of the company. "We don't want to go looking for trouble. But I don't see why them that chooses shouldn't go to the ball. Now let's get some work done, if you please, ladies and gentlemen."

The reading resumed. Prudence was quite satisfied with her secondary part as Constance Neville. Some of the things Young Marlow said to Kate Hardcastle when he believed her to be a servant were decidedly improper. Though Aimée took it all in her stride, Prudence was sure she herself would have been disconcerted, not to say embarrassed. Hampered by her upbringing, she began to wonder whether she was really cut out to be an actress.

Constance Neville and her betrothed, Hastings, were much more decorous. The worst they did was plan to run away together to be married.

Admittedly Prudence had to flirt with Tony Lumpkin, Mrs. Hardcastle's good-natured but loutish son, pretending to be in love with him. However, she had already made it plain to Ben Dandridge that where the stage directions said: *"They retire and seem to fondle,"* he was to observe the "seem," not the "fondle."

All the same, she winced when she thought of Lord Rusholme watching that particular scene. It could only reinforce his assumption that she was a wanton lightskirt.

The reading ended, with Tony Lumpkin jubilantly renouncing Constance Neville's hand in favor of her faithful Hastings, and Aimée coyly accepting Marlow. Mr. Hardcastle sent them all off to start learning their lines. Prudence and Aimée retired to their small shared chamber, perching on the bed for want of chairs.

For a while silence reigned, broken only by occasional mutters. Prudence had no difficulty with this part of the acting business, since many hours of her childhood—the majority, she sometimes felt—had been spent learning Bible verses by heart. To Aimée it was agony, and she soon asked for help. In tutoring, too, Prudence had experience. Aimée was duly grateful.

"I'll lend you a gown for the ball tonight," she proposed. "You haven't got anything pretty."

"I wasn't going to go."

"Course you'll go, Sera! It's not like it was the Cyprians' Ball in London, with all the Fashionable Impures parading about and the gents looking for a new convenient. It's only a bunch of servants, all of 'em as seraphic as you, I daresay. Most, anyways."

"Well, maybe." Prudence did not want to be thought prim or above her company. "But I don't know how to dance."

Aimée gaped at her. "What, not at all? Never mind, me 'n' Ben'll teach you a few steps quick as winking. That's settled then. Lessee, you can wear the lemon yellow crêpe. You're thinner than me, so we'll have to take a tuck or two."

"I'm taller, too." And Aimée wore her gowns well above the ankle.

"It won't take but a minute to stitch a ruffle round the hem. There'll be summat in the wardrobe box we can use. Come on, let's go look."

To Prudence's relief they also found a lace fichu to be pinned into the alarmingly low bodice of the lemon crêpe. The result was not exactly elegant, but prettier than any of her own clothes, she had to admit. Thus arrayed, refusing rouge and powder, she set off for her first ball.

The servants' hall was bedecked with holly and evergreens. Just inside the main doors, a big bunch of mistletoe dangled from the old minstrels' gallery. Opposite the doors, in the vast fire-place, the remains of the Yule log still smouldered, supplemented by a dozen faggots. At each end of the room stood a trestle table laden with food and drink.

The smell of tallow candles was overlaid by the odors of woodsmoke, pine, spiced ale, and oranges. At Christmas Lord Easthaven always provided an orange as a treat for each member of his huge staff and visiting servants.

Entering the crowded room, Prudence managed to dodge Ben Dandridge's kiss, though he landed a peck on her cheek. His breath was redolent of brandy. Aimée's lips met his, and she recoiled with a "Faugh!" wrinkling her nose.

"Come on," she said, "you'd better dance it off." And with that she pulled him out onto the floor.

Hastings, at his most gentlemanly, offered Prudence his arm, and they took their place in a set as the fiddlers struck up a lively air.

With only a single brief lesson to her credit, Prudence lost her way at once, but neither Hastings nor the marquis's servants cared. They steered her about, calling out the steps and encouragement equally. Breathless with exercise and laughter, she survived the first dance and went on to accept First Footman Samuel's invitation to stand up with him for the second.

Her arm linked with his, she was in the middle of a turn when Lord Rusholme appeared under the mistletoe.

"Oh!" she gasped. "Oh, no!"

"What's the matter, Miss Savage?" Samuel peered down at their feet. "I didn't step on your toe, did I?"

"No. It's just . . . I didn't know any ladies and gentlemen came to your ball."

"Some o' the family generally puts in an appearance for a while." He guided her to one side while another pair took their turn. "That's Lord Rusholme, that'll be the next marquis. You had a word with him out in the woods t'other morning, didn't you?"

"Yes," Prudence admitted unwillingly. "He needed help with the children."

"Lady Maria's children. That's her beside him, and Lady Julia, his other sister, along with the gentlemen they married. T'other fellow's Lord Rusholme's friend, Mr. Denham. His wife's sister's after his lordship. Leastways, Miss Wallace is too bashful to chase him like them other two do, but her ladyship'll set her onto him." He laughed. "Looks like he's slipped the leash for half an hour. Hey, come on, it's our turn again."

He tugged Prudence into the center of the set. Her clumsiness, which had been a joke, was suddenly painfully mortifying. She wished she had never come. She wished she could leave without affronting Samuel. She wished she might at least go to sit with the scullery maid, Rosie, in an inconspicuous corner where Lord Rusholme would not see her.

Concentrating on the steps, she tried to avoid looking in his direction. Nonetheless she was instantly aware when she spotted her. At once she turned away, but she felt his gaze burning into her back through the thin, silky crêpe.

When the pattern of the dance made her face that way again, she dared a peek. His head was bowed, speaking to Lady Julia. Prudence scolded herself: what vanity to imagine he was watching her! His interest was of the most casual kind, a matter of chance proximity. All she had to do was keep out of his way.

The dance ended. She could not leave since Rusholme still

stood in the entrance, and she did not know where the other doors led to, so she made for the farthest corner of the room.

Rosie sat there on a bench against the wall. "You're looking ever so pretty, miss," she said, her thin face lighting as Prudence joined her.

"Thank you, my dear." Prudence fanned herself with the fan borrowed from the props box. "I wish I knew the steps properly! Do you?"

"Oh, yes, miss, only there's none but the stable lads'll dance wi' the likes o' me." She glanced down at her red, chapped hands. "It takes 'em a few pints to get up their courage," she explained with a wisdom beyond her years. "I 'specs I'll be dancing later. Meantimes, I likes to watch."

"So do I."

A gentleman's gentleman, stiffly proper in black, approached and begged Prudence for the honor of the next dance. "His lordship has requested a waltz," he said, "which being a new dance and foreign, the lower servants haven't had no opportunity of learning."

"Nor have I," Prudence excused herself. "I'm sure you will be able to find a proficient partner."

But the valet considered it not at all correct to desert a lady he had invited to stand up with him simply because she chose to sit out the dance. He fetched for her—and, at her prompting, Rosie—a cup of lemonade, then hovered over her until she asked him to be seated.

Lord Rusholme waltzed past, Lady Julia in his arms. A wave of longing swept over Prudence. If she could dance, if she were well-born and beautiful and beautifully dressed, if she were one of the young ladies chosen by the marchioness as a suitable bride. . . . What she wanted was to feel his strong arms about her without in any way compromising her principles, and that was clearly impossible.

She turned her attention to the man at her side.

He was employed, he revealed, by Mr. Denham, a good master, but without the figure or the style, he confessed, of his friend

Lord Rusholme. His lordship was a Corinthian of the first stare, a Nonpareil, equally at home on horseback or in the ballroom and always elegant, always impeccable. As the valet waxed enthusiastic, Prudence recalled Rusholme in the woods, bareheaded, hair ruffled, a child on his shoulders; Rusholme wobbling on the lurching Yule log, arms waving wildly; Rusholme seated cross-legged on the floor in his mother's drawing room. She stifled a giggle.

Those were the images in Prudence's mind when the waltz ended and Rusholme, impeccably elegant, swirled Lady Julia to a halt just in front of her. Thus, instead of freezing him with a glance as she had intended should he approach her, when he bowed to her she smiled up at him.

She quickly came to her senses when he failed to introduce her to his sister, whose eyes passed over her as if she were not there. Lady Julia murmured something to her brother and sailed off, the crowd parting deferentially before her.

"Miss Savage, may I have the pleasure of the next dance?"

"Pray excuse me, my lord," Prudence said coolly, "I do not know the steps."

Lord Rusholme looked taken aback. "You don't know yet what it will be," he pointed out, clearly aware she was snubbing him.

She had to make sure he understood that her excuse was the truth, as well as a rebuff. "I don't know *any* of the steps," she explained.

"I saw you dancing earlier."

"My partner and the others in the set all told me what to do as we went along."

"Do you think me less capable of instructing you than my father's footman?" His smile was quizzical, her snub forgotten or disregarded. "I promise to steer you right and not to tread on your toes. Come." He held out his hand.

Half unwilling, half glad to be overruled, Prudence rose, venturing a last protest: "I may tread on yours. You cannot wish to stand up with anyone so clumsy, my lord!"

"I believe my toes and my credit will survive. Besides, however inaccurate, your movements were never less than graceful, I assure you."

"I don't care for Spanish coin, sir," she said tartly, laying her hand on his arm.

He laughed. "I should have guessed that of you, which is why I'd not dare offer it. I shall not, for instance, tell you your gown becomes you."

"I didn't choose it."

"I suspected as much, having already complimented your taste. Your cloak was a good color. Sophie was right, you looked like a wood elf."

Prudence hurried to change the subject. "The children all seem very fond of you."

"I am told I spoil them abominably. The advantage of nieces and nephews is that one need not fear to ruin their characters by overindulgence. That's for their parents to fret about. Children are a great responsibility."

"I daresay there are rewards to having one's own children," said Prudence dubiously. Her father had certainly never appeared to think so.

"I daresay," Rusholme sighed. "I cannot avoid marriage and setting up my own nursery much longer. Perhaps David's little sister-in-law would do," he mused aloud. "She'd bore me to tears, but I'd rather be bored to tears than pestered to death."

Once more they were on dangerous ground. To Prudence's relief the fiddlers started to make preliminary scrapings, and they took their places in the nearest set.

The dance was "Strip the Willow." Prudence and Lord Rusholme were in the middle of the set, so for some time all she had to do was link arms and turn with whichever footman, valet, or groom presented himself, then promenade with his lordship. By the time they moved to the top of the set, she had watched enough to understand the pattern.

Alas, understanding and performing proved to be two different things. Bewildered, she lost her place, offered the wrong arm, turned the wrong way, faced in the wrong direction. She even found herself linking arms with a surprised abigail on the wrong side of the set. Rusholme grinned and cheerfully corrected her. As soon as the servants realized he was not miffed, they all joined in to help. Instead of a humiliating disaster, the dance turned into a merry romp which left Prudence as laughing and breathless as her first efforts of the evening.

The final chord sounded, and she curtsied to Rusholme's bow. His friend Mr. Denham appeared at his elbow.

"Time we were getting back to the drawing room, old chap," he said. "Your sisters left long ago."

"Be damned if I will," Rusholme exclaimed. "I'll only be trapped into turning Lady Anne's music for her, or offering Lady Estella the use of my best hunter. I'll have one more dance first."

As the gentlemen spoke, Prudence had moved back toward Rosie's nearby bench, and they had drifted after her. Now Rusholme looked at her as if he meant to ask her to dance again.

She must not let him single her out so! "If you are seeking a partner, my lord," she said hastily, "I'm sure Rosie will be happy to stand up with you. She knows all the steps." And she indicated the little scullery maid.

Rosie gazed up at him in speechless fright, with just a touch of incredulous hope.

After a start of surprised dismay, quickly hidden, he said smoothly, "Will you do me the honor, Miss Rosie?"

Rosie gasped. Eyes huge, she nodded. As they moved out onto the floor, the scrawny child with her hand on the arm of the tall, broad-shouldered, fashionable gentleman, Prudence watched uneasily.

She could fight her attraction to him, the disturbance she felt in his presence, the flutter at his touch. The trouble was, she *liked* him.

When Rusholme returned the scullery maid to her corner, Prudence was gone. Though she was not there to observe him, he thanked the child with the same punctilious courtesy he would have expended upon a duchess.

She bobbed a curtsy. "Strewth, m'lord," she said, her little face glowing, "I'll never fergit it all me born days!"

He smiled at her, half ashamed that so simple an act could give so much pleasure. He'd never have thought of it without Prudence's intervention.

However, he did not flatter himself that her only motive had been to give the maid something to remember "all her born days." Prudence was almost as eager to evade him as he was to evade the ladies Anne and Estella.

Yet when they were together he felt she enjoyed his company. His original guess that she was playing coy to lead him on was untenable now that he was better acquainted with her candor and openness. No false modesty suggested his person was less attractive to women than his title and his purse. He didn't understand her.

He scanned the room. Nowhere a glimpse of tawny curls nor the dreadful lemon yellow dress. He saw the other actress, Aimée Orlando, in an eye-catching cherry red gown cut so low it was a wonder she didn't spill out. Unnecessarily flirting her fan to draw attention to her bosom, she was looking up saucily at. . . . Devil take it, Henry Ffoliot!

What the deuce was he doing at the Servants' Ball? It was all very well for family to attend, and a close friend like David Denham who had often visited Easthaven in boyhood. But Ffoliot had no business here.

No legitimate business, Rusholme corrected himself. The way he was gazing at Miss Orlando's exiguous bodice was self-explanatory. Well, the vulgar hussy could take care of herself. She was an actress after all. If Ffoliot were to pester the maids, it would be another matter.

The fiddlers started up again. Past time Rusholme returned to his duty in the drawing room. He spent the rest of the evening doing the pretty to Lady Anne while racking his brains for a way to see more of Miss Prudence Figg.

To see more of her in every sense of the phrase.

Yet he did not want to figure in her eyes as a persecutor, nor to draw the attention of family and guests to his interest in her. By the time he went to bed, he still had not contrived a viable scheme.

Five

Rusholme had arranged with some of the gentlemen to go riding early next morning. Somehow Lady Estella learned of the plan and awaited him in the stables when he went down.

Through brook and through briar she stuck to his side like a leech. So when they all returned to the house and the butler told him his mother desired a word with him, he was more thankful than dismayed. He'd far rather listen to the marchioness's strictures on an empty stomach than to Lady Estella's analysis of their ride while he ate his breakfast.

He went straight to his mother's private sitting room, but paused on the threshold to say, "Do you mind my dirt, Mama? I have been out on Salamander. Shall I go and change?"

"No, no, Garth, come in and sit down." Her ladyship was clad in an appalling mulberry-colored morning gown which clashed not only with her favorite green and pink shawl, but with the black and scarlet Chinese furnishings.

Resisting an urge to shade his eyes, her son entered and kissed her cheek. "Good morning, ma'am," he said. "What can I do for you?"

"I wish to ascertain your preference. You do not appear to distinguish either Lady Estella or Lady Anne by your attentions. Which do you favor?"

"Good Lord, neither! If I favor anyone, which I'm not prepared to say, it's Miss—dash it, what's her name?—ah, Wallace."

"Miss Wallace? I have scarcely observed you exchanging a single word with Miss Wallace."

"Have you tried to exchange a word with her, Mama?"

Lady Easthaven frowned. "She is a modest, well-behaved young lady. It is a pity her father is merely a baron and her fortune insignificant. However, I don't mean to cavil at your choice. I shall invite Miss Wallace—and her sister and Mr. Denham, of course—to stay on for a week when our other guests leave."

Aghast, Rusholme jumped to his feet and opened his mouth to protest. At that moment the marquis burst into the room.

"My dear," he cried, "disaster has struck!"

"Sit down, Easthaven, and collect yourself," said his wife, her composure undisturbed. "Is the house on fire?"

"No, no, nothing like that."

"Then there is no need for haste."

"You are quite right, my dear. Hello, Garth, you here? Just wait till you hear!" He turned toward the door and said impatiently, "Come in, Hardcastle, come in!"

Rusholme recognized the man who hovered unhappily on the threshold as the front half of the dragon. He stepped in. "M-my lady," he stammered, "my name is—"

"Tell her ladyship and Lord Rusholme what happened."

"It's Ben Dandridge, my lady. . . ."

"Tony Lumpkin," elucidated Lord Easthaven. "Seems the fellow used to be a circus clown. He got a bit bosky at the servants' hop last night and started doing acrobatics on the table. The long and short of it is, the clunch fell off and broke his leg."

"Has a physician been summoned, Mr. Hardcastle?"

"Yes, my lady. My name is—"

"The fellow will be on crutches for months," the marquis broke in despairingly. "He can't possibly play Lumpkin!"

"Surely you have other actors in your company, Mr. Hardcastle?"

The actor-manager gave up his attempt to rectify his name. "None but those who already have vital rôles, my lady, and those not fit to play aught but servants and such. None to spare that's capable of Tony Lumpkin."

"You see, it's a catastrophe," moaned Lord Easthaven, slumping into a chair. "I have promised our guests a play and I have already invited all the neighbors."

"Nonsense," said the marchioness bracingly. "Our neighbors are always vastly gratified to be invited to Easthaven on Twelfth Night, with or without a performance to entertain them. Not that I believe it necessary to disappoint them. You—"

"I have the solution," Rusholme interrupted before his mother could voice her proposal. He had in fact thought of several possibilities which had not occurred to his impulsive father or the beleaguered manager. One was so glorious, so utterly perfect, he hastened to suppress all others. "I beg your pardon, Mama, but there's no need to rack our brains. I shall play Tony Lumpkin."

Hardcastle blanched and wrung his hands. "But my lord . . . ," he bleated.

"I was forever winning prizes at school for the recitation of Latin verses," Rusholme assured him. "A few speeches in English will be simple to get by heart, and I daresay you can teach me the rest of the business in no time."

"But my lord . . . !"

"Do you know the play, my boy?" his father enquired anxiously. "Tony Lumpkin is no dashing hero; he's a rowdy buffoon."

"I know, sir. I've always had a fancy to try my hand at a bit of farce." The notion had never crossed his mind before, but to further his acquaintance with Prudence, he was even prepared to make a cake of himself in public.

"Impossible," pronounced his mother. Hardcastle cast her a glance of burning gratitude. "It is out of the question for a Warrender to prance about upon the stage."

"Perhaps another part," the marquis suggested. "Hastings is a sedate, gentlemanly sort of fellow. Then the fellow playing Hastings can do Lumpkin."

"Tony Lumpkin or nothing!" said Rusholme. He distinctly recalled Tony flirting with Constance Neville. He and Prudence would have to rehearse a great deal to do it just right.

"Nothing," snapped Lady Easthaven. Hardcastle nodded vigorously.

"Come, my dear, let the boy have a bit of fun. He'll be a staid old married man soon enough."

"More staid than his father, I daresay." With a sigh, she gave in.

"Good, that's settled," said Rusholme. "Hardcastle, if you'd be so kind as to send my lines to the breakfast room, I shall start studying at once."

"Yes, my lord," groaned the unfortunate man, and he bowed himself out.

Rusholme made his escape before his mama could begin again on the subject of his preferences in the way of brides. If she went ahead and invited Kitty Wallace and the Denhams to stay on after Twelfth Night, perhaps he'd be able to pass it off as due to his own desire to hobnob with David.

Or perhaps he'd give in and propose to the speechless chit.

Over ham and eggs and a mountain of toast, he perused his part. As he'd thought, it gave him plenty of excuses to seek out Prudence for rehearsals. Of more immediate use, it gave him an excuse not to listen to Lady Estella, though when she started to praise Salamander's finer points, he found it difficult not to respond. She was an excellent judge of horseflesh, but he was afraid the least encouragement would lead to an endless lecture.

When he turned the last page, she asked what he had been reading, and he explained.

"Oh, famous fun!" she neighed. "I don't suppose there's a part I could take?"

"I'm afraid not," he said, repressing an urge to add that it was a pity the horses were all offstage as she'd do very well in that rôle.

The others at the breakfast table, mostly gentlemen, quizzed him unmercifully, except David, who seemed perturbed. Rusholme finally extricated himself from the good-natured teasing and went to look for Prudence.

In the passage outside the room he met the First Footman, bringing fresh coffee and tea.

"Where can I find the players, Samuel?" he asked.

"They'll be breakfasting, I expect, my lord. They've their own dining room in the northeast wing, being as they're not respectable enough for the housekeeper's room, but a cut above the servants' hall."

Rusholme made his way to the northeast wing, frowning as he pondered the footman's exposition of the actors' place in the household. Though reasonable, it displeased him, and he couldn't decide quite why. Of course, the company was not really part of the household, standing outside the hierarchy, the sequence descending from marquis at the head to scullery maid at the foot.

Was Prudence pleased with him for dancing with the scullery maid? he wondered. Should he tell her what the girl had said? Would it amuse her or would it look too much like conceit?

He'd wait and see how angry she was with him for insisting on playing Tony Lumpkin.

As Rusholme entered the long, narrow Elizabethan gallery where the company sat at breakfast, silence fell, and every head swung round. "Good morning, ladies and gentlemen," he said with a slight bow.

Dismay, resignation, annoyance—no face indicated gratitude for his helping them out of their difficulties, he noted wryly. He sought out Prudence. She looked thoroughly flustered.

When Prudence had learned, half an hour earlier, that Lord Rusholme insisted on taking Ben Dandridge's place, her first reaction was resentment. How dare he pursue her when she had so plainly rebuffed him! Then honesty compelled her to admit she might have confused him by dancing and chatting and laughing with him.

Next modesty came to the fore. She flattered herself to suppose an interest in her had anything to do with his wish to strut upon the stage. Perhaps he hoped thereby to evade those marriageable damsels the marchioness had presented for his choice. Perhaps he didn't want his father to be disappointed, and he had not considered alternative solutions. Perhaps it was merely a whim. That she could understand: after all, a sudden whim accounted for her own acting career.

Nonetheless, the prospect of flirting with him—even in double make-believe, playing Constance pretending to love Tony—alarmed and embarrassed her. Thus, when he appeared in the doorway, the sudden rush of gladness which lifted her heart thoroughly bemused her.

And when his eyes met hers and he smiled, how could she not smile back?

"I hoped for some advice on learning my part," he said, "but I see I am too early."

"No, no, my lord." Mr. Hardcastle sprang to his feet. "Won't you join us?"

"Thank you, I've eaten, but I'll take a glass of ale."

Someone fetched one of the heavy, dark oak chairs from the row against the wall, and the others shifted along to make room for him, just opposite Prudence. He sat down, and Mrs. Hardcastle filled a glass from the pitcher of home-brewed ale.

"May I introduce my people to your lordship?" said Mr. Hardcastle. "If you don't mind, my lord, I'll present them by their rôles so as not to confuse you with their real names."

"An excellent notion," Rusholme agreed. "I confess myself a rank amateur."

Several people nodded in approval. At least the fine gentleman wasn't pretending he knew more than those who earned their living in the theater. Among her other qualms, Prudence had feared he would meet with a hostile reception. She should have known he was quite capable of charming everyone.

"You already know me as Hardcastle, my lord. This is my wife, in real life and on stage, Mrs. Hardcastle. Miss Kate Hardcastle, Miss Constance Neville and a maid, Sir Charles Marlow and the servant Diggory, Hastings, and next to you, my lord, Young Marlow. Then there's wardrobe and props people, and our scene painter. And down the other end there's various servants, who also play the landlord and your lordship's drinking companions, besides shifting scenery and so on."

Rusholme rose and bowed again. "Have done with 'my lord,' " he said, "I am Tony. If you feel particularly respectful, you may address me as Mr. Lumpkin, or Squire."

As everyone laughed, Prudence knew she was right. Rusholme would have them all twined around his little finger in no time. All except her, she vowed.

"If you want help learning your lines, Tony," said Aimée, the first to avail herself of his permission, "Seraphina—Constance Neville, that is—she's been helping me, and she's ever so clever at it."

"Thank you, Miss Hardcastle. May I prevail upon you, Miss . . . er . . . Miss Neville, to give me the benefit of your assistance?"

Prudence bit back a sigh. For the sake of the company she could not refuse. There went her hope of having no more to do with him than strictly necessary. "Of course, my . . . Mr. Lumpkin. I am at your service." She stood up, pushing back her chair. "Over by the windows, I should think, where the light is good."

Pausing, she wondered a trifle derisively whether he would stoop so far as to move two chairs into position himself, or expect someone to do it for him. *She* wasn't going to.

After a moment's hesitation, he lifted one of the solid, unwieldy, old-fashioned things in each hand and carried them to a corner by a window. He placed them far too close together for Prudence's liking. Joining him, she dragged one round with its back to the window. The effort required made her marvel at the strength in his hands, wrists, shoulders, to have carried two so easily.

"You will see better with the light behind you," she said primly.

"True," he responded with a grin and a knowing look.

He held the back of her chair while she seated herself, then took his place. His knees nearly touched hers. She slid back until the edge of the seat pressed into the back of her legs.

"I understood you claimed to be good at memorization," she accused him as he retrieved his part from his coat pocket, "so why are you now asking for assistance?"

"When I read through the part, I realized how difficult it was to learn English prose compared to Latin and Greek verse. It wants scansion."

"Latin poetry depends upon meter rather than rhyme, does it not? I don't know about Greek."

"How the deuce. . . . I beg your pardon. How on earth do you know about Latin poetry? And what scansion is, come to that."

"Oh, I suppose I must have heard someone mention it," Prudence said vaguely. She never had any trouble hiding her education from her fellow actors. With Lord Rusholme she found it impossible to mind her tongue as she had decided she must in her new profession.

"Not someone among the sort of company actresses keep," he said.

Prudence chuckled. "How can you say so, my lord, when I am presently in your company?"

" 'A hit, a very palpable hit.' But I cannot allow you, Miss Figg-Savage-Neville, to address me as my lord when Miss Hardcastle calls me Tony. Come, let me hear it, or better, Garth."

Shaking her head, she considered. Garth was out of the question, and even Tony seemed too familiar for comfort. Lumpkin was too horridly vulgar a name for the elegant, arrogant earl. "In the play," she said, "I call you Cousin Tony and you call me Cousin Con. That will do quite well. Now, let us get to work. We are to rehearse the first act tomorrow."

As they talked, the noise level in the room had returned to normal, not enough to make them raise their voices, but a background hum from which odd phrases emerged.

"Can we not go somewhere more private, Cousin Con?" Rusholme coaxed, glancing round at the breakfasters.

"No," Prudence said firmly. She felt their corner of the long room was already more private than she quite cared for.

"It is a trifle hard to concentrate. Do you learn your lines amid all this chatter?"

Recalling the chilly water she had washed in that morning cooled her rising blush, a trick Aimée had taught her. She had no intention of telling Rusholme she had studied her part in her bedchamber. He just might suggest they repair thither.

"I'm sure you will manage. It may be prose, not verse, but at least it's English. Let us begin with your song, which has both rhythm and rhyme to guide. . . ." She stopped and stared at him in consternation. "Oh, dear, can you sing?"

"I'd have you know I'm in great demand at musical evenings. At least, I used to be whenever one of my sisters needed a partner in a duet. If someone will give me the tune, I warrant I'll follow it tolerably."

"Good enough. Tony Lumpkin is not meant to be an opera singer."

"Do you sing? Other than carols with a group?"

"Tolerably." She played the pianoforte tolerably, too; but that was an unusual accomplishment for an actress, and to admit it could only add to his curiosity. "Now, find the song, if you please. Act I, Scene 2, I believe."

" 'An alehouse room,' " he read. " 'Several shabby fellows with punch and tobacco.' At least I'm at the head of the table, a little above the rest."

"You chose the rôle," Prudence reminded him.

His conscious look, together with his quickness to learn the tavern song, convinced her she had guessed right: he had taken the undignified part and requested assistance in studying it in order to be near her. She could not help but be flattered. She was also angry and not a little alarmed. All her powers of resistance would have to be mustered against such determined pursuit.

If only Rusholme were not amiable as well as handsome and charming!

Partly in revenge, partly to avoid further personal conversation, Prudence made him work very hard. He soon mastered the words of his first brief scene, though she doubted he'd ever attain

Tony's insolent manner toward his mother. It went against his every gentlemanly instinct. She decided to leave it to Mr. Hardcastle to direct him in that.

The alehouse scene was longer. Again Rusholme readily learned his lines, but he had considerable trouble speaking them at the right moments until Prudence advised him to learn his cues as thoroughly as his own speeches.

"Is that what you do?" he asked.

"Yes. In fact, by the time we perform a play, I generally have the whole by heart, even the scenes I don't appear in, simply from having heard it so many times. Aimée says it's a monstrous waste of memory cells. She seems to know by instinct when her moment comes."

Rusholme laughed, but he said seriously, "You are ruled less by instinct than by intellect, are you not?"

"I hope so! Come, let us take this bit again, where you and the landlord are misdirecting Marlow and Hastings."

The difficulty with the cues overcome, Rusholme was word perfect. His half-concealed glee at Tony's prank was perfect, too. When he finished, Prudence clapped.

"You are a born actor, my . . . Cousin Tony," she exclaimed.

"I daresay half of what Society regards as polished manners is acting. I know I'm acting when I bear with complaisance the company of certain of my mother's guests! Undoubtedly, if regrettably, the ability to act smooths one's path through life, as you declared of manners."

"True," Prudence murmured. "Well, I believe you quite capable of learning the rest without my help, so—"

"But the next scene is the one I've been waiting for!" he protested as she started to rise. "The one where you pursue me, coquetting—that is," he hastily amended as she frowned, "where Constance Neville pursues Tony. Coquetting."

"Also the one," she pointed out, "where we stand back to back and you give me a crack on the head."

"Unkind, ungentlemanly, and most unromantic," Rusholme

admitted with a mournful sigh. "I'd forgotten that bit. But you will need to practice your coquetting."

"When you have learned your lines," she said inexorably, postponing the inevitable. "Besides, it's not till Act II."

Mr. Hardcastle came over to see how matters were progressing. Prudence left the unruly earl to him. The coquetting was going to be bad enough. What was she to do when they reached that wretched stage direction, "They retire and seem to fondle"?

She had a feeling Ben Dandridge was very much easier to deter than Lord Rusholme.

Six

Sitting up in bed, her old shawl about her shoulders, Prudence watched Aimée refreshing her face paint, placing the new layer over the old.

"You're really going to sneak up to Mr. Ffoliot's bedchamber?" she asked. "What if you go to the wrong room?"

"His man's s'posed to be waiting to show me the way and make sure all's clear. Don't look so shocked, Sera. It's only a bit of fun."

"Fun!"

"I mean it's not for money. Course he's promised me a nice present, but the servants all say Henry Ffoliot's in Dun Territory. If he gives me anything, it'll be some cheap trumpery bauble."

"Then why . . . ?"

"Why'm I going?" Aimée swung round, hands smoothing the pink satin over her ample hips. " 'Cause he's young and ever so handsome, that's why. It'll be a change from old Sir Enoch, who pays the bills right enough, but ain't got much else to keep a girl happy. He'll never know, and what he don't know can't hurt him."

"I suppose not," said Prudence dubiously.

"Don't condemn what you never had." The actress crossed to the bed, sat down on the edge, and took one of Prudence's hands in hers. "Look, dearie, you're simply not up to snuff. You do know what that Lord Rusholme's after, don't you?"

Prudence bit her lip. "Yes."

"They all want the same thing, and he's got his eye on you, sure enough."

"I wish you hadn't told him I was a good teacher!"

"Won't make no difference, dear. If he wants it, he'll get it," Aimée said fatalistically. "It's the first one a girl remembers, and if it's not him, it'll be someone else, prob'ly not so much to your liking. You do like him, don't you?"

"Yes," Prudence whispered.

"I can always tell. Honest, if I was you, I'd grab him. He's not so good-looking as Mr. Ffoliot, but he's got all the blunt a girl could ask for. With his title, too, I 'spect he could even buy you into a London company. Well, I got to go. Cheer up, Sera, it's not the end of the world."

But Prudence had been brought up to believe loss of chastity was indeed the end of the world, both this world and the next. Suddenly chilled, she huddled down beneath the bedclothes. A poem flashed through her mind, written by Oliver Goldsmith, the very man whose play was bringing her so much trouble.

> When lovely woman stoops to folly
> And finds too late that men betray,
> What charm can soothe her melancholy,
> What art can wash her guilt away?
>
> The only art her guilt to cover,
> To hide her shame from every eye,
> To give repentance to her lover
> And wring his bosom, is—to die.

Men! Prudence thought with loathing. Why should the woman seduced suffer shame and death while mere repentance was expected of the seducer? Aimée's cheerful debauchery was surely saner than that!

Yet Prudence could not easily shake off her principles, the deeply inculcated belief in the virtue of chastity. Perhaps she should have been christened Prude, not Prudence.

Aimée thought Lord Rusholme was bound to attain his ends, and if not he, another, but that only applied as long as Prudence was an actress. She was not suited to the life, she knew it now. She ought to leave at once, to resume the journey interrupted when she had descended from the stagecoach in Cheltenham and read the theater's playbill.

Would he be angry? Would he miss her? Not for long. He himself had told her he meant to marry soon. Even if she did surrender to him, she'd not have him for long.

The realization strengthened her resolve. She would not surrender! Nor would she run away, as if she were at fault. Though after this engagement she'd go back to her old, dull but safe life, for now the company relied upon her, and she'd not let them down. To lose Constance Neville as well as Tony Lumpkin might prove disastrous.

Although, what if Lady Anne volunteered to play the rôle? To judge by what the servants said of her, she'd probably do the coquetting part better than Prudence.

It would serve Lord Rusholme right. Picturing his aghast face, she fell asleep at last with a faint smile on her lips.

"May I beg a last nightcap before I retire, Garth?" David Denham requested, as the marquis took himself off to bed in the wake of the rest of his guests.

"What, not speeding to the side of your bride?" Rusholme went over to the tray of bottles and decanters provided for the gentlemen after the ladies retired. "You haven't stayed up so late since you arrived."

"I want a word with you," Denham said defensively. "I warned Lottie I'd be a bit late."

"Has my mother invited you to stay on after Twelfth Night?"

"No. Is she likely to?"

"Yes."

"Why? And if she does, would you like me to claim urgent business elsewhere?"

"If you don't mind, old fellow. I made the mistake of indicating a slight—a *very* slight preference for Miss Wallace over the other two eligibles. No offense to the lady, nor to you, but I'm not ready to tie the knot yet, with anyone." It would not be fair to court a bride while in hot pursuit of the enchanting, intriguing Miss Prudence Figg. A morning spent with her had only served to confirm her charms.

"Don't worry about offending poor Kitty," his friend advised, accepting the glass of brandy. "She's frightened half to death of you. She hasn't been presented yet, you know, and she needs to acquire a little Town Bronze before she'll be up to your weight. Talking of females, that's a pretty little actress you have your eye on. Not in your usual style."

Denham's casual tone failed to deceive. This was what had kept him up late.

"I have a usual style, do I?" Rusholme enquired, attempting equal casualness. He sat down, lounged back, and stretched out his legs.

"You tend to fall for elegant, languorous brunettes without much sense in their cocklofts. Some real dashers you've had in keeping over the years, I must say. But it's not quite the thing in your parents' house, old fellow. None of my business, of course," he added warily.

"None at all. However, let me assure you that I am not so smitten I cannot restrain my lusts until both the troupe and I myself have left Easthaven." Despite his plans for Prudence, Rusholme found himself revolted to be talking of her in such terms. He took a swallow of brandy. "Tell me, is everyone aware I've taken a fancy to Miss . . . Savage?"

"Lord, I don't suppose so. No one has said anything in my hearing. I was at the Servants' Ball, remember, and I put it together with this crackbrained business of your acting career and a look you gave her after the mummery." Denham grinned. "To tell the truth, if you'd denied it, I'd have believed you."

"Damn your eyes, David!" He frowned, recalling the first meeting in the woods, and the second, with the Yule log. "The servants are as able as you to put two and two together, though, and what they know everyone knows sooner or later."

"I daresay, but from what my man says they're all too agog over Ffoliot and the other actress to notice your comparatively discreet goings-on."

"Damn Ffoliot's eyes! And this time I mean it. If his aunt wasn't a crony of Mama's, I'd have him out on his ear."

"Oh, no you wouldn't, old chap. Not only is he drawing attention below stairs from your little intrigue, he's making some headway above stairs with the Winkworth menace."

"Lady Anne will never have him."

"No, she thinks she's using him to make you jealous. At least he keeps her off your back. Henry Ffoliot is a curst rum touch, but I'd be grateful to him, if I were you."

"I'll think about it."

Denham stood up. "Well, I'm off." Rather pink-cheeked, he looked down at his friend. "You know, marriage isn't so bad. I don't mean you ought to propose to Kitty, or Lady Anne or Lady Estella, but I hope one day you'll find someone you can love as I love Lottie."

He left. Rusholme gazed into the depths of his glass, swirling the brandy as he mused. In the firelight, the tawny liquid was just the color of Prudence's hair. His fingers ached to caress those feathery, rosemary-scented curls.

For all his many mistresses, he had never felt such a yearning before, never felt that one and only one could satisfy him. Nor had he ever felt so protective. He didn't want Prudence to suffer from the scorn of the servants, the animosity of the ladies, the lecherous imaginings of the gentlemen.

It was absurd. No matter what he did those attitudes existed already, because she was an actress and everyone knew actresses were lightskirts. The two words were practically synonymous.

So he had no real reason to be discreet for her sake. However, David was right. To shelter a *chère amie* under one's parents' roof was unconscionably bad *ton*. Although Prudence wasn't yet his *chère amie,* he'd continue to be discreet for his family's sake.

Restless and dissatisfied, Rusholme abandoned his half-full glass and went up to bed.

"Don't fuss so, Sera," Aimée exclaimed as they entered the gallery next afternoon. "After all, it's not like if your precious earl can't act worth a damn he's going to be out on the street in the cold." She gave an exaggerated shiver. The weather was still clear and frigid, with frost-flowers blooming on the bedroom windowpanes in the mornings. "Nor the gentry aren't going to boo and hiss him off the stage."

"No," Prudence admitted, "but how mortifying for him if he is excessively bad."

"How mortifying for *us* if a bloody flash cove turns out as good as us professionals! Anyways, first rehearsals are always a bungle. I'm sure to forget half my lines, even with all your help. Thank heaven it's only the first act."

Lord Rusholme was already there, looking far less anxious than Prudence felt on his behalf. Talking to the Hardcastles, he smiled at her, but did not come to greet her. A slight sense of pique mingled with her relief at not being singled out.

At one end of the gallery, some of the furniture had been arranged for the first scene, a room in Mr. Hardcastle's house. Its old-fashioned shabbiness was perfect for the purpose. Prudence wondered whether it could be carried down to the ballroom for the performance. Those gaudy gilt and royal blue ballroom chairs would never do.

"All right, we're all here for the first scene," said Mr. Hardcastle. "Tony, Miss Hardcastle, Miss Neville, you'll enter stage right, so wait over there if you please."

Prudence and Aimée converged with Rusholme in the indicated corner.

"You remember your cues?" Prudence whispered to Rusholme as the Hardcastles moved to the stage and began their bickering.

"I believe so. And I practiced hallooing when I was out riding this morning, much to my mount's astonishment."

Prudence smiled and Aimée giggled. They fell silent, listening to Mr. Hardcastle enumerating his stepson Tony's pranks.

" 'It was but yesterday,' " said the long-suffering squire, " 'he fastened my wig to the back of my chair, and when I went to make a bow I popped my bald head in Mrs. Frizzle's face.' "

Rusholme grinned, but he pulled a wry face when his ever-loving mother defended him by prating about the delicacy of his constitution. " 'I'm actually afraid of his lungs,' " she said.

" 'So am I,' " said Hardcastle, " 'for sometimes he whoops like a speaking trumpet.' "

"Halloo!" called Rusholme.

"Louder, if you please, my . . . Mr. Lumpkin."

"Halloo!"

"Louder still, and not so much as if you're trying to attract attention, more sheer animal spirits."

"HALLOO!" bellowed the earl.

Hardcastle sighed. "That will do for now. 'Oh, there he goes.' "

Tony strode onto the stage, on his way to the Three Pigeons. Rusholme's superbly tailored morning clothes—buff pantaloons, blue coat, and snowy starched neckcloth—were scarcely suitable, but the natural arrogance of his demeanor was close enough to Tony's bumptious swagger. He remembered his cues and his lines, and his voice carried well. However, Tony's impertinent words to his mother emerged from Rusholme's mouth in the politest of tones, and when he "hauled" her away it looked more as if he was supporting her steps over a rough patch of ground.

As Prudence had suspected, rudeness to a female was utterly unnatural to him. His natural acting ability held only as long as the part was not at odds with his own character.

Hardcastle had them repeat the scene a couple of times, then sighed again and said, "No doubt it'll improve with practice. Are you ready, Miss Hardcastle?"

Aimée muddled her way through, her speeches erratic, but her lively, teasing manner to her indulgent father perfect. Then Prudence joined her, to discuss their respective suitors. She was very much aware of Rusholme watching her, and when she called Tony a "pretty monster" she couldn't help glancing at him with a smile. He grimaced at her.

A moment later Constance Neville was describing her cousin Tony as "a good-natured creature at bottom." Prudence managed not to look at Rusholme, but from the corner of her eye she saw him nodding vigorously. She almost laughed.

Next came the tavern scene. The stagehands shifted tables and chairs and took their places as Tony Lumpkin's low drinking companions. Tony seated himself at the head of the table.

Prudence knew Rusholme had taken the sheet of music of his song for one of his sisters to play for him upon the pianoforte, but she had not heard him try it. She was as surprised and delighted as the rest when she heard his resonant, tuneful baritone. As he finished the refrain of the third verse, "Toroddle, toroddle, toroll!" the players burst into spontaneous applause, adding their bravos to those of his alehouse friends.

"Don't tell poor Ben I said so," Aimée said to Prudence, "but your earl sings a sight better."

"He's not my earl," Prudence said crossly, her pleasure spoilt. Tomorrow they were to rehearse Act II, and she'd have to pretend to flirt with Rusholme. Somehow she must persuade herself to regard him solely as Tony Lumpkin or she would never be able to do it.

Seven

"The gamekeeper says the lake's frozen over, my lord," Samuel announced, bringing a pot of fresh coffee into the breakfast room.

"Hard enough for skating?" Rusholme asked.

"Yes, my lord. He walked all round the edge and right across the middle."

"Splendid," crowed Lady Estella. "I hope you have skates, Rusholme."

"Plenty. The lake—it's more of a large pond, really—quite often freezes during my father's Christmas house parties."

"I'll go with you after breakfast to check that it truly is safe." Rusholme cried off on the grounds of having a rehearsal. Though he was not at all sure he was progressing in Prudence's affections, the play was proving useful for at least one of his purposes. Lady Estella had to be satisfied with the several other gentlemen who offered to escort her.

"If your report is favorable," he consoled her, "I shall certainly skate this afternoon." So, undoubtedly, would a great many other people. There was safety in numbers.

His breakfast finished, he turned his eager steps toward the Elizabethan gallery. Today Prudence had to flirt with him while he rebuffed her. He was looking forward to the switch, anticipating no little amusement.

On the way, he was waylaid by his older nephews and nieces. They had heard about the ice.

"And we want *you* to take us skating, Uncle Garth," said one of the boys. "It'll be much more fun than with our mamas and papas telling us to be careful all the time."

"We don't mind if you bring that lady," William added. "You know, the one who helped us pick holly; the one Sophie thought was a wood elf. She's a Trojan."

"I rather doubt she'd be able to come," Rusholme said with regret. Chatting with an actress met by chance in the presence of his sisters' children had been bad enough. He could not actually invite her to join them.

"Then you *will* take us?" they clamored joyfully.

Having trapped himself, he gave in. "But sliding, not skating," he said, remembering a great many painful falls when he learned to skate. They would fall sliding, too, but with luck do themselves less damage.

"All right. We'll fetch our coats and boots."

"Not yet! I'll take you for an hour before luncheon if you are all ready and waiting. I have to rehearse now."

"Is acting fun? Grandfather says we may watch you on Twelfth Night, but Grandmama says we may not."

"I'll see what I can do," he promised.

The rehearsal had already started when he reached the gallery. As Tony did not appear until near the end of the second act, the delay didn't matter, but Hardcastle looked so relieved at Rusholme's arrival that he resolved never to be late again. The manager must have feared he had deserted them. He had forced himself upon the poor man, and it was up to him not to disrupt the company's schedule.

To his disappointment, Prudence was sitting between Mrs. and Miss Hardcastle, intent on Hastings and Marlow on stage. She gave no sign of noticing his arrival.

Hardcastle returned to the scene, and Rusholme watched Prudence's bright face as she laughed at the misunderstandings of the three men. She was beautiful, and the thought of her in another man's arms was unbearable.

Had she left a lover behind when she came to Easthaven? Had she bid him *adieu* or only *au revoir?* Or, worst of all, was she involved with one of her colleagues?

Marlow and Hastings were both personable young men and competent actors, and she was Hastings' beloved on stage. In fact, she had a scene alone with him before her scene with Tony. Rusholme didn't want to watch it. He wished the children had delayed him longer.

Prudence rose and moved with graceful dignity to take her place in readiness for her entrance. As she passed Rusholme, she nodded soberly and murmured, "Cousin Tony."

"Garth," he whispered.

With a tiny but determined shake of the head, she continued on her way.

The scene was not as painful as Rusholme feared. Hastings met Constance Neville with outstretched arms, but she only clasped his hands briefly. The warmest words they exchanged were "My dear Hastings," and "my dearest Constance." Rusholme saw no sign of a consciousness of intimacy between them, and he didn't think Prudence was a good enough actress to hide it if it existed.

Actually, loath as he was to admit any inferiority in Prudence, Miss Aimée Orlando was a far better actress. In spite of her garbled speeches, Kate Hardcastle's scene with the bashful Marlow was a delight.

Then came the scene Rusholme had been waiting for. To mislead her aunt and guardian, Constance Neville pretended to acquiesce in Mrs. Hardcastle's plan to marry her to her unwilling son. He protested mightily as she followed him on stage.

" 'I tell you, Cousin Con, it won't do!' " Rusholme found it difficult not to grin, impossible to infuse his voice with the necessary petulance. " 'I beg you'll keep your distance. I want no nearer relationship.' "

He fled to the back of the stage, Prudence at his heels. While Hastings buttered up Mrs. Hardcastle at the front, Prudence laid her hand on Rusholme's arm, smiled up at him, a fixed, unnatural smile, and batted her eyelashes. She looked as if she had something painful in her eye.

"Stop," called Hardcastle. "That won't do, Miss Savage. You need a fan. Someone find a fan. My lord—Mr. Lumpkin, I mean—pray turn your back on her, fold your arms and scowl. No, just partway round, the audience must see your face. That's better. Let's take it again from your entrance."

The fan somewhat improved matters, but Prudence remained stiff and clearly ill at ease. She didn't seem to know how to flirt, nor to have any desire to learn. Rusholme wanted to reassure her, to promise he'd not profit from the situation by taking unwanted liberties, to explain that his aim was to win her, not to force her.

This was neither the time nor the place.

"Once more," Hardcastle ordered. "No, you still haven't the way of it, Miss Savage. I suggest you apply to Miss Orlando for lessons in coquetry. All right, we'll go on."

Mrs. Hardcastle called Tony and Constance to come and measure heights against each other. Hardcastle explained to Rusholme how to jerk his head back and to one side while Prudence cocked her head to the other side, to give the appearance of a sharp blow without actual contact. This they managed to his satisfaction.

"Oh, lud!" she cried, "he has almost cracked my head." She clutched her head and stumbled forward in so realistic a fashion Rusholme was afraid for a moment he had really hurt her, though he'd felt nothing.

Turning, she peeked through her fingers at him, eyes a-sparkle. The uncomfortable flirtation over, she was once more enjoying herself. Satisfied, Rusholme exerted himself to respond with churlish sullenness to Mrs. Hardcastle's reproaches.

The women left the stage, and Tony proceeded to vilify Constance to Hastings in thoroughly abusive terms. With Prudence watching and laughing at him, Rusholme let himself go and ended the act with a snatch of song to a burst of applause.

"Not bad, my lord," Hardcastle observed hopefully.

Much as Rusholme wished to talk to Prudence, he had to rush off to keep his promise to his nieces and nephews. Scraped hands, bruised knees, and one bloody nose made him regret not having invited her. She would have known how to cope! However, he returned the children to the house with no limbs broken.

After luncheon, with only a couple of hours left of midwinter's short daylight, he went back to the frozen lake with most of the younger guests and a few of the older. Though an icy breeze blew fitfully from the northeast, the sun shone, and a shrubbery of evergreen laurels and junipers sheltered the lake.

Several people, as soon as they actually saw the ice, decided discretion was the better part of valor and spectatorship the better part of sport. Footmen had carried down chairs to supplement the two wooden benches, so they sat or strolled about.

Two or three ladies not quite bold enough to try skates sat on

chairs to be pushed about on the ice by obliging gentlemen. Lady
Estella regarded these with great scorn. Strapping on a pair of
blades, she set off whizzing across the lake with the same verve
and aplomb with which, mounted, she tackled the highest hedges.

This was a tactical error if she hoped for Rusholme's company.

Lady Anne sat prettily helpless on a chair and held out a dainty
foot in a pink leather half boot.

"If you would be so kind, Lord Rusholme. I have no notion
how to put them on, I vow."

Politeness won. "Of course, ma'am," he said, swallowing a
sigh.

Once the skates were attached, she revealed that she had never
skated in her life. "But I am determined to try it, if you will
support me, sir."

So he gave her his arm, and she clung to it as they made a
circuit of the lake. Her progress was suspiciously free of staggers
and stumbles, although she gave less attention to her feet than
to fluttering her eyelashes and looking up at him adoringly—in
a way Prudence would have done well to emulate. Rusholme was
certain she was a competent skater, but he could hardly call her
a liar.

"I expect you'd like to rest for a while," he suggested hopefully
as they returned to the chairs.

"Oh, no, I am just beginning to master it. Pray let us go round
again."

As the sun's red disk began to sink behind the hills, the air
seemed to grow chillier. The spectators, shivering, started to
stroll back toward the house. Soon skaters were taking off their
skates and departing likewise. Footmen came to remove the
chairs.

Rusholme and his partner once more approached the benches.

"What an excellent teacher you are, Lord Rusholme," cried
Lady Anne gaily. "I do believe I shall venture across on my own,
if you will wait for me at the other side."

No gentleman could desert her alone in the dusk. With the
deepest reluctance, he agreed. He was not in the least surprised

when, reaching the center, she floundered for the first time and subsided gracefully onto the ice.

"Oh, my ankle!" she wailed. "It hurts dreadfully. I fear it is broken."

Rusholme looked around wildly. Not a soul in sight. Whether he carried her home in his arms or stayed with her in growing darkness until someone realized they were missing, Lady Anne could claim she was compromised and demand marriage. What the devil was he to do?

"Go out in the bloody cold when we don't have to," Aimée exclaimed with a shudder, "and all for what? So's we can fall down and get bruises all over! And maybe break a leg like Ben. You know what, Sera, you got windmills in your head."

"I've always wanted to try skating."

"Go ahead, dear, but I'm not going with you. If you're not back by half an hour after dark, I'll send someone to pick up the pieces."

Prudence had much the same reaction from the rest of the troupe. She was determined, however. With visions of herself swooping gracefully across the ice, she went to find the First Footman.

"Yes, miss, I'll find you a pair of skates, and show you how to put 'em on, right enough. If you go down to the lake round about sunset, the nobs'll be leaving and you'll have it all to yourself."

"None of you servants skate?" she asked.

"After Twelfth Night, maybe. With all the people in the house and the New Year's Ball coming up, we've none of us a minute to call our own. A couple of the under-footmen'll go to fetch the chairs, though. You can go with them."

So Prudence set off with an escort of three smart footmen in puce livery. One carried the skates for her, curly-toed steel blades attached to wooden soles, with leather straps to fasten them to the feet. As they approached the lake, they heard voices coming toward them. With a whispered word of thanks, Prudence took her skates, and stepping off the path, she slipped in among the bushes.

She found a spot where she could watch without being seen. Several people were leaving already, but a number of skaters still skimmed and whirled across the ice with varying degrees of expertise. It was a delightful scene, the ladies in vivid-hued velvet pelisses with fur pelerines and muffs, the gentlemen with their coattails flying.

Quite against her will, Prudence's eyes sought out Lord Rusholme. She had not the least difficulty recognizing him, though he was on the far side of the lake, a lady in ruby velvet clinging to his arm.

As they moved around the perimeter toward her, Prudence recognized Lady Anne. Her beautiful face, framed by golden ringlets and aglow from the exercise, was raised to gaze adoringly up at Rusholme. Prudence watched her smile, pout, delicately flutter her eyelashes, then tap him on the cheek with one gloved finger.

So that was how it was done, though admittedly Rusholme did not look as if he were enjoying the flirtation. In fact, he seemed to be trying to hurry while she held him back.

By then the rest of the skaters had taken off their blades and set off for the house, chatting hopefully of tea and hot chocolate. The footmen gathered the chairs and trudged after them. Rusholme and Lady Anne stopped on the ice near the benches.

"What an excellent teacher you are, Lord Rusholme," cried Lady Anne gaily. "I do believe I shall venture across on my own, if you will wait for me at the other side."

"It's getting dark. You had best try it tomorrow."

"There may be a thaw, or I may have lost the knack by then. I want to do it now."

She let go his arm and started straight across the lake, her movements not fast, but with none of a learner's precarious balance. From behind her juniper, Prudence heard Rusholme softly groan.

Hands on hips, his stance the essence of exasperation, he watched Lady Anne for a moment, then set off after her. Reaching the center, she suddenly faltered, waved her arms, and sank down onto the ice.

"Oh, my ankle!" she wailed. "It hurts dreadfully. I fear it is broken."

Rusholme swivelled on his skates and looked back, peering through the gathering gloom. His shoulders slumped. He turned and headed for Lady Anne, deep reluctance in every line of his body.

Prudence decided it was time to intervene. Dropping her skates on the nearest bench, beside a greatcoat draped over its back, she set one tentative foot on the ice.

"May I be of assistance?" she called.

Rusholme swung round. "Miss Savage! Thank heaven! Lady Anne has injured her ankle."

His skeptical voice echoed Prudence's thoughts. However, when she set her second foot on the ice and realized just how slippery it was, she began to feel more charitable. Lady Anne had undoubtedly deliberately contrived to be left alone with Lord Rusholme, but it was just possible her fall and her injury were genuine.

Sliding one foot forward at a time, Prudence made her way toward the pair. Lady Anne scowled at her.

"Allow me to present Miss Savage," said Rusholme, always the gentleman even in the most unpromising circumstances.

"My lady." Prudence embarked upon a curtsy and quickly changed her mind as one foot slithered a few inches.

"I don't care to consort with actresses," said Lady Anne coldly.

"Don't be caperwitted," Rusholme snapped at her, and she gasped in shock. "Miss Savage, if you wouldn't mind supporting me while I take off my skates, perhaps between us we might help Lady Anne off the ice."

Prudence willed her feet not to slip out from under her as he put one arm round her shoulders. He stood on one leg, reached down to unbuckle the straps on the other foot, then reversed the process. The weight of his arm was warm and somehow comfortable. She thought he gave her a brief, one-armed hug before he released her, but she couldn't be sure.

Crouching, he removed Lady Anne's skates. "I cannot carry you across the ice," he said. "We should both go flying. With Miss Savage on one side and me on the other, I hope we can lift you so that with support you can hop to the bank."

"I can't possibly," she moaned.

"You cannot stay here. The ice will begin to melt beneath you. I shall have to drag you."

Picturing Lady Anne sliding on her bottom across the ice, Prudence suppressed a giggle. Perhaps the girl envisioned the same undignified posture, for she said ungraciously, "Oh, very well, then, I shall try to hop."

Fortunately Prudence was beginning to get the knack of walking on ice. Somehow they made it to the bench without worse than a few wobbles. Lady Anne touched down with her supposedly bad foot two or three times, each time letting out a gasp a trifle too late to be quite convincing. She plumped down on the bench with a martyred sigh.

"Here, this will keep you warm." Rusholme took his greatcoat from the back of the bench and spread it over her, then turned to Prudence. "Thank you, Miss Savage. Would it be too great an imposition to ask you to keep Lady Anne company while I go for help?" *Please,* his tone begged.

"Of course not." Prudence hoped her amusement was hidden by the darkness, now near complete but for a glimmer of starlight reflected off the ice.

"You stay with me, Lord Rusholme," said Lady Anne. "She can go for help."

"I shall go much faster," he pointed out, "and as it is my home I know what orders to give and to whom to give them."

Not, Prudence noted gratefully, "No one will take any notice of an actress's orders." What a dear he was!

Before Lady Anne could think up some credible reason to keep him at her side, he strode off up the path. Lady Anne sat there in a silence from which sulkiness emanated in waves. Prudence pulled her cloak about her and strolled up and down, unwilling to risk a rebuff if she dared venture to share the bench.

After a few minutes, Lady Anne said petulantly, "I daresay I may as well go after him."

"What of your ankle, my lady?"

"I only twisted it, after all. It is quite better now."

"Shall I walk beside you in case it fails again?"

"No!" Without further ado, she flung off Rusholme's coat and stalked away.

Prudence watched her go. No one could have said there was a spring in her step, but she walked without any sign of a hobble, not even pretending to favor her supposedly twisted ankle. Grinning, Prudence shook her head.

About to follow, she realized it was growing lighter instead of darker, as a nearly full moon edged above the woods to the east. Sitting down, she strapped on the skates.

Two tottering steps and she was on the ice. She sat down again, hard.

Perseverance, she told herself sternly, struggling to her feet. In her effort not to go over backward again, she overcorrected and landed on hands and knees. "Ouch!"

"Miss Savage?" Rusholme's voice, at once followed by Rusholme's roar of laughter. "Methinks you need my arm."

Cautiously she knelt up and turned her head. "What are you doing here?" she asked crossly.

Coming over to set her on her feet and help her back to the bench, he explained. "I'd scarce reached the house when I met Lord and Lady Winkworth setting out after their daughter. I told them what had happened. Lady Winkworth turned back to organize a rescue party, which she seemed oddly reluctant to do. Lord Winkworth and I set out down the path and met a miraculously recovered Lady Anne. He turned back with her. I came on."

"They must have thought that odd."

"I insisted on fetching the two pairs of skates we'd left in the middle of the lake, in case they are needed tomorrow."

"Either they would still be here tomorrow," Prudence pointed out dryly, "or it will thaw, in which case they'll sink, but you won't need them."

"True," he said, sounding crestfallen. "I hadn't thought of that. Still, I don't expect they will, either."

She smiled. "You should have said you came for your coat."

"She left it here?" He turned his head and saw it, where Prudence had laid it over the back of the bench. "The little . . . ahem! Of course, I really came back to see that you were all right. Were you going to try to skate in the dark?"

"It's not dark. There's a beautiful moon. I shall go on trying a little longer, but it's more difficult than I thought," she confessed.

"May I help you? Let me, Prudence."

Her prosaic name sounded almost romantic on his lips. The moonlight was romantic; the vast starry vault above was romantic; his dark eyes gazed down at her, filled with mystery and romance. She dared not. "No."

He took her hand. "I promise—I swear by the honor of a gentleman, I shan't force my attentions on you."

With a sigh for her own weakness, she acquiesced. After all, it was far too cold for serious misbehavior. What harm could there be in taking a couple of turns about the lake?

He fetched the abandoned skates, put his on, and led her onto the ice. Concentrating on her feet and his instructions, at first she was too busy to pay much heed to his closeness. Then she found the rhythm and her balance. Exhilaration swept through her.

As if Rusholme sensed it, he speeded up. Gently, irresistibly, he drew her with him in a soaring, swooping flight that seemed to last forever—or no time at all before, both hands at her waist, he swung them to a halt in the middle of the lake.

Laughing with delight, she gazed up at his smiling face. His smiled faded. In the magical moonlight his face was intent, eager.

He pulled her closer, into his arms, and the fragrance of sandalwood filled her nostrils. Her heart thudded in her breast as his
head bent toward her.

The crunch of feet on gravel sounded loud in the stillness.
"Seraphina? Aimée sent me to see. . . . Oh, beg pardon, I'm sure.
I didn't mean to interrupt anything."

"No! Wait! I'm coming."

Lord Rusholme gave her his arm to the bench. He crouched
to take off her skates, and gentlemanly to the last, when she
shivered he draped his greatcoat about her shoulders. Then all
three, in silence, walked back up to the house together.

Eight

Act III: Tony Lumpkin promises to help Constance flee with
Hastings and even steals her jewels for her from his mother's
bureau.

" 'My dear cousin!' " Constance cries fervently.

To quell the blush that threatened when Rusholme grinned at
her, Prudence had to imagine falling through the ice into the
frigid water below. He knew how nearly she had succumbed to
moonlight and his kiss. If Hastings had not arrived at precisely
the wrong moment. . . . The *right* moment, she corrected herself.

But right or wrong, he had arrived. She was on her guard now,
aware of her own susceptibility. Unfortunately, that was not going
to help her tackle him about the stage direction that had been
preying on her mind ever since he had taken Ben's part.

She was happier now about the coquetting business. Copying
Lady Anne rather than Aimée, she need not fear she would do
anything to make him think her unspeakably vulgar.

Though if he thought her unspeakably vulgar, perhaps he'd
lose interest in her, a situation devoutly to be wished. Was it not?

Determinedly she turned her attention back to the stage, where
Marlow flirted with Kate Hardcastle under the impression that
she was a servant. All coy encouragement, Aimée actually re-

membered most of her lines. On stage she seemed playful, not vulgar, whereas Lady Anne's attempt to entrap Rusholme into marriage was highly improper. Once more perplexed, Prudence sighed.

Beside her, Ben Dandridge echoed her sigh. His broken leg stretched before him, he had watched the rehearsal lost in gloom, especially when Tony plagued Mrs. Hardcastle. Impudence came naturally to him, and Rusholme's attempt to counterfeit it pained him more than his broken bones.

"Tell his lordship I'd like a word with him after," he said in an undertone to Prudence when she joined him.

"You will give him some advice?"

"Gad no! Me advise an earl? That's a laugh."

Rusholme saw them whispering and wondered if Dandridge was pointing out to her how badly his substitute acted. More likely he considered that too obvious to mention and was simply venting his bile. The poor fellow had a right to chagrin, though not to blame Rusholme for his plight. He might well wish for a more adequate replacement.

The rehearsal ended and Prudence approached Rusholme. Her gaze fixed on his middle waistcoat button, she said, "Can you spare a moment to speak to Ben, my lord?"

Her return to strict formality surprised him. After the way she had responded to him last night, even though she had drawn back at the last moment, he had expected at least acknowledgment of the attraction between them. Instead, she behaved like a modest, respectable woman afraid of her own impulses.

She was an actress, he reminded himself. The rôle of a proper young lady came easily to her, witness her Constance Neville. Maybe she was lost in the part, so involved she reacted like Constance on stage and off.

In which case he wished his father had chosen *The Beggars' Opera,* with Prudence as the promiscuous Polly Peachum!

But he could afford to wait. In any case, despite being sorely tempted last night, he had no intention of proceeding to the actual seduction scene under his parents' roof. In the meantime, it might prove amusing to treat her as the virtuous damsel she presently felt herself to be.

"Certainly, Miss Savage," he said gravely. "After I have spoken to Dandridge, may I beg for a word with you?"

"Yes." She glanced quickly up at his face, then down again, looking adorably flustered. "I must talk to you about . . . about Act IV."

Aha, the fondling business. A smile tugging at the corners of his mouth, Rusholme went to see the injured actor.

Dandridge reached for his crutches.

"Don't stand up, man. What can I do for you?"

"I just want to thank you, my lord," Dandridge said gruffly.

"Thank me?"

"If they'd had to hire another actor, he'd've had to be paid, out of my share. I'd not've got a penny."

"I see! I can't claim I realized that, still less that my motive was to aid you, but I'm glad it has worked out well for you. Are you getting proper care?"

"Better'n I'd get anywheres else. I'm told these crutches were your lordship's."

"I thought they looked familiar." Rusholme laughed. "I'd like to be able to say I came off my horse attempting a daring jump, but the fact is I stumbled going down the stairs in a hurry."

Dandridge grinned. "It happens to the best of us, my lord," he said, gesturing ruefully at his splinted leg.

Waiting a few paces off, Prudence saw Ben smile. Rusholme had cheered him up when he could so easily have condescended, or even sneered at the ex-acrobat for his clumsiness. The earl was considerate and amusing as well as perilously seductive. How was she to fight him?

He came over to her. "Before we discuss Act IV, Miss Savage," he said seriously, "may I request your counsel? I'm all too aware I make a sorry botch of Tony's scenes with his mother, so I asked Dandridge to advise me. He said he couldn't possibly. Do you know why?"

She responded to his seriousness with frankness. "In part it is because you are a nobleman. He would not presume to instruct you. But I believe it's mostly because he is not conscious of how he does what he does. Since he does not analyze his method, he cannot teach it."

"Then I am sunk, since Hardcastle merely tells me I am not rude enough, unless you can help me?"

"I can only suggest you try to think of yourself as Tony Lumpkin, not as Lord Rusholme playing Tony Lumpkin. That is not very helpful, I fear."

He smiled wryly. "I'll try, but I suspect I am too self-conscious, quite the reverse of Dandridge. Now, what is the difficulty with Act IV?"

"I expect you can guess."

"You don't care to abuse me to my face?" he teased.

"Constance is perfectly willing to abuse Tony, I assure you."

"But, if I'm not mistaken, Constance is not willing to fondle her dear cousin."

"The stage direction reads *'seem* to fondle,' " Prudence reminded him firmly.

"Did I not promise on my honor not to force my attentions on you? Tony stands by Rusholme's word. Come, now, let us see what we can work out which will satisfy Hardcastle and our audience without offending your sensibilities."

Her heart swelling with gratitude, Prudence agreed. It wasn't his fault that his hand at her waist made her quiver inside and her hand on his shoulder burned at the feel of the hard muscle beneath the blue Bath cloth. As he pointed out, they were no closer than a thousand couples waltzing in fashionable ballrooms.

The Easthavens' New Year's Ball was tomorrow. Rusholme would be waltzing with Lady Estella, Miss Wallace, even Lady Anne, not with Prudence.

The wind changed that night, bringing warm, moist air from the southwest. Before breakfast on New Year's Eve, Prudence walked down to the lake. The ice was rapidly melting. Soon the spot where Rusholme had nearly kissed her by moonlight would be just another patch of rippling water reflecting the gray overcast.

The rehearsal of Act IV went well enough for Mr. Hardcastle to declare a holiday on New Year's Day. Rusholme continued to treat Prudence with absolute courtesy, not once hinting at any desire for an improper relationship. Of course she was glad, but she could not help wondering. . . .

Was he simply fickle? Had her admittedly equivocal behavior on the lake convinced him of her respectability? Had his parents somehow learned of his gallantries and forbidden them? Or did discretion, honor, and kindness alike dictate an end to his hopes of an illicit liaison because he had made up his mind to offer for Miss Wallace?

The last possibility so cast down Prudence's spirits that Aimée remarked upon it. "Cheer up, Sera," she said. "Maybe we aren't invited to the nobs' ball, but you wouldn't enjoy it anyways with all them high-and-mighty ladies looking down their noses at you."

"I know. I don't want to attend, but I should like to see it."

"Then go and peek through the windows," Aimée suggested.

So that night Prudence crept downstairs and slipped out through a side door. She made her way around to the terrace outside the ballroom. The weather was so much warmer than it had been that though December was about to become January, she was quite comfortable in her woollen gown and green cloak.

She moved up the steps, between the stone gryphons standing guard on pedestals at the top. The strains of a country dance floated out into the night air. Silently Prudence flitted from one window to the next until she found one where the crimson velvet curtains did not quite meet. Through the narrow slit she glimpsed a gentleman's black-clad shoulder, the pretty face of an unknown lady with pearls entwined in her blond hair, and several bobbing heads beyond.

She wanted to see Lord Rusholme, she confessed to herself. She wanted to know the identity of his partner, whether he was lavishing attention on Miss Wallace, galloping around the floor

with Lady Estella, or under attack again by Lady Anne. The
servants said Lady Anne had taken up with Mr. Ffoliot since her
mishap on the lake, but he was ineligible. Beautiful as she was,
she might hope in her ballroom finery to dazzle Rusholme.

Prudence moved on to one of the French window bays. No
one would venture out to the terrace at this time of year, she
thought. Expecting to find the door locked, she turned the handle.

The door opened. The noise was suddenly loud: music of
strings, spinet, and flute; voices and laughter; the thump of feet
on polished parquet. Closing the door behind her, Prudence stole
over to the curtains. Here she was, skulking behind the arras
again!

This time she could bolt if anyone approached. Parting the
curtains the merest trifle, she put her eye to the gap.

A swirl of color met her wondering gaze. Beneath chandeliers
ablaze with hundreds of wax candles, jewels sparkled, gold
gleamed, spangles shimmered. Lady Easthaven crossed just in
front of the curtains, glittering with a king's ransom in diamonds
and amethysts—which clashed abominably with her claret red
gown. She stopped no more than a yard off to exchange a word
with a gentleman. As he turned his head, Prudence recognized
the marquis, his red face beaming.

"I'm good and ready for my supper, my dear," he said.

"Just as soon as this set is finished," she assured him. "You
really must speak to Garth. He keeps dancing with his sisters
and his friends' wives."

Lord Easthaven merely chuckled. Prudence at once decided
she liked him.

She could not see Rusholme, peer as she might. Miss Wallace
was nearby, partnered by her brother-in-law, Mr. Denham. Lady
Anne tripped across Prudence's field of vision, arm linked with
Mr. Ffoliot's. She was indeed dazzling in a rose silk gown with
a white lace overskirt, cut quite as low at the neck as Prudence's
captive-princess dress. But she was not with Rusholme, and to
judge from Lady Easthaven's words, he had not danced with her.

The music came to an end. People began to stream toward the

pillared exit to the anteroom, presumably on their way to supper. Prudence sighed—she had seen all she was going to see.

She was turning away when she heard Lady Anne's voice, close by. "No, I am not hungry. La! It is too horridly hot in here."

A man spoke. "Perhaps a breath of fresh air? The weather is amazingly warm for the season."

"Well, just for a moment, if the doors are not locked. I feel quite faint. I am sure Mama could not object to my stepping out just for a moment."

Prudence leapt for the door. Closing it behind her with a distinct click, she ducked to her right. As the curtains parted and light flooded forth, she crouched down in the angle where the bay met the wall.

A moment later, Lady Anne and Mr. Ffoliot stepped out onto the terrace. She was fanning herself vigorously, as if to lend color to her words. He pulled the door shut, offered his arm, and led her away from the stream of light.

"It is colder than I thought," Lady Anne complained. "I believe I shall go in."

"Never fear, my dear, I shall keep you warm." Mr. Ffoliot swept her into his arms.

"Let me go!" she exclaimed. "You go too far, sir, indeed you do."

"I shall let you go," he assured her, sounding amused, "as soon as we are discovered. I daresay your parents will be glad to accept my suit when you are found out here in my embrace."

Prudence stifled a chuckle. Lady Anne was caught in the net she had cast for Rusholme.

"But I don't want to marry you!"

"I'm not eager to tie the knot myself, but you've a devilish attractive fortune, my dear. Come, I'll teach you to love me." He drew her closer.

"No!" she cried, beating on his chest as he bent his head to kiss her.

Deciding matters had gone far enough, Prudence stood up and

took off her cloak. She folded it over her arm and approached the couple.

"My lady, your wrap," she announced in a loud voice. "You'll catch your death."

Ffoliot jumped back. "What the deuce?"

Prudence draped her cloak around the sobbing girl and thrust a handkerchief into her hand. "Go on in," she said gently. "I shan't tell."

Lady Anne fled. Prudence watched to be sure she was safe inside.

"You're no abigail," said Ffoliot. "Who the devil are you?"

Not deigning to respond, Prudence turned away.

He seized her arm and pulled her into the light. "The other actress, by all that's holy! Miss Savage, isn't it? Well, you've savaged my chances with Lady Anne. You can't compensate me for loss of her fortune, but a little compensation for loss of her person will not come amiss."

"You already have Aimée," Prudence pointed out. "You cannot want two mistresses at once."

"You'd be surprised." He reached for her other arm.

She wrenched herself free and dashed toward the terrace steps. As she reached the top, he caught her. Grasping her shoulders, he swung her around and backed her against the pedestal. His body crushed her against the stone.

"Not so fast, little savage. I want compensation, and if you won't give it, I'll take it."

Struggling in vain, Prudence knew the helpless fear Lady Anne must have felt. In saving the girl she had ruined herself.

Last in the procession, his sister on his arm, Rusholme scanned the supper room. He didn't want inadvertently to find himself seated beside Lady Anne, Lady Estella, or Miss Wallace after taking so much trouble to avoid them in the ballroom.

There was Kitty Wallace, with David and Mrs. Denham as usual, poor little mouse. There was Lady Estella, apparently quite content with a noisy group of hunt-mad fellows. No sign of Lady Anne.

Nor any sign of Henry Ffoliot. He had seen them dancing together. What the deuce was Ffoliot up to? He could not be trusted to observe the proprieties. Perhaps Lady Anne deserved to be trapped into marrying him, but she was a guest at Easthaven. Rusholme acknowledged a certain responsibility for her well-being in his parents' house.

He sighed. "I'm afraid I'm going to abandon you, Maria. I daresay I'll miss the toast to the new year, but if Mama asks, I'll be back shortly."

As he reached the empty ballroom, a female figure rushed in from the terrace, wrapped in a leaf green cloak and weeping into a handkerchief.

"Prudence!"

The woman raised her head: startled blue eyes awash with tears, framed by golden ringlets.

"Lady Anne? What's happened?"

"Mr. Ff-f-foliot," she wept. "He tried to k-kiss me. Miss S-savage saved me."

"She's out there?" Not waiting for an answer, he strode past her, his heart in his throat.

Beyond the wedge of light from within, the night was inky black. For a moment Rusholme paused, wondering which way to turn, afraid he was too late. Then his eyes adjusted. Against the pale stonework was a deeper shadow, Ffoliot's black coat and Prudence's dark dress merged into one silhouette.

Oh, God, did she *want* Ffoliot?

"No!" A strangled cry. "Let me go!"

"Let her go."

Ffoliot jumped. Slowly he turned, still gripping Prudence's arm. "Rusholme? What the devil is it to you?"

"Let her go."

"Oh, so that's it, is it? You're not usually so possessive of your bits of game."

"I said, let her go. Unless you wish to make the intimate acquaintance of the goldfish pond at the foot of the steps."

"I fancy you'd not have it all your own way if we came to cuffs!" said Ffoliot, piqued. "Still, she's hardly worth a darkened daylight to either of us. She's only another actress."

"An unwilling actress, and a guest in my home." Rusholme stepped forward, and at last Ffoliot hurriedly let go Prudence's arm. "To my sorrow, you also are a guest in my home. However, I have an odd premonition that in the morning you will suddenly recall an urgent appointment elsewhere. Do I make myself plain?"

"Quite plain. What a tempest in a teacup over a tuppenny lightskirt! I wish you joy of the doxy." He sauntered past Rusholme and into the house.

Prudence huddled by the gryphon, her face hidden in her hands. Gently Rusholme pulled her into his arms and held her like a frightened child. How had she grown so dear in so short a time? He stroked her rosemary-fragrant hair until her shaking ceased.

"Better? I shan't let him harm you."

With two fingers he raised her chin, scanning her pale face for signs of fear. No glint of tears in the faint light from the windows. Her mouth trembled. It was the most natural thing in the world to bow his head and kiss her.

She twisted from his embrace. "Don't! I thought you were different. You're all alike, every one of you!"

Sobbing, she stumbled down the steps and disappeared into the darkness.

Nine

After sinking into blessed oblivion the moment her head touched the pillow, Prudence woke at daybreak. She felt stifled. She had to get out of the house, *his* house, where somewhere in the distant unknown corridors he lay sleeping—or plotting her downfall.

She turned her head. Aimée was lost in slumber, a sweet, innocent smile curving her lips. How could one ever guess what lay behind another's mask?

Prudence slipped out of bed and quickly dressed. Lady Anne had her green cloak, the one *he* said made her look like a wood elf. No matter, she had thriftily kept her old brown cloak which looked as drab as she felt. Wrapping it around her, she made her way to the side door and stepped out into the gray dawn.

To her right lay the lake, to her left the Yule log's path, straight ahead the woods where the holly grew. Haunted by memories, she'd never be able to decide what to do. She trudged around the vast mansion and set off down the drive.

Today was a holiday. She need not see Rusholme until tomorrow, Act V, when he'd take her hand only to reject her. That would be bad enough. She had rather never set eyes on him again. But in the days to follow, again and again she must flirt with him, pretend to fondle, smile and pretend she didn't care.

She couldn't! Somehow the company must manage without her.

They had been so kind to her, giving her a chance when she had never acted in her life, teaching and encouraging, applauding her successes and glossing over her failures. How could she let them down?

She came to the end of the drive. The gryphon-posted gates stood hospitably open, as always when the family was at home. The brick lodge to one side was silent, still, the only hint of life a thin wisp of smoke from the chimney. Prudence crossed the lane and started along a grassy ride through the bare woods on the other side.

A light rain began to fall. She scarcely noticed. Lost in doubt and misery she plodded on.

A squirrel chattered at her from a tree. Somewhere a woodpecker drummed briefly, paused, and drummed again, a hollow tock-tock-tock. Closer, behind her, a muffled thudding sounded like a subdued echo.

Not an echo, hoofbeats on damp grass. Prudence swung round as the tall bay slowed to a stop beside her. Her gaze travelled up the glossy top boot, the muscular thigh, the straight torso clad in a caped greatcoat. She knew who it was long before her eyes reached his face, before Rusholme's voice said roughly, "So it *is* you."

She backed away, clasping her arms protectively across her breast.

"Don't run from me!" His words emerged as a cry of pain.

On the verge of turning to flee among the trees, she stopped. She was tired of running away. Somehow, however hard it was to say it outright, she had to convince him that she would never be his mistress.

"Look, I'll dismount. We'll walk with Salamander between us. He's a pretty effective barrier."

"Salamander? Not named after the lizard, surely. A fire elemental?"

"For his color and spirit."

"He should have taken the part of the dragon in the mummers' play." It was all too easy to fall into friendly conversation with him, to forget past and future in the pleasure of his company.

"I'd give a monkey to have seen my mother's face if Salamander had pranced across her drawing room. No, I suspect he'd be an even worse actor than I am."

Prudence wished she could see his face, but the horse's nose was between them. She took a deep breath. "I shan't be acting any more after Twelfth Night."

Rusholme was silent for three paces. Then, "It's my fault, isn't it?" he said quietly.

"Only in part. As Aimée said, if it was not you, it would be another. I was woefully naïve to think I could become an actress without sharing the general reputation of actresses."

"You have not been with the company very long, have you? I couldn't sleep last night. I went over and over everything you ever said to me. I remembered you told me you had too little experience to play Kate Hardcastle."

"Just a few months."

"What will you do next? You have relatives to turn to?"

"No." Prudence could scarcely speak for relief that he had asked such a question rather than offering his protection.

"Then how will you live?"

"I shall go back to being a governess."

"A governess!" He stopped stockstill and bent to peer at her under Salamander's neck. "You!"

She smiled, at the picture he presented and at his disbelief. "A life of the utmost respectability, and dullness."

"You were a governess?"

"For nearly ten years."

"That explains a good deal, your clothes, your way with children, your manners, your education."

"I was educated to be a governess. I had a choice of that or finding a curate to marry. My father was a clergyman, you see."

"I do indeed begin to see," he said thoughtfully. Salamander tossed his head, and Rusholme started walking again. "I don't blame you in the least for champing at the bit, but what on earth made you kick over the traces?"

"I suppose I'd have to say coincidence and caprice. The youngest child of the family who employed me was sent off to school. Seeking a new position is always an uncomfortable business, so I was rather moped. On my way to London I had to change stagecoaches in Cheltenham, and I happened to see a theater bill, which happened to have a notice in small print saying the company needed an actress. Much as I like children, it sounded far more interesting and exciting than being a governess."

"Undoubtedly."

"I must have been mad."

"Do you regret it?"

"No . . . ," Prudence said uncertainly. She thought for a moment of all that had happened since that day, then said more decidedly, "No, I don't."

"I'm glad. But what made you imagine you could act?"

"I had been acting all my life! My father thought me pious and dutiful. My employers thought me humble and obedient, and grateful for the pittance they paid me."

"As any number of tedious and exasperating ladies and gentlemen think I am delighted to welcome them to Easthaven." He stopped again as they reached the edge of the wood. "All this will be mine one day," he said with a sweeping gesture.

The track had gradually risen. Before them spread a wide valley, a tidy, hedged checkerboard of pasture dotted with fat cattle, and brown plowland, some striped green with winter wheat. Spinneys and copses, a stream lined with willows and alders, a prosperous-looking whitewashed farmhouse with barns and stables, all would be his one day.

Lord Rusholme could not have found a more tactful way of making his point: he was heir to a marquis. Whether Prudence was actress or governess, she belonged to another world.

"Will it be difficult to find another post?" he asked abruptly.

"I doubt it. I am an excellent governess, and I have first-rate references."

"No one will question the missing months?"

"Unlikely. If they do, I shall say I had to nurse my father on his deathbed. It's true enough, only it happened several years ago."

"So you have no relatives to take you in."

If Mr. Ffoliot had spoken thus, in that meditative tone, Prudence might have feared abduction. Perhaps she was a complete addlepate, but she trusted Rusholme. From his point of view, last night had been no different from the night on the lake, when she had so nearly welcomed his kiss. Had she not just been assaulted by Ffoliot, she'd not have reacted so violently.

Now that the earl knew who she was, she dared to hope he would not try to take advantage of her susceptibility, of which he was certainly well aware. For the next few days they could be friends, working together to produce the best performance of which they were capable.

Then she must return to the staid tedium of the schoolroom, but at least she'd have memories to sustain her through the endless years to come.

"You were never on stage in London?" Rusholme asked.

"Only in Cheltenham, and here, of course." Roused from her musing, Prudence realized the mizzle had slowly but surely seeped through her threadbare cloak, damping the shoulders of her gown. She shivered.

"My dear . . . Cousin Con, you will be soaked to the skin! I'll not offer to take you up on Salamander, but we must turn back."

"I don't want to cut short your ride."

"I can ride later, if you will allow me to escort you."

He said no more while he turned the horse. Prudence fell into step beside him. She no longer felt any need to keep the great beast between them. They started down the slope between the dripping trees.

"I haven't yet apologized for last night," said Rusholme, his gaze straight ahead. "I'm not really like Ffoliot, you know."

"I know. If he had not just frightened me, I wouldn't have been so angry, and I'd never have said that."

"Can you forgive me?"

"I already have, if there is anything to forgive. You had no reason to believe me different from any other actress."

"I had every reason!" He turned his head to smile at her. "Did I not say the first time we met what an unusual actress you are? Nothing since has given me any cause to change my opinion, and now I know I was right. You are no more an actress at heart than I am an actor."

"I have enjoyed it, most of it, but I realized several days ago that I'm not really suited to the life," Prudence admitted.

"Which is not to say you are as bad at it as I am. Though I cannot regret it, I ought not to have insisted on taking Tony's part. I shall let you all down."

"Not at all, it's just. . . . Oh, I have an idea. Your trouble is you cannot bring yourself to be rude to your mother—Mrs. Hardcastle, that is. Suppose you pretend to yourself you are speaking to Mr. Ffoliot?"

"Ffoliot!"

"I've never in my life heard so insolent and contemptuous a tone as you used to him last night."

Rusholme stared at her, then laughed. "It might work."

"Then at least something good would come out of my unpleasant experience."

"Something good already has," he said softly. "I have found a new friend."

Which was precisely what Prudence had wished for, so why was she filled with discontent?

The rest of the way back to the house, they talked about a myriad of subjects. When they parted at the arched entrance to the stable yard, Rusholme said sternly, "Go straight in and change into dry clothes."

Prudence curtsied, smiling. "Yes, my lord."

"Baggage! *Please* go and change. If you take ill, how shall I play Tony without my Cousin Con? And have a hot drink."

She glanced back as she walked on to the side door. He still stood there, rubbing Salamander's nose but watching her. He waved and turned away.

When she reached the bedchamber, Aimée was dressing. She swung round, her face agog with curiosity.

"Don't tell me you been out for a walk already," she exclaimed, "and in the rain! You're sopping wet."

"Just damp." Prudence took off her brown cloak.

"You're crazy. Sera, what the deuce happened last night? Ffoliot was in a devilish temper and said he had to leave today, but he wouldn't tell me why. Then a few minutes ago Lady Winkworth's abigail brought that, for you." She gestured at the dressing table.

Thankfully, Prudence saw her green cloak, which she had feared might be gone for good. On top of it lay her handkerchief, a plain square of white cotton, washed, ironed, and neatly folded.

"Your Ffoliot tried to compromise Lady Anne," she said as

she picked up the handkerchief to put it away. Beneath it was another, a dainty thing of finest linen, lace-edged, with a posy of violets embroidered in one corner. "Oh, bother! Here's one of her handkerchiefs. I shall have to return it."

"You caught them on the terrace and foiled his plan?" Aimée laughed. "Poor fellow, he'll have to look elsewhere for a fortune."

Prudence nodded absently as she discovered, under the second handkerchief, a sealed letter and a tiny package wrapped in tissue paper and tied with a scrap of ribbon. She opened the package first, and sat down on the dressing table stool with a gasp. "A brooch," she said blankly, staring down at a gold butterfly with amethyst eyes, its wings set with seed pearls.

Aimée joined her. "Pretty. Looks like Lady Anne is proper grateful, which ain't something you can count on with the nobs."

With her sewing scissors, Prudence slit the seal on the letter. Aimée was ready to paint her face, so Prudence left the stool and moved to the bed to read Lady Anne's hurried scrawl to herself.

Miss Savage,

I shall never forget what you did for me. Please accept the brooch as a token of my gratitude. We are leaving Easthaven today, but I hope we shall meet again so that I can thank you properly.

I am very sorry I was rude to you down by the lake. I was angry, but I know now that you were right and that you saved me then, too, from a loveless marriage. Lord Rusholme would have hated me forever.

If there is ever any way I can help you, please do not hesitate to call upon me.

Your most humble, grateful well-wisher, Anne Winkworth.

P.S. I think Rusholme is in love with you.

Startled, Prudence reread the last line. What could have given Lady Anne such a notion? Rusholme had hoped to make her his mistress. Now he considered himself her friend. Never a word of love had been spoken.

She wanted his love, she at last admitted sadly. She'd never be his mistress, and friendship was not enough. Yet even if he loved her, she could never be his wife.

He was heir to Easthaven, and she was—at best!—a governess.

Salamander gave Rusholme a reproachful look and snorted in disgust as they entered the stable yard. Rusholme laughed, feeling in his pocket for a lump of sugar.

"That was not much of a ride, was it, old fellow! I'm sure Lady Estella will be delighted if we go out again later."

He turned his mount over to a groom and went on into the house, his step light, humming his tavern song. His irrepressible cheerfulness puzzled him somewhat. Prudence was an innocent. He ought to be disappointed that he could no longer justify seducing her, for he had not desired any particular woman so much since his first calf-love for a pretty opera dancer.

Instead he was relieved, joyful even. As he approached the breakfast room he had to restrain himself from warbling out loud: "Toroddle, toroddle, toroll!"

Not until after breakfast did Rusholme recollect that Hardcastle had declared New Year's Day a holiday. No rehearsal. No excuse to see Prudence until tomorrow. And then only five days before she left Easthaven.

If she were staying with the troupe, he might find some excuse for frequent trips to Cheltenham; he must have friends who lived in Gloucestershire. Not that it mattered. She was leaving the stage. She was going to be a governess, and therefore virtually inaccessible to anyone, especially a young, unmarried gentleman.

Perhaps he could persuade one of his sisters to hire her. Then at least he'd see her when he stayed with Maria or Julia. What was more, they frequently reproached him for not visiting more often. But a few words sneaked in the schoolroom with his nieces and nephews all around was not what he wanted, nor could he bear the notion of Prudence as a servant to any of his family. Besides, it scarcely seemed fair even for her sake to deprive either Maria's or Julia's present governess of her position.

Of course, he'd be able to see Prudence in London while she sought a new post. Rusholme brightened at the recollection. Then he began to worry about whether she had enough money to keep herself in Town. She would never accept a penny from him; of that he was quite sure. She had too much pride, and he had no right to insist on taking care of her.

"It's stopped raining." David's voice interrupted his thoughts. "Coming for a gallop, Garth?"

Kept busy entertaining his guests all day, Rusholme had no opportunity for further reflection. Having scarcely closed his eyes the previous night, he fell asleep the instant he climbed into bed. He awoke late, and had only time for breakfast before the rehearsal was upon him.

In the fifth act Tony Lumpkin and Constance Neville appeared together only at the very end. Rusholme took Prudence's hand, pleased to see her smile at him without the withdrawal he had always sensed before when they had to touch on stage.

" 'I, Anthony Lumpkin, Esquire, of Blank Place,' " he said, " 'refuse you, Constantia Neville, of no place at all, for my true and lawful wife.' "

He fancied a fleeting sadness crossed her face, but she quickly turned away to give both hands to her faithful Hastings. Hardcastle joined Kate's and Marlow's hands likewise, and the play reached its happy ending.

Hardcastle had a list of scenes in need of practice before they would be ready to run through the whole play from beginning to end. They worked hard and Rusholme stayed to take luncheon with them in the gallery so as not to lose time. The flirting scenes with Prudence went smoothly now that she was comfortable with him, knowing he'd not take advantage. Also, the director was much pleased with his improvement in the scenes with Mrs. Hardcastle.

"I followed your suggestion," Rusholme told Prudence when they both took a break at the same moment. "I pretended I was speaking to Henry Ffoliot."

She chuckled. "I hope you are properly grateful to him. He has done me a favor, too, in providing another new friend, if I may be so bold to call her so."

"Who?" he asked, intrigued, as she pulled a much folded sheet of paper from her reticule.

"Lady Anne. I want you to read the note she wrote me. I know you don't care for her—"

"Don't care for her!"

"Oh, very well, you positively dislike her, and with reason, I admit. But I hope this will prove to you she is not so disagreeable after all." Her cheeks a trifle pinker than usual, she added, "Only, pray don't read the last line—you see I have folded it over. It is personal."

What a sweet nature she had, to wish him to think well of Lady Anne! He took the letter, read it, and nodded. "She appears to repent of her determination to become Countess of Rusholme and Marchioness of Easthaven. That's enough for me. She's forgiven."

As he handed the paper back to her, Hardcastle called, "Miss Savage, your first scene once more, if you please, and we'll see if Miss Orlando can remember her words at last."

Distracted, Prudence dropped the letter. Rusholme bent to pick it up. The bottom of the sheet had come unfolded and, his eye drawn by his name, he had read the single line written there before he could stop himself.

"P.S. I think Rusholme is in love with you."

In a daze, he handed the letter to Prudence. Her attention already on the stage, she noticed nothing amiss, but took it with a word of thanks and hurried off.

"P.S. I think Rusholme is in love with you."

How the devil had Lady Anne guessed, when until that moment he hadn't even realized it himself?

Ten

Snow. All evening big, soft, fluffy flakes drifted down, and nervous guests spoke of leaving while the roads were passable. The marquis fretted: half his audience liable to disappear and the other half perhaps unable to arrive. His wife and son soothed him. Most guests had no objection to being snowbound amid the luxuries of Easthaven. As for the neighbors, in three days who could guess what the weather might be doing?

In the morning, a pale sun shone on a blanket of sparkling white. On his way to the stables before breakfast, Rusholme was waylaid by his nieces and nephews.

"A snowman!" they cried. "We need you to help us build a snowman. We'll have a snowball fight, too."

Rusholme promptly sent a footman running to request Prudence's attendance. She came, a little anxious, wrapped in her green cloak.

"I don't think I ought—"

"I need your help with these brats," he informed her as Sophie took her hand and William restrained his enthusiasm long enough to bow. "And I'm going to want someone on my side when it comes to a snowball fight."

"Please come, ma'am," William begged. "It'll be fun."

It was fun. Prudence soon forgot her qualms and ran and shouted with the rest. Rosy-cheeked and laughing, she said as she walked beside Rusholme back to the house, "I've been behaving disgracefully childishly, I fear. But I haven't enjoyed myself so much since . . . oh, forever!"

With difficulty he refrained from kissing her on the spot and promising she should enjoy herself a great deal in the future.

They parted, she to the gallery, the children to the nursery,

Rusholme to the breakfast room. There Samuel brought him a summons from his mother.

In her private sitting room, surrounded by the Chinese black lacquer and scarlet silk, Lady Easthaven wore lemon yellow with her eternal green and pink shawl. Rusholme was too intent on preparing his arguments to wince.

As usual his mother came straight to the point. "Must you spend so much time with the actors, Garth? Our guests scarcely set eyes on you yesterday."

"I have to rehearse my part, Mama. I don't want to let Father down."

"No one will expect a gentleman to attain a professional standard of acting. If you are attempting to prove to me your lack of interest in the young ladies invited for your benefit, there is no need. I have relinquished all hope of seeing you wed."

"Unnecessary. I spend time with the actors because I wish to marry, not because I don't."

The marchioness raised her eyebrows. "Then it is true," she said caustically, "as my dresser informed me, that you invited one of the actresses to join you with the children this morning? I told her she was certainly mistaken. You would not expose your sisters' children to a female of that sort."

"But I did. My future wife is fit company for anyone."

"Warrenders of Easthaven do not marry actresses."

"She's not really an actress, Mama. She has only been on the stage a few months and intends to quit after Twelfth Night."

"Naturally, if she supposes you will marry her."

"She doesn't know that," Rusholme said softly, "and I'm by no means sure she'll have me."

"Come now, you cannot imagine an actress is in the least likely to refuse an earl!"

"Prudence might. And she's not an actress. She was a governess for many years."

"A governess? Scarcely more suitable for a Warrender."

"She's not really a governess, either." He grinned at his mother's baffled face. "She left her last post months ago and has not yet applied for another. She is a clergyman's daughter and a guest at Easthaven."

"That tale will not serve for those who spent Christmas here, nor for those who have seen her on the stage!"

"She has only been on the stage at Cheltenham, thus seen, I have no doubt, only by provincial nobodies. As for our guests, when she appeared in the mummery she wore that odd medieval headdress concealing her hair, and for *She Stoops to Conquer* she'll have on a wig as well as a cap. Her hair is her most distinctive feature by far—if you disregard her character."

"And what, precisely, is her character?" Lady Easthaven enquired with a hint of sarcasm.

"Don't ask," Rusholme advised, "unless you wish me to go into raptures. Suffice it that she is every inch a lady."

"Supposing I believe you, what of her relatives? You cannot wish to ally your family to a common clergyman who probably possesses hordes of still commoner, even vulgar relatives."

"She has no family living. Mama, I—"

"My dear!" The marquis burst in. "Essex insists on leaving, although it has stopped snowing, and he's taking the duchess and Lady Estella with him."

"In the present circumstances," said his wife tartly, "it scarcely signifies. Pray speak to your son, Easthaven. He has an answer for everything. I wash my hands of him."

"Hello, Garth, you here? Told your mother you're not coming up to scratch, have you?"

"Not with Lady Estella, sir. I have another bride in mind."

"Splendid, my boy. The Wallace chit?"

"No, sir, Miss . . . er . . . Neville."

"Constance Neville, hey? A respectable young woman, though she did think of running off with Hastings."

"Easthaven, she is an *actress!*" the marchioness pointed out.

"No, she is *not*." Rusholme went through all his arguments again.

"By Jove, you're right, my dear," cried the marquis. "Garth

has an answer for everything. We'd best have Miss Neville up and welcome her to the family."

While his mother raised her eyes to heaven with an exasperated sigh, Rusholme shook his father's hand vigorously. "Just two things I ought to mention, sir," he said. "I haven't actually asked her yet, so you'll have to postpone welcoming her to the family. And her name isn't really Neville."

"Not Neville? Dash it, I daresay it's not. As for the rest, I shouldn't worry, my boy." He patted his son's arm encouragingly. "Don't imagine she'll take exception to a fine, well-set-up young fellow like you."

Rusholme was not so certain. Not that he thought Prudence had any objection to his person—he'd had too many hints to the contrary. But he knew the marchioness's resistance was by no means conquered, not to mention his sisters' when they found out. Though he was quite prepared to defy them, Prudence might well refuse him rather than set him at odds with his family.

The estate carpenter finished the stage in the ballroom just in time for the dress rehearsal. Unfortunately, no one had thought to check the curtains in advance. Stored in an attic since Lord Easthaven's previous theatrical Christmas, they were found upon hanging to have provided a feast for moths. Every maid in the mansion capable of wielding a needle was set to darning and patching.

The dress rehearsal proceeded without a curtain. To everyone's dismay, the marquis came to watch. Worse, in the middle of the second act the marchioness joined him.

Aimée forgot every other line. Rusholme's vigorous baritone emerged as a cross between a squawk and a croak. The stage-hands put a chair in the wrong place, and Marlow stubbed his toe on it, whereupon he hopped around the stage loudly damning them. Mrs. Hardcastle's cap and wig slid down over her nose when her son hauled her offstage. And Prudence was so discon-

certed to be flirting with Rusholme under his parents' gaze that
she poked him in the eye with her fan.

Squinting at her through involuntary tears, he whispered with
a wry smile, "The way things are going, you might as well stab
me to the heart and put me out of my misery."

"They say a bad dress rehearsal means a good performance,"
she whispered back, making him miss his cue.

When at last they stumbled through to the end, the cast found
a lavish afternoon tea set for them in the circular, pillared anteroom.

"Knew you'd need something to cheer you up," the marquis
explained jovially, undeterred by the prospect of disaster.

The marchioness, in lilac with cherry red ribbons, seated herself behind the tea table. Rusholme introduced each of the players
to his parents. Prudence was greatly taken aback when Lady
Easthaven coolly asked her to help pour the tea. Having presided
over her father's tea table for years, and taught the correct eti-
quette to more than one small girl, Prudence had no difficulty—
but suppose her ladyship had asked Aimée!

They made polite conversation about the weather, Christmas
traditions, such of the countryside round about as Prudence had
seen. Prudence felt oddly as if she were being interviewed for a
position, though Lady Easthaven asked no searching questions
about her abilities upon the pianoforte, her knowledge of French,
or the proper use of the globes. She wondered whether Rusholme
had spoken of her intention to return to governessing. Perhaps
the marchioness would recommend her to a friend, or even one
of her daughters.

If Lady Julia or Lady Maria employed her, she'd see Rusholme
now and then. What more could she wish for?

The last cup of tea was poured and drunk, the last biscuit and
slice of cake consumed. Still coolly gracious, the marchioness
thanked Prudence for her assistance. Whether she approved or
disapproved, Prudence could not guess.

As she rose and curtsied to her ladyship, the marquis came
over. "Miss Neville, Garth swears your encouragement has kept

98 *Carola Dunn*

him up to the mark," he said genially, taking her hand and patting it. "I've you to thank if he don't ruin the show."

"Lord Rusholme exaggerates, my lord. He has worked very hard."

"That's what I mean, my dear. He has a natural talent for most skills he's had to master; but for this he has exerted himself, and it's all to the good. Wasn't sure he had it in him, so I thank you."

Prudence smiled at him. Though tempted to credit Rusholme's exertions to her genius for encouraging children to learn, she said candidly, "I believe his motive has been to avoid making a cake of himself before an audience, sir."

Lord Easthaven laughed. "Very likely, but he didn't have to volunteer for the part in the first place, did he? What put that notion into his head, I wonder?"

His eyes had a teasing twinkle very like his son's. Prudence suspected he knew Rusholme had hoped to seduce her, but he did not seem to hold it against her or he'd never have let her sit down with his wife.

Mr. Hardcastle came to thank Lord and Lady Easthaven for the tea party. The rest of the company were leaving, so Prudence went after them. Rusholme stopped her.

"Shall you walk early tomorrow?" he asked. "Otherwise I may not see you before the performance. My mother requires my presence tomorrow as our guests will leave the day after, weather permitting."

"Weather permitting, I shall walk."

"Then I shall pray for sun, though I know rain does not daunt you."

"It depends how hard it rains! I must go. Aimée wants my help with her lines."

At the door she glanced back. Rusholme was talking to his parents, a noble family at home in their magnificent mansion. The sight reminded her—as if she needed a reminder!—that not only the guests were soon to depart. The day after tomorrow the company would be on their way back to Cheltenham, and Prudence would be on the stagecoach to London, heading for a future bereft of the man she loved.

Both Prudence and Rusholme were very late for breakfast the next morning. To Salamander's displeasure, they had walked for miles, sometimes talking, sometimes silently enjoying each other's company. At least, Prudence was quite content simply being with him, and she assumed he could have found an excuse to turn back had he wished to.

She did not see him again until just before the performance. Surrounded by the rest of the cast in the space behind the stage, they smiled at each other.

"Careful with that fan!" he whispered.

"Don't knock Mrs. Hardcastle's wig off!" she retorted.

The play proceeded without a hitch. Young Marlow, sent by his father to woo Kate Hardcastle, lost his way and stopped at the Three Pigeons. Tony, ever mischievous, directed him to the Hardcastles' house, but told him and his companion, Hastings, it was an inn. Meeting Kate there, as if by chance, Marlow was so desperately shy he never raised his eyes to her face. However, when he saw her later in the old-fashioned dress her father preferred, he took her for a barmaid and eagerly pursued her.

Prudence, her own part going smoothly, for the first time was struck by the parallel between Marlow's attempt to seduce Kate and Rusholme's pursuit of herself.

The differences were more to the point, she decided sadly. Marlow fell in love with Kate and offered marriage, defying the supposed disparity in their stations. Kate's renunciation, her fear of his father's disapproval and his own regrets, were all in fun since she knew herself his equal and their parents' favor was assured.

Nothing could be less like the situation between Prudence and Rusholme.

Nor that between Constance Neville and Tony Lumpkin! *Their* flirting had been solely to mislead the interfering Mrs. Hardcastle. In the last scene Tony joyfully surrendered his Cousin Con's hand to Hastings.

" 'I, Anthony Lumpkin, Esquire, of Blank Place,' " he said, " 'request you, Constantia Neville, of no place at all, for my true and lawful wife.' "

Prudence blinked at Rusholme. His memory had not faltered throughout the play. How could he suddenly confuse "refuse" and "request"?

Self-consciously avoiding her eyes, he finished his speech. She turned to Hastings. Either the others had not noticed his mistake or they were all too good at carrying on regardless of blunders to show it. The play ended to tumultuous applause.

They took their bows. Rusholme was quickly surrounded by laughing, congratulating friends. As they bore him off, he looked back at Prudence, grinned, raised his eyebrows, and gave a helpless shrug.

"Later," he mouthed.

She turned away. She was not sure she wanted to see him later. There was nothing to say but goodbye.

Slipping away from the cheerful hubbub of the Elizabethan gallery, Prudence made her way back down to the ballroom. By the light of her single candle, the guests' chairs and servants' benches stretched in untidy rows back into the gloom. The stage was a dark cavern.

She perched on the edge of the stage, set the candle down beside her, and hugged her knees. Twelfth Night: just two weeks since a tall, arrogant gentleman with amusement in his voice had discovered her lurking behind a curtain.

If she had known beforehand she was going to fall hopelessly in love, would she have stopped in Cheltenham that day last summer? Yes, she thought defiantly. For a few months her dull, friendless life had blossomed with the comradeship of the company, the thrill of walking out on stage before an audience. For

a few days she had known the painful joy of being so in tune with someone his very presence made her happy.

She saw again his laughing face, his quizzical look, his free, self-confident stride. She recalled his kindness to the children, to Ben Dandridge and little Rosie; and the way he had rushed to her defense against Henry Ffoliot. She heard his voice, warm, teasing, sympathetic.

His final speech on stage echoed in her head. That slip of the tongue would live on in her dreams through the lonely years ahead.

She buried her face in her hands.

The soft thud of footsteps crossing the ballroom swiftly approached. "Prudence, don't cry!"

"I'm n-not c-crying," she said fiercely as Rusholme sat down beside her and his arms encircled her.

"No, love, of course not, but take my handkerchief anyway." His forefinger under her chin, he raised her face and blotted the tears, then thrust the handkerchief into her hand.

She blew her nose. "I didn't mean to cry."

"It's my fault. I should have spoken sooner, but it would have been so awkward for you if . . . if you don't. . . ." He took a deep breath. "I, Valentine Tregarth Warrender, Earl of Rusholme, request you, Prudence—"

"You don't have to propose to me just because your tongue twisted at the wrong moment."

"Shall I tell you why it twisted? Because I'd been practicing. After trying to contrive a pretty speech of my own, I decided to take the easy way and adapt Goldsmith's, but I didn't mean to say it on stage. It's lucky 'request' slipped out—a possible confusion—not beg, entreat, implore, any of the others I've considered. Dearest Prudence, will you marry me?"

Their two candles gave just enough light for her to see the hope, the longing, the diffidence in his eyes. For a moment, acceptance hovered on her lips. Goldsmith came to the rescue, Kate's speech, imprinted by constant repetition. She pulled away.

"No, my lord. 'Do you think I could suffer a connection in

which there is the smallest room for repentance? Do you think I would take the mean advantage of a transient passion to load you with confusion? Do you think I could ever relish that happiness which was acquired by lessening yours?' "

" 'By all that's good, I can have no happiness but what's in your power to grant me.' " He, too, had learned the lines. " 'Your beauty at first caught my eye, but every moment that I converse with you steals in some new grace, heightens the picture and gives it stronger expression.' Oh, bedammed to Goldsmith! Prudence, I love you. If you can say with absolute candor that you don't love me, never will, and abhor the thought of being my wife, then I shall leave."

She couldn't. Reaching up to lay one hand against his cheek, she said softly, "I do love you, Garth, but how can I marry you and condemn you to the anger of your parents and the contempt of your equals?"

"To misquote—" he smiled, so tenderly that Prudence's heart lurched—"for my equals, those whose opinions I care for are those who care for me and who can only rejoice in my happiness. As for my parents, when I told them my hopes, my father wanted to welcome you to the family without further ado. I must warn you that he is in some confusion and may continue to address you as Miss Neville for some little time."

"That is preferable to . . . my real name," Prudence declared, then asked hesitantly, "And your mother?"

"I will not pretend Mama is overjoyed. After all, I have just rejected the three unexceptionable brides she found me. However, I have persuaded her to regard you as the daughter of a respectable clergyman, and she complains bitterly that I have answers to all her other objections. When I set out to search for you, she was giving orders to the housekeeper to prepare a guest chamber for you—Lady Estella's, I believe."

"She is very certain I shall accept you!"

"But I am not. Please, Prudence, put me out of my misery!" But his eyes laughed, and his arms had somehow sneaked back around her while she was not attending.

Well, not attending closely.

"Oh, Garth." With a sigh, she laid her head on his shoulder. "I cannot think of anything more heavenly than being your wife."

"The very first thing I learned about you was that you have excellent taste!" he said triumphantly, hugging her so hard she squeaked. "I wonder how soon I can talk Mama into letting you redecorate the ballroom?"

Prudence laughed. "Not until she is accustomed to having an ex-actress for a daughter-in-law."

"Then the sooner she begins to grow accustomed, the better. When shall we be wed? Dash it, I foresee one last difficulty."

"What?" she asked, dismayed.

"Since I must insist on an unquestionably legal marriage, the banns must be read not for Constance Neville, not—thank heaven—for Seraphina Savage, but for Prudence Figg. Can you bear it, my love?"

"For your sake, and considering I need never hear my odious surname again, I shall endeavor to bear the ignominy."

"Ignominy! I do believe I fell in love with your vocabulary before I paid any heed to the rest of you. The rest deserves a little attention now." And so saying, he pulled her onto his lap and kissed her.

Fire in her veins, Prudence melted. If she had known his kiss was like this, she'd never have been able to resist there on the ice, or out on the terrace. Yet how much sweeter now. . . . Reason faded away and she was all sensation.

At last Rusholme raised his head. He looked dazed. "My wood elf," he murmured, "my wildfire. I shall dress you in russet, and violet, and apricot, and laurel green."

"Oh, Garth, not all at once!"

"No, one harlequin in the family is sufficient. First I shall dress you in russet, and then I shall undress you, and then. . . ."

About the Author

Carola Dunn lives with her dog in Eugene, Oregon. Her many Zebra regency romances include: SCANDAL'S DAUGHTER, THE TUDOR SECRET, THE LADY AND THE RAKE, HIS LORDSHIP'S REWARD and THE CAPTAIN'S INHERITANCE. Carola's newest regency romance, THE BABE AND THE BARON, will be published in January 1997. Carola loves hearing from her readers and you may write to her c/o Zebra Books. Please include a self-addressed stamped envelope if you wish a response.

UNDER THE MISTLETOE

Karla Hocker

One

As the gilded clock on the mantel chimed midnight, Susan Cavendish unfastened the long row of jet buttons at the back of her gown. Christmas Day was past.

Two years of mourning were over. Two years of feeling guilty as sin.

The sleeves were tight. Susan shrugged and tugged, impatient to be rid of the garment. Scratchy dull gray thing, designed to keep her in a suitably mournful frame of mind.

The gray wool joined gray dimity and lavender silk, black gloves and ribbons, and the black bombazine and crepe of her first year of mourning, all tumbled haphazardly in a deep wicker hamper. She dropped in her black slippers and closed the lid.

There. That was done. She could feel easy now, unburdened by guilt.

Susan stood, waiting for the uplift of spirits that surely must follow the shedding of her widow's weeds. But she only felt cold. Donning a wrapper over her stays and petticoats, Susan drew close to the fireplace where a fire still burned hot. Yet she shivered.

Rubbing her arms, she looked at the wide four-poster bed occupying a major part of her chamber. At eleven o'clock, a maid had slid hot bricks between the sheets. The bricks would still be warm. Surely, tonight, she would be able to sleep at long last.

She advanced on the bed. As she reached out to turn back the coverlet, she heard it—the dreaded sound of a footstep, a voice muttering darkly.

"A pox on you," she said under her breath, feeling as shaken as the first time she had heard the sounds. She assured herself that they could not be real, were merely the imaginings of a guilty conscience. But, imagined or real, she could not climb into the bed. Not now.

For the past seven months Susan had scarcely slept more than three or four hours a night, with an occasional brief rest in the afternoon. She had hoped that with the ritual of putting away all reminders of mourning and half mourning, she would also rid herself of guilt and shame, and had expected never to hear those chilling sounds again.

Stepping into house slippers, she gripped a slim, domed night lamp and started on what would undoubtedly be only the first of many nightly rounds of the house. No wonder her mother-in-law pointed out at every opportune and inopportune moment that she looked positively hagged. In the morning she'd look worse than ever. And guests arriving! Elizabeth and Clive, who planned to stay through Twelfth Night.

Susan tiptoed past her mother-in-law's rooms, though there was little danger that the dowager Mrs. Cavendish would hear anything short of a cannon shot above her lively snores. Traversing the portrait gallery, Susan resolutely kept her eyes on the light in her hand. Two of the paintings depicted her late husband, and she did not want to catch even an accidental glimpse of Frederick. But she listened, alert to the slightest whisper of a sound.

She hastened her pace. It was all so ridiculous . . . the listening the imagining of sounds, a voice, a footstep, a door closing. Frederick was dead. He could not speak to her, or follow her.

A floor board creaked, and she all but tumbled down the stairs. Stupid! 'Twas her own hurried tread that made the wood creak.

Heart racing, Susan stopped in the great hall, the only chamber in the manor house bearing the imprint of her artistry and labor. Her fingers and wrists still ached from years of stitching tapestries, rugs, and chair covers, but her efforts had been worthwhile and had turned a cold, soot-darkened vault into a favorite gathering place. If the hall at Cavendish Manor was not as majestic as the great hall of Stenton Castle, Elizabeth and Clive's home, it certainly was every bit as beautiful. And this year, the dowager had deemed it proper to decorate for the holidays again and to hold the tenants' Boxing Day dance as in the years prior to her son's death.

The night lamp's dim light did not reach the kissing bough suspended from a chandelier high above Susan's head, but it fell upon branches of fir studded with slim white candles, silver ribbon bows, and clusters of red holly berry—a Christmas tree, as Susan had first seen it at Stenton Castle, the medieval stronghold of the Rowlands that rose high above the chalk cliffs of Beachy Head. Beyond the Christmas tree, the occasional flicker of flame showed the Yule log, properly banked and screened, and a garland of evergreens and red velvet looped along the vast mantel.

For a moment, Susan stood enveloped in the fir's rich, pungent scent and gave herself up to memories of the Christmas when Frederick had visited a gambling friend and she had traveled the twenty-odd miles to Stenton with her mother-in-law. It was the first anniversary of Elizabeth and Clive's wedding. Elizabeth had glowed with happiness. And Clive . . . such a proud, attentive, and deeply caring husband.

Some distance to her left, in the drawing room, the tall-case clock struck the half hour past midnight. Twelve-thirty, and all was well.

Or was it? Was that a footstep she heard?

"Susan."

She spun, the lamp in her hand shaking and weaving so violently that the flame was extinguished. Her light was not needed. The man striding toward her, shirt tucked haphazardly into buckskin breeches, carried his own lamp.

"Frederick! Leave me alone!"

"Devil a bit! Are you sleepwalking, Susan? Or ill?"

No, she was daft. She had made a fool of herself. As if it wasn't bad enough that she was caught sleepless. Again.

"Dash it, Andrew!" Her voice was too sharp, but better that

than trembling. "How you startled me! You should not creep up on a female in the dark."

Andrew Cavendish raised his lamp and scanned the pale features of his late cousin's widow. "You called me Frederick."

There was unmistakable concern in his voice, but it was of no comfort to Susan at this moment of embarrassment.

"It is hardly my fault that I am rattled. Stop watching me and following me around as if I were a sneak-thief."

"Why aren't you asleep? And don't turn away, Susan. Or ask why *I* am not asleep."

"Very well, I shan't."

"But neither will you answer?"

They stared at each other, the silence thick and heavy, quite out of proportion to the simple exchange. But nothing was ever simple between them.

A click, like a door closing, broke the stillness. Then a dragging sound, a muffled imprecation.

Susan did not move, only drew a sharp breath, her eyes widening.

"You heard it?" Andrew's voice was scarcely more than a whisper. "The salon, I think."

The salon, between the drawing room at the front of the east wing and the dining room at the rear, was set aside for the dowager's exclusive use. No one should be in it at this time of night.

Susan did not resist when Andrew took the lamp from her and set it down. Neither did she object when he clasped her hand. If she had not learned in past years to exercise restraint, she would bury her face in the soft lawn of his shirt and draw comfort from the broad chest, so conveniently close. But she was Frederick's widow, and Andrew was her late husband's cousin. Theirs was not a relationship that tolerated impulsive acts, a giving in to momentary weakness.

There was the dragging sound again. And no doubt about it, Andrew heard it, too. His grip tightened.

"Shall I see you to your room or will you come with me, Susan?"

"I'll come."

She should feel pleased to know that she hadn't fallen prey to a disordered mind, that it wasn't imagination when she heard sounds in the night or awoke, hearing her name spoken. But even Andrew's company could not quell her apprehension as they approached the salon.

At the door, Andrew thrust her behind him before he burst into the room. Advancing, he swung his lamp in a wide circle. There was no one. Nothing was out of place. If a chair or table had been dragged, it now stood in its original place.

"Every window is closed and locked." Releasing the drapes on the last window he had examined, Andrew faced Susan. "I could have sworn the sound came from this room."

"It did." She looked at the high racks of shelving built into the paneling on either side of the fireplace. "The dragging sounded like a priest's hole closing."

"Impossible. I disabled every opening to a priest's hole or hidden passage when the boot boy got lost."

"Somebody could have removed the nails."

He shook his head, but went to the rack left of the mantel and twisted one of the bosses mounted on the frame. Nothing happened. The shelving did not pivot.

"Everything tight and secure. And let me assure you, it isn't a mere few nails that keep the hidden doors fast."

She vacillated between disappointment at not discovering the source of the sounds and relief that the worst of her nightmares had not come true.

"And the noise we heard, Andrew?"

Shining the light once more in a circle, he returned to her side. "In truth, I've come to think 'twas nothing but the settling of timber. You know how old the house is, Susan. No doubt there's a length of rotting beam somewhere."

"It did not at all sound like rotting timber."

"I shall search the house, and if we have an intruder, I'll dispatch him speedily. Now, please allow me to see you to your room. I promise I shan't let you or my aunt come to harm."

His voice, deep and warm, was comforting, but her apprehension was too deep-rooted to be expurgated with a few reassuring words. Perhaps she should tell him now that this wasn't the first time she had heard something. That it started after he had sealed the passages. Or, perhaps, it was best to wait until Clive and Elizabeth arrived, for she must tell them, embarrassment or not. Elizabeth Rowland, Duchess of Stenton, would demand an explanation for her friend's haggard appearance. And His Grace, the Duke of Stenton, must be made to swear on his oath that Frederick—

"Susan?" Andrew raised his lamp. "Can you not trust me?"

She met his eyes, dark like Frederick's but kinder than her husband's had ever been. Andrew's broad shoulders and strong limbs were like Frederick's, too. The difference was that she had never seen Andrew misuse his strength or his power.

Yes, she trusted him. But, although they had shared a house for almost four and a half years, they did not live on intimate or even comfortable terms. The fault was hers. She had kept him at a distance since he discovered her, early on, during a moment of weakness and vulnerability when she was hiding from Frederick.

"Susan, would it help if I promised that regardless of my aunt's wishes, I shall not discomfort you with an unwanted offer?"

Her breath caught, and before she could reply, Andrew spoke again.

"I do most solemnly promise, my dear."

Unaccountably, hot tears stung her eyes, but did not spill as, just as swiftly and just as irrationally, anger loosened her tongue.

"A rash promise I may or may not want to hear!" What on earth was she saying? She did not understand herself, knew only that this evening, this night when she could officially cease mourning, was turning into a disaster. "Good night, sir. I need no escort to my room."

"Susan, wait. What did I say or do wrong?"

"Nothing!"

He reached out, clasping her hand, but she tore away, aware

that her behavior was undignified, yet unable to stop herself. Andrew was not like Frederick. She should at least try to explain, but she had never in her life been called upon to express her feelings—feelings that were mixed and tangled and totally incomprehensible. And thus she kept running, in complete disregard of her matronly status, not bothering to fetch her lamp and light it. In the dark, she fled to the chamber where sleep was all but impossible, where, undoubtedly, since Andrew had touched upon the subject, she would be compelled to think about the dowager's suggestion for a second marriage.

Andrew Cavendish also suffered through periods of painful reflection while diligently searching the house, as promised, for a possible intruder. As he had expected, he discovered neither an intruder nor an answer to the question whether Susan would or would not be repulsed by a proposal of marriage.

In the morning he was heavy-eyed when he joined Augusta Cavendish at the breakfast table.

"Been out gallivanting?" the dowager asked dryly as she poured tea. "You look downright haggard."

He grimaced. "That is the line you usually reserve for Susan. Where is she? I've not known her to be late."

Majestic in stature and demeanor, Augusta gave her nephew a shrewd look. "She's not ill, if that is what you fear. She has ridden out to meet the duke's carriage."

"At eight o'clock? Devil a bit! She used to be a sensible girl."

"Woman," Augusta corrected. "Susan is one-and-thirty."

"But these past six months or so—"

"Seven months, to be precise."

"Six months or seven—what does it signify? The point is, she has displayed lapses of rationality that have me quite worried."

"You amaze me." Augusta ogled the empty toast rack, but this was not the time to ring for a fresh supply. "For a man who professes to be worried, you do very little to divert her from whatever it is that troubles her."

"What would you have me do? She has not precisely been at ease in my company since you suggested she should marry me when she's out of mourning."

"Which she is, as of today." Augusta raised a delicately darkened brow. "But I dropped the hint only last Christmas, while Susan has shown reserve and unease in your presence since well before Frederick's death."

"I stand corrected." Andrew pushed back his chair. "May I serve you from the sideboard? Eggs? A sliver of sirloin?"

"No, thank you. I've always wondered what could have happened. If I did not know you so well, I'd suspect you made improper advances."

He said nothing, but directed his attention to the silver dishes on the sideboard.

His aunt's remark came close to the truth, yet nowhere near it. Four years ago, when he returned to Cavendish Manor after Waterloo, he had fallen in love with Frederick's wife.

Of course, he had met Susan earlier, during brief furloughs, but at that time he could think of nothing but the war and the need to trounce Napoleon. He had scarcely paid attention to the quiet young woman. After Waterloo it was different. He had seen Susan and within the first twenty-four hours had known that he was in love. There was no question of his leaving before his wounds had healed. Cavendish Manor had been his home since his earliest memories. He and Frederick were raised as brothers. Had he expressed a desire to recuperate elsewhere, his aunt would have declared him crazed and blamed it on the raging fever contracted in the incessant rains in Brussels while he awaited transport.

Also, he had believed he could handle the situation. He was an officer, after all, and a gentleman. And he had, indeed, comported himself with propriety toward Susan until, almost a year after his arrival, he had found her crying. He could not now remember why she cried. It was of no consequence. He'd had time to observe the countless acts of unkindness, even cruelty, Frederick directed at her, had on numerous occasions admonished and berated his cousin, had come to blows with him. When he saw Susan cry, he had simply taken her in his arms and held her close until the tears dried and the heartrending sobs stilled. Then, as she started to apologize, he had kissed her. And Susan had returned the kiss with a passion that set his blood afire.

"You love her," said Augusta, watching him from her chair at the head of the table. "Have loved her for a long time."

"I should have left as soon as I was well."

"Perhaps." Augusta waited until he had returned to his seat. "But you never truly had a choice, did you?"

"There is always a choice, Aunt."

"Indeed. You could have chosen to leave and condemn Susan and me to the almshouse."

At his startled look, she gave a dry laugh. "I am Frederick's mother, but I was never blind to his faults or deaf to the clamor of his creditors. Nor was I ever bird-witted."

A reluctant grin tugged at his mouth. "On the contrary. You're as sharp as a pin, my dear aunt. How long, do you suppose, will it take Susan to realize that her friends cannot possibly be here before ten o'clock?"

"Don't change the subject. As long as you wish to keep up the pretense that I am the owner of Cavendish Manor and you are my steward, you had best do as I bid. Now, let us clear the air between us. 'Tis more than time to do so."

"Devil a bit! It seems there's nothing left to clear."

"Perhaps not, but I want no misunderstanding between us. Andrew, I know for a fact that you had no choice but to stay when you were well enough to hobble about and saw how Frederick had mismanaged the estate. You may believe 'twas your secret and Frederick's, but I know 'twas your selling-out money that staved off the creditors."

"As I said, sharp as a pin. And now we need never mention it again."

"I also know 'twas you who compelled Frederick to give up gambling."

"That wasn't at all difficult once I held his writ." He swallowed bitterness. "But I could not compel him to give up cruelty."

"Neither could I."

When Andrew made no reply, she said, "My dear boy, there is no law that governs a man's deportment toward his wife as long as he does not endanger her life. And though I don't doubt that he struck her, she was not seriously hurt or injured."

"No." In a sudden gesture of revulsion Andrew pushed away the plate he had just filled. "He would have made certain the bruises did not show. And mostly, I think, his cruelty found expression in other ways. Do you remember Susan's puppy, Aunt?"

She paled a little. "My memory is as good as yours. But there is also no law granting a mother or a cousin or anyone the right to interfere between husband and wife."

"There were times when I should have acted without the backing of the law."

"Considering Frederick's broken nose on one occasion, a blackened eye on another, I must assume that you did act."

"I could have done more."

"What, Andrew?" Augusta gave him a level look. "What could you have done, short of calling him out? Your cousin. My son."

Andrew's face grew uncomfortably hot, and the clatter of hooves in the cobbled yard was a welcome distraction. He rose.

"Pardon me, Aunt. You will understand that I had rather not face Susan with that question on my mind."

"You can hardly avoid meeting her. She'll be in the hall before you reach your sanctuary in the west wing. But you know that, and it isn't Susan you don't want to face." Again, that level look. "I understand, dear boy. After all, I raised you."

He went to her and kissed her, first on the proffered cheek, then on the swath of white that ran through her dark brown hair just above the left ear.

Augusta patted his hand. "We must forget the past so that we may get on with the present. We have a feast to celebrate! Now, go and catch Susan before she can escape upstairs. Send her in to me, will you? Tell her not to bother changing."

Andrew was tempted to ask her not to meddle, but merely bowed and left. Augusta would do as she pleased. And if it had not yet occurred to her to intercede on his behalf with Susan, his request could serve only to put the notion in her mind.

He started across the great hall, slowly, anticipating the opening of the front door. When it did, he stopped. Susan had almost reached the wide, open stairway before she saw him. For a moment it seemed as if she would continue on her way and run upstairs. Then she stopped, too.

The ride on a cold, crisp December morning had done her good. Her face, though a bit too thin and with shadows of sleeplessness under her eyes, had a rosy glow. The color deepened as she looked at him.

"Hello, Susan." He wanted to put her at ease, but hardly knew how. He feared to say the wrong thing—as he had done last night, when he had wanted only to reassure. "You were out and about early."

She drew a deep breath.

"Good morning, Andrew," she said brightly, as though she had never stormed off in a passion when he made his ill-conceived promise in the middle of the night. Or, as if she had resolved to be cheerful. "Am I late for breakfast?"

"Not late enough to signify. Augusta hopes you won't insist on changing before joining her."

Susan inspected her boots and the skirt of her riding habit, which showed traces of snow. "I stopped in the copse," she said, shaking out her skirts, "and built a snowman. I may be just a bit too damp and bedraggled."

A snowman. Would he ever understand her? He wanted to do

and say just the right thing, but could not tell what she expected. Susan was not a woman who wore her heart on her sleeve, though last night she had clearly been angry. She might simply wish to ignore that encounter. On the other hand, if she expected an apology or a retraction of his rash promise, she would not mope or demand that he apologize. No doubt then, for the present, it behooved him to proceed with caution.

"Take off your hat," he commanded, striding toward her.

When she had done so, he brushed the snow from her long golden brown hair. It had probably been tied or pinned when she left, but was now tumbling about her shoulders in silken abundance.

"There. That should do." Keeping his voice matter-of-fact, he added, "You have lovely hair."

"Thank you." She sounded calm, if a trifle breathless. "Andrew, I've done a vast amount of serious thinking this morning. We must talk."

"Yes, indeed."

"About us. Augusta's plans for us."

He wanted to tell her they were his plans, too. Wanted to take her in his arms and kiss her until she agreed to marry him. But as he well knew, a kiss snatched on impulse could misfire disastrously.

"Whenever you wish, my dear, I shall be at your disposal."

A flicker of irritation crossed her face. "What I wish is that you would not call me 'my dear' in that horridly avuncular manner. You're scarcely three years older than I, yet you address me as though you were a graybeard."

"I apologize. The sad truth is, I'm tongue-tied today. I scarcely dare address you at all."

"You? Timid? That does not sound like the Andrew I know."

"But you know nothing of me. Except—" He paused deliberately. "Except that I kissed you once, a long time ago."

Once more her color deepened, but she did not speak.

"If I were not timid, I would kiss you again. You're standing right beneath the mistletoe."

She glanced at the chandelier above her head. "I had forgotten the kissing bough. It seems much longer than two years since we were able to celebrate Christmas the way it's—but you're trying to divert me, and you shan't succeed. Andrew, I know that you are very brave. You don't boast of your feats, but the Duke of Wellington does not commend a timid man."

"A military commendation does not equip me to deal with you."

"Yes, indeed," she said, her voice colorless. "I am a difficult woman to deal with. Frederick always said so."

"The deuce, Susan. That is not what I meant."

"No. Perhaps not."

"You must know by now that I am not adroit with words."

This drew a fleeting smile. "I know nothing of the kind, though you can be a man of *few* words when it suits your purpose. But I must learn not to be so sensitive. I will remember that when we talk again. Now I had better join Augusta. She'll wonder why I do not go to her."

"Let us talk now. Augusta will understand."

But she shook her head and moved away.

"Susan." He followed. "Will you answer a question?"

"What question?"

"When you stood under the mistletoe, did you want me to kiss you?"

She started to speak, her mouth shaping to say no. Then she looked at the kissing bough and back at Andrew.

"I fear 'tis my turn to confess a sad truth. I do not know what I want, Andrew. Not with certainty."

"Not precisely the answer I hoped to hear." He smiled ruefully. "But I can hardly fault you for honesty."

"I am more than thirty years." Wonderment filled her voice. "And I don't know what I want. I've never asked myself what I want. No one has ever asked."

"Then I must be glad I did. Go now, before Augusta raises the hue and cry that I've abducted you."

"She would not, as you well know. She'd be only too pleased. Which is one of the reasons why decision making is so very difficult."

Two

Conscious of Augusta's watchful gaze on her, Susan tried to do full justice to a hearty breakfast of ham and eggs. She did not feel like eating, but if she did not want to be cajoled and questioned, it would not serve to fall into a brown study while she pondered the conversation with Andrew.

After the extensive soul searching during the night and early morning, Susan had believed herself prepared to meet him with composure. That she had blushed when she saw him might be excused. After all, she had behaved badly during their previous encounter. But that he could overset her so easily with a question . . . such a deceptively simple question.

Susan, did you want me to kiss you?

And she had not known the answer. Admittedly, she had been tempted to taste his mouth again, feel his arms around her. Feel cherished. But only for the briefest of instants, the span of a heartbeat. Just as that other kiss, years ago, had thrown her mind into great disorder, so would his kiss under the mistletoe have done. Years ago, while she was a married woman, she had to struggle with shame and guilt when the kiss was over. Now, as a widow, she would face a quite different problem.

Now, a kiss might convey to Andrew that she was amenable to Augusta's suggestion. And Susan did not know whether she wanted to marry again. Ever. She did not know what she wanted to do with her life. Had never considered the possibility that she might be in a position to choose what she wanted.

"Here we come a'caroling. . . ." The old wassail song, rendered in the dowager's slightly rusty but energetic voice, brought Susan up with a start.

Augusta chuckled. "I had to catch your attention somehow, and it has been far too long since we've enjoyed a merry tune. Susan, do you remember the Christmas we surprised the tenants?"

"When *we* wassailed them? Indeed, I do." Susan smiled. "Mrs. Eldridge was so flabbergasted, you had to remind her to offer the wassail cup."

Her smile faded. She also remembered the aftermath of that innocent joke she and Augusta had played on the tenants. Thank goodness, Augusta never learned of Frederick's displeasure.

"Is something troubling you, Susan?"

"No. Well, perhaps. Mother Augusta. . . ." Susan took a fortifying sip of tea.

"Out with it, Susan! Don't turn missish on me."

"When Mr. Quitiquit read Frederick's will, there was no mention of me—not that I expected it. I know the estate is yours. But the dowry I brought, if I remember correctly, my father told me the money was to be settled on me. Was it, Mother Augusta? Is it mine?"

"To be sure it is," Augusta said promptly, and with such forcefulness that it earned her a sharp look from Susan. "Frederick signed the settlement papers. A sum in the amount of your dowry is yours to do with as you please and, since we have no dower house, the tenancy for life at Cavendish Manor."

"Frederick did not gamble the dowry away?"

"Certainly not."

"Forgive me, but—" Susan floundered. She had never before doubted her mother-in-law's word, never before felt that the imperial tone and proud demeanor were used to hide something from her. "Frederick lost constantly. I cannot believe he did not touch my dowry. I asked, only he resented questions so much that I did not persist. I *should* have. 'Tis my right to know."

"Yes, it is." Augusta rose. "Come with me, child. I have some

explaining to do, and I feel I have endured the breakfast table
long enough."

Susan followed the older woman upstairs. In her sitting room,
the dowager went straight to a painting of Cavendish Manor,
commissioned several years ago by Andrew and presented to his
aunt as a birthday gift. Behind the painting, Susan knew, was a
safe.

"Mother Augusta, if you're planning to give me the money,
pray don't! That was never my intention."

"I don't have the money. You'll have to apply to Andrew for
that."

"Andrew . . . yes, of course. Your man of business." Susan
sank into the nearest chair, a square, ornately carved monstrosity
reputed to be as old as the manor house. "I don't know what I
was thinking. When I saw you reach for the painting. . . ."

Having lifted the painting off its hook, Augusta Cavendish
unlocked and opened the safe. She turned to Susan.

"There's something you ought to know about Andrew and the
estate. He owns Cavendish Manor, not I."

Susan felt as if she had been slapped. If the estate belonged
to Andrew—but Augusta must be wrong. 'Twas all a mistake.
Or was it? Her mother-in-law made very few mistakes.

Struggling to keep her composure, Susan said, "I do not understand. How is this possible? Frederick bequeathed his portion
to you, and you already owned the other half."

"And wasn't it just like Frederick not to change his will in
your favor? I was quite annoyed at the time. When I saw the
ledgers, however, I realized he had no right to bequeath anything
to anyone. He had mortgaged the estate."

"Could he do that without your consent?"

"He did not go to our banker, who would have known that I
owned one half. No, Susan. The estate books show that a Mr.
Throckmorton of Bishopsgate in London held the mortgage."

"A money lender?"

"I expect so. And Frederick, no doubt, gambled with the sum
he borrowed. And lost."

Susan sat stunned. Frederick had always seemed to lose. Every bit of jewelry she inherited from a great-aunt had found its way to the gaming tables. Her mother's pearls. The Consols her father had left her. Then her wedding ring. But his own mother's home!

"Andrew redeemed the mortgage," said Augusta. "In fact, he paid all of Frederick's debts."

"And now he owns everything," Susan said tonelessly. "I am living on *Andrew's* charity. Not yours."

"Rubbish! Would you call *me* his pensioner?"

Encountering the dowager's indignant look, Susan rallied. "Yes, indeed. It seems we're his pensioners."

"Pishtosh!" Augusta did not sound quite as assertive as earlier. "In any case, on paper the estate is still mine since I've not yet signed it over. Though, in truth, I ought to do so without delay. Now, pray do not distract me further or I may forget why I opened the safe."

Briskly, she turned and, reaching into the wall cavity, removed a blue velvet pouch, an inch wide and two inches long.

"My ring!" Susan half rose, then sank back. "But it cannot be. That, I know for certain, Frederick lost at play."

"Andrew retrieved it. He gave it to me for safekeeping so Frederick would not be tempted again."

Susan accepted the pouch. For a moment, she merely looked at it, reluctant to face the token of Frederick's pledge of troth. She shook the ring into her palm. The large pink pearl gleamed softly. The diamonds surrounding it caught the light from the window and sparkled enticingly.

What hopes and dreams she had cherished when Frederick slipped the ring onto her finger—dreams spun by a very young and naive girl and destroyed within the first few months of marriage.

Augusta said, "I did not mean to keep it so long. Not after Frederick died. I was waiting for the right moment, but that moment never seemed to come. Did I do wrong?"

"No, indeed." Susan returned the ring to the pouch. "Even

now I do not want it. Perhaps at some later time. Will you keep it a little longer?"

"Because 'twas Andrew who retrieved it?"

"Partly for that reason, but mainly because—please, Mother Augusta! Won't you put the ring away?"

Augusta obliged and, when the painting once more hid the safe, took a seat facing her daughter-in-law.

"Believe me, Susan, I understand. You do not want the ring because it serves as a remembrance of your marriage. Now that you're out of mourning—"

Susan cut in. "I never was in mourning! I wore black gowns and ribbons, I accepted condolences, yet I did not feel bereaved."

"No, how could you? But you did not flout the conventions, and for that I am grateful."

"Lud! I am so sorry!" Susan could scarcely speak for shame. "I should never have spoken to you as I did."

"Rubbish. I should always wish you to be honest with me."

"You're his mother!"

Augusta suddenly seemed much older than her sixty years. "And as his mother I mourned not his death, but wept only for the man he could have been, yet never was."

Their eyes met.

Augusta said, "I should have been a friend to you. A confidante."

"You were—you *are* my friend, Mother Augusta."

"Oh, I know I wasn't the ogre a mother-in-law is reputed to be. But I never invited you to confide in me when you were in need of a friend." Her voice sank to a whisper. "Even now, I don't ask questions, and I know you're still troubled by the past."

Susan rose and started to pace, past the bedroom door and the heavy oak credenza, to the window, and back to the carved chairs by the fireplace. She had heard the apology in Augusta's voice, the admission of guilt, and wished she could reassure her. Alas! Her skills at translating feelings into words were poor.

In frustration, she burst out, "Frederick is dead! Why must we continue to feel guilty? Ashamed!"

"You have no need to feel ashamed, Susan. You were everything a dutiful wife should be."

"The shame lies in the very fact that the marriage was not a good one. If it had been forced on me, or on Frederick—but neither one of us had any objections to the arrangement. And had I protested from the start, I doubt even that could excuse my failure."

Augusta shook her head so violently that a pin came loose and dropped into the folds of her shawl. She ignored it. "Oh, I know, we are raised to succeed at marriage, and I would have agreed with you had I not witnessed my son's conduct. I am aware I did not see or hear the half of it. Your rooms were at a distance from mine. You had no maid to carry tales. But what I did see quite convinced me that we must revise our thinking about a woman's duty to her husband."

Susan could only stare in astonishment.

"Don't look at me as if I have suddenly grown horns!"

"Why! Mother Augusta, you've turned into a revolutionary."

"Nonsense! Though I do admit 'twas the writings of a female revolutionary that set me on the road to seeing sense. I must have had the books for twenty years or more, but did not read them until recently, more's the pity. Hadn't even cut the pages."

"Who is this female revolutionary?"

"Was. Her name was Mary Wollstonecraft. You ought to read her works. See what you think. And read her husband's *Memoir* of her as well. 'Tis enlightening. There's also a daughter, who is a writer of sorts. But that's neither here nor there. It's *A Vindication of the Rights of Woman* I particularly want you to read. I wish I had done so years ago!"

"Very well, I shall read it. But you must stop thinking that you could have helped me more than you did. You're Frederick's mother. Admit that there are matters we could never discuss."

"I should have let you know that you could discuss *anything* with me."

"It would have been an intolerable burden on you and might have doused the warmth you showed me when I most needed it.

I would not have risked that, no matter how much you might have pressed me to confide in you. So there's no point blaming yourself."

Augusta Cavendish was not given to displays of emotion, but now she rose and enfolded her daughter-in-law in a fierce embrace.

"And you, child, must allow yourself to grasp at the chance for a little happiness."

Susan stepped back, giving Augusta a quizzical smile. "You're referring to Andrew, are you not? Does it mean so much to you that I marry him?"

"It does not matter what it means to me. It's what *you* want that you must consider."

"Indeed," Susan said wryly. "Nothing could be simpler than deciding what I want."

"If you will only apply your mind to it, you'll not find it so very difficult to consider your own wishes."

Turning to leave, Susan was conscious of a flutter of excitement. 'Twas strange how much better, how much more alive she felt. Perhaps it was the talk with Augusta. Or perhaps it was because she had resolved earlier, while shaping a snowman in the copse, that she would no longer live in Frederick's dark shadow. Though, undoubtedly, that was easier said than done.

"I only wish I knew," said Augusta, following her to the door, "why you cannot sleep. Since June I've watched you grow paler and thinner, and I cannot for the life of me determine what caused you alarm—save for the boot boy getting lost in the passages. And he's in fine fettle, the rascal, so there's no need for you to be fretting over it."

"I never told you that I cannot sleep. Has Andrew been carrying tales?"

"Andrew is as worried as I am, but he does not carry tales. Never you mind how I know that you wander around the house at all hours of the night. Just tell me what I can do to help."

"I think Clive can help, Mother Augusta. At least I hope he

can. Gracious! Look at the time! If I don't hurry and change, I may have to receive their Graces in riding dress."

The Duke of Stenton's traveling chaise did not roll into the courtyard until noon. Susan, who had stationed herself by the crackling Yule log in the great hall, flung down the crochet shawl she was working for Augusta Cavendish and dashed outside.

The wind had picked up since her ride, and a fresh layer of snow covered the cobbles swept early in the morning by the grooms, but Susan would not have remained in the shelter of the portico had a blizzard blown across the yard. Elizabeth Rowland, Duchess of Stenton, was alighting from the coach, and whenever Susan saw Elizabeth, she felt young once again, and daring—like the girl who ran barefoot and climbed trees in the orchard of Elizabeth's home.

Neither did Elizabeth stand on ceremony. Picking up her skirts, she ran to meet Susan halfway on the flagged path leading to the portico and front door. They embraced, crying and laughing and wishing each other a merry Christmas all at the same time, and it wasn't until they finally turned toward the house that Susan noticed something amiss.

"Where is Clive?" She looked back at the coach, where two footmen were unstrapping Elizabeth's trunk. "And little Lizzy?"

"They stayed home. Last night, the east tower started to crumble, and Clive did not think he should leave."

Until she tasted the bitterness of disappointment, Susan did not realize just how much she had banked on speaking with Clive.

"But—Elizabeth, it's the anniversary of your marriage! Does he not wish to celebrate with you?"

Elizabeth smiled. "We did celebrate royally, I assure you. And since I could not bring my husband and daughter, I decided to bring someone else."

Susan once more looked back at the coach. No one had alighted. The door was shut, and the footmen were about to lift the single trunk and Elizabeth's crested traveling bag.

"But there's no one."

"Yes, there is." Elizabeth sounded as if she was stifling laughter. "It's Annie. She must have slipped inside while we were hugging. Doesn't feel comfortable out in the open, poor thing."

Susan blinked. "You mean—"

"Yes, silly! Annie Tuck, my little ghost."

"But—that's impossible." Susan could never quite believe in the presence of a ghost at Stenton Castle, except, perhaps, for the short while that she was witness to the mysterious lighting of the Christmas tree candles by an unseen hand. "Ghosts do not travel."

"Annie does. Not well, mind you. A few years back, she spent several months in London. But let us step inside, I beg. I am freezing in a fur-lined pelisse, and you don't even have a shawl."

"Indeed, my teeth are chattering."

The dowager and Andrew were in the great hall. Greetings must be exchanged and the explanation for Clive's absence repeated.

"To be sure," said the dowager, "your husband must do what is necessary. But could you not have brought the child?"

"You would not ask, ma'am, had you heard Clive on the subject." Unfastening her pelisse, Elizabeth turned a mock-tragic look on her hostess. "He did not seem to mind parting with his wife, but live without his daughter during the Christmas revels he could not."

The dowager harrumphed. "Lizzy is three, is she not? Undoubtedly a handful of trouble since neither of you believes in keeping the child in the nursery."

Andrew excused himself, saying he would just make certain that the duke's horses had not suffered from the twenty-six-mile journey on winter roads.

Susan followed the tall figure with her eyes and almost missed Augusta's next question to their visitor.

"Are you increasing again, my dear?"

"It's early days yet, ma'am. But, yes, I believe I am."

"There's something about your face that told me so. My felicitations, Elizabeth."

"How wonderful," said Susan, not without envy, but pleased on her friend's account. Elizabeth, who had married quite late, would be the mother of two before Susan had ever conceived.

Augusta waved both young women toward the stairs. "Susan will show you to your room, Elizabeth. You ought to rest awhile, and no doubt you two have much to say to each other."

"Indeed, ma'am. It has been far too long since I saw Susan. Last February!"

They had ascended the stairs no more than two or three steps when an exclamation of annoyance from Augusta made them turn.

"I do declare!" Retreating, the dowager pointed to the chandelier and kissing bough swinging to and fro above her head. "The maids are turning more addle-pated with every passing minute. If I told them once I must have told them a thousand times *never* to open the window at the end of the portrait gallery."

"I doubt your maids are at fault," said Elizabeth. She frowned at the kissing bough. "Annie, where have you been? Pray come down and make your curtsy to Mrs. Cavendish and Miss Susan."

Susan was torn between amusement and irritation. At Stenton Castle she had found it easy to smile when Elizabeth fell into conversation with an invisible being, but now she wished Elizabeth had left Annie, whether she truly existed or was imagined, at the old fortress. Cavendish Manor was already overcrowded with spirits of the past.

Neither did Augusta appear pleased, due, no doubt, to a recollection of a long and wearisome afternoon at Stenton, when the duke's uncle, Lord Decimus Rowland, had invited her to play three-handed whist. The third player, invisible to Augusta, had been Annie Tuck—or so Lord Decimus had insisted.

"Annie?" The dowager's voice was pained. "My dear Elizabeth! Can it wait? I find I have the headache all of a sudden."

Chuckling, Elizabeth picked up her skirts and continued upstairs. "Come along, then, Annie. We've been properly snubbed."

"And well you deserve it." Susan followed her friend. "I should think that Annie, if she must accompany you, would at least have the courtesy to show herself."

She felt a stir of air, as if someone brushed past. Yet Elizabeth was ahead of her.

"Oh, I will, Miss Susan," someone said in a high, clear voice, yet no one but Elizabeth was around. " 'Tis just that it takes a bit longer with some than it does with others. But I'll tell you straightforward that I do not like this place. I'm not at all certain I'll wish to stay."

Susan could only gasp and blindly thrust out her arms in hopes of finding something to clutch for support.

"Annie!" Directing a look of reproach over her shoulder, Elizabeth saw Susan, white-faced, clinging to the banister. "You heard! I am so sorry. I had no notion you could hear the little prattlebox. I always thought you did not—never mind! Come, lean on me. I still remember how my skin crawled and my heart leaped into my throat when I realized for the first time that I was hearing a ghost."

Recovering, Susan forced a smile. "Keep your arm to yourself. I may be a widow, but I'm not in my dotage. Just give me warning, if you please, whenever I should expect to be addressed by someone I cannot see."

"Annie is gone." Elizabeth scanned her surroundings as they proceeded up the stairs and into the east-wing corridor. "And I must say I don't see what she doesn't like. The house may be a bit dark, but what beautiful furnishings! What artists they were, those Jacobean craftsmen!"

"Wait until you see your bed. 'Tis covered with gargoyles and coiled serpents, heads raised to strike."

Elizabeth stopped in the door Susan had opened.

She took one look at the canopied bed and gasped. "I see what you mean. I suppose I might have borne it had Clive been with me, but I fear 'tis out of the question that I sleep here alone. I wouldn't want to give the babe a nightmare."

Susan did not hesitate. "Please share my room."

"Splendid!" Elizabeth turned sparkling green eyes on her. "We'll talk and laugh all night just as we did when we were girls and you visited me at home. Lud, I am so very glad I came, which is amazing when, I confess, this morning I did not want to leave without Clive and Lizzy."

"I, too, wish that Clive had accompanied you. And, of course, your daughter."

Elizabeth cocked her head. "There's more to your regret than pity for me that I must make do without my husband."

"Perhaps. But as you say, we can talk all night." Susan closed the guest room door. "Let me see you settled now and rested. And a footman must fetch your trunk to my rooms."

"By all means," Elizabeth said cordially as they followed the corridor to the last suite of rooms. As soon as they entered, she closed the door and faced Susan.

"But first, my love, you will explain the note of disappointment when you spoke of Clive." Her look quizzed. "Lest you want me to believe that you pine for the sight of my husband?"

"If I thought I could convince you . . . after all, I am a young and lonely widow."

They both laughed a little, but Elizabeth was not slow to note that Susan's laughter lacked true merriment.

"What is it, Susan? I do not like to say it, but you look—"

"Positively hagged. No need to spare me. I hear it almost daily."

"I meant to say ill, not that it makes any difference." Elizabeth lightly brushed a hand over Susan's hair. "Something is amiss. Please tell me."

"I had hoped to question Clive about Frederick's death."

Elizabeth frowned. "I was sure we told you. Frederick was shot and fell off the cliffs. We believe he had dealings with the free traders, who regard the stretch of coast below the castle as their very own. That night Frederick must have run afoul of them. There was a falling-out."

"I remember what you told me. But I wanted Clive to assure me that Frederick is truly dead."

"Of course he is." Elizabeth was becoming quite concerned. "What megrim have you taken into your head?"

"Did you see him?"

"Frederick? No, I did not. For the same reason that Clive would not allow you and Mrs. Cavendish to see him. His injuries . . . the fall from the cliffs . . . he was horridly maimed, Susan."

"Could it have been someone else at the foot of the cliffs?"

Elizabeth clasped Susan's shoulders and shook her none too gently. "Stop it. Frederick is dead, and if you will not believe me, why do you not ask your cousin? He helped Clive carry your husband to the castle."

"My cousin," Susan repeated numbly. She did not have a cousin.

"Andrew Cavendish," said Elizabeth.

Susan had always thought of Andrew as Frederick's cousin, though of course he must be considered hers, too. Cousin by marriage. And he had been at Stenton when Frederick died.

"Pray excuse me, Elizabeth. I must see Andrew immediately."

Three

Andrew Cavendish heard the study door open, but did not look up until he had completed an entry in the stable log regarding the duke's carriage horses.

"Susan!" He rose, mastering his astonishment that she had sought him out in the room Augusta called his sanctuary. "My apologies. If I ignored you, 'twasn't meant—"

"It does not signify," she said impatiently. "Only tell me that you can spare a few moments of your time!"

"All the time you need."

He stepped around the oak desk that all but stretched from wall to wall in this narrow chamber at the rear of the west wing. His heart was beating in a manner strongly reminiscent of the moment before battle. Yet Susan did not look to be in a fighting mood, but in a state of considerable agitation—which made it the second time in less than twenty-four hours that she dropped the reserve she had shown him since he kissed her, an incident more than three years in the past.

Despite the air of urgency that accompanied her, she did not seem to know what to say or how to start, which gave him leisure to scan the features so dear to him, the shapely mouth, a rounded chin with a small dimple, the graceful curve of neck and shoulder, and the slender figure, alluring in some soft fabric of a deep apricot shade.

"This color becomes you, Susan. It gives your hair a burnished look."

"Does it?" Her voice was breathless. "Then I thank you, but pray don't distract me. I learned from Elizabeth that you were at Stenton the night Frederick died. I want to know what happened. All of it!"

Whatever he had expected, it was not this. And not now, before he had even proposed to her, let alone been accepted. If the subject of Frederick's ignominious death had to be discussed at all, a more propitious moment could have been found *after* they were married.

Or else the tale should have been told two years ago.

"Andrew!" She shook his arm. "Don't you dare ignore me now! Or fob me off. I want to know if Frederick is dead!"

"What?" He could scarcely believe his ears. "Of course he's dead. We brought him here and buried him."

"But did you recognize him?" she demanded. "The body was—Andrew, how did you identify him?"

"His clothes. The signet ring. Devil a bit! What is all this about, Susan?"

"You must have been misled by appearances. I believe—" She drew a ragged breath. "I believe that Frederick is alive."

"You cannot be serious!"

Holding herself stiffly, she met his incredulous look. "Since you closed off the passages, I've heard footsteps at night. His footsteps. I've heard him call my name."

"So that is why you do not sleep."

Slowly, gently, as if she were a child that must not be frightened, he clasped her hand. And as he did so, he realized that it was the attitude he instinctively assumed toward her since he had seen that a married woman could be as vulnerable and in need of protection as a child was. But it was the wrong attitude now. Susan was no longer captive in an intolerable marriage, nor was she a child. If she needed protection, it was from a well-meaning bungler as he had proven to be.

He spoke with authority. "It was Frederick. Though the features were unrecognizable, I could not be mistaken. Do but recall that I knew him since earliest childhood. And we had the smugglers' testimony. They had no reason to lie."

"I want to believe you. Lud! How desperately I want to believe!"

Pressing her hand briefly, he let go. "It is absurd to fear that Frederick is alive—and I use the word fear with purpose, Susan, for it is time we stop pretending that your marriage was nothing out of the ordinary."

She met his gaze for a fleeting moment, then turned abruptly. Hugging her arms to her chest, she stepped close to the fire he had rather neglected.

Andrew was content to let the matter rest. He had read acknowledgment in her clear gray eyes and, he believed, relief that he had swept aside an implicit taboo against the discussion of such a volatile topic as a man's treatment of his wife.

Seemingly absorbed in contemplation of the sluggish remains in the grate, she said, "I did not know you were at Stenton. Tell me what happened. I never quite understood about the smugglers. Was Frederick trading with them?"

"He was part of them."

She cast a startled look over her shoulder. "He was a smuggler himself?"

"I had convinced him that he could no longer gamble for high stakes. Free trading was his revenge on me, for there was nothing I could do about it short of turning him in."

"Yes, that must have pleased him very much," she said, turning back to the meager fire. "Why, then, did he have a falling-out with the smugglers? At least, Elizabeth said that is what happened."

"Boredom, I expect. Trade wasn't as brisk as it was during the war." Andrew chose his words with care. "Too many nights spent in the chief smuggler's tavern with cheap drink and no diversion more exciting than rolling the dice for chicken stakes. Or courting the tavern keeper's daughter. Or fighting."

"Fighting *over* the tavern keeper's daughter, no doubt."

"Yes, I suppose so. You see, she was betrothed to a local fellow. One of the smugglers. But, apparently, she preferred Frederick."

"No need to sound apologetic. Though he did not tell me about the smuggling, he made no secret of his conquests. I knew there was someone in East Dean."

Andrew looked at the straight back, the proudly held head.

She faced him. "Please, Andrew. Tell me what happened. I promise I shan't have a fit of the vapors."

He indicated a settle beneath one of the windows overlooking the pristine whiteness of the gardens. "Shall we sit?"

"No, but you might add a little coal to the fire. Or, perhaps, there is something else you can think of to delay telling the rest of the tale?"

He flung up a hand in the manner of a fencer acknowledging a hit. "If I hesitate, 'tis because I'm not certain that this is the time to rake over past history. But so be it. Anything will be better than having you believe Frederick is still alive."

She gave a crooked little smile. "You were there, and you assure me he is dead. It is impossible, I find, to maintain doubts when faced with your certainty. Only tell me all."

"Very well, then. Frederick decided to elope to France with

the tavern keeper's daughter. Jed Beamish, the father, got wind of the plan at the last moment and would have none of it. He and the girl's betrothed and a handful of their smuggling friends caught the pair in the estuary beneath the castle as they were about to set sail."

"Alone? I remember that we had quite a gale blowing that Christmas Eve. It must have been worse at Stenton, and they would have needed a crew, I should think."

"Three of the smugglers agreed to go with them and bring back the boat later. That's how Beamish heard of it. A wife or mother or sweetheart—I don't remember which—could not keep a still tongue in her head."

"The daughter—what is her name?"

"Mary. I understand she set up quite a screech when her father plucked her from the boat."

"She should count herself lucky, poor girl. So what happened then?"

"A fight broke out."

Andrew joined her at the fireplace. He picked up some lengths of wood, a fuel he preferred to coal, and arranged them on the glowing embers.

Watching him, Susan said, "A fight. Go on. That was when Frederick was shot? But no, that happened on the cliff path. Do tell, Andrew!"

"Frederick stabbed Jed Beamish." Andrew straightened. "In the arm, but the men said he was aiming for the heart. Mary's betrothed shot at Frederick but missed. Then Frederick drew one of his pistols—he had the pair of Mantons on him. He did not miss."

"He wouldn't. He could shoot the pip out of a playing card. Whom did he kill?"

"Mary's betrothed. Then he took to his heels, with Beamish and his men in pursuit. Apparently, Frederick intended to seek refuge at the castle. He chose the cliff path instead of the longer but safer carriageway. His last gamble, you might say."

For a moment Andrew watched the flames as they flickered

and rose around the fresh fuel. Susan was silent as well, but between them, as though spoken aloud, hung the phrase, "And as always, he lost."

Finally Andrew said, "On his way up the cliffs, Frederick shot and killed a second man. The smugglers gave up the pursuit—except for Jed Beamish. He did not have a pair of fancy dueling pistols, but he had an old blunderbuss pistol loaded with lead shot and small scrap. Before Frederick could make it to the top, Beamish fired."

"And Frederick fell." Despite the increasing warmth from the fireplace, Susan shivered. "That, I knew. But why wasn't I told the precise circumstances?"

"We—His Grace and I—thought it best to spare you the sordid details. His Grace conferred with the magistrate, who agreed that there was little purpose in arresting Beamish. 'Twas his daughter Frederick tried to ruin, and his boat he tried to steal. You could hardly blame the man for shooting Frederick."

"And, at least, there was no scandal. I am glad for Augusta's sake. Does she know the . . . sordid details?"

"She does."

"Yet I, his widow, was not told."

"You," he pointed out, "did not ask."

She flinched.

"Why not, Susan? Why did you not ask a single question?"

He thought she would not answer, for she turned away, hands clenching at her sides.

But she faced him again, her expression one of defiance mingled with shame. "I did not care enough to ask. I had no curiosity, no interest in the circumstances of his death. I felt only relief."

"Quite understandable."

She stared at him, gave a dry little laugh that ended in a strangled, choking sound. "Lud, Andrew! Did you not listen? I was glad! *Glad* that he was dead!"

"As any woman in your position would have been."

From the vicinity of the fireplace came a loud thud, a sound very much like a booted foot kicking wood.

Susan whirled, staring at the racks of shelving that flanked the mantelpiece—shelving that was a feature installed in almost every room of the house and designed to conceal a priest's hole or the entrance to a hidden passage.

The thud rang out again, louder, and repeated twice more in rapid succession. With a muffled cry, she jumped back only to be caught up against a solid chest. Before she could cry out again, strong arms closed around her. Andrew's voice, deep and reassuringly close to her ear, told her to quit struggling and be still so he could listen.

Obeying the first part of the command, she said, " 'Tis Frederick! I told you he's alive!"

"Rubbish!"

Andrew wanted to say considerably more. However, he heard the study door open.

The dowager entered, saying, "Andrew, I want you to send for Quitiquit first thing—oh, my dears! This is a sight I've longed to see. Susan, I am very pleased to know that you have finally come to your senses."

"I beg your pardon—" With an effort, Susan broke Andrew's close hold. " 'Tis not what it seems, Mother Augusta."

"Oh? I did not see you in Andrew's arms just now?"

"No. At least, it wasn't an embrace as you perceived it." No further sounds emitted from the secret passage. Unwilling to speak of Frederick to his mother, Susan looked to Andrew for help.

He either could not or would not understand her plea. Would not, most likely, for he was smiling, a brow raised in bland inquiry.

"Wretch," she whispered before facing the dowager again. "A small mishap. I tripped and Andrew caught me."

It was near enough to the truth that only a hint of betraying warmth touched her face. But she could not trust herself to utter yet another fib without blushing deeply should her mother-in-law decide to question her further.

"Pray excuse me. You have business with Andrew, and I should return to Elizabeth."

"But don't you want to marry Andrew?" asked Elizabeth when the full tale, starting with the nighttime encounter with Andrew and the reason for Susan's sleeplessness, had been poured into her ears.

"Whether I do or don't, what does it signify? Elizabeth, don't you understand? Frederick is alive!"

As it befitted her interesting condition, the Duchess of Stenton was reclining against a mountain of pillows, but now she sat up to stare at her friend, huddled at the end of the bed, feet tucked beneath her skirts, arms folded tightly.

"Susan, you are my dearest friend. I have known you far longer than I care to admit. I don't deny that in your salad days you dreamed up some quite bizarre and madcap adventures for us to act out, but—"

"Ha! And *you* did not?"

"We are not discussing me," Her Grace replied with dignity. "It is you who gives cause for concern." Dignity slipped. "Dash it, Susan! Overall, you used to be sensible!"

"I am being very sensible now. I'd consider it foolish beyond measure knowingly to contract a bigamous marriage."

"Then you *do* wish to marry Andrew."

Susan reached for a thick plaid shawl Elizabeth had earlier discarded. Wrapping it around her shoulders, she said, "I don't know if I would wish ever to marry again."

"Nonsense. I've seen you with Lizzy. I know you want a child."

"I would not be the first woman who cannot have what she wants."

Elizabeth hesitated. "You never said anything, never complained, but—your marriage was not a happy one, was it?"

Susan wanted to deny this, as had been her habit when someone presumed to comment on her marriage. But what about her resolve to live no longer in Frederick's shadow—whether he was alive or dead, she must try to stand by her decision. And Elizabeth was her friend. It was hardly presumption when she asked a question.

Elizabeth said, "Your silence is answer enough. I have long suspected that Frederick . . . did not treat you as he should, but Clive said I mustn't ask. It would only make it worse for you."

Susan's face flamed. "Yes, I knew you were concerned and, at the time, I appreciated your reticence. It was horrid having to parry questions, no matter how innocent or well meant. And the whispers!"

"It was no reflection on you that there was speculation."

"Was it not?"

Elizabeth evaded the skeptical, lightly mocking look that made her remember occasions when she had caught the ladies of neighboring estates in whispered conversation about the young Mrs. Cavendish. Some of the comments had been unkind if not downright malicious, and the whispering had always ended in abrupt silence when the ladies noticed the Duchess of Stenton was close enough to overhear.

"Of course not, silly!" she lied, wishing every gossip to perdition. "Given Frederick's reputation, and the fact that he would not allow you to accept an invitation unless he was home to attend with you—which was not often!"

"I was so careful when I declined and prayed no one would notice anything amiss."

"You even declined some of *my* invitations. And except for that one time when you and Mrs. Cavendish spent Christmas with us, you did not come for a visit."

"I spent a week with you in February and the summer before last."

Elizabeth waved a dismissive hand. "I'm referring to the years before Frederick's death. Surely he would have made an exception for a visit to an old friend?"

"Especially *not* to an old friend. Lud!" Susan slid off the bed. "The tenants' dance tonight! Excuse me, Elizabeth. There are a dozen things to see to, and I don't want Mother Augusta to wear herself out."

"You forget I have more than a nodding acquaintance with your mother-in-law. Mrs. Cavendish will not wear herself out, but will long since have delegated any remaining tasks. Come, Susan. Don't cry craven now that you've begun to confide in me again."

Susan gave her friend a rueful look. "But I don't want to speak of Frederick."

"No, indeed. Let us speak of Andrew."

Before Susan could decide whether to admire or scold Elizabeth for her tenacity, a clatter made her start. Instinctively, her eyes sought the shelving next to the fireplace. But this time she could have sworn the noise had not come from the passage hidden away behind the shelves.

"Annie!" Elizabeth said with exasperation. "What on earth is the matter? I've never seen you behave like this. Please pick up everything immediately."

There was an unintelligible mutter, and as Susan turned in confusion, she saw her brushes and Elizabeth's jump off the polished floor boards and fling themselves onto the dressing table. The sight made her feel queasy and weak-kneed, but she refused to give in to a craven impulse to run.

"Annie?" Her voice was no more than a hoarse whisper, and she hastily cleared her throat. "I had no notion you were here. In the room."

"Neither, apparently, did anyone else." Indignation filled the disembodied voice. "I might have been invisible for all the attention Miss Elizabeth paid me."

Despite her uneasiness in Annie's presence, Susan gave a choke of laughter. "But you are invisible."

"Not to her."

"Stop it, Annie." Elizabeth drooped back against the pillows. "A young lady does not show petulance."

"I'm a nursery maid, not a young lady. And I don't like it here. I want to go home."

Susan ventured a step closer to the dressing table, where, presumably, Annie Tuck stood. But, perhaps, a ghost floated. Or hovered. "You're afraid, I think. I hear it in your voice."

"I want to go home."

She sounded like a child, thought Susan. "How old are you?"

"Seventeen. Or eighteen. What does it matter?"

"Why do you want to go home?" asked Elizabeth. "You told me you were moped at Stenton. You said you were looking forward to the visit."

Annie made no reply.

"Is she still here?" whispered Susan.

"Yes, I am," came the disgruntled response from the dressing table. "But if I were you, Miss Susan, I'd find myself another house. This one has an evil spirit."

"Fiddlesticks!" cried Elizabeth.

Susan did not protest. She could not deny that Annie was at least partially correct, for Frederick's evilness still lingered.

Elizabeth said, "I'd be the last to deny the existence of ghosts and spirits. But *two* in the same house! It boggles the mind."

The little ghost gave an indignant sniff. "I'm a visitor. And who said anything about another ghost? I was speaking of an evil spirit, the kind Miss Caroline told me about when I was in London."

"Annie is referring to Caroline Renshaw," Elizabeth explained. "Caroline grew up in Haiti—Saint Domingue, as it was known when she lived there. But those evil spirits of the dead have to do with voodoo. It is utter nonsense to think we'd have anything like it in England."

Susan scarcely listened. "Annie, would you know if there was another ghost in the house? I mean—would you be able to sense him? See him?"

"I don't know." Annie sounded slightly mollified, now that she was definitely included in the conversation. "I never encountered another ghost, and I don't even understand why *I* am one. I've been at Stenton Castle some forty-odd years and don't understand the purpose of it, and want *you* to know if I can sense another ghost!"

Elizabeth slid off the bed. "Susan! Did you say *him?* Are you—you cannot mean *Frederick's* ghost!"

"No?" Seeing Elizabeth's horrified expression, Susan suddenly felt like laughing. Not that she did, and not that it was a laughing matter.

She said, "It is strange, is it not? I cannot even now feel easy about Annie, and yet I'm wishing that Frederick were a ghost. But I promise you, I would definitely like it much better—and find it less frightening, too—than believing that Frederick is alive."

Elizabeth became pensive. "Well . . . put that way, it doesn't sound half bad. Indeed, it doesn't. And it would explain those strange noises you heard, and your name being called."

She looked around. "Annie? Oh. You're on the bed. That's where I should be. *You* shall have a mission. A purpose for your visit. Find out if this house has its own ghost."

Four

Though by no means pleased that she would not be able to leave Cavendish Manor, Annie Tuck willingly flitted off to scour every chamber and hallway, the secret passages, attics, and cellars for signs of a ghost. There wasn't much she would not do for the young Duchess of Stenton, and especially did she like being given a mission. One never knew, but a simple human mission might lead to the discovery of her overall mission—the reason she was still entangled in worldly matters.

Annie had perished in a fire that broke out in the nursery wing at Stenton Castle more than forty years earlier. She had died in the vain attempt to save the fourth duke's three children—those of his first marriage. Even though she had not succeeded, and the duke's wife and seven others of the staff had perished as well,

surely her efforts must be counted as a good deed. Surely she
ought to be able to rest in peace.

Regardless of *her* feelings in the matter, she was still very
much involved in the affairs at Stenton, where the present duke,
issue of the fourth duke's second marriage, was doing his best
to render the long neglected estate self-sufficient and, at the same
time, create respectable positions for the men in East Dean and
other villages all too likely to engage in smuggling when times
were rough. The duke had even reopened the old salt mines, and
Miss Elizabeth was supervising the leasing of two castle wings—
with resident ghost—just as if they were houses for hire in
Brighton or Worthing. With that and the gardens and little Miss
Lizzy, the duchess had her hands full, which was the reason she
had not seen as much of Miss Susan as she would have liked.

Now that Annie had been at Cavendish Manor several hours,
she was convinced Miss Elizabeth should have paid a visit much
sooner. Ghost or no ghost, something was amiss, and above all,
Miss Elizabeth understood how to put things to rights. As did
Annie, especially if it involved reluctant lovers. Annie was very
curious to meet a certain gentleman named Andrew, whom Miss
Susan seemed just as hesitant to discuss as the one who might
be a ghost.

Annie vaguely recalled a tall gentleman in the great hall at the
time of their arrival, but she had been too intent on exploring the
manor house to give him more than a cursory glance. His hair
was quite dark, she thought. She did not know whether he was
young or old, for she had not seen his face. She knew only that
he was of an admirably powerful build. When she returned to
the hall later, he had left. But there was to be a dance that night,
the tenants' Boxing Day dance. If she did not encounter the gentleman earlier, surely she would meet him then.

"What does Annie look like?"

"Quite ordinary," Elizabeth replied drowsily. She and Clive
had risen before dawn to celebrate the anniversary of their wed-

ding day before her departure. Now, as much as she detested pampering, she would dearly like to indulge in a nap. Pointedly, she closed her eyes.

"How ordinary?" Susan persisted. She stepped closer to the bed. "Like you or me? Like Augusta? Like Squire Appleby's plump daughter?"

"More like a wraith."

"A wraith? And ordinary. What does an ordinary wraith look like?"

Elizabeth opened one eye. "If I tell you, will you promise me something?"

"Anything."

Elizabeth smiled. "The same reckless reply you used to give years ago. I am glad you haven't changed."

"I have, though. It is only with you that I feel safe to be myself. To be outgoing. Or a little rash once in awhile. Or lighthearted."

Elizabeth opened both eyes. "There are others you can trust. And I'm not speaking of my husband, for that is understood."

"I know. You're speaking of Augusta and Andrew." Susan was intent on smoothing the long, narrow sleeves of her gown. "I love Augusta dearly. . . ."

"But she is Frederick's mother," Elizabeth finished when Susan's voice trailed into silence. She added dryly, "You can hardly blame her for that, poor lady."

"I'm not such a dimwit! 'Tis only that sometimes, around her, I cannot help but feel ashamed. She is so kind. And the feelings I harbored—still harbor for her son! And not only that. I am ashamed of everything that happened in my marriage. And I did not mourn as a wife should. It makes me feel so . . . so *base!*"

"Great heavens!" Elizabeth was moved to sit up again. "If you aren't Frederick's inconsolable widow, no one can be blamed for it but he. Augusta will certainly not hold it against you. Now, don't be tiresome, Susan! For, I vow, if you have turned into a tragedy queen, I shall leave this instant!"

Shocked and hurt, Susan could only stare at her friend, but gradually, under Elizabeth's dark glower, her feelings eased.

"Dash it," she said weakly. "Why must you always be in the right? I've been tiresome even to myself. I am weary of moping and feeling guilty and ashamed. It has become a habit, I think." Her mouth firmed in resolve. "One that I shan't indulge any longer."

"Good." Elizabeth flashed a dazzling smile. "Then I can finally take my nap? Or, perhaps, you will tell me why you cannot be yourself around Andrew?"

"No, I shan't do that." Susan imitated the scowl Elizabeth had directed at her earlier. "And you may *not* go to sleep until you've described Annie Tuck."

Descending to the kitchens fifteen minutes later, Susan found herself looking around, peeking into corners, in the expectation of discovering a wraith of a girl in an old-fashioned striped cotton skirt with an overdress of some dark blue material, a huge mobcap all but hiding a thin little face framed by wisps of dark curls. Not that she particularly wanted to see Annie Tuck; conversing with a ghost quite sufficed for her. But the conversation had eradicated any lingering doubts in Annie's existence, and Susan was no longer uneasy. She was prepared, if must be, to endure a face-to-face encounter.

She felt a lightness of heart she had not experienced since she was a young girl, a liveliness of spirit that even a possibility of meeting Frederick's ghost could not dampen. Only Frederick alive could bring that about, but on this menacing thought she would not dwell. If she retained a shred of doubt about his death, she must not let it show. No one else deemed it at all possible that he was alive.

When she resolved early that morning to escape Frederick's dark shadow, she had discovered it no simple feat. Fortunately, Elizabeth had shown her that part of the shadow was of her own making, and Susan was confident that anything of her own doing, she could undo. She could believe for the first time in the possibility of future happiness.

The kitchens and pantries were a-bustle. Cook, housekeeper, and butler assured her, ever so politely but quite firmly, that she need not waste her time or concern on the nether regions. The china and crystal had been washed, the silver polished, the meats and pies were baking, and there were enough Christmas puddings to serve twice the number of guests they expected. Perhaps madam would be so kind as to inspect the great hall?

The request was no more than a sop to her dignity; neither Susan nor the three heads of staff entertained any doubts that the hall would be found in fine shape. Yet, deference must be shown and accepted.

"Indeed, I will." With a nod, Susan turned. In the vaulted kitchen doorway, she could not resist a look over her shoulder at three satisfied faces which quickly assumed looks of polite inquiry.

"Was there anything else, madam?" asked the butler.

"If there were, Tredwell, would you be able to think of yet another ruse to hasten my departure from your domain?"

He bowed. "Madam likes to jest. If I may say so, I am glad to hear it."

"You may say so, indeed." She smiled. "It is entirely possible, however, that you will regret it tonight, when I shall claim revenge and ask you to sing."

The butler looked pained, but cook and housekeeper were unanimous in their approval. Tredwell was by far the most gifted singer in the neighborhood. When he could be persuaded to lend his rich baritone to lead the caroling, the tenants' dance was bound to be a success.

As Susan climbed the stairs to the great hall, it occurred to her that despite the dowager's order to decorate and proceed with the Christmas celebrations as in the years before Frederick's death, she had heard neither song nor laughter from the staff. And how jolly the maids and footmen used to be at Christ-

mastime! Not even Frederick, if he was home, had succeeded in
dampening their high spirits.

Frederick had died in the early hours of Christmas Day two
years ago, when black crepe had to replace the decorations in
the great hall. One year ago, Christmas had marked the end of
full mourning, yet no festivities were planned. But this year. . . .

Tredwell had told her he was glad to hear her jest. Elizabeth
had warned her that she had turned into a tragedy queen. Augusta
felt guilty because Susan wasn't confiding in her. The longer
Susan thought about it, the more clearly she saw that she had not
only hurt herself these past two years, but she had also poisoned
the atmosphere for those around her. *She* had succeeded where
Frederick could not. *She* had banished the spirit of Christmas
from the house.

Very well, that, too, would change.

No one was in the hall when Susan entered. While she was
with Elizabeth, footmen and maids had set up refreshment tables,
had rolled up rugs, and moved pieces of ancient armor and the
heavy settles, chairs, and tables carved from oak and mahogany,
to clear a respectably proportioned dance floor in the center of
the hall. More garlands had been strung, some of spruce and
holly, others of fir entwined with red ribbon, and the Christmas
tree near the foot of the open stairway was adorned with fresh
white candles.

Indeed, everything was in readiness for the tenants' entertain-
ment, which would begin at six with the presentation of gifts to
the children, who would then be fed and bedded down in the
servants' hall. By eleven, the majority of the guests, since they
had to rise at four or five to tend the milking of their cows, would
be taking their leave and receive their own gifts. Only the staff,
joining the celebration after they carried in the flaming Christmas
puddings, would feast and dance till midnight.

Susan was about to go upstairs when Andrew came out of the
corridor that opened near the vast fireplace and bisected the west
wing, which was considered his domain and was quite unlike
the east wing, where Susan and the dowager had their apartments

and where the rooms on the ground floor opened directly onto the great hall.

"A pretty scene," he said.

"And high time." Turning slowly, Susan watched his approach. "We should have held the dance last year."

"Why do you look at me like that?" Andrew cocked his head. "As if you had never seen me before?"

"Sometimes when I look at you, I also see Frederick. Your build and coloring, even your features—no! I don't mean that. Even though you resemble Frederick, *your* eyes are kind. *You* smile, whereas he sneered."

"Thank God for small mercies." The smile she had lauded was notably absent. "So this is what I'm up against. My resemblance to Frederick is what keeps you from marrying me."

She had meant only to explain feelings that were horribly tangled, but had probably looked at him like the tragedy queen Elizabeth had deplored.

"Really, Andrew!" She managed a smile—a determined effort at mending her ways. "In the first place, you have not yet proposed."

"That can be remedied."

"Don't, pray don't be precipitate! I told you this morning that we must talk, and that still holds."

"Let us talk now." He drew her toward the fireplace and turned two chairs so that they faced each other. "Give me a reason—other than my resemblance to Frederick—why I should not propose this instant."

"Because," she said calmly, "I don't know my own mind."

He studied her for a long moment, then relaxed. "I shall take this as encouragement. How long do you suggest I should wait? No, don't answer that. Tell me what it is that keeps you from making up your mind."

"We don't know each other."

"Indeed," he said dryly. "We have shared a house for a mere four years. Naturally, we do not know each other."

Again she managed a smile and found that it came much easier.

"We have shared a house but not our minds. And if you will recall, this morning it was you who said I know nothing about you. Andrew, I did not even know that Cavendish Manor is yours."

"It isn't. If you marry me, you'll be marrying Augusta's man of business."

"You're quibbling. Just because she has not yet deeded the estate to you—but never mind that. Earlier today, I asked Augusta about the money that was settled on me. She assured me Frederick did not gamble it away, though I cannot believe it."

"One thousand pounds," he confirmed. "Yours to do with as you please."

She shook her head. "Seven hundred pounds. The amount of my dowry."

"Seven hundred pounds invested in the funds are bound to earn interest, my dear."

"Almost half again of the capital? I don't believe that either. But never mind." She frowned. "I think I may have mentioned it before, your calling me 'my dear' in that horrid, avuncular manner. I wish you would not do it."

"Then grant me the right to call you my love."

"Don't!" she said hastily. "You made a solemn promise last night."

"A damnably ill-conceived, rash promise!"

"But I shall hold you to it. Andrew, there is something I must know. Do you *wish* to marry me, or is it that you do not like to disappoint Augusta?"

"Devil a bit!" Leaning forward, he gripped her shoulders. When she flinched and tried to draw back, his clasp gentled, but he did not let go. "Don't, Susan. Don't shrink from my touch. You have nothing to fear from me."

She did not look at him. "I know, and I did not mean to jump. But, do you see now? It is but part of the reason I hesitate to marry—provided, of course, that I am truly free."

He released her. "I feared we would come back to that bit of nonsense. Of course you're free. If it will help, I'll open every passage, every priest's hole, to prove to you that Frederick is not hiding somewhere."

"Please do it. You think me foolish—I even agree with you! I did not mean to speak of it again, but only consider, if I were to marry you and suddenly Frederick appeared!"

"If you were to marry me . . . I shall take that as yet another encouragement. Have a care." Quizzical. "You will be committed before you realize it."

"You would not hold me to something so vague as a supposition."

"Would I not? No doubt about it then; you do not know me at all. But I did not answer your question. You asked if I *wish* to marry you. How can you doubt it? The kiss we shared—did it not prove what I feel for you?"

Her eyes widened. "That kiss, it was madness! I was distraught at the time . . . and you took pity."

"The deuce it was pity!"

"I was married! I should never have—"

"But you did, Susan. You responded passionately. Or do you deny it?"

She sat silent, her gaze on the Yule log.

When she spoke, her voice was soft. "I do not deny it. I felt cherished, Andrew. And for that reason, at that moment, I loved you."

"At that moment," he repeated.

Slowly, he rose, drawing her with him and enfolding her in his arms. "Let me cherish you again. Like this, Susan."

His mouth covered hers. There was no demand in his kiss, no harsh pressure; only the slow warmth that had marked the moment when he drew her into his embrace. It was his tenderness that was her undoing, for there seemed to be no reason to protest. Her arms closed around him of their own accord, drew him closer until she felt the beat of his heart close to her own, felt the strength of that powerful body and the response of her own as habitual aloofness changed to supple, lissome pliancy.

But this was the same delicious madness that had gripped her three years ago. Dangerous . . . designed to deprive of rational thought. He would take it as further encouragement. She could not allow that.

There was no need to struggle. As her arms dropped from his waist, Andrew released her. He did not speak, but searched her face closely before he stepped back, turned, and walked away.

Susan was still in a daze of confusion when she dressed for the evening. He had simply walked away. There was no understanding it. Still less did she understand herself. She had melted in his arms just as she had done three years earlier. She had felt cherished and sheltered—and wished fiercely to hold on to those feelings. Just as she had felt and wished three years ago. And that was simply impossible, for her circumstances now were quite altered.

Elizabeth received absentminded or no replies at all to comments and questions and finally gave up trying to draw out her friend. Since neither had a personal maid, Elizabeth from inclination and Susan still from the habit of eleven years of marriage when Frederick had denied her the services of a maid, they dressed each other's hair as they had often done in their youth. Only now, due to Susan's preoccupation and, perhaps, advanced sobering years, there was a marked absence of giggles and laughter. Not even Annie made an appearance to provide a diversion. Elizabeth was heartily glad when it was time to join the dowager and Andrew in the great hall.

She saw Susan grow pale, then blush at the sight of Andrew Cavendish and drew some very shrewd conclusions on her friend's state of mind. She had met Cavendish only twice, once at a dinner—she could not even recall when or where—and, of course, at the time of the infamous Frederick's death. But what little she had seen of him, she had certainly liked. As had Clive.

"Your Grace." Andrew Cavendish was bowing over her hand. "I hope you have recovered from your journey."

She laughed. "If anyone were to hear you, they would think

I traveled one hundred twenty-six miles instead of a mere twenty-six. But please, let us not stand on ceremony. You shall call me Elizabeth if I may call you Andrew."

"My pleasure. Will you join us in receiving our guests, or would you rather sit by the Yule log?"

"You will sit, Elizabeth," the dowager commanded. "It is better for you and less intimidating for everyone else."

There was no time for more since a footman at that moment opened the doors to a steady stream of arrivals that lasted for perhaps half an hour. The dowager and Susan welcomed each family, who was then shepherded toward Elizabeth by Andrew.

The men, farmers mostly, and the miller and blacksmith, whose properties were leaseholds, appeared stiff and ill at ease. The women, not usually shy, were quiet and watched their hosts uncertainly on this first grand celebration since their bereavement. The children, whether in awe or by power of parental threats, seemed to be struck dumb. But only until Susan clasped a small girl's hand and bade the other children form a chain so they might sing and dance around the Christmas tree before the gift giving. As if a dam had broken, squeals and laughter and jubilant young voices burst forth and washed away their elders' reserve.

"Well done," said the dowager, sitting down beside Elizabeth. "I hoped I need not intercede, but that Susan would cast off her shackles at last."

Elizabeth transferred her gaze from Susan and the children to Augusta Cavendish. "And under no circumstances must she be allowed to slip them back on. What can I do to help?"

"I don't know. Or, perhaps, I do. Susan is not one to bare her soul, but I do believe—and this may be mere wishing on my part—that she is more inclined toward a second marriage than she is willing to admit."

"Or capable of recognizing?"

"Whatever the case may be, you could make her see sense."

Susan's clear soprano, eagerly supported by the children's bright voices, filled the hall with "Be Merry, Be Merry."

Elizabeth said, "Sometimes it's best not to meddle, dear ma'am, but we shall see. You have, I presume, a specific marriage in mind?"

"Indeed. And knowing your perspicacity, I need not name names, need I?"

Elizabeth smiled. "Why don't we join Susan, or would the children regard me as an unwelcome interloper?"

"Not with that impish look, my dear. But you go alone. Or take Andrew. I am glad to be sitting for a spell."

And thus, the Duchess of Stenton joined hands with a red-faced, plump boy of about ten and a dainty little girl of her own Lizzy's age. Andrew went straight to Susan's side, but encountered resistance when he tried to break into the ring that had formed around the tree.

"Take your place between the Eldridge boys," said Susan, not looking at him but further increasing the pace of the children's energetic hop. "Then they won't be able to come to fisticuffs."

"You cannot be so cruel." Andrew trotted alongside the erratically weaving circle. "Those boys pinch!"

"Well, you cannot join here. George and Nell are quite happy holding hands with me."

On Susan's right, four-year-old George's scowl convinced Andrew that he need not look for support there. Holding Susan's left hand was Nell, George's twin, who did not seem to share her hostess's and her brother's reluctance, but smiled invitingly.

The song ended, and the whirling children came to a stop. Andrew seized his opportunity.

"A happy, wonderful, magical Christmas to you, Miss Nell. May I have the honor of holding your hand?" He bowed. "And Miss Susan's?"

Giggling, the small girl tugged herself free to reach out to the tall gentleman with the merry eyes. He took the hand—and Susan's—and bent to speak to his young benefactress.

"Thank you, lovely lady. Has anyone told you yet that you're absolutely ravishing?"

He was rewarded with another giggle.

"And you are shameless," whispered Susan when he straightened. "Now sing."

"You know I cannot carry a tune."

"It is the forfeit you pay when breaking into the circle."

"Look!" said Nell, slipping her small hand from Andrew's clasp and pointing to the top of the Christmas tree. "Magical."

Andrew smiled at the glowing upturned elfin face. "That's what I wished you, pretty lady. A wonderful, magical Christmas."

More children, eyes ever-widening and mouths shaping a silent "oh!" stared up at the tall fir tree. Even Susan looked spellbound.

Puzzled, Andrew followed their gazes. "The deuce!"

"No," said Nell. "An angel."

Andrew blinked and looked again, but his eyes had not deceived him. A long wax taper held by an unseen hand was moving from candle to candle, one by one setting them alight.

"Stop!" said Elizabeth when the upper third of the candles were lit. "Do the others later. We don't want the children to catch their hair on fire while they dance around the tree."

The flame on the taper flickered, then died. Slowly, the taper floated across the hall, past faces registering the gamut of emotions from awe and astonishment to startled incredulity, even fear, until the taper reached the mantel shelf, where it settled gently.

"Forgive me," said Elizabeth, smiling at the crowd. "I should have warned you that I brought the Stenton ghost. You may have heard of Annie Tuck? She is the reason so many families are willing to pay a fortune to lease a wing of the castle. But I did not expect her to show off where she is a visitor. I do hope she did not frighten you."

No one wanted to admit to fright, and after a few moments, when nothing else strange and spooky happened, conversation was resumed among the adult guests. After all, they were in the presence of their betters—one of them a duchess, no less—and they could hardly voice their opinions of ghosts and such things or of the persons who believed in them. Possibly, later, they might venture to ask Mr. Andrew Cavendish how he had arranged the spectacle and still kept a straight or, rather, an astonished face at the sight of it.

The children were less easily calmed, especially the older ones, who pelted Her Grace with questions, wanting to know if Annie clanked chains and if she had scared anyone witless at the castle or driven anyone to throw himself or herself off the towers.

Andrew grinned. "Quit nagging Her Grace, you little ghouls. One more question, and you won't need a ghost with chains to toss you off a tower."

The children snickered at such a threat from Mr. Andrew, who gave rides on horseback or piggyback, carved whistles from hazel switches, and always carried a pocketful of pennies when the wandering fair set up at the crossroads. But the inquisition stopped.

"Let's go on with the caroling," said Susan. "Mr. Andrew cannot wait to join in."

"If I must," muttered Andrew, for her ear alone. "Though I had much rather quiz Elizabeth on that trick of lighting the candles. I understand she does it at Stenton, too. You've seen it, haven't you?"

"Sing!" commanded Susan, who had no intention of explaining Annie Tuck.

"On your head be it."

The next song was the old favorite, "Here We Come A'Caroling." Andrew's voice was sometimes bass, sometimes baritone, or somewhere between the two, but always it was loud. One by one, the children fell silent; even Elizabeth stopped singing and stared in speechless wonder until Susan signaled Tredwell to take her place and all but dragged Andrew from the circle.

"I warned you," he said.

"You did that on purpose! You did not sing quite so badly in past years."

"Lack of practice made it worse, I expect."

Taking the lead, he drew her away from the crowd and the

blaze of light from the chandeliers, into the shadows cast by the open stairway.

Abruptly, he said, "I wish to report that I have closely examined the grate and the rocks that barricade the garden entrance to the secret passages."

"Oh." She kept her eyes on the children. "Is that why you left so precipitately?"

"I left because I recognized that you were having second thoughts about kissing me."

"You were kissing *me."*

"I feared you might box my ears. So I went off to earn my reward."

She felt breathless, and it was not because she had danced around the Christmas tree.

"Andrew, you're still holding my hand."

"Yes. I'm rather afraid in the dark."

"You are never afraid, and it is not precisely dark here. Just a bit dim."

"I am afraid in dim light as well."

She was silent, her heart beating much too fast. She could either withdraw, as the habit of several years dictated, or she could break the old pattern forced by circumstances—an undertaking she might unwittingly have already begun when she allowed him to kiss her again.

"Perhaps," she said, still not looking at him, "I am a little afraid, too."

Hands twined, they stood and listened to the decorous murmur of adult conversation and the squeals and noisy chatter of the children lining up in front of the dowager to receive their gifts.

"Holding hands," Susan said softly, "makes me feel young again."

"Indeed," he said gravely. "Such an old crone as you are."

This, finally, made her turn her head.

"For shame, Andrew! You're laughing at me!"

"And what is it that I see dancing in your eyes, even in this dim light? Certainly not tears!"

Susan was vividly aware of his hand, the strength and warmth that flowed from him to her. It was a good feeling, one that encouraged her to persevere in her efforts to dismantle the barriers of reserve she had erected between herself and Andrew.

"I am one-and-thirty," she said lightly. "Do you think that is young, then?"

"In years, it is just right. Not too young and not too old. Measured by feminine arts and graces, however, you're younger than little Miss Nell."

"What do you mean? The child is *four!*"

"And already understands the importance of graciously accepting a man's hand and heart."

The words might give her pause and remind her of the as yet unresolved question of their marriage, but the quizzing tone of voice reassured her. For the present, at least, she need not take him seriously.

"You're abominable, Andrew! Will you have me take lessons from an infant?"

"Hardly an infant. Miss Nell was born a minx."

"And I was not? How can you be certain?"

"I'm sure of it. And having observed you and Miss Nell together, I perceived instantly that I would have to adjust my courtship of you."

"Your courtship! Is that what you're doing? You are courting me?"

"But of course. How else could I make you change your mind about marriage?"

"Oh, my heavens—" It was Annie's voice, awed and scarcely above a whisper, but it startled Susan.

"What is it, Susan?" asked Andrew. "Surely there is no need to jump when marriage is mentioned."

Annie said, "Isn't he the most toothsome gentleman imaginable?"

Susan did not know what to say or where to look . . . at Andrew, who was watching her with a puzzled frown, or in the direction of Annie's voice behind her.

"If he was courtin' me. . . . ," breathed Annie.

"Susan?" Andrew's voice held concern but also a note of impatience. "What the deuce have I said to put you in a trance?"

"I beg your pardon. I thought I heard—"

"Heard what? Those nocturnal sounds that have been plaguing you?"

"It was nothing. I was mistaken."

"Of course were mistaken, else I would have heard it, too. And since the garden entrance to the passages showed signs of tampering, I made certain alterations at the hidden door to my chamber. I expect I'll know before the night is over who is playing tricks on us."

Annie said, "I wish your Andrew was a ghost like me."

"No!" Susan said sharply.

"What do you mean?" demanded Andrew. "Don't you want me to discover the culprit?"

"Yes . . . yes, of course." Susan's head spun. She wanted to fix her thoughts on what he had—oh, so casually—dropped about the garden entrance to the passages, but Annie's strange wish still echoed in her mind. Wishing that Andrew were a ghost!

"Good," said Andrew. "Then I'll solve that little puzzle. And there's also something I must explain. About the night Frederick died."

Annie said, "Step back, Miss Susan. Perhaps eight steps or ten, and you'll have him beneath the kissing bough."

Susan closed her eyes. *Go away, Annie! You're distracting me.* Someone gripped her arm. Her eyes flew open.

"Come with me," Andrew said curtly. He, who had shown her only kindliness and concern in the four years she had known him, looked quite thoroughly exasperated.

"For goodness' sake, Andrew! We cannot leave. The guests . . . Augusta."

"The children are about to go below stairs. We shan't be missed during supper, but, if we must, we'll make our excuses to Augusta and Elizabeth. Anything to get you away from whatever it is that's distracting you here!"

"Very well, though I don't see what could be so urgent that we must leave the festivities."

"Did you not listen? The night Frederick died— I must tell you why I was at Stenton."

Five

"That Christmas Eve two years ago, I followed Frederick." Having lit the lamp on his desk, Andrew shut the study door. "He had infuriated me. I intended to drag him back by the scruff of his neck."

"I don't understand. Drag him back . . . did you know he planned to go to France with Mary Beamish?"

"Yes. He left a note."

Susan crossed her arms. It was cold in the room. The fire had been allowed to burn out since no one expected the study to be occupied on the evening of the tenants' dance.

Andrew faced her. "A note, meant for you."

"For *me?* Then you must be quizzing me. Frederick never accorded me the courtesy of a message, but always left without warning or farewell."

"This note was not a courtesy."

"Then, surely, if there was such a note, you would have given it to me?"

"I burned it." He said no more, but started to pace, a practice quite uncharacteristic of him.

Susan was still flustered from the encounter with Annie and the unfamiliarity of seeing Andrew lose patience. Now, his restless prowl following on the heels of a curt response made her feel distinctly uneasy.

"For goodness' sake! This is not the time to be a man of few words. It wasn't I who insisted on leaving the festivities so that you might explain something. *You* carried me off will ye nill ye."

"Peace!" He stopped, holding up a hand. "I was merely gathering courage."

"I see. Without a doubt, then, Frederick's message was an insult." She shrugged. "You need not let it bother you. His insults lost their power years ago. I'm only sorry you had to see the detestable thing."

"It was propped on the mantel shelf in the hall, and it was neither folded nor sealed, nor did it have a salutation. I believed it for me, but about halfway it said something like 'so, you see, my sweet and dearly beloved wife. . . .' "

Susan compressed her lips. It was the salutation Frederick had used in his most vile moods. That Christmas Eve, shortly before ten, when Augusta opened the family Bible for the Christmas reading, he had demanded, icily polite, that he be spared the message of a joyous birth when it was obvious that he would never share in the experience. Without a word, Augusta rose and left the hall. Susan, ignoring Frederick's order to pour wine, followed her mother-in-law to the salon. She never saw Frederick again.

"No need to tell me I shouldn't have read on," said Andrew. "I know 'twas inexcusable."

"Well, I shan't hold it against you. What does bother me, however, is that you rode after Frederick to fetch him back!"

"I could not allow him to disappear. Susan, he did not plan to return—wanted to start a gaming hell somewhere on the Continent. But he had no intention of setting you free."

"What do you mean?" Her eyes widened. *"Divorce?"*

"The taunt of no divorce—that's why I thought the note was for me." Andrew resumed the pacing. "If he did not release you, how could I marry you?"

Her breath caught. Even then, before Frederick's death, Andrew had thought of marriage.

"I cannot believe what I am hearing! You *told* Frederick you wished to marry me?"

"No, of course not." He stopped by the window and looked at her. "However, I did once suggest divorce, and he resented what he called my championship of you. The next day—" His voice tightened. "You found your puppy dead."

She flinched. "Don't! Just stick to the point, if you please."

"The point. Yes. After I burned the note, I set out after him. To make him apologize to you. To initiate the procedures for divorce."

She sank into the nearest chair. "But . . . *divorce!* Andrew, even if I had not been ostracized . . . considered quite beyond the pale . . . a second marriage would have been impossible. Bigamous!"

"Not if you petitioned Parliament and were granted an absolute divorce."

"Indeed . . . ," she said dazedly. "How well informed you are. However, that is neither here nor there. If Frederick is dead, I shan't need a divorce."

"He is dead."

Andrew started toward her. "I stood atop the cliffs when Frederick with the smugglers in pursuit came scrambling up."

"Then you do know for certain that it was Frederick who died!"

She started to rise, but thought better of it. Perhaps it was the set look of Andrew's face, or whatever the reason, her legs felt as if they had turned to rubber. A thought crossed her mind . . . that it should have occurred to her that morning to ask what he was doing at Stenton the night Frederick was killed.

"I, too, carried a pistol, Susan."

Yes, she thought, that was why I did not rise. Why I did not even think to ask this morning. I feared. . . .

"Andrew." Her voice would scarcely obey her. "Did you shoot Frederick?"

"No."

She let out the breath she had inadvertently held. "Thank God!"

"Though I don't deny I had murder in my heart. If I had discovered him in East Dean and he proved obstinate—but I did not find him there, only a great number of harried females and crying children afraid for Beamish and the men he had persuaded to help him catch Frederick."

"I am glad. If Frederick had to die—thank heavens it wasn't by your hand!"

He did not speak, and she rose, doubting no more that her legs would carry her.

"Thank you for telling me. I know you did not find it easy, but now you need not give it another thought. As I said, even two years ago Frederick could no longer hurt me with his vile tongue—or pen. And he cannot now."

"Susan, it wasn't only the message I must explain."

"Quick, then. We must return to the hall. They'll expect us to open the dancing."

"I could have stopped Beamish."

And if he had . . . ! She felt the blood drain from her face and return with a rush of heat.

"The clouds parted, and for a brief moment we had full moonlight. I saw Beamish aim the blunderbuss."

"Don't, Andrew!" She stepped back. "Don't say any more. It cannot matter now. After two years!"

"I was wrong to keep it from you."

"I wish you had kept it from me forever. What am I to think now? Should I be sorry you did not save my husband? Or should I be glad?"

"Must it be one or the other?" Fleetingly, he touched her heated face. "Can you not simply accept it?"

She gave him a searching look. "Have *you?* But you may not have been close enough to make a difference. And the moon—I doubt the moon was visible for long?"

"Long enough, Susan."

In the flash of time it takes to draw breath, Andrew saw himself atop the cliffs suddenly bathed in moonlight. Two men on the steep path below. He saw the second man drop to his knees and raise the blunderbuss. Frederick's cape filling like a sail in the gusting wind and hiding his pursuer from view. The cape dropped, and Beamish—mayor, tavern keeper, smuggler, mainstay of a struggling village—had not yet fired. And in East Dean, Mrs. Beamish and three younger daughters had begged Andrew to lock up his dastardly cousin so they could get on with their lives.

He met Susan's troubled gaze. "In battle, a man learns to make a decision in less time than it takes to cock a gun. There was time to shoot. But I did not. And they did not hear my shout in the gusting wind and the noise of the firing blunderbuss."

"Then, if you had no trouble deciding, why on earth must I be tumbled into a welter of confusion now?"

"Are you saying you would rather that I had shot Beamish to save Frederick?"

"And what good would that have done? Dash it, Andrew! I don't know what I am saying. I don't want you to have shot anyone. But I do wish you had never started to explain."

"I want honesty between us. Truth."

"Lud! The truth is that I want to forget everything to do with Frederick. So let us say no more." Squaring her shoulders, she turned to the door. "We must return. I am determined that nothing shall mar the Boxing Day festivities."

He followed her. "This morning when you learned that I was at Stenton, I feared you sought me out to ask *why* I was there. You did not—perhaps, because we were interrupted. I was relieved. But after I kissed you, I knew I must not wait for you to ask."

She said quietly, "There is no need for further explanation—or justification on your part. It's not the decision you made atop the cliffs that has me horrified, but my response when you said you might have stopped Beamish."

"Susan—"

"I shan't discuss it. Frederick is dead, and I've put it from my mind."

It was agreed by everyone present that the tenants' Boxing Day dance was the merriest in more than a decade. And if the young Mrs. Cavendish danced just a trifle too exuberantly and laughed a little too gaily for the more prim-minded among the guests, deep in their hearts, none could blame her for her vivacity. Nothing had ever been said aloud, but they all knew, didn't they, that Miss Susan had had no easy life, married as she had been to Frederick Cavendish. And having to bear two years of mourning on top of it! Well, 'twas finished, and all the best to her.

When Tredwell rose to lead them in the final carol, "Welcome, Sir Christmas," the tenants joined in gratefully. They expected and enjoyed their Boxing Day dance, but all good things must come to an end. In truth, it was rather a strain having to mingle with the gentility, let alone the nobility—though it couldn't be said that Her Grace had put on airs any more than Miss Susan did. Her Grace was a right 'un, they had decided. Gave sensible advice on vegetable and flower gardens.

Now, if only she showed a mite of sense about ghosts, too. But Her Grace stuck to the story of the Stenton ghost, Annie Tuck, whom Her Grace could see—or so she said—and whose voice had been heard by a few others. She had convinced most of the womenfolk; but the men, less gullible by nature, knew the ghost was a trick to get wealthy merchants to lay down their blunt for the lease of a few rooms in a crumbling old fortress. A clever fabrication, mind you. But a bouncer nevertheless.

Having welcomed my lord, Sir Christmas, with a last joyful burst of "Noel, noel, noel, noel!" the tenants accepted their parting gifts with appreciation and gratitude, collected their offspring from the servants' hall, and hurried home to snatch a few hours' sleep before duty called them to stables and barns.

The dowager retired immediately. Elizabeth, attacked by a sudden craving for something kippered or pickled, went off with the housekeeper to explore the pantries. Andrew made certain the punch bowl had not quite run dry, and Susan stayed long enough to bid a maid fetch another platter of pasties to sustain the staff during the remaining hour of revelry.

Having kept an eye on Susan, Andrew saw her walk toward the stairs and set out after her.

"Susan." His long stride permitted him to catch up without looking like an overeager schoolboy. "You cannot retire without giving me the chance to tell you how extraordinarily beautiful you are tonight."

She looked startled, then smiled—a smile that lit her eyes and, indeed, her whole face.

"Thank you, Andrew. But don't you mean ravishing? Or does that apply only to minxes like little Nell?"

"It applies to a minx of any kind."

"Ah! If I were to prove myself a minx . . . ?"

"Then you will be the most ravishing of all."

"Indeed? Perhaps, then, I shall be daring tonight." Her smile turned mischievous. "If I tell you that you look extraordinarily handsome, will that do?"

"No. But it earns you a token of my appreciation."

He drew a short, slim, tissue-wrapped item from his coat pocket. "A merry Christmas, Susan."

The small package was so light, it might have been empty, except that she could feel whatever was inside. She closed her eyes, exploring the delicate something by touch.

"It makes me think of filigree work. No, of . . . leaves or blossoms made of thin metal. A sprig of some kind . . . lavender, perhaps? Or violets?"

"Why don't you open it," he said, amused by the look of fierce concentration on her face.

"This is so much more fun than mere looking."

"If your guesses don't improve, you'll still be at it tomorrow morning."

"I think you're trying to mislead me. I'm not far off the mark, I wager." Her fingertips explored once more, moving slowly all around the tissue paper. "Most certainly, this is a sprig. If not a flower, then . . . no, not pine or fir. I don't feel needles."

"Give up?"

She opened her eyes. "A sprig of mistletoe!"

"And I was sure I could surprise you!"

"Then I am correct! And yes, you did surprise me. It is a rather unusual gift. But perhaps not, considering that it is Boxing Day."

She unwrapped a finely hammered silver sprig with small mother-of-pearl berries. "How beautiful! Thank you, Andrew."

"You are to wear it in your hair."

"Oh, I am, am I?"

"So I may kiss you any time I wish."

The mischievous look was back. "Not just at present. I must first prove myself a minx."

"And how will you do that?"

She glanced at a point above his head, then toward the fire-place, where the staff were opening the gifts she had helped Augusta box and wrap and exchanging small gifts among themselves. No one paid any heed to the couple at the foot of the stairs.

"By asking you to step slightly to your left, which will place you precisely beneath the kissing bough."

He had never moved faster.

Laughing softly, she placed her hands on his shoulders, raised herself on tiptoe, and brushed her lips against his.

"Merry Christmas, Andrew!"

"Not so fast." He captured both her hands when she would have stepped back. "That was but a trifling kiss. You'll have me believe you a flirt as well as a minx."

"I doubt you can be one without the other. Or, if you can, is a flirt worse than a minx?"

He was about to say, "Not if she flirts only with me," but her suddenly wistful look gave him pause.

"Do you dislike it, Andrew? When a woman flirts?"

"No, indeed. How could I dislike it? I rather enjoy a bit of flirtation myself."

She smiled. "Yes, so I noticed—when you spoke with Miss Nell."

"And it wouldn't be fun if the lady did not respond."

"You were outrageous."

"You don't sound outraged."

She was silent for a moment as if uncertain what to say next.

"It was my being termed an incorrigible flirt that precipitated my marriage."

She had spoken in an off-handed manner, as if she were merely pointing out that Tredwell, whose rich baritone once more filled the hall, had obviously been persuaded to sing again. And Andrew, in the hope of encouraging further confidences, took care to respond in kind.

He raised a quizzing brow. "What a shame, then, that I wasn't around. I would have delighted in flirting with you. Were you in London? Being 'brought out'?"

"I used to call it 'trotted out' like one of many brood mares at an auction. I thought it hilarious and rather good sport and enjoyed myself tremendously. At least, to begin with. But because I laughed and had fun and did not take any of the young beaux and dandies seriously when they danced with me or asked me out for a drive, some of the society matrons disapproved."

"And called you an incorrigible flirt." He raised first one, then the other of her hands to his lips. "Pure spite, my love, and jealousy."

Momentarily distracted, she looked at her hands, as if she realized only now that they had been held captive all this time. Gently, she freed herself.

"You're generous to call it spite and jealousy. Society was not so charitable, and the sobriquet stuck. Mama cried, and Papa began to believe it true."

"And thus, to save your reputation and their good name, they married you off to the first man asking for your hand? How gothic!"

She gave a choke of laughter. "How outraged you sound. But, believe me, had it been your daughter, you would have done the same."

He let that pass. "Again I say, what a shame I wasn't around at the time. I would have beaten every suitor to the door of your father's house."

"Pishtosh! I was married well before my eighteenth birthday.

You were a mere cornet, caring for nothing, I don't doubt, but gaining a lieutenancy."

"I daresay. But Frederick was ten years older than you!"

"I liked that. As did my parents. They felt I needed guidance."

He was hard pressed not to show the anger welling in him. But he would match Susan's tone and mood if it gave him an apoplexy.

She said, "You mustn't think that I was forced into the marriage. I had no objections. After all, 'twas the reason I had gone to London. Only it did not work out the way I thought it would. I believed Frederick liked me as I was then . . . but he called me unseemly when I laughed or joked, and wicked when I flirted with Squire Appleby. But you know how much the squire enjoys it! He would never take liberties, only call you a saucy baggage and be as pleased as the cat who got into the cream. Perhaps, if I had tried a little harder to mend my ways. . . ."

"But you did." His voice was so soft, it could scarcely be heard. Restraining his voice was the only way to prevent fury from boiling over. Fury with his cousin, who, if he weren't dead, would be in dire straits now.

Susan gave him a questioning look. "Andrew? Are you unwell?"

"Exercising my brains. I am trying to recall my first furlough—it couldn't have been more than six months after your marriage—but I don't remember much about you at all. Such a quiet thing you were. You must have mended your ways most speedily."

"Well, yes. But it made no difference."

"Precisely. So stop blaming yourself for Frederick's misconduct!"

She made no reply, but seemed to withdraw into herself.

Her distraction did not last. "And would you believe it? I am now mending my ways once again. I am trying to find my old self, though at times it's nigh impossible to recall what my old self was."

"That is hardly astounding. I don't recall what I used to be at eighteen."

"Possibly," she said demurely, "it would be too embarrassing to recall?"

"Are you referring to me or to yourself?"

She laughed and turned toward the stairs, then stopped and faced him once more, all laughter wiped out.

"Perhaps I made you understand just a little why I am hesitant about marriage? I hardly know who I am or what I want, and I do not think that I am ready to place myself and my life in another's keeping once more."

Her life in another's keeping. . . . Andrew stood motionless and silent and watched her run up the stairs. It looked very much like flight. Not encouraging at all.

Or was it? She had at last shown candor regarding her marriage. She had not rebuffed him that afternoon when he kissed her, had even kissed him just now—if such the fleeting brush of lips could be called. If it was flirting, it pleased him well. For he knew with certainty that Susan was not the hardened, incorrigible flirt who teased and kissed, meaning nothing by it, save to lead some poor fellow a merry dance.

He had been a fool not to have claimed another kiss while they stood beneath the kissing bough. She needed to be shown that she was desirable, that a man's touch could be tender and caressing. She had told him that she had felt cherished when he held her in his arms three years ago, and for that she had loved him, if only for a short moment. He must make her feel cherished again, must awaken the love he had kindled once before.

Andrew looked up. He still stood in the right place for a kiss, and much good did it do.

He had scarcely finished the thought when he felt a breath of air against his face. A chaste kiss dropped on his cheek, another on his brow.

He shook his head to clear it. If he didn't know better, he'd think he was bosky. Imagining that Susan was kissing him, merely because he wished it were so! Only a man in love could be so daft. And his imagination hadn't even conjured the kind of kiss he wanted from her.

Soft lips brushed against his mouth, very much the way Susan's had done when she wanted to prove herself a minx.

Devil take it! If he wasn't drunk, he must be going crazy. Guardedly, Andrew looked around him, but no one was nearby who might have, through means unknown, played some dastardly trick on him. Behind him, the wide area cleared for dancing lay bare and empty. Some distance to his left stood the Christmas tree, but a casual stroll around it proved no one hiding there. The staff were still gathered by the Yule log, the footmen and two of the maids beginning to stack plates and cups on large trays.

Ah, well. He'd blame his fantasies on the Duchess of Stenton's ghost—which reminded him that Susan hadn't explained how her friend contrived the trick of lighting the candles. But that could wait. It was going on midnight. Time to lie in wait for a trickster of an altogether different ilk, one who haunted hidden passages and had spooked Susan into believing that Frederick was still alive.

Six

Susan was relieved to find her bedchamber empty. Elizabeth would not be long, but that was all right. A moment or two was all she required—though for what, she did not quite know herself. She was perfectly composed. It had not distressed her to speak to Andrew of the past. She did not resent that he assumed she was blaming herself for Frederick's failings. It was precisely what she had been doing. But no longer.

She did not even wish time to herself so that she might ponder the disclosures Andrew made in the study, the brief moment of horror when she realized that had he leveled his gun at Beamish, and pulled the trigger, Frederick would still be alive. Her gaze strayed to the bookshelves by the fireplace. Every time she had heard footsteps in the past, a voice calling her name behind the hidden door, she had lived through the nightmare of believing Frederick alive.

But no more. Frederick was dead. This, she finally believed wholeheartedly, and she was done beating her breast and tearing her hair over her lack of proper feelings.

She set Andrew's gift on the mantel shelf. A sprig of mistletoe. To be worn in her hair. Smiling, she picked it up again and unwrapped the delicate silver sprig. It truly was beautiful. On impulse, she pinned it into the cluster of curls Elizabeth had so carefully arranged earlier that evening.

And now a fire, in case Elizabeth wished to revive the old girlhood habit of staying up half the night. Careful of her gown, a blue velvet and lace confection Augusta had commissioned for her two years ago for the Boxing Day dance that had to be canceled, Susan knelt on the hearth rug. One of the staff had placed everything in readiness: kindling, wood, tinderbox. She had only to light a match, and a very short while later a satisfactory warmth spread from ash logs and pine.

Ash . . . the wood of the Yule log in the great hall, where Andrew had kissed her, then walked off without another word, leaving her in a welter of confusion about the feelings his embrace evoked. Feelings and emotions similar to those she had experienced three years ago. Yet this could not possibly be so. Andrew's kiss then, and her passionate response, had been triggered by the circumstances of the moment.

Andrew had found her crying. She was not generally a watering pot, but that had been the day she had received the news of her father's death. When she had sought solace from her favorite book of poetry, Frederick had taken offense at her idleness and ripped the pages. A trifling matter in itself, yet, added to an already heavy accumulation of past hurts and grief, the despoiling of beautiful verse had brought her to tears. And the only way she could deny Frederick the satisfaction of watching her pain had been to hide.

Frederick did not trouble to search for her; he knew she could not escape for long. But Andrew chanced upon her. He did not say a word, merely enfolded her in his arms and held her close. When her tears finally dried, his coat and shirt were soaked. Gathering her wits, she started to apologize—and he kissed her. It seemed the natural conclusion to his tender comfort.

And she kissed him back with a passion born of desperation and gratitude for his kindness. Her heart was filled with love for the man who gave warmth and tenderness, who made her feel alive and cherished and pulled her from the abyss of despair. She would have kissed jolly, corpulent Squire Appleby had he comforted her in that hour of need. Or so she believed.

But gratitude could not explain her feelings when Andrew kissed her earlier by the Yule log. She had not been in despair then.

"Or," said Annie Tuck, "when *you* kissed him under the mistletoe."

Susan hardly gave a start. Her eyes still on the fire in the grate, she asked, "Do you read minds, Annie?"

"Why do you think I left you alone when Mr. Andrew was a-courting you? Closed your eyes, didn't you? *Go away, Annie! You're distracting me.* Isn't it what you told me in your mind?"

"I offended you." Susan looked over her shoulder at the bed, unoccupied, the covers undisturbed. But it was where Annie's distinctly huffy voice had originated. "I apologize. Unfortunately, I found it very difficult to listen to two speakers at the same time, and Andrew had just mentioned the garden entrance to the hidden passages."

"Who cares about stuff like that when a gentleman like Mr. Andrew is offering marriage!"

"He wasn't."

"He said he's courting you. He said he wants you to change your mind about marriage. And you don't think he was making an offer! Pooh! You don't deserve him, Miss Susan!"

"Why are you so angry?"

There was no reply and no way of telling whether the little ghost was still in the room.

"Annie, you know I cannot see you. Do me the courtesy, at least, of letting me hear you."

Susan heard a sniff right beside her, where she still knelt on the rug.

"Are you trying to make me jump?"

"No," said Annie, her voice a bit gruff but not necessarily angry any longer. "I'm trying to keep an open mind."

"About what?"

"About helping reluctant lovers."

Susan shifted her weight from her knees to a more appropriate part of her anatomy.

"It's something I'm very good at," said Annie. "If I have a mind to do it."

"I don't doubt it."

"So why are you reluctant, Miss Susan? Usually, it's the gentleman that needs a bit of prodding."

"I consider myself cautious rather than reluctant."

"What's there to be cautious about? Did you ever see such a fine-looking gentleman as Mr. Andrew? Those shoulders! Such an elegant leg! And not, as with some town dandies, thanks to buckram padding!"

"Looks are not everything, Annie."

"As if I didn't know! There's two paintings that caught my attention in the gallery. The man has the looks of Mr. Andrew— you might say he's the more handsome of the two. But there's something about him . . . I can't explain, but I just know the painter didn't paint him right. Or the painter couldn't see what he's truly like."

"Not many could."

"Aye, you would know, being a member of the family. He is a cad, isn't he? A knave. A bounder."

"Frederick Cavendish, my late husband. Andrew's cousin."

"Oh."

In the ensuing silence, the hiss and crackle of the fire sounded unnaturally loud. Susan was about to reach for another piece of wood to place atop the dwindling stack in the grate, when a length of split pine rose out of the wood box and floated into the fireplace. Then another.

"Thank you, Annie."

"That man in the paintings—" The little ghost sounded out of breath. "If he's the one whose ghost I'm supposed to find, I'm mighty glad to say I've seen neither hair nor hide of him. Nor do I want to. But Mr. Andrew! Why, I could swoon just catching sight of him."

Susan smiled. "I think you're more than half in love with Andrew."

"And if I am, what's it to you?"

"Nothing . . . I suppose."

"You suppose. Aren't *you* more than half in love with him? You were holding hands all the while I saw you!"

"You don't have to be in love to hold hands."

"No, but that doesn't answer my question."

Susan rose. "I am too old to sit on the floor so long. And much too old to be questioned about love."

"You don't know if you're in love! That's what it is! But you were a married lady. It's not as if you was like me, who has never had a beau!"

"I haven't had a beau either. And I certainly did not learn about love while I was married to Frederick."

If Annie made a reply, it was drowned in a sudden clatter of noise behind the shelving next to the fireplace.

For an instant, Susan stood stockstill. A surge of anger that left no room for fear welled in her. She flung herself at the shelves and tugged and twisted the boss that would open the secret door. Nothing happened. The door did not budge, which was as it should be since Andrew had disabled the mechanism. But he had said something about changing that, or had he?

The rapping and stomping in the passage continued.

"A pox on you!" she shouted.

The reply was a burst of laughter, a voice, strangely flat and muffled, calling, "Susan! Susan!"

"It's not Frederick's ghost," Annie whispered in Susan's ear. "I just took a peek."

"I did not think it was."

Neither could it be Frederick in person. Furious, Susan twisted and pulled the boss again. It snapped off in her hand.

"The devil take you!" Only Andrew's vocabulary served in the heat of her anger, but it did not get her into the passage to confront her tormentor. In frustration, she flung the bit of carved wood into the fire.

The garden entrance! Tampered with! That's what Andrew had said.

Clutching the full skirt of her gown, Susan rushed from the room, past Elizabeth, who was about to enter but stopped, wide-eyed, and demanded an explanation.

"Annie will tell!" Susan called over her shoulder as she pelted down the hallway toward the stairs.

And very proper behavior it was for a lady of matronly status! Also, she ought to take a light. But time was precious. Any moment, the culprit might tire of noisemaking and flee.

Susan did not bother with the heavy doors in the great hall. They would be locked and bolted and take too long to open. Besides, the kitchen door was closer to her goal.

Running down the basement stairs, she was greeted by the rattle of dishes and silverware and a few tired voices rendering a languid version of "Nowell Sing We." Sleepy faces turned to her as she raced through the pantry and the kitchen and out the back door. Too late did it register that the stable lad who jumped back from the door at her pell-mell approach had clutched a lantern in his hand.

At least she would reap the benefits of a quarter moon. On she raced, through the snow in the rose garden. Slippers and skirts were icy wet in no time at all, but she did not care. If her feet and legs turned to icicles, she would catch the trickster who had plagued her since June.

She burst into the maze, constructed of prickly laurel and other evergreen shrubs and short stretches of high rock wall. There, in a blind path, lay the entrance to the secret passages. The disguising rocks had been moved, and the grate Andrew had secured when the boot boy got lost in the passages was resting against a laurel bush. The opening, dark and sinister, yawned at her feet. A quarter moon did not beam sufficient light to penetrate to the rungs of an iron ladder below ground, but served to reveal the trampled snow in the path. Proof of a very human intruder.

Her heart pounded. Her breath came in short, ragged gasps. But she did not hesitate to lower herself into the gaping darkness. She had descended a mere five or six steps when she heard feet thudding in the passage below. Someone in a hurry. And he would collide with her on the ladder unless she retreated.

She thought she saw a glimmer of light below and scrambled upward, more difficult even than descending in heavy, sodden skirts. At the top, she tripped, sprawled into the snow. Lud! If Augusta were to see her now!

The footsteps were close, heavy shoes or boots on the iron rungs of the ladder . . . more than one person. A thread of fear appeared above the anger fueling her energy. She rolled aside, hiding as best she could behind the rocks that should have covered the grate.

What now? She had made no plan, developed no strategy when she rushed off to confront the intruder. Now there were more than one.

Out of the opening they burst; two dark figures, one after the other. If they had carried a light below ground, they did not have it now. Susan caught no more than a glimpse of flapping cloaks as the two plunged through a length of hedge and disappeared. And she crouched in the snow, shivering in the cold, and felt extremely foolish.

Picking herself up, she shook the tumbling mass of hair and slipping pins from her face and brushed her hands over the snow clinging to her gown. Velvet and lace. 'Twas sure to be ruined. For nothing. Or was it?

A pox on them! That was a third set of steps clattering up the iron ladder. She clenched her hands in a fresh burst of anger and

vigor. So she was a fool, a feather-brained widgeon lost to all
sense of decorum. But she would, at least, make sure of the identity of one scoundrel.

As the third figure pushed out of the ground, Susan lunged at
him, wrapping her arms around his neck in a choke hold while
he had one knee on the ground and one foot still on the ladder.
A muffled exclamation was the only sign that she had taken him
by surprise. His arms flailed in a struggle for balance as together
they hovered on the brink of crashing into the pit.

He gave a mighty heave, propelling them away from the
treacherous opening. Again, Susan lay sprawled in the snow, this
time on her back. The scoundrel's powerful shoulders pressed
into her chest and stomach, making breathing nigh impossible.
But she still had his neck imprisoned, and if breathing was difficult for her, it was worse for him, for his head rested at an
awkward angle beside her own, his face buried in her hair.

He lay absolutely still, and if she hadn't felt his breathing, she
might have feared that she had strangled him. But, indeed, he
was very much alive and all but crushing her with his weight.
He did not wear a cloak like the other two. When she had lunged
at him, there had been no time to consider his state of dress or
undress. But now, her rather restricted view of his back and shoulders confirmed the pristine whiteness of a shirt gleaming in the
moonlight. And there was some elusive scent . . . shaving soap,
perhaps.

She turned hot all over. Lud! She had truly cooked her goose
now! But, perhaps, she was wrong. Her arms tightened around
his neck as she tried to get another whiff of the aromatic, faintly
spicy fragrance. Sandalwood.

"Andrew!"

He muttered into her hair.

"Get up, Andrew!" Embarrassment sharpened her voice.
"You're crushing me."

He stirred, gripping her wrists and awkwardly forcing her arms
apart to free his head.

"Devil a bit!" He sounded amazingly cheerful. "How could

I move with you bent on strangling me? Or was it suffocation you had in mind? Though, in truth, there are worse fates. Your hair, my love, is pure silken enchantment. And your embrace is sheer delight."

Again warmth spread through her, despite the icy chill of the snow. With difficulty, she collected her wits. "What are you doing here? I thought I was catching one of the tricksters."

"But for your heroic if somewhat misguided efforts, *I* would have caught them." He rose, drawing her with him.

"Listen." He lowered his voice. "Someone's here, in the maze."

She whispered, "Do you think they're returning?"

"Helloo!" A woman's voice. "Susan!"

"It's Elizabeth." Ruefully, she added, "Come to scold me, I wager."

"As should I."

A beam of light darted into the blind path where they stood.

"There you are!" said Elizabeth, turning the corner with the stable lad and his lantern. She was bundled in a long cape and wearing a pair of sturdy boots, such as the maids pulled on when they were sent outdoors in inclement weather.

Elizabeth's face was a mixture of concern and curiosity as she hurried toward them. "Are you all right, Susan? Did you get them? I did not want to believe it when Annie said you were planning to go into the garden. But she insisted that you'd been thinking of the garden entrance to the hidden passages. And when I asked in the kitchen, this boy offered to light the way. And Andrew here, too! Where did you spring from?"

Not waiting for a reply, she addressed Susan again. "Didn't I say you haven't changed? If I weren't so pleased, I would scold you. Sensible as can be one moment, an impulsive little madcap the next. They might have hurt you! Where are they? Isn't anybody going to tell me what happened?"

"Inside," said Andrew. "We cannot stand about exchanging information while Susan turns into a glacier."

"Or you!" Elizabeth chuckled. "What a pair you are! One as bad as the other. You may share my cape, Susan. Only hurry!"

Susan looked at Andrew. "What about the opening?"

"I'll put the grate back for now. Go and change. Will you meet me in the hall in half an hour?"

She wished she could see his face more clearly. A meeting at this late hour? But she was growing numb with cold and disinclined to linger and ask questions.

"Very well. In half an hour."

"You are blue with cold!" Kneeling, Elizabeth took the towel from Susan's stiff fingers and rubbed her friend's feet. "So, are you going to marry Andrew?"

On a stool as close to the fire as possible without singeing her back, Susan dropped the brush she was about to apply to her hair. "I thought you wanted to hear about the men we tried to catch."

"Well, you did not catch them. What else is there to know?" Elizabeth rubbed with increasing vigor. "I want to hear about you and Andrew. Holding hands in the shadows beneath the stairs. So romantic! Then leaving together."

"There was nothing romantic about the talk we had in the study."

"You didn't quarrel, did you?"

"We did not. Ouch!" Susan pulled her feet out of Elizabeth's reach. "My toes may be frozen, but that doesn't mean you should scrub off the skin."

"Ingrate. Turn around. I'll brush your hair while you tell about the hand holding."

"I did not realize it was so obvious or that anyone paid attention."

"Perhaps no one did. That is, no one besides Mrs. Cavendish and me. But I wouldn't count on it. I learned from the staff that you and Andrew kissed."

"I made sure no one was watching!"

"They saw you." Elizabeth smiled. "The only reason they did not felicitate you there and then was the kissing bough above your heads."

Silence reigned as Elizabeth concentrated on several particularly recalcitrant wet tangles in Susan's hair.

With her toes, Susan nudged the sodden lumps that used to be a pair of satin slippers. Silly to think they could be saved. The gown, perhaps, was not quite beyond salvation. The blue velvet, draped across a screen, looked black where the snow had soaked it, but with slow, careful drying and a good brushing. . . .

And no matter how long silence was maintained, eventually Elizabeth would repeat her question about Andrew and marriage. Susan knew it as surely as she knew that the mummers would visit Cavendish Hall on New Year's Eve.

She said, "I suppose I must come to a decision."

Elizabeth had no difficulty following her friend's trend of thought. "You do not sound enthused. Yet you appeared to enjoy his courtship."

"He makes me feel alive again . . . young even, and pretty. It is strange, is it not? I think I could not bear to have him stop courting me—perhaps return to the old distant, formal manner. And yet I fear the inevitable conclusion of courtship. I don't know that I can promise myself in marriage again."

"For better, for worse," murmured Elizabeth. "Till death us do part. It is so final, isn't it? Irrevocable."

"Marriage is captivity. A life sentence without reprieve or escape. For, no matter where you turned, you would have to be restored to the man who holds your life in his keeping."

Not a sound from Elizabeth, not even a movement of the hairbrush.

Susan gave a choke of wry laughter. "Listen to me. The tragedy queen! And even though I did not mean it, I am insulting Andrew with such talk."

"I am glad to hear that you're aware of it. Marriage to Andrew would not in the least resemble your old marriage."

"I know that."

Another silence reigned.

Pensively, Elizabeth said, "If you refuse him, or even if, somehow, you contrive to prevent his making an offer, it would be
awkward living under the same roof."

"It would be impossible. Living on his charity!"

"The estate is his?"

"It will be. And I could not face Augusta. You see, Andrew is
a son to her."

"You cannot marry to please Augusta!" Elizabeth tilted
Susan's head so that she could scowl at her. "Marry to please
yourself or don't marry at all."

"I have a little money. I wonder if I could live somewhere,
very modestly, in a small cottage, perhaps. I could earn a living
with needlework. You saw the tapestries and rugs I stitched for
the great hall. And the chair covers."

"Would that be preferable to marriage with Andrew?"

"It is an option I did not know I had until yesterday. I believed
that Frederick lost the money at the gaming tables. Perhaps, he
did. And Andrew made good the loss, as he made good all of
Frederick's debts."

Elizabeth tied Susan's hair at the nape of her neck. "You had
better put on stockings and shoes if you still plan to meet Andrew
in the hall."

"You think me foolish, don't you? For not jumping at an offer
of marriage."

"It does not matter what I think. The decision is yours alone.
If you cannot like Andrew—"

"Of course I like him!" Susan rose. "I hold him in esteem and
deep affection!"

"But you do not love him."

"*Love?*" said Susan, as though it were a foreign word. "Mama
assured me I would learn to love Frederick once we were married."

She sat on the bed to pull on stockings. "You and Clive are in
love. What does it feel like?"

"Lud, Susan! There are so many facets to the feelings and

emotions encompassed in the single word love that it might take an hour or more to list and describe them all."

"Just name a few." Susan tied her slippers. "Is it a special feeling when he touches you? Or holds you? Or kisses you?"

"Oh, yes! But that is only one narrow aspect of love, a small part of the physical side. There should also be a spiritual closeness. Not necessarily that you think and feel alike, but that there is understanding, a sharing of thought, of dreams. . . ."

The clock on the mantel chimed once.

"Susan, you'll know that you love someone when you face the possibility of a life without him, and the mere thought of it fills your heart with bleakness and desolation. And now you ought to go."

Susan embraced Elizabeth. Then, arranging a shawl around her shoulders, she left quickly. A moment later, she poked her head back in the door.

"Where's Annie? Did she not accompany you into the garden?"

Elizabeth turned from the dressing table, where she was removing the pins from her hair. "Annie does not feel comfortable out in the open. She said she would explore the passages once more. Why? Do you miss her?"

"I want to scold her for not warning me that I would meet *two* men escaping through the garden entrance."

Annie had, indeed, been in the passages. That was after she had told Miss Elizabeth all she knew, and Miss Elizabeth had left to ask the butler about the garden entrance. Annie had then joined the two noisemakers in the passage behind Miss Susan's chamber. She wanted to frighten them, but away from Stenton Castle, her powers were greatly diminished. Lighting the Christmas tree candles had been difficult; adding wood to the fire had all but exhausted her. Now, no matter how hard she yelled and screeched, she could not make the scoundrels hear her.

Finally, she managed to wrest the lantern from the slighter of the two, who let out a scream that was neither scoundrelly nor manly and ran off. The other cursed but stood his ground and after a few more colorful oaths snatched the lantern back. Then Mr. Andrew came around a bend in the passage. He saw the cloaked and muffled intruder and stormed forward, which made the scoundrel take to his heels at twice the speed of his departed friend.

Naturally, Mr. Andrew followed in pursuit, with Annie trailing behind, though not so far behind that she could not give him a shove when he and Miss Susan were in danger of toppling down the opening. Shaking from the exertion, Annie sat on a rung of the iron ladder. She heard Miss Elizabeth arrive and leave with Miss Susan. She heard Mr. Andrew drag the grate back over the opening and depart.

And, of course, she heard that he and Miss Susan planned to meet in the great hall.

Seven

Andrew was waiting.

Quite calm until she saw his dark silhouette at the foot of the stairs, Susan descended slowly. Surely, the sudden racing of her pulse was a good omen. Surely, if it were apprehension about an imminent proposal, she would feel quite numb. And if it were embarrassment over the garden incident, she would be more reluctant to meet him.

The great hall was dim. The candles in the chandeliers were snuffed, and only the candelabra on the mantel shelf cast pools of light near the fireplace.

Andrew extended a hand to assist her down the last few steps. "I half expected you to change your mind. I am glad you did not."

"I may be undecided at times, but I am not fickle."

"Then let us embark on an adventure. A clandestine, romantic adventure."

"An adventure? Then, I daresay, you invited me so that you need not be afraid in the dark?"

"No, my love. That was before you wrestled me to the ground." He placed her hand in the crook of his arm. "And before I heard Elizabeth say that you hadn't changed, still were an impulsive little madcap."

"Only occasionally." But she did not want to speak about that. "Andrew—no doubt you'll think me petty, but it is not at all proper that you address me as 'my love,' which you've done repeatedly this evening."

"Quite improper. However, you will have noticed that I do so only when no one but you can hear. Now, what was I saying?" He started toward the fireplace, where a fresh log had been placed atop the old Yule log. "Ah, yes. Elizabeth's reference to you as a madcap. It made me realize that I was still going about my courtship in quite the wrong way."

"If you're trying to say I should not have run outside, you needn't. I am well aware it was a foolish thing to do."

"And yet you ventured into the night to chase who knows what kind of villains. Do you mind explaining why?"

She wished it were not quite so dim. The tone of his voice, light, almost bland, did not tell her what he felt.

"I heard them, Andrew! In the passage behind my chamber. They made such a racket, and then they laughed. I was never so angry! And you had mentioned the garden entrance. So I went out to confront them—or him, because, at the time I had no notion that there were more than one."

"And you could not depend on me to catch them for you?" he asked quietly.

They had reached the light shed by the candles on the mantel, and Susan keenly searched his face.

"I thought you meant to scold me for undignified and foolish behavior. But you are offended that I did not go to you for help."

"Not offended. Disappointed, yes. And I might have been discouraged had I not learned early in my career that falling prey to discouragement is the fastest, surest way to defeat. Thus, I promptly reassessed and regrouped."

"Lud! I don't know whether to laugh or cry. Is courtship a military exercise? Am I the enemy to be conquered?"

He cocked a brow. "I am most grateful, I assure you, that you don't charge again in a full-blown attack."

"I would not dare. It was a different matter in the garden. The man who climbed out of the opening was unprepared and defenseless. If you remember, you had one foot still on the ladder."

"Do I remember! I feared we'd both fall and break our necks."

"A small miscalculation on my part. But you recovered nicely."

"My guardian angel at work. Or yours."

Susan thought she heard a sniff nearby, but could not be certain. In any case, she refused to be distracted.

She sat down on a wooden settle. "Earlier, I tried to make you understand that the quiet woman you know is not the true me. If my impulsiveness offends you—"

"Not at all. Did I not assure you that your embrace was sheer delight? I wish you would follow that impulse more often."

"If it had been an embrace, yours would be a most improper suggestion."

"But suitable in a clandestine, romantic meeting." He leaned against the mantelpiece. "Before we go off on such a delightful tangent, however, promise me something."

"And what would that be?"

"My love, you disappoint me. A madcap's reply to the demand for a promise should always be 'anything.' "

"I apologize. But, you see, Elizabeth cautioned me about the habit just this morning."

"She could not have meant a promise to me!" In the candlelight, his teeth gleamed brightly as he gave her a quick grin. "Swear to me you will remember from now on that I am utterly trustworthy and dependable. When I say I will catch the trickster, or tricksters, as the case turned out to be, then I shall do so."

"Did you say that?"

"I did. When you were holding my hand beneath the stairs. I also hinted that I had unbolted the secret entrance to my chamber. But I recall you were distracted at the time."

"Not at all."

Another sniff, such as Susan had heard from Annie, sounded nearby.

Susan ignored it. "Did you expect them to enter your room?"

"Alas. Fortunately, I did not waste all night waiting, for it did not take me long to realize my mistake. It was the east wing they'd enter. If they were regular visitors to the west wing, I would have heard them before."

"We heard them in the study."

"True. But that was the only time they were in my part of the house."

"I would not know. It certainly was the only time I heard the noise during the day. Usually they came midnight or later."

"Will you swear, then, to let me catch the scoundrels?"

She smiled. "You are persistent. Very well, I swear it."

"Vow that from this day on you will rely on me to fight your battles for you."

"That is . . . rather comprehensive, wouldn't you say?"

"Vow. Or do you wish to see me turn gray before my time with worry over what you may be doing next?"

"Now *that* would be wicked of me. Very well, I vow I shall rely on you when necessary."

"No qualifying, please."

Pushing away from the mantel, he started toward her, but stopped, still some distance from her, on the tapestry rug Susan had stitched years ago.

He said, "And promise to spend every moment of every day with me until I have convinced you that I am the right husband for you."

"Don't!" Annie's voice. "For I doubt *you* are the right wife for him."

Susan's head jerked a little, but she did not turn toward the voice, nor did she speak in rebuttal.

"Surely that is not too much to ask," said Andrew.

"It is asking for all I can give." Susan took a deep breath. "I promise you opportunity to convince me."

"Good." With the candlelight at his back, his face was shadowed, but there was no misreading the deep huskiness of his voice. "And now I should kiss you. But you're not wearing the mistletoe."

"But I—" Her hands flew to her hair, brushed smooth and neatly tied with a ribbon by Elizabeth. "I lost it! I was wearing it when I ran into the garden."

"I'll find it at first daylight. Kiss me, Susan."

She looked up at him. It did not matter that his face was still shadowed. She knew every feature, the square, determined chin, strong nose, mobile dark brows, the fan of laugh lines at the corners of his eyes, the mouth that could smile so broadly and kiss so tenderly.

Yes, she wanted to kiss him. Wanted to feel her pulse race and her blood turn warm. Wanted to feel her body grow pliant and mold to his.

She had never felt this longing with Frederick, and that was as it should be. Nothing in the relationship with Frederick had been good. What she felt for Andrew—a deep affection, respect, trust, even the blatant physical attraction—all of these feelings were good and right. Promising ingredients for a marriage. Fertile ground for a rich and fulfilling life. Certainly more fulfilling than stitching tapestries in a cottage.

Cavendish Manor had been her home for eleven years. During Frederick's absences she had known contentment, even a measure of happiness. Augusta had trained her in the management of the household and, over the years, relinquished a large part of her duties as mistress of the manor. Susan took pleasure and pride in her work, the efficiency of kitchens and stillrooms, the new design of the rose garden, the small school for tenant children.

She could not begin to imagine leaving. It was much easier to imagine staying on. Perhaps this was what Elizabeth meant when she spoke of love.

Andrew had not asked for a commitment. Only for a kiss. But Susan knew, if she kissed him now, she would feel bound to accept the offer he would certainly make almost immediately. She would gain so much. She'd have Andrew's devotion . . . Augusta's continued friendship. Perhaps there would be a child.

Slowly, she rose.

Andrew's arms were waiting, and she ran forward to be engulfed by his warmth. She raised her face, and the look in his eyes was confirmation of the words he spoke.

"I love you, Susan. Have loved you since my return. I have carried the thought of marriage in my heart from the moment I read Frederick's note and knew he planned—"

"Don't speak, Andrew. Kiss me."

The violent flicker of light and a resounding crash made them both start and spin to face the fireplace. A candelabrum, a five-branch solid brass piece, had toppled off the mantel and smashed onto the hearth stone. One candle, still alight, had come loose from its socket and rolled near them on the tapestry rug. In the brief moment it took them to turn and grasp the situation, the flame, fueled by the wax-soaked cotton, had burned a hole the size of a small cabbage.

Andrew thrust Susan toward the settle. "Keep back! Watch your skirts!"

Deftly, he folded the rug, then stomped on it with his glossy Hessian boots until he could be certain the flame was extinguished. Even then he was not satisfied. Folding the rug still smaller, he picked it up.

"The snow will do the rest." He saw Susan standing motionless by the settle. "You're not frightened, are you? There's no danger now."

"I'm fine."

"I shan't be a moment."

She watched him stride to the front door. In the quiet of the night, she heard the scrape of the heavy bolt, the grating of the large brass key, the slight creak of the hinge that no matter how frequently it was oiled would always betray the movement of the door. She felt the cold draft through the crack Andrew left open, heard his boots clatter down the steps. But above all, she heard Annie's wailing.

"I'm sorry, Miss Susan. I truly am! I never meant to set the rug afire. I only wanted a crash. You were going to kiss him. And then you were going to accept his offer! But you don't love him, Miss Susan! It isn't right what you're doing. He deserves better!"

Susan stood still and silent. *He deserves better.* She felt as if she had tumbled into the icy waters of the Channel. She felt so numb, she could not even be angry with Annie.

And she had no reason, for goodness' sake, to be angry. It wasn't the little ghost's fault that she could read minds.

She felt a fleeting touch on her arm, heard a sob, a watery sniffle.

When she looked, she saw the sprig of mistletoe Andrew had given her and two hair pins straddling the silver stem suspended in the air at shoulder height. She brushed a fingertip against the finely hammered metal, but when she grasped it and tried to pull it toward her, she encountered resistance.

"*I* am wearing it." Tears and defiance made Annie's voice tremble. "I found it at the foot of the iron ladder."

" 'All good to me is lost,' I suppose?"

"What does *that* mean? You only lost the mistletoe."

Susan turned away. "Only? Yes, and I am being melodramatic. A tragedy queen once more."

"Are you still going to marry him?" asked Annie. "Knowing you'll break his heart when he discovers that you don't return his love? That you married him because it was convenient?"

"What I will or won't do is none of your business." Susan walked toward the front door where Andrew should reappear at any moment.

"What are you going to do?"

"I shall suggest to Andrew that we continue our conversation in the garden or some other outdoor place where we are unlikely to encounter an eavesdropping ghost."

"You can't go outside! You aren't dressed for it!"

"I am not now, but I will be tomorrow." Susan drew her shawl tight as a gust of cold night air pushed the door farther open. "And the mistletoe was a gift to me. I expect it returned by morning."

Only Augusta was at the breakfast table.

Susan kissed her cheek. "I hope you rested well."

"Too well, it seems. I understand from Tredwell that I missed some great excitement in the maze. He was, however, unable to enlighten me as to the precise nature of it. He also reported a burn in one of the rugs in the hall."

"I will explain. Only, if you don't mind, not right at present. There is . . . a rather important matter I must resolve first."

"That is just what Andrew said."

"Did he?" Susan took her seat on Augusta's left. "Do you know where he is?"

"Looking for mistletoe, if you will believe it. As though we didn't have enough of it in the hall!"

"Not the kind Andrew is searching for. But that, too, must be explained later." Accepting the tea Augusta had poured, Susan gave her mother-in-law a quizzing look. "For now, I shall say only that Annie has it and won't give it back."

"Annie!" Augusta gave a sniff almost as disdainful as that of the little ghost she refused to acknowledge. "But I shall let that pass. Is Elizabeth not joining us?"

"Not for breakfast. However, she promises to eat for two at luncheon."

Augusta nodded absently. "Susan—forgive my prying—did Andrew propose last night?"

"Not in so many words." Susan gave assiduous attention to the spreading of marmalade on a piece of toast. "I feel certain he was about to propose formally when we were interrupted."

"And who could have been so totty-headed? But never mind. Will you accept him?"

"That is what I led him to believe."

Augusta narrowed her eyes. "A plain yes or no I would have understood. But this! Pray, Susan, leave the toast and look at me."

Susan obliged.

"Well?" A hint of testiness sharpened Augusta's voice. "Tell me how I am to interpret your reply."

"Perhaps Andrew deserves better than a wife who, though she holds him in affection, does not return his love to the degree he feels for her."

Augusta blinked. "I suspect I ought to ask you to repeat that. But never mind. I think I have the gist of it. You're trying to measure your affection—as you call it—against his love. And, pray, what standard of measure would you apply?"

Susan shook her head. "Forgive me. I should not have spoken. 'Tis something I must resolve on my own."

"Might I suggest you resolve it with Andrew? He may feel qualified to judge what he deserves."

Susan rose. "Pray excuse me."

"My dear child." Augusta's voice softened. "I will not meddle in your affairs, but before you make a rash decision, will you listen to me for just a moment?"

"But of course."

"So polite," muttered Augusta. "And wishing me to perdition, no doubt."

Susan's mouth twitched.

"That's better. Now I need not fear I condemned you to listen to a pronouncement of doom. Susan, are you aware how long Andrew has loved you?"

"Since his return, he told me."

"Four and a half years he has acknowledged and maintained his love for you. And it would not be unnatural if the thought of marriage occurred to him as soon as he knew that Frederick was dead."

Although Augusta paused expectantly, Susan said nothing.

After a moment, Augusta continued. "Now consider yourself those four years, two of which you were married, and two in mourning. What I am suggesting, Susan, is that while Andrew loved you, *you* fell into the habit of taking his presence for granted."

Susan was startled into a response. "Impossible! It's . . . absurd."

"Is it? You were obviously comfortable maintaining the relationship as it was when Frederick was alive. And you were quite taken aback when I mentioned the possibility of marriage between you and Andrew last Christmas."

"But how can you interpret that as my taking Andrew for granted?"

"That is all I wished to say, and I shan't detain you any longer." The dowager smiled. "I believe you were about to meet Andrew? Or did I misunderstand?"

Susan gave a wry little laugh. "I never said I'd meet him, but I will. Lud! You're as bad as Annie—reading my mind!"

Susan encountered Andrew leaving the maze as she was about to enter. He looked preoccupied, but the sight of her brought a smile to his face.

He caught her in his arms. "I must have been mad last night to let you escape. Today you'll have to come up with a much better excuse than sudden fatigue."

"There won't be an excuse."

She was breathless, as happened so often in his presence. And, as also happened in his presence, she felt vibrantly alive, aware of frosty air nipping her face, snow crunching beneath her feet, children caroling in the distance. It was Christmas. And she was free.

She met his gaze. "Last night . . . I was struck by sudden cowardice."

"Then it definitely was not the time for an adventure." He stepped back. "Show me your shoes. Are they sturdy?"

"Why?" Susan displayed ankle boots beneath the fur trim of her pelisse.

"They'll do. And if not, I'll carry you."

"Carry me where?"

"What if I said Gretna Green? Stop asking questions that will spoil the adventure."

She laughed. "One of the nicest things about you is that you never make me feel embarrassed or ashamed. After last night—"

"Forget last night. I am a much wiser man today than I was yesterday."

She gave him a questioning look.

"Susan, I was a fool to rush you. But I have loved you so long, and this Christmas marked the end of interminable waiting. I think—nay, I know I lost my head. I overlooked that only a night and a day had passed since, for the very first time, I openly spoke to you of marriage."

"When you promised not to discomfort me with an unwanted offer?" She added ruefully, "You chose a most importune moment. I had packed away all my mourning gowns and expected an uplift of spirits. But nothing happened to me, except that I heard those sounds again. I feared it was Frederick."

"No wonder you were distraught." His wide smile flashed. "You should have boxed my ears for my presumption. I was a coxcomb to assume you spent the past year wondering whether I would or would not make an offer. Especially once I knew you feared that Frederick was alive!"

"Andrew, would you say that I take you for granted?"

He raised a brow. "Something warns me not to answer hastily. But, in truth, I hope you do take my presence in your life for granted. 'Twas the reason I insisted on your promise to depend and rely on me."

Susan met his gaze, so candid and warm. Why should she doubt and hesitate when he did not? Andrew loved her and wanted her. He did not fear that his love was not returned. Why should she?

Shyly, she laid a hand on his shoulder. "If you like, you may propose to me now."

Something leaped in his eyes, a flame that warmed her even in the frosty morning air.

But he said, *"What!* When I just confessed myself a fool for rushing you? No, my love. This morning you shall have the adventure I promised last night."

"Why? Are you so certain I shall wish to hear your proposal at some other time?"

"Quite certain. You told me yourself that you're not fickle."

"Lud, Andrew! What havoc you wreak just when I thought I finally knew my own mind."

"You'll know it better still when I'm done courting you."

"Someone should warn you of a lady's prerogative."

"To change her mind? I've no fear of that happening."

She was undecided whether to let it go or demand outright that he make his offer here and now. How could he be so sure of her? Perhaps, for his sake, a continued courtship would be best. It would give him opportunity to discover her shortcomings. Give him time to reconsider. It was not a prospect she found pleasing.

Andrew, gloveless, blew into his hands. "And surely you must see that kneeling in the snow might somewhat cool my ardor."

"Whereas a rug aflame beneath your feet would fire it?"

Laughing, he drew her into the maze. "I shall take care not to have candlelight when I propose to you. The devil of it is, I cannot discover what happened. The mantel shelf is wide and smooth. How can a heavy brass piece topple? Even if it stood close to the edge!"

"Quite inexplicable."

"I suppose, we can always blame it on Elizabeth's ghost."

"Indeed." She deemed it time to change the topic. "Andrew, are you taking me into the passages?"

"Can you think of a better adventure than exploring?"

"I did that years ago. The passages are dark and damp. And

cold, even in the heat of summer. But I shall go with you. After all, I promised not to make excuses."

"I want to show you something I discovered last night. In the priest's hole off the salon."

"That's where we heard the scraping sounds."

They turned into the blind path, where the opening to the passages was located.

Andrew said, "I did not find the mistletoe. But if you lost it here, it'll show up when the snow melts."

"I expect so."

Only if Annie stopped moping. The little ghost had not made an appearance since the previous night, because, Susan suspected, she feared Elizabeth would demand the return of the silver mistletoe.

Susan's gaze fell on the grate which, as on the previous night, was leaning against a laurel bush. Beside it stood two lanterns.

She said, "You've been down already. Or did the scoundrels return after we left?"

"I went in to fetch my lantern, which I left last night when I got close to your chamber and heard a string of oaths that could not possibly be yours. The other lantern must be theirs. I found it at the foot of the ladder."

He extended a hand. "Are you game?"

"Yes."

Andrew, carrying a lantern, went down first. Susan followed and found the dark tunnel as damply cold as she remembered it from her explorations shortly after her arrival at the manor. It looked like an old disused mine shaft with timbers at irregular intervals and boards shoring parts of the chalk rock walls and ceiling. The wood was splintering and dark with age, but now and then, reassuringly, a new beam and fresh boards stood out.

"It is safe, isn't it?" she asked.

"Quite safe. Frederick had no interest in the running of the estate, but he was obsessed with the passages and their upkeep." Andrew held up the lantern. "Though I must admit I expected to see more new timbers. When I think of the number of trees he ordered cut!"

They continued in silence, Andrew stooping, and still he scraped his head occasionally.

The ground was fairly smooth, the lantern light steady. There was no reason for apprehension, yet Susan was glad of Andrew's guiding hand. Perhaps it was the mention of Frederick that made her uneasy. She had not known of his obsession with the passages, and now her imagination ran wild, calling back the dark shadows she had believed banished.

A narrow door marked the entrance to the interior passages. Andrew pushed it open, and they stepped into the hollow wall between the root and the wine cellars.

"Perhaps," said Susan, "all passages ought to be permanently sealed and the tunnel beneath the gardens filled in."

"I will do just that as soon as I've removed what Frederick left behind."

"Frederick again. Why am I made to think of him more often now, it seems, than when he was alive?"

Andrew stopped. He could not straighten, but he put an arm around her and drew her close, his chin touching her hair.

"Not much longer, I promise. After today, his name will be a mere memory etched on his tombstone."

"And, perhaps, in Augusta's heart."

"Shall we go on? Behind me is the ladder to the ground floor."

"Of course we'll go on. You would not expect me to retreat when we're so close to our goal!"

She stepped away from him, immediately missing the comfort and strength of his arm. And immediately conscious again of unease.

She cocked her head. "What is that sound? I cannot tell whether it's behind us or beside us."

Andrew listened. "I hear nothing. But just as we could hear sounds from the passages when we were in the house, we would now hear Tredwell in the wine cellar or one of the kitchen maids in the root cellar."

"Of course. That must be it."

Or it was Annie, coming in search of them. But Annie did not make a sound when she moved. Only when she toppled candle-sticks off the mantel shelf.

Gathering her cloak and skirts in one hand, Susan awkwardly climbed the almost perpendicular steps to the ground floor. Andrew followed with the lantern.

"We go left," he said. "Then right."

"Let us speak softly. We don't want to frighten Augusta. Or the staff."

"Come close, then." Taking her hand, he led the way once more.

She whispered, "I had forgotten what a rabbit warren this is."

"A masterpiece of Jacobean architecture. Or folly, I suppose. Every wall from the ground floor up is hollow."

"Augusta told me the family was Catholic back then."

"Here." The light of his lantern danced across a solid door of fairly new wood planks. "Do you know where this is?"

"You did mention the salon and the priest's hole. So I assume this is it. But the door is new."

Andrew opened it. In the narrow space were three stacks of long, flat wooden crates, one stack reaching close to the ceiling of the priest's hole, the other two only three crates high.

"Hold the lantern."

She took it and watched in silence as Andrew raised the top on one of the crates.

"Earlier, I pried open several. Look at this, Susan."

She squeezed into the doorway with him. In the crates, carefully packed in straw, were guns. And bayonets.

She frowned. "Those are military guns. Muskets?"

"Rifles. The 95th used them."

"And you believe Frederick hid them? But where would he have found so many rifles? And why would he have wanted them?"

"Where, I don't know. As to why—he was a free trader, Susan."

"He smuggled guns to France?" Her voice had risen, and she quickly lowered it to a whisper. "Surely not during the war!"

"I doubt that. Until I put a stop to his gambling, he probably had no more traffic with free traders than Squire Appleby or the vicar. And then only with the land smugglers who'd deliver the wine or brandy and collect payment."

Susan stared at the crates. "We're saddled with a cache of rifles. Lud! If that doesn't put us in the suds!"

Eight

"It rather does, I fear." Andrew closed the crate. "The rifles are almost certainly stolen."

Susan's hand clenched on the lantern grip. "It makes no sense. If Frederick committed this villainous theft and planned to sell the guns in France, why did he leave them behind?"

"I don't know. But it wasn't a regular run he was making. It may have been a bit risky to carry a full cargo of English army rifles."

"Do you think he sold some on previous crossings? There are seventeen crates in one stack. Only three in each of the other two. Who in France would purchase smuggled guns in times of peace?"

"Napoleon sympathizers. And make no mistake about it, there are many who would see Napoleon escape from St. Helena and restore the empire."

Susan backed out of the priest's hole. "Andrew, we must be rid of them! Just think if they were found! Lud! The intruders—"

Andrew placed a finger across her lips. "Listen."

From the salon, they heard Augusta's voice raised in song. *"Now make we mirth, all and some, for Christmas now is y'come, that hath no peer. Sing we all in'fere. Now joy and bliss they shall not miss that maketh good cheer. Now joy and bliss. . . ."*

Andrew shut the door on the crates.

Susan whispered, "For Augusta's sake, this must never be known. Do you think those two men who roamed our passages were sent from Whitehall? To search for the guns?"

"Not likely."

"Clive was a Whitehall agent during the war."

"The Duke of Stenton? You don't say!" Andrew took the lantern. "No harm, then, asking his advice."

"No harm at all. It's not as if he didn't know Frederick for what he was."

Andrew guided the way back to the ladder, descended swiftly, then lighted the steps for Susan.

Once she was safely in the cellar passage, Susan said, "Did you hear how happy Augusta sounded? Andrew, promise you'll never tell her!"

"I'm thinking I should never have told or shown you either. I have quite spoiled Christmas for you, haven't I?"

"No! Don't say that, Andrew. Don't even think it."

Susan stopped. They stood within sight of the narrow door leading to the garden tunnel. It was cold and damp in the passage, and icy air streaming in through the open door made her shiver. But deep inside her spread a warm glow.

She said, "This Christmas began most inauspiciously for me. But it all changed on Boxing Day . . . when you kissed me by the Yule log. And it steadily improved. No matter what happens, Andrew, this Christmas will live in my memory as the feast of rebirth."

"I love you, Susan."

Tears pricked her eyes. In the low passage, she had no need to rise on tiptoe to brush her lips across his brow.

She whispered, "Have a care, Andrew Cavendish. I may just marry you without a proposal."

"And you, Susan. Have a care." Setting down the lantern, he drew her into his arms. "Before long you may just be saying you love me."

He gave her no opportunity to make a retort, but claimed her mouth in a kiss that took her breath away. On Boxing Day, his tenderness had made her feel cherished and sheltered and wish that those feelings would last. Now, his ardor awakened sensations that were quite unfamiliar and infinitely exciting. His passion made her feel beautiful. Desirable. It empowered her with a new knowledge of herself.

From somewhere in the passages, or, perhaps, the adjoining cellars, came scuffling, scrambling sounds. Susan gave a start, but did not relinquish the tight hold she had somehow or other taken of Andrew's coat. He broke the kiss, reluctant to do so, still cupping her face in his hands, still trying to maintain the closeness they had shared. But irate voices, male and female, sped them from enchantment to reality. The nightly intruders, seemingly engaged in a wrestling match, had appeared just outside the doorway.

"I will *not* be still!" The female, muffled and cloaked like her male companion, struggled against his restraining hold. "I want what's mine, and I don't give a fig if we're caught! I'm tired of sneaking about."

"Fine words!" Susan took a step toward the two. "We shall see if you mean them."

She did not speak loud, but the muffled figures stopped their wrangling, stared, and after a quick look at each other took to their heels.

"Stop!" Susan ran after them.

Andrew snatched the lantern. Running stooped, he learned to his chagrin, diminished the advantage of a longer stride. They were halfway into the garden tunnel before he caught up with Susan, about twenty paces behind the fleeing pair.

"Let them go, Susan!" He reached for her, encountered a fold of her cloak and held on.

"Andrew, hurry!" She tugged to free herself. "We almost have them."

He slowed. "It does not matter. I know now who they are."

But she was pressing forward. His grip on her cloak slipped, and she fell against a timber. He saw her arms close around the rough gray wood for support. And he heard the warning creaks and groans of protesting lumber.

He did not know he had moved or set down the lantern, but he was beside her, prying her arms off the treacherous old timber, thrusting her, to the accompaniment of splintering, cracking, rumbling noises and a cloud of dust, toward the garden entrance.

The timber snapped, hit his chest and shoulder, knocked him down. Boards tearing off the ceiling smacked against him and settled heavily. He felt the impact of rock and gravel hitting the boards. There was some pain, but nothing unbearable. Only, he could not shift the load pressing on him. At least, not from the awkward, crouched position in which he was caught against the tunnel wall.

"Andrew!"

"Susan, are you all right?"

"Yes. Where are you?"

"Stay away!" The dust made him cough. "Dashed if I know what happened! That timber snapped like a dry twig."

"My God! So much rubble! Andrew, are you hurt? I cannot see you!"

He grimaced ruefully. He could scarcely see himself. And the sounds he heard were not reassuring.

He spoke quietly and calmly. "I am beneath the boards that were supposed to shore the ceiling. I'm all right, but I cannot shift them by myself. So you had better fetch the grooms to help me out of here."

"I'll help you."

"No, Susan. Please do not come close or touch anything. I don't know what the ceiling looks like above me, but I wouldn't wish to precipitate a burial just when we're getting along so famously."

For a long moment he heard nothing but the slide and fall of gravel. He was beginning to wonder if she had left when she spoke again, so softly he could barely make out the words.

"I see your hair, Andrew. I'm going now. I'll bring help. Only please don't move."

"Never fear. I'll be as still—" He did not go on. Chalky dust bit his throat, and a coughing fit was anything but desirable in the narrow confines of his prison.

"Andrew, I just want to say . . ."

He waited.

"I love you, Andrew. I love you with all my heart."

You'll know that you love him when you face the possibility of a life without him, and the mere thought of it fills your heart with bleakness and desolation. Elizabeth had said it. And Susan was facing the possibility now. The thought of it was unbearable.

I love you, Andrew. I do!

Leaving Andrew in the tunnel was the most difficult thing Susan had ever done. Only the certainty that it would take several men to shift the boards and the debris covering Andrew gave her the strength to turn her back on him. That, and the knowledge that Annie was there.

Brushing at the tears blurring her sight, Susan picked her way through fallen rock. Finally, the path was clear. Running the last stretch to the iron ladder, climbing, then running again, all the way to the stables, she kept her mind on Andrew, trapped in the tunnel. On Andrew's voice. On the thatch of dark hair visible through a gap in the boards. And on the silver sprig of mistletoe beside it.

She had to keep her focus narrow. Just on Andrew and the little ghost. Paralyzing fear would return, and she'd never make it to the stables if she allowed herself to think of anything else she had observed . . . the cross beam in the ceiling that had split and was pulling away from the iron spike anchoring it . . . the deep fissures that made scraping, creaking sounds and rained chunks of chalk rock onto the boards below . . . the weight of debris already piled on the boards and still increasing.

But she would not think of that. Only of Andrew. And Annie. And fetching help.

Annie saw Miss Susan wipe away tears as she left. "I love you, Andrew," Miss Susan had said—now, when it might be too late.

A fresh shower of rock and gravel dumped on the boards, and Annie braced herself against the impact. If only she didn't feel so weak. If only she hadn't been still miffed at Miss Susan. She should have told her to hurry. But, surely, Miss Susan knew better than to dilly-dally.

"Talk to me, Mr. Andrew. Take my mind off this load that seems to weigh as much as a mountain."

They were so close that if she were a human, he'd tell her not to crowd him. But he still did not hear her. Not for the first time, Annie wished it were him instead of Miss Susan whom she could reach with her voice.

But wishing paid no toll. She had better concentrate.

More rock fell. Heavy pieces. Even Mr. Andrew felt them and groaned, despite her efforts to cushion the impact.

"I'm sorry." Annie was panting. "It's just that I'm so tired. Away from the castle, my powers fade."

She shouldn't have left Stenton. But if she hadn't, she would never have met him. Would never have known that even the heart of a ghost could skip a beat at the sight of someone very special. Would never have experienced that delicious shiver brought on by the sound of a voice.

And there it was, the voice. Mr. Andrew's.

"Susan, my love. Delight of my heart. What the deuce is taking you so long?"

Annie felt the boards tremble. Or was the trembling inside her?

He loved Miss Susan. She had known it all along. But knowing something did not stop pain.

It was strange that she could feel a pain of the heart and not feel any aches of the body. The weight on her back and shoulders was crushing, yet gave her no pain, only a feeling of being without strength, without resilience. She had always been able to pass through wood, rock, anything solid, but now she felt as if the boards and debris she supported would push through her.

If that happened, if her powers faded to nothing. . . .

If Mr. Andrew died, would he be a ghost, like her? Would he

oam the passages and be lonely and wonder why he could not
est?

"You won't be lonely. I promise. I'll be with you, Mr. Andrew."

'Twas a lovely thought, being with Mr. Andrew. Forever.

Annie heard a groan, quickly stifled. Horrified, she saw that
Mr. Andrew crouched lower than before. The boards with all
their weight of fallen debris were pressing him down.

She was failing him!

Frantically, Annie pushed against the boards. She saw them
lift a fraction, heard Mr. Andrew let out a breath of relief. But
she was tired, her strength ebbing. She felt like a half-blown soap
bubble at the end of a straw. Not light enough to take off and
dance in the air, but simply hanging there, slowly dissolving into
a drop of liquid uselessness.

And, at the back of her mind, but becoming bolder and more
prominent, the insidious thought that, perhaps, the purpose of
her visit to the manor might not have been to help reluctant lovers
but to find her own true love.

"Devil a bit, Susan!" said Mr. Andrew. "Will you hurry! What
good will it do you to love me when I'm no longer around!"

A rumbling noise . . . more rock falling. A crushing weight.

Annie had struggled too hard, too long already. She had no
strength left, could not be expected to go on.

She heard Mr. Andrew's ragged breathing, felt him stir slightly.
And she heard his voice once more.

"I'll be dashed," he said weakly. "I've found the mistletoe."

In the stables, the head groom took competent charge, sending
his underlings for ropes, planks, blankets, buckets, hammers,
axes, all of which were assembled more quickly than it took
Susan to catch her breath. And then she was running back to the
maze with them and saw them disappear below ground with their
paraphernalia.

She was about to follow when someone spoke to her.

"I wouldn't. You'd only be in the way."

Susan turned to face the female intruder, who had stepped ou
of the shadows cast by the shrubs. Until then, Susan had not ever
noticed that the sun was shining.

"Tim went down earlier," said the young woman, who looke
to be no older than twenty. She spoke civilly enough, but there
was no mistaking the anger and hostility in her eyes. "He's th
one you saw with me."

Susan merely gave her a distracted look and turned back to
the opening. She heard the men's voices, but could not make ou
what they were saying. Heard hammering and ominous rumbling
sounds.

She must go down.

The woman said, "Tim used to work in the mines. Knows wha
he's doing, but he wouldn't let me go down with him. And there's
all the others now. They can work faster and better without you
underfoot."

Susan closed her eyes. If only she could shut out those awful
terrifying sounds from below. Dear Lord, please let him be al
right!

She tried to concentrate on Annie, down there beside Andrew
Surely, the little ghost was there to protect him, to ensure that
the falling rock would not crush him. But she could not concentrate. Fractions of thought skipped around in her mind. Parts of
a conversation with Elizabeth. About love. About bleakness and
desolation. Then she thought of the carol Augusta had sung.

Now make we mirth, all and some, for Christmas now is
y'come. . . . Now joy and bliss they shall not miss that maketh
good cheer.

It had been Christmas when Frederick was killed. And she had
been glad.

Now it was Christmas again. And she had just found her love.
But he was trapped beneath some flimsy boards covered with
rock and debris.

Now make we mirth. How ironic.

She heard soft laughter behind her, then a muffled, eerie,
"Susan!"

She spun. "Stop those childish tricks!"

The young woman tugged the thick knitted scarf from her nose and mouth. She looked embarrassed, but also still angry.

"You're Mary Beamish."

"And if I am?" Mary set her jaw belligerently. "I want the guns Frederick hid. They're mine now."

Susan heard more rumbling in the tunnel and rushed to the opening.

Mary jerked her back. "Don't be daft! There's seven men down in that narrow tunnel. And that's not counting your lover. If it all starts to go, they'll want to be out in a hurry. Not wait for some prim and proper lady to gather her skirts and daintily pick her way."

Trembling, Susan sank onto the pile of rock that used to cover the grate.

Softly, she said, "I wish I had not taken so long to recognize that I love him. I don't even know if he heard me when I told him. I wish we *had* been lovers."

"Frederick said you were."

Susan looked at Mary. "Why did he leave the rifles behind?"

"So that Tim and his friends could bring a few at a time when we ran out of money. Not that it's any of your business!" Mary tossed her silver-blond curls. "Me and Tim have been carrying them off, two each visit, for over a year. Didn't stop us when you blocked the entrance. Just made it a cursed nuisance coming and going, always having to mess with the rocks."

Susan listened, but there was no sound from below. Surely, a good sign?

Mary said, "I was mad as a hornet. That's why I started waking you up nights and scaring you. And you were scared out of your wits, weren't you?"

Still not a sound from below. Susan started to shake again. Yes, she was scared out of her wits. If only Andrew was all right! If only she could tell him again that she loved him. Why did she not know it sooner? Why only when she saw him buried under rock and debris? When, perhaps, it was too late!

But she mustn't think like that. He was all right. Annie was with him. And the grooms were strong and capable. And Tim, who had worked in the mines. He'd know what to do.

She looked at Mary. "It's a long way from East Dean just to carry off a rifle or two. And after the passages were sealed, I heard you most nights."

"Didn't come from home. Went into service at Squire Appleby's. So did Tim."

Hammering started up again in the tunnel. Some terse shouts or commands.

Susan's hands clenched. She saw Mary twisting and untwisting the ends of the scarf around her neck.

"Tim will be fine, too," Susan said gently.

For a moment, their eyes met and held.

Then Mary shrugged. "A few nice words won't make me think better of you. I know what you are. Frederick told me all about you."

"Does your father know about the rifles, Mary? And that you're stealing them from here?"

"I'm not stealing. They're mine now! And if you tell my father, I'll scratch your eyes out!"

"So he doesn't know."

Again, Mary shrugged. "He'd have my hide if he knew I was out nights, sneaking in your house. And he'd kill me if he ever found out about the guns."

The shouting in the tunnel grew more frantic. Susan jumped up and started to pace, up and down the short blind path, along the evergreen shrubs and the stretch of rock wall, and always keeping her eyes on the tunnel opening. She dared not turn the corner and lose sight of it. Lud! If only she knew what was happening!

Mary said, "I want them all now. All twenty-three crates. Me and Tim want to be married and start our own tavern."

"You cannot have the rifles. They were stolen from the army." Tearing her gaze from the tunnel opening, Susan studied the young woman. "How old are you, Mary?"

"What's it to you?"

"How old?"

"Going on twenty."

Two years ago, when Mary planned to elope with Frederick, she had been just the age Susan was when she married him.

Susan said, "Forget about the rifles, Mary. You'll be much happier wedded to Tim and saving for a tavern than spending the rest of your life in Newgate. Or Botany Bay."

Mary blanched, though she still tossed her head and looked belligerent.

Suddenly the men's voices in the tunnel were closer, more distinct. Mesmerized, Susan stared at the opening.

The head of a groom appeared. As he jumped out, and a second groom emerged, the rumbling started up again. Susan felt the earth tremble beneath her feet. She saw the evergreen hedge sway. Shouts rang in her ears.

She tasted fear. Dear God, keep him safe. Keep them all safe.

A third man came out of the opening. Mary's young man. He knelt and stretched out his arm to someone on the ladder. A thatch of dark hair covered with chalky dust showed above the opening.

"Andrew!"

The earth trembled again, but it did not matter. Her feet scarcely touched the ground anyway. There was a crashing, sliding noise some distance away, then silence. She was intent only on hearing Andrew shout her name. Dust streaming from the opening filled her nose and mouth, but she felt his arms closing around her and tasted only the sweetness of his kiss.

He held her at arm's length, his eyes devouring her. "I thought I'd never see you again. Lud! What a narrow escape."

"I love you, Andrew."

She tasted tears as she spoke, but they were tears of relief. Tears of happiness. Tears that might have been waiting since that moment three years ago, when she had loved Andrew for his kindness.

"I told you in the tunnel, but you may not have heard."

"I heard." Gently, he kissed the tears away. "It gave me the strength of a giant. The men said 'twas a miracle I wasn't crushed."

"It is Christmas. A time of miracles." Still, she could scarcely speak for love, for sheer happiness, for gratitude. Thank you Lord. Thank you, Annie.

Andrew looked over his shoulder. The grooms, grinning widely, were watching him and Susan with unabashed interest.

"Good. Everyone made it out. I am very grateful to all of you. Have a rest and some grog, and then we'll see what damage the cave-in did. My guess is, we'll find a crater in the rose garden."

As the men filed past to reach the main path of the maze, he said to Susan, "This wasn't what I had in mind when I said I'd have the tunnel filled in, but whatever our plans, the process has begun."

"Now that you're safe, I don't care how it started. Just finish the work as quickly as possible."

She saw Mary and Tim, standing hand-in-hand in the shadows of the evergreen hedge. Mary's eyes met and held hers for a moment. Then Mary turned. Pulling Tim with her, she disappeared through a gap in the shrubs.

"You hurt your head." Andrew's thumb caressed Susan's right temple. "You must have hit against the timber."

"I don't feel it. Andrew—tell me that you love me."

"With all my heart and soul. Susan, will you marry me?"

"At once." She gave a shaky laugh. "If only you had proposed when I asked you earlier. I'm sure we would have gone to tell Augusta instead of exploring the passages."

"But then I would not have found this." Taking the sprig of silver mistletoe from a much torn coat pocket, Andrew pushed it into her tumbled hair. "I don't know how it ended up in the passage, and it doesn't matter. When I saw it, I knew I'd get out, if only to return it to you."

Gently Susan touched the ornament. "Thank you."

She meant it for Annie as well.

About the Author

Karla Hocker lives with her family in San Antonio, Texas. Her Zebra regency romances include LADY MARYANN'S DI-LEMMA, AN IMPROPER COMPANION and JUNE LOVE. Karla loves to hear from her readers and you may write to her c/o Zebra Books. Please include a self-addressed stamped enve-lope if you wish a response.

THE
CHRISTMAS
BEAU

Joy Reed

One

Miss Melanie Hartman gave a last touch to the cluster of blond ringlets at the back of her neck and sat back to examine the effect in the glass.

"You look beautiful, Mellie." Her sister Nina spoke enthusiastically from the foot of the bed. Nina was the younger of the two girls, having just turned fourteen. Like Melanie, she had soft blond curls, blue eyes, and a fair complexion. To be sure, Nina's figure at the moment was still that of a schoolgirl, remarkable chiefly for the length and angularity of its limbs, but of late it was beginning to show promise of filling in as satisfactorily as her sister's had done.

Melanie gave another touch to her hair and smiled at her sister in the mirror. "Thank you, Kitten," she said. "I wish you could come downstairs for the party tonight."

"I wish I could, too. But Mama says I may next year, perhaps, when I am fifteen—and at least I can watch tonight from the gallery, even if I can't join the fun. That is such a pretty dress, Mellie. You look as elegant as a queen in it."

"It is pretty, isn't it?" Melanie regarded her reflection complacently. "I am very pleased with the way it made up. I still can't believe Temple let me have it cut after that plate we saw in the *Repository*. In general, you know, she will not let me bare so much as a collarbone."

Nina nodded sagely. Temple was their mother's dressing woman and the acknowledged arbiter of fashion in the Hartman household. Her opinions about the style of dress suitable for young ladies were both conservative and extremely rigid. For the past two years, Melanie had begged and coaxed in vain to be permitted to wear décolleté dresses, such as were illustrated in the pages of her mother's fashion journals.

Temple's concession on the present occasion had therefore been very gratifying to Melanie, and not a little unexpected. As she looked down at her white satin and net evening dress with its short sleeves, flounced hem, and low square neckline, she felt quite the epitome of elegance and sophistication.

"You look very grown-up, Mellie," said Nina, echoing Melanie's own thoughts. "I am sure Lord Colby will think you the prettiest girl at the party."

This, too, was an echo of Melanie's thoughts—or of her hopes, at any rate. But she turned her sister's words aside with a laugh. "Oh, I can hardly expect to be that, Kitten. You know Augusta Madison is coming tonight."

"Miss Madison is certainly very handsome," allowed Nina. "But to my mind, Mellie, she's not a bit prettier than you are."

Melanie laughed again to hide her pleasure. "Oh, Kitten, you will swell my head if you keep showering me with compliments that way! And indeed, they're not at all deserved. Even if I was as handsome as Augusta Madison to start with, I couldn't hope to compete with her diamonds and French silks and I don't know what else. Jeannie Marsh was telling me the other day that Augusta has all her dresses made by a London dressmaker, and that all her hats come straight from Paris. It's enough to make me wish our papa had been a wool merchant, too, instead of merely a gentleman farmer."

Nina acknowledged this with a sigh. "But of course the Madisons are rather vulgar people, Mellie, even if they are very nice," she added in a consoling voice. "I'm sure Lord Colby would never marry a wool merchant's daughter. Besides, I heard Mrs. Madison tell Reverend Farley yesterday that Augusta is engaged to an M.P. over in Kent."

"Is she indeed?" Momentarily diverted from her toilette, Melanie turned to look at her sister with surprise. "Why, I never would have thought the Madisons would be satisfied with such a match as that. It's common knowledge that Mrs. Madison was hoping to get a lord for Augusta, or at least a baronet. But perhaps she felt an M.P. was almost as good as a lord—and to be sure, with Mr. Madison's money behind him, there's no saying but he might start out an M.P. and end up Prime Minister. I must be sure and tell Charles when he gets here. I hope it won't be too great a disappointment to him. I've always suspected he rather admired Augusta."

"I think all the gentlemen admire Miss Madison, but I don't believe Charles really cares a fig for her, Mellie. If he did, he would have made more of an effort to attach her, I'm sure."

"Yes, but you know how thoughtless Charles can be, Kitten. He just drifts cheerfully along, taking it for granted that everything will work out very well without his lifting a finger. And if by chance something doesn't work out as he likes, he never does anything about it until the last possible moment and sometimes not even then. Look at this business of his going up to London. He might have gone any time these six months to see his attorney, but no, he has to wait until this week, with Christmas only days away and our party going on tonight. I just know he won't get back in time for it, whatever he may have written in his letter. Something will happen to delay him, and then we will have to manage without him. Charles can be very inconsiderate sometimes."

"Oh, Mellie, I am sure he'll be here in time for the party," said Nina, looking distressed. "He will be the host, after all, and he knows how much Mama depends on him now that Papa's gone. I expect he'll be here any minute, if he isn't already. I thought I heard the sound of a carriage in the drive a few minutes ago."

"Yes, now that you mention it, I thought I heard a carriage a few minutes ago, too. Why don't you run down and see if it's him, Kitten? I'll be down in just a few minutes, once I get this one curl fixed so it doesn't keep poking out."

"All right," said Nina, sliding obediently off the bed. Midway to the door, she paused to bury her nose in an exquisite bouquet of roses that stood on her sister's commode. "Mmm . . . what lovely roses. I'm sure Lord Colby's gardener grows the best roses in the county. You mustn't forget to bring them when you come downstairs, Mellie."

"I won't," said Melanie, who indeed would sooner have forgotten her slippers, or her gown. She waited until her sister had left the room, then rose from her dressing table, went over to her desk, and took from one of its drawers a small leather-bound notebook.

This was Melanie's diary. At the age of sixteen she had first begun to keep a record of her daily activities, together with such moral reflections and resolutions as occurred to her in the course of recording them. She had been recording them faithfully now for more than two years.

Melanie smiled as she read through some of those early entries:

"Resolved: not to giggle or gush in company, as I did at the Marshes' last night,"

and

"Resolved: to practice the pianoforte two hours a day, so that I may play as well as Lucretia Potter."

With such girlish resolutions as these, Melanie had filled the first hundred or so pages of her diary. But even here among the resolutions might be glimpsed an occasional admiring reference to the elegant manners and masculine beauty of Lord Colby. As the diary went on, his name cropped up more and more often, until at last it dominated nearly every page.

Lord Colby was the scion of a noble family whose ancestral home, Colby Castle, lay only a few miles from the Hartmans' property. Melanie had known him since her early girlhood and, like the rest of the neighborhood, had taken a strong interest in his doings. But her interest in those early years had been more critical than admiring, for she had entertained scant regard for the pale and supercilious youth who had once encouraged his dog to tree her pet kitten and who was wont to ride past her and the other girls of the neighborhood as though they were beneath his notice.

All that had changed a few years ago, however. At the age of twenty-one, Lord Colby, like several generations of Lord Colbys before him, had been sent to acquire such worldly wisdom and polish as could be obtained by a few years on the Continent. His return had coincided with Melanie's sixteenth birthday. When she had seen him that day, his fair hair gleaming beneath his dashing high-crowned hat as he drove his curricle through the village in a splendid whirl of dust and flying hooves, she had lost her heart to him on the spot. He had seemed to her like nothing so much as a young Apollo, sweeping along in his divine car.

From then on she had caught fairly frequent glimpses of Apollo as he drove through the village in his curricle or cantered along the country lanes on his thoroughbred hack. Each of these encounters had been faithfully recorded in Melanie's diary, though in truth they could hardly be dignified by the name of encounters. Lord Colby remained almost as oblivious to his young neighbor's existence as he had previous to his European venture. The circumstance of his favoring her once with a casual nod and a touch of his hat brim had been sufficient to inspire several pages of impassioned prose in Melanie's diary.

It had been a year ago, almost to the day, that she and Lord Colby had first made each other's formal acquaintance. Melanie had been seventeen then, old enough to attend a local Christmas party along with her mother and elder brother Charles. On this occasion the entire Colby family had also been present. This was by no means a common occurrence, for though invited as a matter of course, the residents of the castle were more apt to decline than accept the invitations of their neighbors. But they had all been in attendance that night: the Dowager Lady Colby, dazzling and dignified in green silk and emeralds; the Honorable John Colby, an undersized and unwholesome-looking young gentleman whose face was disfigured by a perpetual sneer; and of course the young god himself, the Right Honorable Lord Colby.

Melanie could still see him in her mind's eye as he had appeared that night—although, to be sure, if her memory had failed her, she might easily have refreshed it by referring to the appropriate page of her diary. Lord Colby had been wearing a blue topcoat, a white-and-gold-striped waistcoat, and a pair of white Inexpressibles. All of these garments were molded closely to his body in the current fashion, a fashion that might have been divinely ordained to set off his Apollonian figure. Bereft of hat, his hair was seen to gleam like new-minted gold, his chiseled features were set in an expression of pleasant condescension as he looked around the room, and his aristocratic bearing would have set him apart in the crowd even had not his appearance utterly eclipsed that of every other gentleman present.

Melanie had been unable to take her eyes off him. She had been taking part in a country dance when Lord Colby had made his entrance, and so intense had her preoccupation been that she had nearly come to grief when it came time for her and her partner to take the lead. But her momentary discomfiture had been replaced by incredulous delight when, at the conclusion of the dance, Lord Colby had followed her to the corner where she and her mother were sitting and begged for the privilege of dancing with her.

Melanie blushed now to remember how she had stammered in responding to this petition. But her eagerness to accept it must have been clear to Lord Colby, even if her speech was not, for he had smiled and led her onto the floor. There he had addressed to her those words that had promptly won over all that yet remained unconquered of her heart:

"Do y'know, Miss Hartman," he had said, "I've been watching you this half hour, and I'm dashed if I don't think you're the prettiest girl in the room."

Even now, as Melanie reread the words in her diary, she felt a thrill of pleasure. The thrill had been a hundred times greater at the time. And it had been amplified to a state of near euphoria when Lord Colby had asked her to dance a second time that evening, an honor he had accorded to no other woman in the room.

All this had been very flattering, but unfortunately the rest of the evening had been in the nature of an anticlimax for Melanie. Upon finishing their second dance together, Lord Colby had strolled into the card room and remained there the rest of the evening, denying her any further sight of his magnificence. In an effort to occupy herself in his absence, she had accepted a dance with a clumsy young gentleman whose wayward feet had done material damage to her dress. And when she had gone to the ladies' retiring room to make repairs, she had been captured on the way back by the Honorable John Colby, who had seized upon the proximity of a nearby branch of mistletoe as an excuse to kiss her.

Melanie had found kissing the Honorable John a highly distasteful experience. It was not merely that he had a wet, loose mouth whose touch was like the contact of a raw oyster. Most families have a black sheep, and the Honorable John was widely known to fill this position in the Colby family. Since adolescence, he had been notorious for his amorous exploits among milkmaids, milliners' assistants, and other low females. Melanie was not pleased to be numbered with such company, but she comforted herself by reflecting that a kiss under the mistletoe was a relatively innocent business as such things went. For the sake of his noble brother, she was willing to forgive and forget the Honorable John's offense.

There was, indeed, not much Melanie would not have forgiven for Lord Colby's sake, after he had singled her out in front of the whole neighborhood in such a flattering manner. Her former admiration for him immediately blossomed into a full scale devotion. His devotion in return was not quite so marked, but though he did not especially pursue Melanie in the months that followed the Christmas party, neither did he forget her entirely. If they met by chance in the village, he invariably smiled and raised his hat to her. On occasion he would even pause to exchange a few words with her, and once, when they happened again to attend the same party, he repeated his former flattering behavior by twice asking her to dance with him. But it was not until a couple of months ago, in the fall of the present year, that his attentions had become really particular.

Melanie could remember exactly when the change had taken place. The Colbys had spent most of June and July at Brighton, as was their invariable custom. This had meant a long, boring summer for Melanie, but when August came, Lady Colby had returned to the castle with her retinue of servants. She was followed a few weeks later by her sons, who had come down for the start of the shooting season. It was then that Melanie began to sense a more purposeful direction in Lord Colby's attentions.

She had at first been unable to credit a change that seemed like the realization of her most extravagant daydreams. When Lord Colby had been staying at the castle before, he had been content to see her whenever their paths crossed without making any effort to see that they did. Now he began to actively seek her out, calling upon her at her home, taking her out driving in his curricle, and bestowing upon her a number of pretty trifles. Only a few days ago he had given her an exquisite hand-painted fan depicting a courting couple in a gondola. The fan had instantly become Melanie's most treasured possession, but even more did she treasure the words with which Lord Colby had accompanied his gift. She had transcribed them into her diary as soon as he had taken leave of her, but this was more because she needed an outlet for her feelings than because she feared to forget what he had said. She felt quite certain that the whole conversation was engraved upon her heart.

"Oh, Colby, it's beautiful," Melanie had said, first examining the fan with delight and then looking up to smile at him. They had progressed by this time beyond the formal "Miss Hartman" and "Lord Colby." Only the week before he had respectfully requested the privilege of calling her Melanie, while at the same time begging her to call him familiarly by his title. Of course his request had been blushingly granted. "Oh, Colby, it's beautiful," said Melanie again. "I won't dare use it, I know. In any case, it's much too fine for any of the parties around here."

"Aye, so it is. This is an accursed slow place," Lord Colby had agreed with a grimace. Melanie was rather hurt by this speech, which seemed to reflect upon her as well as her native village, but her hurt vanished with his next words. "I'm glad you like the fan, Melanie. It reminded me of you when I saw it. A pretty thing, and pretty dear, too, don't you know."

"Oh, Colby!" Melanie had been so much overcome by these words that for a moment she could find no adequate reply. "Oh, Colby, indeed you should not have," she said, with a smile trembling on her lips. "If it was so dear as that, you ought not to have bought it for me. But I can't help being glad you did. It is the very prettiest fan I have ever seen. Is it supposed to show a scene of Venice?"

"Aye, that's right. That's the Grand Canal there, and you can see the Ca'd'Oro in the background." With a knowledgeable air, Lord Colby pointed out these landmarks to Melanie. "You ought to see Venice sometime, Melanie. It's the prettiest place in the world, 'pon my word. Paris ain't half bad either, of course, but for my money, it's Venice every time. Especially at this time of year. Ever since I came back from the Continent, I'm half killed by these blasted English winters."

"Are you, Colby?" said Melanie sympathetically. "To be sure, it is very chilly out today, with the wind blowing so sharp. It must be lovely to live in such a place as Venice, where it is sunny and warm the year round. And I am sure it must be a very beautiful place. 'A fairy city of the heart, Rising like water-columns from the sea,' as Lord Byron says. I wish I could see it."

"By George, I wish I could show it to you." Lord Colby had looked down at Melanie thoughtfully and rather assessingly. Half confused, she had looked back at him for a moment, then looked down at the fan with a soft flush staining her cheeks. "I've been wanting to get back to Italy, but I'm not quite my own master at the moment, worse luck," he had explained to her with an air of gravity. "I'm of age, of course, and I've got the title all right and tight, but as for money—well, the terms of my father's will were deucedly odd, not to put it any stronger. I think the old man must have been a bit gaga toward the end. He left things tied up so my mother has full control of the purse strings until I'm thirty. At the moment, I haven't a shilling to call my own."

There was cold anger in Lord Colby's voice as he spoke these last words. Melanie made a sympathetic noise, which seemed to recall him to a sense of her presence. He forced a smile to his lips and took her hand in his. "It's a dashed nuisance having to beg my mother for every farthing, as you can probably imagine. But the thing is, Melanie, I've reason to believe she'd untie the purse strings a few years early if I were to marry. She's always after me to find some nice girl and settle down. Lately I've been thinking I might just take her advice. What do you say, Melanie? I can't think of a better honeymoon spot than Venice."

"Oh, no," Melanie had said in a failing voice. Lord Colby had smiled again and pressed her hand.

"You understand, of course, that I've got to discuss things with the old lady before making any formal offer. Not that I think she'll make any objection. For a while there she was trying to make a match between me and Lady Madeleine Seale, but I told her flat out I wasn't having any part of that business, and I think it's gone off by now. She'll be glad enough to see me tie myself up without much bothering about the who and how of it. I tell you what, Melanie: I'll have a word with her as soon as I get home tonight. If she's agreeable to the notion, she can come call on you and your mother sometime here during the holidays. It's an awful bore, I know, but there's no getting around it, I'm afraid."

"Oh, no, Colby! Indeed, I should be very honored to have your mother call upon me."

"Should you?" Lord Colby looked indulgently down at Melanie. She had felt sure some avowal of devotion must be forthcoming, perhaps even some display of devotion, but all he had said was, "Very well, then. I suppose I ought to be toddling off now. I'll see you at your mother's party Monday night,

Melanie." And having saluted her hand with punctilious courtesy, he had gotten up and taken his leave.

Although Melanie was disappointed not to be able to record her first kiss with Lord Colby in her diary, she found plenty of other matter for her pen. Her lover's words, amounting to a proposal, had all to be carefully set down, analyzed, and exulted over. And in due time, this had given birth to a brand-new resolution, to wit:

> "Resolved: that I shall study Italian for at least an hour each day and also make a thorough study of the geography and customs of the country."

Melanie smiled wistfully as she reread this resolution. It was a resolution she had kept faithfully during the past few days, though she had experienced a few qualms about doing so. Melanie was not unduly superstitious, but it seemed almost like anticipating good fortune to begin her study now, when a word from Lady Colby might result in its all being for naught.

To be sure, Lady Colby was well known to be an indulgent parent in all matters not pertaining to money. Her indulgence had indeed been such as to bring criticism upon her from some quarters, but this circumstance gave Melanie hope now. It seemed most unlikely that Lady Colby would refuse to countenance her son's chosen bride if her son were really set upon his choice. So Melanie told herself, but still she had been on pins and needles during the three days that had passed while she was waiting to hear her fate.

Those three days had been the longest and most nerve-wracking of Melanie's life. It did occur to her now and then, as she endeavored to study, sew, or practice the pianoforte, that Lord Colby might have sent her a line or two to end her suspense. But as soon as her thoughts began to take on this reproachful tone, her heart sprang up to defend him. Perhaps he was merely awaiting a favorable moment to approach his mother. Or perhaps he had already done so and was now anxiously awaiting her decision. Or perhaps he was busy with some other, unrelated matter. Such an important man as Lord Colby must have a great deal of business in hand at any time, Melanie reasoned. But whatever its cause, her suspense had continued until that very morning, when the bouquet of roses had arrived from the castle bearing Lord Colby's card.

This had in a large measure set Melanie's fears to rest. He would not be sending her bouquets if his mother had been opposed to the idea of their marrying, she told herself happily, as she had carried the precious bouquet up to her bedroom. Once there, she had examined the bouquet carefully, on the chance it might contain a note from Lord Colby. Although she was quite, quite certain now that the interview with his mother must have had a favorable outcome, still she would have been glad to have some written confirmation of the fact.

The bouquet proved to contain nothing but flowers, however. With flowers Melanie had therefore to be content, and she was content, once her first disappointment was past.

"I will see him at the party tonight, after all," she told herself. "And that's much better than any note could be. In a note he would have had to be very roundabout and discreet, lest it fall into the wrong hands. It will be better to hear the news from his own lips. Not that I'm afraid it will be bad news. I'm sure he would not have sent the bouquet if Lady Colby had advised him against marrying me. Who knows? Perhaps she has already given her consent, and he will formally propose to me tonight!"

The idea sent a little shiver down Melanie's spine. For the most part it was a shiver of delight, but mingled with it was an element of apprehension. The events of this evening might well determine the entire future course of her life. Nothing could be more delightful or desirable than a proposal from Lord Colby, of course, but the acceptance of such a proposal would inevitably mean leaving all that was familiar behind her and embarking on a new and unknown existence. For a moment, Melanie felt almost frightened to consider how different that existence might be.

"But that's foolish, Melanie," she told herself firmly. "Of

course it will be a change, but a change for the better. There isn't a girl in the neighborhood who wouldn't jump at the chance to marry Lord Colby."

Drawing the diary toward her, she picked up her pen and dipped it in the ink bottle. "December 20, 6 P.M.," she wrote. "Lord Colby has sent me a beautiful bouquet of roses, for which I will thank him at Mama's party tonight."

As she sat debating whether to add something of her hopes and fears, she heard the sound of her brother's voice ring out below. Melanie dipped the pen in the ink bottle and wrote quickly, "Charles has just arrived, late as usual. We have been waiting dinner for him this hour. I must go down now, but shall finish this later, after the party, when perhaps I shall have more news to record."

Having put the last period to this sentence and underscored the word "more," Melanie blotted her words carefully, then restored diary and writing implements to the drawer. The sound of the dinner bell ringing below stairs gave impetus to her movements. Shutting the drawer hastily, she rose from her desk, snatched her bouquet from the commode, and hurried out of the room.

Two

As Melanie ran down the stairs, she heard the sound of masculine laughter ring out from the direction of the drawing room. Supposing that her brother was closeted there with Nina and her mother, and that the three of them were awaiting her own arrival before going in to dinner, Melanie quickened her pace still further and hurried across the hall to the drawing room.

As she went, she was considering how best to break the news to her brother about Miss Madison's engagement. It was not that she supposed the news would really crush him. The Hartmans might not be so aristocratic a family as the Colbys, but their name was quite as well respected and (if one wanted to be particular) of considerably greater antiquity. Charles, for all his free and easy manners, had as much regard for what was due that name as had his father before him.

The Madisons, on the contrary, were definitely humble in their origins. Their daughter might be a beautiful, agreeable, well-dowered girl, but Melanie was confident that her brother would never have seriously considered allying himself with a family who had gained their fortune through trade. He had expressed enough admiration of Miss Madison on former occasions to make it a legitimate topic for teasing now, however, and as Melanie threw open the drawing room door, she was rehearsing in her mind exactly what she would say to him.

"Oh, Charles," she cried, entering the drawing room with a hasty step. "You shall have to order yourself a suit of mourning, Charles. Prepare yourself for a shock: we just received word today that Miss Madison is engaged to an M.P. over in Kent."

Melanie had barely spoken these words when she became aware that she was not breaking in upon a family party, as she had supposed. There was no sign of her mother or sister in the drawing room, only Charles and an unknown gentleman in boots and riding dress who turned to look with surprise at her mock-serious announcement.

"Oh, I beg your pardon," said Melanie, covered with confusion.

Charles smiled tolerantly. He was a good-looking young gentleman of twenty-five with a lean, athletic build and the same fair coloring as his sisters. Like the gentleman beside him, he still wore breeches and riding boots in token of his recent journey, though a dampness about his temples showed he had made some recent effort in the direction of washing up. His golden hair had been ruthlessly combed back from his forehead in an effort to discourage its tendency to curl, a tendency that it shared with his sisters', to his own great disgust.

"Hullo, Mell," he said. "If you're hoping to shock me with that news, my girl, you're a bit slow off the mark. I heard about

Miss Madison's engagement two days ago when I was up at Town."

"Oh," said Melanie. It was all she could think to say. She was unnerved by the steady gaze of the strange gentleman, whose eyes had continued upon her all the while she and her brother were speaking. "Won't you introduce me to your friend, Charles?" she said, attempting a light tone. "I don't believe we are acquainted."

"Oh, aye, to be sure. I meant to introduce you, only it slipped my mind when you came in all of a pelter. Mellie, this is my friend Will McCraig from University. I ran across him while I was in Town and insisted he come back with me to spend the holidays. A Scotchman in London is of no use to himself or anyone else, eh, Will?"

Mr. McCraig made no acknowledgment to this jest, but bowed gravely to Melanie. His eyes, dark brown and deep-set beneath heavy dark brows, dwelt unblinkingly on her face.

"Will, this is my sister Melanie," continued Charles. "You remember me talking about her at school, I daresay."

"Indeed," said Mr. McCraig, bowing again. "I'm verra pleased to make your acquaintance, Miss Hartman."

His voice was deep and mellow, with a pleasant Scotch burr. Melanie, looking him over critically, decided it was the most attractive thing about him. Some people might have considered him handsome, she supposed, but it was a rough-hewn kind of handsomeness that bore no comparison to the chiseled perfection of Lord Colby's features.

In size, too, the two men bore no comparison. Mr. McCraig was a good half-head taller than Lord Colby and much broader across the chest and shoulders. Melanie, who had always considered Lord Colby to represent the *beau idéal* in this respect, felt there was something not quite genteel about a man being so large. It made him look more like a prizefighter than a gentleman, she thought. But she was forced to admit that where Mr. McCraig's barbering was concerned, nobody could have mistaken him for a prizefighter. His dark hair was worn long rather than close-cropped—not so long as gentlemen had worn it in the previous century, to be sure, but long enough to reach past his coat collar in back. His complexion was nearly as dark as his hair and hinted at a life spent largely out-of-doors. Melanie, surveying him dubiously, felt he presented altogether a very rough and uncouth appearance. But she nevertheless smiled and curtsied politely in response to her brother's introduction.

"I am very pleased to make your acquaintance, too, sir," she told the Scotchman.

Mr. McCraig did not return her smile, but continued to look solemnly down at her. Melanie was disquieted by his steady gaze and rather annoyed by it, too. It seemed to her rude conduct, but she reminded herself that Mr. McCraig came from Scotland, a notoriously uncivilized country by all she had heard and read. In all probability, he was unused to the ways of polite society. So she smiled upon him in a friendly way before turning again to her brother.

"I am glad to see you home, Charles. I was beginning to think you might not return in time for our party tonight. We have all been very worried about it, I assure you."

Charles grinned. "You mean *you've* been worried about it, Mell," he said acutely. "Nina hasn't any stake in the business, and as for Mama, you won't catch her worrying about such a trifle. Why, she ain't even dressed for dinner yet. I sent Nina upstairs a few minutes ago to hurry her along a little."

"I hope you'll excuse our not changing for dinner, Miss Hartman," put in Mr. McCraig, in a deprecating voice. "Your brother wouldna hear of it, on account of our being a bit behind our time, but—"

"Oh, that's all right, Will," interrupted Charles, drowning out the civil rejoinder Melanie was about to make. "The party don't start till eight. There'll be plenty of time for us to change before then, assuming we sit down to dinner pretty soon. I hope Mama don't keep us waiting too much longer. I haven't had a bite to eat since we left London this morning."

He had not much longer to wait, for only a moment later the

drawing room door swung open, admitting Nina and Mrs. Hartman.

"Good evening, Charles," said Mrs. Hartman, smiling upon her son with her usual serenity. "Nina said you had just arrived. I trust you had a pleasant journey." Having kissed him affectionately and received in return a hasty peck on the cheek, she looked doubtfully at Mr. McCraig.

"Will McCraig, Mama," said Charles, with an airy wave of his hand. "Daresay you remember me mentioning him when I was up at Cambridge. I found him wandering around London like a lost soul and brought him back to spend the holidays with us. Will, this is my mother." Having thus summarily disposed of the matter of introductions, and having given neither party a chance to respond to them, Charles seized his mother's arm and began leading her toward the dining room.

Mr. McCraig appeared rather perplexed at being left with two young ladies to squire. At last, with an air of hesitancy, he gave one arm to Nina and the other to Melanie. The three of them followed Charles and Mrs. Hartman into the dining room. As they went, Melanie tried to catch Nina's eye to communicate her amusement at their escort's naïveté. But Nina was smiling sympathetically up at Mr. McCraig.

"It must be very difficult to spend Christmas away from home," she said. "Do you have a great deal of family back in Scotland, sir?"

Mr. McCraig shook his head. "Nay, 'tis only myself and a few aunts and uncles and suchlike," he said in his deep voice. "I've no immediate family living." He helped Melanie and Nina seat themselves at the table, then went to take his place at Mrs. Hartman's right hand.

As soon as they were all seated, Charles took up the ladle and began portioning out the soup, a bisque of fish served from a tureen at table.

"Thank you, Charles," said Mrs. Hartman, accepting a plate of bisque from her son. She was a plump woman in her late forties, gray-haired now but still retaining remnants of the beauty

234 *Joy Reed*

that had made her famous in the London of thirty-odd years ago. She had been the Honorable Miss Milford then, with a pedigree to match her beauty, and with so many advantages to her name, it had been widely expected that she would make a very great match indeed.

The surprise had therefore been great when she had chosen to marry the late Charles Hartman. Her parents, her sisters, and her friends had all done their best to dissuade her from throwing herself away upon a mere country gentleman. But though unshakably placid in temperament, Miss Milford had possessed a fund of obstinacy that had carried her triumphantly against every obstacle that her family and friends could put in her way. She had married her chosen bridegroom and, having married him, had never thereafter been heard to speak a word against him or the lot in life that had been hers in his company.

This was not so much a testament to Mrs. Hartman's stoicism as to her contentment with that lot. She had been devoted to the late Mr. Hartman, and he to her, and his death a few years ago had been one of the very few events to ruffle the equanimity of Mrs. Hartman's temper. But though her husband's death had come as a great shock to her, it had had little effect on the outward form of her life. She had continued on in much the same way as before, occupying herself in her tranquil fashion with her children, her household, and such society as the neighborhood afforded.

It was true that most of that society was a good deal lower than that she had been born to. Mrs. Hartman's birth would have entitled her to take precedence of every other woman in the neighborhood if she had cared to assert herself. But Mrs. Hartman had never chosen to assert herself in that particular way. Among the neighborhood women, it was Lady Colby who was generally given the precedence, while Mrs. Hartman went her own way: calm, dignified, and for the most part unrecognized. As she patiently explained to her daughter whenever the subject arose, the conviction of one's own superiority ought to be enough for one, whether or not that superiority was recognized by other people.

Melanie did not quite sympathize with these sentiments, but she loved and respected her mother very much in spite of Mrs. Hartman's distressing lack of pride. A much more serious lack, in her opinion, was her mother's lack of social ambition.

For years Melanie had been begging her mother to take her to London for the Season, but on this subject Mrs. Hartman was as adamant as she had been on the subject of her marriage. Country living amid the familiar environs of Hartman Hall suited her best. Melanie had often deplored this want of enterprise on her mother's part, but of late she had become reconciled to it. To be presented at court as Lord Colby's bride would be an even greater triumph than to make her bows there under the aegis of the Milfords, she thought.

The thought was in her mind now as she finished her soup and embarked upon the fish course that followed it. Charles provided most of the conversation during the meal. The meeting with his attorney had gone well, and he was full of triumph as he detailed his adversary's approaching discomfiture.

"Adamson says he hasn't a leg to stand on," he told the others exultantly, between mouthfuls of mutton and potatoes. "He expects the case will come to session in the Hilary term, and there shouldn't be a doubt as to the verdict. That'll teach that old fool Brooke to threaten me with lawsuits!"

Mrs. Hartman shook her head. "Indeed, I cannot think why anyone would want to go to law," she said. "It seems to me a very uncomfortable business. Was it legal business that brought you to London, too?" she inquired kindly of Mr. McCraig, who had been quite mute during the meal thus far. It had not escaped Melanie's notice, however, that he had looked in her direction several times.

"Aye, we met at Lincoln's Inn," said Charles, answering for his friend and in the process rendering useless his mother's kindly stratagem. "And dashed glad I was to see him again, too. It's been years since we was up at Cambridge together. He was a couple of years ahead of me in his studies, you know."

Melanie made note of this statement, which tended to confirm her own observations. Mr. McCraig appeared a few years older than Charles, nearer thirty than twenty, she thought.

"Poor old Will had business at the Assizes after New Year's and didn't want to travel all the way back to Scotland between now and then," continued Charles. "So I told him he might just as well come home with me. Passing Christmas in a hotel is a dashed dreary business when all's said and done."

"Aye, and I'm much obliged to you for putting me up," said Mr. McCraig. The words were addressed to all the Hartmans and not merely to Charles. Once more Melanie felt his eyes upon her, as he went on in an earnest voice. "Indeed, if I had known you were entertaining this evening, I wouldna have thrust myself amang you." His burr gave a strong emphasis to the "r" in "thrust," as though emphasizing the gravity of the offense. "I doubtna it's making a deal of trouble for you all."

"Oh, but we are very glad to have you, sir," responded Mrs. Hartman graciously. "We always have room for one more at Christmastime. And as for trouble, I assure you there is none. Simply make yourself at home and think no more about it."

Mr. McCraig did not look as though this speech much reassured him. He said no more on the subject, however, and the conversation soon evolved into another discussion of Charles's lawsuit. As might have been expected, it was Charles himself who bore the largest part in this discussion. But though his friend spoke little, he was assiduous in helping the ladies to the different dishes on the table. In this respect he compared favorably to Charles, who was too busy talking to pay much attention to the needs of his mother and sisters. Melanie, as she accepted a wing of fowl from Mr. McCraig, was pleased to note his gallantry of manner. If only he had not persisted in staring at her in such a disconcerting way, she would have been tempted to modify her first unfavorable judgment of him.

After dinner, the gentlemen went upstairs to change their boots and breeches for evening dress. Nina, too, excused herself with a regretful sigh.

"I do so wish I could stay downstairs for the party," she told Melanie in a whisper. "But I hope you have a lovely time, Mellie. You must come by my bedroom afterward and tell me all about it."

"I will, Kitten," promised Melanie. As Nina left the drawing room with dragging feet, she turned to smile at her mother. "Poor Kitten! I don't blame her for not wanting to miss the fun. The house looks lovely, doesn't it, Mama? I think it's even prettier than last year."

"Yes, very nice," agreed Mrs. Hartman, looking around the drawing room with placid satisfaction. Beyond it lay another drawing room of equal size. Normally the two were divided by a set of double doors, but on this occasion, the doors had been thrown open so that the two rooms were joined into one. Most of the furniture had been cleared away to make room for dancing, and everywhere were ropes and wreaths of Christmas greenery and the blaze of innumerable candles. In the far drawing room, the fiddler who had been hired to provide music for the occasion was setting up his instrument and music stand in a businesslike manner.

The sight of this individual aroused a twinge of discontent in Melanie's breast. She would have preferred to hire a proper orchestra for the occasion, an orchestra capable of playing the latest quadrilles and waltzes instead of merely old-fashioned country dances. Indeed, she would have preferred to go a step further and transform the party itself into a full-scale ball, with a supper afterward and everything done in the most lavish fashion. It was thus that the Colbys entertained. But she consoled herself by reflecting that though her mother's party might not be up to the standards of Colby Castle, the Colbys had nevertheless signified their intention of attending it. And with Lord Colby as a partner, even a country dance was a thing not to be disdained.

"Oh, I can hardly wait," said Melanie aloud. "Listen, Mama,

I hear the clock striking a quarter to eight. People ought to start arriving any minute."

"Indeed," agreed Mrs. Hartman. "I trust Charles will be down soon. And that young man he brought home with him. What was that young man's name, Melanie? Charles introduced us in such a hurry that I did not catch it. But there, I am very stupid with names anyway, I am afraid."

"His name is McCraig, Mama: William McCraig. It's just like Charles, isn't it, to bring home a perfect stranger on the night we're having a party and expect us to make a fuss over him? And such a stranger, too! A rude Scotchman with no notion of polite behavior."

"Did you think him rude, my dear? He seemed to me to have very nice manners. To be sure, he is not so conversable as he might be, but gentlemen very often are not, you know, particularly when they are not quite at home in their surroundings. Your father was just the same, as I recall. I barely exchanged two words with him the first evening we met, but later, after I had come to know him, I found him quite talkative, I assure you."

Mrs. Hartman looked rather pensive as she made this statement, and at the end of it she drew a deep sigh. Melanie, who was familiar with the signs, knew that her mother's thoughts had reverted once more to the subject of her late husband. It was a subject on which Mrs. Hartman was wont to dwell to the detriment of her spirits. Melanie was therefore very grateful when the drawing room door opened and the gentlemen came into the room.

Both had changed their riding clothes for formal black and white evening dress. Melanie was surprised to see that Mr. McCraig was dressed with quite as much taste and elegance as Charles. Indeed, he looked quite gentlemanly; only his long hair and swarthy face proclaimed his uncivilized origins. Melanie looked him over with grudging approval and decided he must have purchased new clothing while he was visiting in London.

As he and Charles joined her and her mother near the door, she shielded her eyes with pretended alarm. "Such visions of

elegance," she said. "Mama, aren't they dazzling? Miss Madison
will be regretting her M.P. when she sees you two."

Charles bowed solemnly. "You do us too much credit, Mell.
As a matter of fact, you look pretty fine yourself." He critically
surveyed his sister's décolleté evening dress. "Setting up as a
regular dasher, ain't you? That's a pretty dress, Mell. But don't
you think it's a bit on the skimpy side?"

"Temple said it was perfectly proper," said Melanie with dignity. She could not help blushing, however, the more so because
she could feel that Mr. McCraig was also looking at her.
"Wretched man," she told herself indignantly. "Why must he
stare at me so? You'd think he'd never seen an English girl before!"

Charles, meanwhile, had turned to his mother. "You'll do me
the honor of standing up for the first set with me, won't you,
Mama?" he said. "I'm afraid the competition will get too hot
for me if I wait till later on."

Mrs. Hartman tranquilly assented to this proposition. Melanie
was pleased to see that Mr. McCraig had manners enough to
follow his friend's lead and request the second dance of her
mother. Her pleasure turned to dismay at his next words, however.
"And it would give me great pleasure if you would stand up with
me for the first dance, Miss Hartman," he said, looking down at
her gravely once more.

Melanie bit her lip. She would have given anything if she might
have declared herself already engaged to Lord Colby for the first
dance. But since Lord Colby had not taken the precaution of
engaging her for that or any other dance, she could make no such
declaration. It was quite possible that the Colbys would not arrive
until after the dancing had begun, and she would look foolish
sitting out the first dance at her own party.

"Oh, very well," she said shortly. Mr. McCraig silently bowed
his thanks and walked away. There was no very kind feeling in
Melanie's heart as she watched him go. She had not much time
to dwell upon her sense of ill-usage, however, for the first party
of guests had just been ushered into the drawing room by the

butler. Summoning up a hospitable smile, Melanie went forward to greet them along with her mother.

For the next hour she was so busy greeting friends and neighbors that she forgot all about the Scotchman's ill-timed invitation. But it came home to her forcefully when the Colbys made their entrance, a little before nine o'clock.

Lady Colby came in first, with the self-important air that attended all her movements. Behind her came Lord Colby, handsome as Apollo in his blue topcoat and pristine white trousers. Last of all came the Honorable John, the sneer prominent on his loose-hung lips as he looked around the drawing room.

Melanie's heart sank a little at the sight of the Honorable John. She had been hoping against hope that he would not feel it necessary to accompany his mother and brother to the party that evening. But she had taken precautions against such a contingency just the same by carefully noting in advance where all the branches of mistletoe had been hung. She might not be able to avoid him altogether, but she was resolved that this year at least he should have no excuse for kissing her. Of course, if his brother cared to kiss her, that would be quite a different matter! Melanie's lips curved into a smile as she watched Lord Colby advance toward her across the drawing room.

Lady Colby, having been the first to enter, was likewise the first to reach her hostess. "Good evening, ma'am," she said, greeting Mrs. Hartman with a brisk but civil nod. "And good evening to you, too, Miss Hartman. Fine night you've got for your party. I hope I shall have as good fortune for my own party at New Year's. Here's these two sons of mine. Colby, John, you must tell Miss Hartman how pretty she looks. I'd tell her myself, but I'll wager she'd rather hear it from you than an old woman like me."

The Honorable John took Melanie's hand familiarly in his own and murmured something to the effect of "Dashed pretty, Miss H., upon my word." All the while his eyes roved boldly over the exposed portion of Melanie's bosom. Melanie was discomfitted by this greeting and turned with relief to Lord Colby, who had meanwhile been engaged in greeting her mother.

" 'Evening, Melanie," he said, smiling down at her. "Indeed, I think Mama is in the right of it. You look charming tonight, 'pon my word: a regular Incomparable."

"Thank you," said Melanie, curtsying first to his mother and then to him, with a shy smile. "Indeed, I am obliged to you all for your compliments."

Lady Colby returned these thanks with a smiling nod, then turned back to Mrs. Hartman, whom she had been regaling with an account of some difficulties she had been experiencing with the castle staff. The Honorable John had strolled off in the direction of the refreshment room, and Melanie and Lord Colby were left in comparative privacy.

"Upon my word, you do look well tonight," he said again, surveying her with critical approval. "Pity there's nobody but a bunch of provincials to see you. You'd make a regular sensation if you was presented in London, dashed if you wouldn't."

"Thank you, Colby," said Melanie, blushing with pleasure. "It's very kind of you to say so."

"It's the truth, upon my word." Lord Colby glanced toward the far drawing room, where a line of couples were beginning to take their places on the floor. "Ah, I see the dancing's about to start. You'll stand up with me for the first set, of course?"

These words were like a dash of cold water on the glow of Melanie's pleasure. "Oh, Colby, I wish I could," she said in a voice like a wail. "But you see, I am already promised for the first dance. Mr. McCraig asked me earlier, and since he is a guest in our house, of course I could not refuse him."

"Mr. McCraig?" Lord Colby looked around the drawing room with a frown. "Who the devil's that? Never heard of the fellow."

"No, you probably wouldn't have. He's a Scotchman, a friend of Charles from University. Charles met him while he was in London this week and brought him home for the holidays."

"Oh, a Scotchman," said Lord Colby dismissively. "I've no

opinion of Scotchmen. Had a Scotch tutor once, and he was the
stiffest, prosiest fellow you ever saw."

"Then he was nothing like Mr. McCraig! I am sure *he* has the
rudest manners of anyone I've ever met," said Melanie, delighted
to have a chance to vent her feelings on the subject. "And his
appearance is so outlandish, too. He looks a perfect ruffian, not
like a gentleman at all. I declare I would be quite afraid of him
if I met him while I was out walking."

Even as she was speaking, she saw Mr. McCraig's tall figure
moving through the crowd in her direction. Lord Colby saw it,
too, and his brows drew together. "What, you don't mean to say
that's him there?" he exclaimed. "That great overgrown fellow
with the long hair?"

"Yes, he looks a regular wild man, doesn't he? I wish I did
not have to dance with him. But I must, you know. He is Charles's
particular friend, and Charles would never forgive me if I were
rude to him. Indeed, Colby, I would much rather dance the first
dance with you than him. But since I can't, perhaps we could
dance the *second* dance together?"

"Oh, aye, just as you like," said Lord Colby, with a tolerably
good grace. "I daresay I can find somebody else to stand up
with. Hullo! Here's Miss Madison. I wonder if she's engaged for
the first set?" Not waiting for Melanie's reply, he set off across
the drawing room toward Miss Madison, who had just walked
through the door in company with her mother and father.

Melanie watched with swelling heart as Lord Colby and Miss
Madison greeted each other. The wool heiress had made herself
very fine in honor of the Hartmans' party. She was wearing her
famous diamonds, a dress of silver-spangled gauze, and half a
dozen plumes in her jetty curls. The face beneath the plumes was
an uncommonly pretty one, with dimples, rosy cheeks, and merry
dark eyes.

Although Miss Madison's manners might have been criticized
as lacking in refinement, they were equally lacking in pretension
or malice, so it was impossible to dislike her. Melanie felt all

this gloomily as she watched Miss Madison accept with unmistakable pleasure Lord Colby's invitation to dance.

"This will be our dance, will it nae?" said a voice in her ear. Mr. McCraig, unobserved, had reached Melanie's side and was holding out his arm to lead her onto the floor.

At that moment, Melanie felt she almost hated him. If it had not been for him and his unwelcome invitation, she would have been walking out with Lord Colby instead of standing by helplessly as he led out Miss Madison.

"I can't dance right now," she said, turning away from Mr. McCraig coldly. "The Madisons have just arrived, and I must stay and greet them."

"Oh, no, dear, you go on and dance," said Mrs. Hartman, overhearing this speech. "I will greet the Madisons. Charles is still over there in the corner talking to Admiral Spicer, so I imagine it will be a few minutes before he can come to me. He and I will join you in the dancing later on."

Without a word, Melanie took Mr. McCraig's arm and accompanied him onto the dance floor.

She had expected that he would be an awkward dancer, but this did not prove to be the case. He went through the movements of the dance with quiet assurance and was surprisingly light on his feet for such a large man.

"You dance very well, Mr. McCraig," said Melanie, surprised into tribute by his unexpected skill. "You must do a great deal of dancing in Scotland. I beg your pardon, did I get your name wrong?" she asked.

A flicker of surprise had crossed Mr. McCraig's face at the beginning of her address. He started to speak, hesitated, then shook his head. "Nay, the name's McCraig right enough," he said in his low, mellow voice. "You're a cantie dancer yourself, Miss Hartman."

"Thank you," said Melanie. He said nothing more after that, and she said nothing more either, judging that she had done her duty by him in exchanging those few words. She was still feeling resentful toward him for having engaged her for the first dance.

It had not escaped her notice that Lord Colby and Miss Madison seemed to be having a wonderful time together and were quite gay and smiling as they went down the line of dancers.

She felt better when the dance was over. Lord Colby, having returned Miss Madison to her parents, came strolling over to where Melanie and her partner stood on the floor. "Hullo, Melanie. Ready for our dance?" he said, extending his arm to her.

"Oh, yes, thank you, Colby," said Melanie fervently. To Mr. McCraig she gave a nod and a brief, impersonal smile. "I am engaged for the next set and must take leave of you now, sir," she told him. "Thank you very much for the dance."

"Nay, it's I that should be thanking you," he said, with a formal bow. "I hope I will have the pleasure of standing up with you again soon, Miss Hartman."

There was a faint questioning note in his voice which Melanie thought it better to ignore. With another brief smile and nod, she took Lord Colby's arm.

Throughout this exchange, Lord Colby had been studying Mr. McCraig with a derisive smile, as though he were a raree-show put on for his amusement. Now the Scotchman's dark eyes flashed to Lord Colby, and for a moment their gaze met and held. It was Lord Colby who looked away first. With a hint of color in his cheeks, he gave Mr. McCraig a curt nod, drew Melanie's arm further within his own, and led her out onto the floor.

"Insufferable fellow," he said under his breath. "Did you see the way he looked at me back there? By God, I've a mind to thrash him for his insolence."

"Yes, but never mind that, Colby. We are together now, and there are so many things I need to ask you about. I'd rather not waste a minute talking about a half-bred Scotchman."

Lord Colby assented to this, though he still seemed inclined to dwell upon the insult done him. "What sort of things was you needing to ask me about?" he said, frowning as he looked after Mr. McCraig's retreating figure.

"Why, about us, Colby. Have you spoken to your mother yet?"

"Spoken to my mother?" said Lord Colby absently. "Spoken about what?"

Melanie felt herself blush. "About what you were talking about last time we were together, Colby," she prompted timidly. "About—well, about your showing me Italy, you know."

"Oh, that! Lord, yes, that's all settled. Mama means to come and call upon you sometime within the week."

"Oh, Colby, how wonderful! She spoke to me so kindly this evening that I couldn't help hoping, but it is such a relief to know it for a fact."

"Aye, so it is. I'll be glad when the whole business is settled and done with, so that we may be off to Italy. I was thinking that if we have the wedding right after New Year's, we ought to be able to set sail next day and reach Venice within a week or two. That would give us a good month and a half before Lent begins. That's the only bad thing about Italy, y'know. Being a popish country, things pretty much shut down there after Carnival. But it's lively enough up till then, I warrant you!"

"Oh, Colby! You mean we should be married *next month?*"

"Why not?" said Lord Colby, a trifle impatiently. "I mean to say, if I'm willing and you're willing, what's the point of waiting?"

Melanie was silent a moment as she adjusted her ideas. She had taken it for granted that if the tentative agreement between her and Lord Colby ever blossomed into a formal engagement, there would follow at least a couple of months before the wedding would take place. She had been counting upon an interval in which to arrange for her bride clothes and to enjoy the envy and congratulations of the other neighborhood girls.

Now it seemed as though she were to be denied her season of triumph. This was naturally a heavy disappointment to Melanie. And yet, at the same time, she was shocked by the depth of her disappointment. She was marrying Lord Colby because she loved him, not because she wanted to flaunt her position before all the other neighborhood girls, wasn't she? Of course she was, Melanie told herself firmly. And that being the case, she ought to be flattered rather than dismayed by his eagerness to make her his bride.

"You are quite right, Colby," she told him, summoning up a smile. "If we are both willing, of course there is no point in waiting."

"That's the dandy," said Lord Colby approvingly. "I'll be glad to get away from this damned cold weather, I can tell you that. As I said, my mother'll be calling upon you within the week, and once that's over with I can make you an offer in form, all right and tight. Then we'll only have to wait for the settlements to be drawn up before tying the knot and heading off to Italy."

Melanie did not feel equal to replying to this speech and so only smiled and nodded. The dance ended a few minutes later, and once Lord Colby had delivered her back to her mother's side, he strolled off to join his brother in the refreshment room.

Three

Melanie had been greatly agitated by the conversation that had taken place between her and Lord Colby while dancing. It had been a shock to learn that he was wanting to marry her so soon and carry her off to Italy. And though she assured herself over and over that it was a pleasant shock, still she found that it had rendered her unfit for ordinary social intercourse. When one of the neighborhood boys begged the favor of standing up with her for the next set, she put him off with the promise of the set to follow and escaped to the ladies' retiring room on the pretext of pinning up a loose curl.

In the ladies' retiring room, Melanie had hoped to find solitude in which to reflect on Lord Colby's proposition. When she reached her hoped-for refuge, however, she found it already occupied. Miss Madison was there, standing before the glass inspecting her face with an anxious, rather critical air. She turned around as Melanie came in, and her anxious expression gave way to a relieved smile.

"Oh, Miss Hartman, you're just the person I was wanting to see," she exclaimed. "You'll think me very silly, I daresay, but—would you mind giving me your opinion on something? Something rather personal?"

"Why, of course I would not mind, Miss Madison," said Melanie, wondering what possible subject Miss Madison could want her opinion on. "What can I do for you?"

"It's these plumes." Once more Miss Madison surveyed her reflection in the glass. "Do you think they're too much, Miss Hartman? Mama insisted that I wear them, but I can't help seeing that nobody else is half so dressed up."

"Oh." The frankness of Miss Madison's question put Melanie in a quandary. She did in fact feel that the wool heiress was overdressed for a simple evening party and had been uttering some very scathing (though silent) criticisms on the subject while that young lady had been dancing with Lord Colby. But it was difficult to communicate those criticisms now, with Miss Madison's eyes upon her. There was such a disarming blend of hope, trust, and anxiety in those eyes that Melanie could not bear to hurt her feelings.

"I am really no authority, Miss Madison," she hedged with an uneasy smile. "I'm sure you would know better than I, having spent so much time in London."

"But that's just what I don't know, Miss Hartman. London is one thing, and the country another—and indeed, I don't know that I do so very well in London either, if the truth be told. Mama means well, but she has the idea that a girl ought always to be dressed to the nines whenever she shows herself in public. I like pretty things as much as anybody, but I can't help seeing that other girls aren't half as dressed as I am most places we go. James is always teasing me about it—James Attenborough, you know, my fiancé. When he saw me at the Prices' party last week, he told me I looked like a walking jeweler's window."

"Oh, yes, I had heard you were engaged, Miss Madison," said Melanie, happy to turn the conversation to this unexceptionable subject. "Mr. Attenborough is an M.P., is he not? From the county of Kent? They say the country around Kent is very beautiful. I'm sure I wish both of you very happy, Miss Madison."

Miss Madison accepted her wishes with every sign of gratification, but to Melanie's distress she soon reverted to the subject of the plumes. "What do you think honestly, Miss Hartman? I wish you would be frank and tell me just what you think. You always look so elegant and ladylike yourself, and everyone says your mama has the best taste in the county. I'm sure you could advise me better than anyone else, if only you would."

"Oh, dear! Well, if I am to be honest, Miss Madison, then I should say that your plumes are probably better suited to the opera or the Queen's drawing room than to a party like this one. But indeed, I don't mean to criticize. They are perfectly lovely plumes in themselves, and your dress is perfectly lovely, too. I've been admiring it ever since you came in."

Miss Madison laughed. "And I've been admiring *your* dress," she said. "Isn't that a funny thing? But thank you for the compliment, Miss Hartman—and thank you also for your plain speaking. I was pretty sure my poor plumes weren't really the thing at a party like this, and I'm glad to find your opinion's the same as mine. Now I must decide what I'm going to do about it. Ought I to go ahead and take the silly things off, do you think? I'd do it in a minute, only I'm afraid that now everyone's seen me in them, they'd laugh at me more for taking them off than if I continued to wear them."

"Yes, I see what you mean. Perhaps it would be better to brazen it out and wear them for the rest of the evening. Or no—I have an idea!" Melanie clapped her hands and looked at Miss Madison with dancing eyes. "The thing to do is to take them off gradually, Miss Madison. One now, you know, and another a little later, and so on throughout the evening until they are all gone. And if anyone makes any remark about it, you can tell them that you are molting!"

Miss Madison laughed heartily at this idea and vowed to adopt it on the spot. "Molting," she chuckled, as she plucked one of the plumes from her hair. "A molting goose, I'm afraid. For I am a goose, Miss Hartman. I was pretty sure all along I oughtn't to wear these things, but I let Mama talk me into it. Ah, well, after I am married and have a home of my own, I expect I shall go on a great deal better. James has very good taste and always knows exactly what is what. He's such a comfort to me, you can't think, Miss Hartman."

"I am sure he must be, Miss Madison. I wish you had brought him down with you, so that he might have come to our party this evening," said Melanie. She spoke sincerely, for the uncharitable feelings she had been cherishing earlier toward Miss Madison had entirely passed away. Indeed, she found herself feeling something remarkably like friendship for the other girl. The feeling appeared to be mutual, for Miss Madison turned from the glass and laid her hand impulsively on Melanie's arm.

"Oh, Miss Hartman, I do wish you would call me Augusta," she said. "We've been acquainted with each other such a long time, and though I've never known you so well as I would have liked, I have always felt I would like to have you as a friend."

Melanie laid her hand over Miss Madison's and squeezed it warmly. "To be sure I shall call you Augusta, and you must call me Melanie," she said, smiling at the other girl. "It's a pity we waited this long to become friends, isn't it? I'm only just getting to know you, and now I suppose you will be marrying and moving away to Kent."

"Yes, but not until June. And of course I will be back here quite often to visit Mama and Papa. So we may continue to be friends even after I am married—and after you are married, too, I hope. But perhaps you won't care to know me when you are Lady Colby."

Melanie blushed. "Oh, but really, you mustn't say that, Augusta. Nothing is settled yet between me and Lord Colby. And even if it were, I am sure I should never be too proud to be your friend."

Miss Madison looked rather surprised by this speech. It seemed to Melanie that she had been more surprised by the first part of it than by the last. "Not settled yet?" she repeated dubiously. "But Lord Colby was talking about it when we were dancing together just now, and I am sure he spoke as though it were quite a settled thing. He said that the wedding would be after New Year's, and that you were going to Italy for your honeymoon."

"Yes." It was Melanie's turn to sound dubious. She supposed she ought to be pleased that Lord Colby had confided his wedding plans to a third party. At the very least, it would tend to confirm that his intentions were serious. Yet she could not help being a bit offended that he had apparently spoken of those plans as settled before he had even discussed them with her, his bride-to-be! She loved Lord Colby, of course—there could be no doubt about that—but she was still not entirely comfortable with the idea of marrying him in such haste.

"Yes," she said again, with an edge of reserve in her voice. "He spoke of some such plan to me, but it is not completely settled as yet, Augusta. Indeed, he has not even formally proposed to me yet—and I have not formally accepted."

Miss Madison surveyed her with an interest verging upon awe. "But you intend to, don't you? Only think of turning down a nobleman like Lord Colby! But perhaps there's somebody you prefer even to him, Melanie. I couldn't help noticing that terribly handsome gentleman you danced the first dance with."

"Who, Mr. McCraig?" Melanie burst into peals of laughter. "Good heavens, Augusta! I hope I am not such a zany as to prefer *him* to Lord Colby. Do you really think he's handsome?"

"Oh, yes," said Miss Madison with conviction. "He looks exactly like what I've always imagined a corsair must look like."

Melanie's first impulse to this speech, as to Miss Madison's previous one, was laughter. Upon consideration, however, she was obliged to admit the justice of the comparison. There was indeed something rather wild and corsairlike about Mr. McCraig's appearance, though of course he could bear no other resemblance to Lord Byron's romantic hero.

"I suppose Mr. McCraig *does* look a bit like a corsair," admitted Melanie grudgingly. "But he isn't one. His name is William McCraig, and he comes from the wilds of Scotland—the very wildest of the wilds, to judge by his behavior. My brother knew him at Cambridge."

This speech, far from dampening Miss Madison's enthusiasm, seemed rather to intensify it. "Oh, a Highland laird," she said delightedly. "But that's nearly as good as a corsair, isn't it? In fact, I'm not sure it's not better. You must introduce him to me when we go back to the party, Melanie. I would like above anything to talk to a real live Highland laird."

"I don't think Mr. McCraig is a Highland laird, but I'm sure you're welcome to talk to him if you like. You mustn't blame me if you can't make out what he is saying, however. He has a dreadful Scotch accent."

Melanie felt a twinge of conscience as she made this statement, for Mr. McCraig's accent was pleasant rather than otherwise and in no way injurious to the clarity of his speech. But in some obscure way, she found herself resenting her new friend's enthusiasm for the Scotchman. Perhaps it was because it went against her own expressed opinion, or perhaps it was simply because she was tired of his very name by this time. In any event, she hoped this speech would put an end to all discussion on the subject of Mr. William McCraig.

Miss Madison was unwilling to relinquish the subject without a definite promise of an introduction, however. "And so you will introduce us, Melanie?" she asked anxiously. "I do wish you would. Of course I am engaged to James now, but I don't see that that's any reason why I should not talk with attractive gentlemen, or dance with them either, if they ask me. Perhaps Mr. McCraig will ask me to stand up with him if I make myself very agreeable!"

Again, Melanie found herself resenting this speech, though there was certainly no reason why she should have done so. "Very well," she said shortly. "Come along, and I'll introduce you now, Augusta." Having given a perfunctory twitch to her curls in the glass, she turned and led the way out of the retiring room.

The corridor that ran between the retiring room and the drawing room took the ladies past the small parlor where refreshments had been laid out. They had just come up even with the doorway to this room when they became aware that something untoward was taking place within its precincts. Melanie's first intimation of disaster was the sound of two masculine voices raised as though in altercation. One of these voices was high-pitched and nasal, and Melanie recognized it instantly as belonging to the Honorable John. The other voice was deeper and spoke with a noticeable Scotch burr. This voice Melanie also recognized, with a sinking feeling in her heart.

"And what business is it of yours if I *do* say so?" demanded the Honorable John contemptuously. "Your threats don't frighten me, fellow. I said it before, and I'll say it again—"

"You'll not say it again within my hearing, you skellum dog," roared the second voice. There was a yelp of protest from the Honorable John and then a mighty splash, followed by the sound of Lord Colby's voice upraised in furious protest.

"What the hell do you think you're doing, you damned Scotch upstart?"

Melanie waited to hear no more, but pushed open the refreshment room door. As she did so, she nearly collided with the Honorable John, who came rushing out of the room with a face so contorted by anger that he entirely failed to see her and Miss Madison standing there. His hair, his face, and the whole of his neckcloth and shirtfront were dripping wet, and as he passed, the pungent scent of champagne punch came strongly to Melanie's nostrils.

"Oh, my," said Miss Madison, looking after him with avid interest.

Melanie spared him hardly a glance, for her attention had been riveted by the scene she had glimpsed within the refreshment room. Over the nearly empty punch bowl, Mr. McCraig and Lord Colby stood glaring at each other with clenched fists and set jaws.

"You damned Scotch upstart," said Lord Colby again. "I'll see you're called to account for this if it's the last thing I do."

Turning on his heel, he stalked after his brother, brushing past Melanie and Miss Madison without a word, though he could hardly have failed to see them.

Melanie stared after him in dismay, then turned to look at Mr. McCraig. His face wore a look sheepish rather than furious now. Almost he was smiling.

"I'm afraid I've gone and couped the cran now," he said in a humble voice.

Miss Madison laughed. Melanie, however, gave him a look of deepest reproach, then turned and hurried out of the room.

Four

How Melanie got through the rest of that evening, she never knew. It was for her an evening of unparalleled mortification.

Miss Madison, with great good nature, had promised to say nothing of the contretemps she and Melanie had witnessed in the refreshment room. But when the two girls rejoined the party in the drawing room, it was evident that news of it had preceded them there. A few couples were still out on the floor doggedly performing country dances, but most of the guests were gathered in little groups about the room, talking excitedly and casting speculative glances toward the refreshment room door. As Melanie came into the room, her mother hurried over to her with her mild features drawn into a look of concern.

"My dear, there is the most extraordinary story going about," she said. "They say that that young man your brother brought home with him from London—really, I cannot recall his name—"

"Mr. McCraig, Mama."

"Yes, Mr. McCraig. It seems that he and John Colby got into a disagreement in the refreshment room, and that Mr. McCraig put John's head in the punch bowl. Upon my word, I can hardly credit it. I would not have supposed a guest in our house could so far forget himself to do such a thing. And indeed, he seemed like such a polite, well-behaved young gentleman—"

"I am afraid the story is quite true, Mama," said Melanie bitterly. "I was there in the refreshment room when it happened—or immediately after it happened, anyway. And I saw and heard enough to know that it is all true."

"Did you indeed? I wonder what can have possessed Mr. McCraig to behave in such an extraordinary way. Ah, here is Charles. I expect he will be able to tell us all about it."

Charles was threading his way purposefully through the crowd in their direction. He veered off before he reached them, however, and made instead for Lady Colby, who alone of the guests seemed unconscious that anything out of the way was taking place. Drawing the dowager aside, Charles said something to her in a low voice. A look of cold outrage spread across her patrician features. She gave Charles a curt nod, gathered up her skirts, and sailed out of the room without looking to the left or right of her.

There was a grin on Charles's face as he watched her go. When she had passed out of the room, he turned and made his way toward Melanie and Mrs. Hartman.

"Lord, what a dust-up," he said, as he joined them. Melanie noted with resentment that there was open enjoyment in his voice. "I don't expect we'll see *her* back here again in a hurry. Bad-tempered old dragon! You'd think it was me who put her precious son's head in the punch bowl, and not poor old Will."

"But, Charles, I do not understand," said Mrs. Hartman plaintively. "*Why* did your friend put Mr. Colby's head in the punch bowl?"

Charles started to speak and then hesitated, with a sideways look at Melanie. "It was something John said," he said at last, in a repressive voice. "Something about Mellie."

"Something about Melanie? But how very odd, Charles. Do you mean to say John insulted her?"

"Not insulted her, exactly," said Charles, still rather repressively. "Fact of the matter is, he made a—er—personal remark about her that Will thought he shouldn't have."

"That idiotic Scotchman," said Melanie, unable to contain herself any longer. "Do you mean to say he claims to have done it on *my* account? Of all the overbearing, interfering *pests*—"

"Here now, Mell, you've got no call to go criticizing poor old Will. When you come right down to it, it's your fault as much as his. I told you when we came downstairs that that dress was a dashed sight too skimpy in front."

"You said no such thing, Charles! And how dare you say that it was *my* fault that your rude, pestiferous friend—"

"That is quite enough children," said Mrs. Hartman, breaking in upon this argument with calm authority. "It will be better if we say no more about it just at present. The Colbys may be gone, but we still have our other guests to think of, and we must all do our best to try to smooth over this unfortunate incident."

Thanks to Mrs. Hartman's capable management, the incident *was* largely smoothed over. The departing guests took leave of the party with many thanks for the Hartmans' hospitality and only an occasional jest about the Honorable John's discomfiture.

Melanie, however, was still seething when she went up to bed that night. Although she obtained some relief by unburdening herself first to Nina and later to her diary, she continued to feel considerable hostility toward Mr. McCraig.

It was wretchedly inconsiderate of him to have done such a thing at such a time. Indeed, it was the timing of the incident that annoyed her more than anything. Had it happened a few months earlier, Melanie felt she could have overlooked and perhaps even appreciated it. The Honorable John was no favorite of hers, and though the punishment he had received was probably disproportionate to his offense on this occasion, it was likely that he deserved punishment on general grounds anyway.

Melanie never doubted that the punishment was, on this occasion, disproportionate to the offense. For after all, had not Lord Colby also been in the refreshment room when the altercation had taken place? And though Charles was annoyingly vague about the exact nature of the remark the Honorable John had made about her, he had admitted under pressure that it had been addressed to Lord Colby. To Melanie, this was sufficient to assure her that the whole episode had been a misunderstanding. The Honorable John had undoubtedly made some perfectly innocent remark about her which the Scotchman had overheard only in part, and which he had misinterpreted to be insulting to her honor.

Melanie was therefore quite comfortable in her mind in regard to this matter, but she was much less comfortable when she considered the future implications of the episode. It disturbed her that Lord Colby and his mother had left the party that night without saying a word to her or her mother. Surely they did not mean to visit Mr. McCraig's bad behavior on the family of his host? Surely they would not use it as an excuse to break off the relationship that had been developing so nicely between her and Lord Colby?

It was questions such as these that made Melanie feel she could have cheerfully strangled Mr. William McCraig. In the absence of such relief, however, she contented herself with pouring out her vexation in the pages of her diary, and in resolving to avoid him as much as possible during his remaining stay at Hartman Hall.

It was nearly noon before Melanie came downstairs on the day after the party. This was partly because she had spent so much of the morning writing in her diary, and partly because she did not wish to encounter Mr. McCraig at the breakfast table. But her precaution proved superfluous. On the way downstairs, she met her mother coming up and learned from her that both Charles and his guest had gone out hunting for the day.

"We shall have to put back dinner again tonight, I expect," said Mrs. Hartman with a sigh. "I've never yet known Charles to return home from a hunt before five o'clock, unless the foxes refused to draw."

On this occasion, the foxes must have proved recalcitrant indeed. It was barely two o'clock that afternoon when the gentlemen returned to Hartman Hall. The ladies in the drawing room were first alerted to their arrival by the pounding of hooves beneath the window and the sound of Charles's voice calling for his groom.

Melanie, who had been busying herself in a half-hearted way with some needlework, rose and went to the window. Below on the lawn was her brother, just dismounting from his favorite bay hack. Beside him sat Mr. McCraig astride a big black gelding. The gelding's flanks and Mr. McCraig's top boots were generously splashed with mud, but he made an impressive figure nonetheless. Melanie was reminded of Miss Madison's remarks about his resemblance to a corsair. But there was resentment in her heart as she watched him swing himself down from his mud-splattered mount.

As he did so, he must have caught sight of Melanie in the window. He paused a moment, his hand still on the pommel, looking up at her. While he was standing thus, Charles turned and addressed a laughing remark to him. He smiled in return, but his eyes never wavered from Melanie's face. For a moment longer he stood looking up at her, then raised his hat to her with a tentative air.

Melanie felt her face go red. She drew back hastily from the window. "Mama, I think I will walk down to the village," she said rapidly. "There's plenty of time before dinner, and I can buy some more of that red embroidery wool you were wanting."

"Why, that would be very kind of you, my dear. Although, to be sure, I don't suppose I will need it for another few days yet. And since Temple was planning to go to the village tomorrow anyway—"

"I need the exercise," said Melanie, and closed the argument by hurrying out of the drawing room. She was resolved not to endure any more of Mr. McCraig's civilities than she could help that day.

After hastily donning her shawl and bonnet in her room, Melanie slipped down the back stairs, went out through the side door of the house, and set off toward the village. It was a fine day, bright and cloudless but rather chilly, as befitted a day in late December. Melanie walked briskly, not only to stay warm, but to work off the annoyance she felt when she thought over the events of the previous evening.

She was more successful on the first account than on the second. Every time she thought of Mr. McCraig's assault on the Honorable John and its possible consequences to herself, her resentment rose anew. And just when she had succeeded in putting the worst of it behind her and was achieving a more cheerful state of mind, she was aggravated to discover that in her hurry to quit the house she had neglected to bring her reticule, making it impossible to buy the wool which had been her excuse for leaving.

"Oh, for heaven's sake," said Melanie aloud. "If that isn't just the way things have been going lately."

She was almost within sight of the village now. As she stood hesitating, wondering whether to turn back or to continue with her walk even though its object should be in vain, she heard the sound of hoofbeats coming up the lane behind her.

Melanie drew over close to the hedge to let the rider pass. The hoofbeats slowed as they approached her, however, and when she looked around she saw that the horseman was Mr. McCraig. She drew herself even closer against the hedge and turned her face away, hoping that he would not recognize her and feel it necessary to stop. But it seemed that he had and did, for he reined in his horse beside her.

"Good afternoon, Mr. McCraig," said Melanie. Hoping to discourage him, she began to walk toward the village once more, keeping her face turned toward the hedgerow.

Mr. McCraig did not return her greeting. Instead, he swung himself down from the saddle and planted himself squarely in front of her, so that Melanie was forced to stop walking. "I *beg* your pardon," she said frostily, still keeping her face turned toward the hedge.

"Nay, it's I that beg *your* pardon," he said, in a voice so humble that Melanie was surprised into looking at him directly. "You must be thinking me an unco' fool for the way I behaved last night. In trowth, I'm verra sorry, Miss Hartman," he said, looking down at her with a penitent expression.

"Oh, that's all right," said Melanie, with a frigid smile. "Think nothing of it, Mr. McCraig." Having given him another chilly smile by way of absolution, she would have walked on, but he continued to bar the way.

"I hope you can find it in your heart to forgive me," he said, sounding if possible even more humble than before. "I don't usually conduct myself like such a menseless fool, but what with one thing and another—well, an impulsive temper's been my besetting sin, ever since I was a lad. Last night was an aberration on my part—a verra great aberration."

His Scotch burr was so strongly in evidence during these last few words as to prolong them several syllables beyond their natural length. It sounded so quaint to Melanie's ears that she could not help smiling. Mr. McCraig saw her mouth curve upward, and an answering smile at once broke forth upon his own lips.

"Come, that's muckle better," he said approvingly. "You may laugh at me all you like, only say you'll forgive me, Miss Hartman. Will you forgive me, though I did spoil your party?"

He looked and sounded so exceedingly penitent as he made this petition that Melanie was quite unable to maintain her resentment. Indeed, she was hard put to keep from laughing. There was something almost ludicrous about a man so large and formidable-looking begging pardon for his sins like an errant schoolboy.

"And after all, his sins were not such very serious ones," reasoned Melanie to herself. "He was wrong in his actions, to be sure, but it must be a point in his favor that those actions were performed in a lady's defense, upon a gentleman who eminently deserved them. The Honorable John really is the most odious little toad. And I must not be forgetting that Mr. McCraig is a Scotchman. I've always heard that the Scotch tend to be rather puritanical in their morals. And of course everyone knows how hot-tempered they are!"

Looking at the situation from this lenient point of view, Melanie was able to absolve Mr. McCraig of any intentional wrongdoing. She was sure that the Honorable John would never have said anything really indecent about her with his brother standing by, but it was quite possible that he had made some remark subject to an immoral interpretation. In that case, it could be no wonder that Mr. McCraig had reacted to it so fiercely. And though it was certainly inconvenient that he had done so on this particular occasion, Melanie had begun to take a more hopeful view of the situation. Lord Colby had undoubtedly been offended by the injury done his brother under her roof, but it was unlikely that his resentment would be long-lasting, or that he would be so unreasonable as to visit it upon her personally.

Having reached this comfortable conclusion, Melanie laughed aloud and held out her hand to Mr. McCraig. "Yes, of course I forgive you," she told him. "You needn't apologize any more, Mr. McCraig. I have rather an impulsive temper myself, as it happens, and I can readily understand how it was."

Mr. McCraig smiled again and took the proffered hand. Melanie, looking up at him, observed for the first time that he had rather an attractive smile. It lighted up his deep-set eyes and did a great deal to soften the harsh lines of his face. "Nay, I canna allow that you share any of my faults, Miss Hartman," he said. "If you can forgive me for the brulzie I caused last night, there's nae doubt but you must be an angel incarnate."

"Hardly that, I'm afraid," said Melanie, smiling back at him. He continued to look down at her, grasping her hand in his. The warmth of his expression made Melanie vaguely uncomfortable. Without analyzing the matter very much, she saw that he was inclined to admire her, and it seemed to her that she ought to say some word to prevent his admiration from becoming inconveniently great. With a little laugh, she gently withdrew her hand from his.

"I forgive you most readily, Mr. McCraig, but I'm afraid that the Colbys' resentment is likely to be more long-lasting," she said. "I only hope you will not receive a visit from Mr. Colby's second this morning, seeking satisfaction for his injuries."

Mr. McCraig's smile at once vanished. "I'll give him any satisfaction he likes, the clarty carle," he said darkly. "Begging your pardon, Miss Hartman, but when I heard him going on about you in such a way—well, it was more than any decent man could stand, I trow. Satisfaction—aye, I'll give him satisfaction! I'll give him his kale through the reek, that's what I'll do."

Melanie was not exactly sure what this expression signified, but it sounded violent and even improper. "Yes, but I am sure there must have been some misunderstanding, Mr. McCraig," she said, drawing herself up the least little bit. "I am sure Mr. Colby could not have said anything about me that was as offensive as all that. His brother was with him, you know." Melanie cast down her eyes as she made this last statement. In a prim voice, she continued, "Perhaps you did not know it, but Lord Colby is a friend of mine, Mr. McCraig. A very *close* friend. And so, you see, if his brother said anything improper about me, it would be his job to reprimand him and not yours."

She just glanced at Mr. McCraig as she spoke. There was a singular expression on his face, compounded of doubt, disbelief, and some emotion Melanie could not identify. All he said, however, was "Nae doubt," and then folded his lips together grimly as though determined to say no more.

The silence that followed made Melanie feel very uncomfortable. Not knowing what else to do, she began to walk on toward the village once more. Mr. McCraig at once fell into step beside her, leading his horse by the reins. In an effort to relieve a silence that she felt was becoming oppressive, Melanie spoke again, lightly.

"You must not be getting an exaggerated opinion of my virtues, Mr. McCraig. Charles is always saying I am the most henwitted creature alive, and I begin to think he is right. I came into the village this afternoon on purpose to buy some wool for Mama, and now that I'm almost there, I find I have forgotten to bring any money with me! And Mrs. Loomis, who owns the shop, is very stiff about giving credit. I will be ashamed to look Mama in the face when I return empty-handed."

The grim expression on Mr. McCraig's face relaxed a little at this speech. "Ah, but there's no need to disappoint your mother, Miss Hartman," he said. "I've my own purse with me. You're full welcome to draw upon it for aught you like."

"You are very good, Mr. McCraig, but I really cannot take your money, you know."

"You're verra welcome to it, I assure you, Miss Hartman. Indeed, you might say I owe it to you and your mother by way of reparation. I doubtna I must have wasted near a gallon of your mother's good punch in washing Mr. Colby's face for him last night!"

Melanie laughed. "Indeed, I don't expect you to make reparation for that, Mr. McCraig," she said. "That matter is all forgiven and forgotten. But since you insist on making me free of your purse, I tell you what I shall do. If you will *loan* me the money for the wools, I will repay you from my own purse as soon as we get home."

Mr. McCraig shook his head with dissatisfaction over this proposition, but consented to it in the end. "I doubtna you drive a hard bargain, Miss Hartman," he grumbled, taking her arm companionably in his. "But if you canna do better, I suppose I must abide by your terms."

It was only a few minutes later that they turned from the lane into the village high street. Melanie entered the small shop where Mrs. Hartman commonly purchased her wools, while Mr. McCraig delayed a moment outside to tether his horse to the railing. He joined her at the counter a few minutes later, looking singularly out of place among the rolls of lace and ribbons and other feminine fripperies. Melanie purchased the necessary wools, admired a new shipment of Indian muslins that had just arrived that day, and then left the shop, bidding the proprietress a civil good day.

"You are very good, Mr. McCraig," she told him, as they began to retrace their steps homeward. "Charles always complains if he has to wait five minutes while I buy a reel of thread. You may have an impulsive temper, as you say, but your patience is exemplary!"

He smiled and drew her arm within his once more. "Well, I dinna just ken about that," he said. "It's a new turn to find myself amang ladies' nicknackets, but I can see well enough the subject would stand a closer study. You'll hardly believe me, Miss Hartman, but until today I was ignorant as to the difference between a mulled muslin and a tamboured one. Now if you'll be good enough to enlighten me as to what distinguishes the twa of them from a jaconet, I'll be much obliged to you."

Melanie laughed and set about enlightening him. They were passing once more along the lane, whose hedgerows were beginning to cast long shadows across the surrounding ditches and pastures as the sun sank in the west. Looking ahead of her, Melanie saw a small party of people on foot coming down the lane toward her and Mr. McCraig. As they drew nearer, she saw that they were half a dozen countrymen and women, hobbling along slowly in the direction of the village. All of them were old, most of them seemed to have some infirmity or other, and by their dress they appeared to be extremely poor.

"Good day, miss. Good day, sir," said the foremost of the group, a wizened old woman who addressed Melanie and Mr. McCraig with an ingratiating smile. "Have you aught to give of alms this eve? We've come a-Thomasing."

"Oh, it is St. Thomas's Day, isn't it?" exclaimed Melanie. To Mr. McCraig, who was surveying the group with a dubious eye, she explained in a low voice, "It's the custom around here that on St. Thomas's Day, the poor in the parish go about collecting provisions for Christmas." Turning back to the old woman, she said regretfully, "I'm afraid I haven't any money with me, ma'am. But if you apply at Hartman Hall, my brother's house, I am sure he will give you something for your Christmas dinner."

The old woman nodded, but it was obvious from her expression that she thought Melanie's words a mere put-off. She answered civilly enough, however, "Ah, 'tis no matter, miss. A merry Christmas to you and the gentleman all the same."

"Merry Christmas," said Melanie wistfully. As the group of Thomasers drew their ragged garments about them and prepared to pass on, Mr. McCraig took the elderly spokeswoman aside and said some words to her. He spoke too low for Melanie to hear, but she saw his hand go to his pocket and caught the gleam of gold as he laid something in the woman's hand.

"God bless you, sir! And a very merry Christmas to you and your good lady," said the woman, her face wreathed in smiles. "Tom, give 'em a bit of that holly there, won't you?"

With a palsied hand, the old man so addressed took two sprigs of holly from a basket he was carrying and presented them solemnly to Melanie and Mr. McCraig. Melanie accepted hers with an embarrassed smile and watched as he and the others started off down the lane. As the last of the group was passing, however, an ancient woman whose white hair lay in wisps across an otherwise bald pate and whose eyes were clouded by cataract, Melanie reached out impulsively and caught her by the arm.

"Here, ma'am, you need this more than I," she said, pulling off her shawl and wrapping it around the woman's frail shoulders. "Merry Christmas," she added awkwardly, as the woman stood stroking the rich cashmere with wondering fingers.

"Ah, 'tis wondrous fine! Wondrous fine indeed. I'm much obliged to you, miss," said the woman in a quavering voice. She flashed a blind, toothless smile in Melanie's direction, then hobbled off down the lane after her companions.

After they had gone, Melanie and Mr. McCraig continued on their way in silence. Melanie was feeling rather embarrassed about her recent impulsive act and cast one or two glances at her companion as she walked, but it was impossible to tell from his face what he was thinking.

"You must be thinking me very foolish, Mr. McCraig," she said at last. "As you can see, you're not the only one with an impulsive temper! But I did hate to let them go without giving them anything at all, especially after you had been so generous."

"Foolish? Nay, I dinna think you foolish. That was a kind thing you did back there, Miss Hartman. I doubt many girls would be so generous. But I'm afraid you'll feel the lack of your mantle before we reach home."

"Oh, no," said Melanie, valiantly repressing a shiver. The next moment she found herself swathed in a blue broadcloth riding coat which, being suited to its owner's proportions rather than her own, covered her as thoroughly as a full-length pelisse would have done, though with rather less of *à la modality*.

"You must take my coat, Miss Hartman. It wouldna do for you to take a chill on the way home."

"I'm not cold," protested Melanie, attempting to remove the coat from her shoulders. "And I'm sure you're as likely to take a chill as I am, going about without your coat, Mr. McCraig. There's no reason why you should suffer, when I was the one who was so foolish as to give away my shawl."

"Ah, but I willna suffer from such a trifle as that, Miss Hartman. I can do without my coat verra well for the bit walk to your brother's place."

"So can I," said Melanie, pulling off the coat and holding it out to him with a determined air.

Mr. McCraig eyed her and it for a moment, and apparently reached the conclusion that a change of strategy was necessary. When he spoke again, it was in a grieved voice, such as a parent might use in addressing a stubborn or unruly child.

"Ah, well, Miss Hartman, I ken well enough you don't care to take favors from me. After what happened last night, I suppose I canna blame you—"

Melanie assured him with energy that she held him no grudge for his actions of the previous evening. "Then you must prove it by taking my coat," he said triumphantly. "Wrap yourself in it well, Miss Hartman, and I'll put you up on my Ajax here. If you ride and I walk, we can reach your home all the sooner, and I willna feel the cold a bit."

"Oh, but I can't allow you to do that, Mr. McCraig! It's bad

enough that I should deprive you of your coat without taking
your horse, too.”

"Didna you hear me, lass? I'll stay a deal warmer walking
than I would on horseback. And you needna fear for your safety,
for my Ajax will carry you as doucely as a lamb. 'Twill be a
welcome relief for him, poor beast, after the load he's used to
carrying."

Melanie alternately laughed and protested for some minutes
more, but in the end she found herself wrapped in Mr. McCraig's
coat and perched precariously crosswise atop Ajax's saddle. Ajax
turned to regard her with an air of mild surprise, as though wondering at the spectacle she presented.

"You may well stare, sir," she told him with a smile. "I'm sure
I look perfectly ridiculous, but you see I hadn't much choice in
the matter. And to think people talk of the Scotch being stingy,"
she went on, smiling down at Mr. McCraig. "From what I've
seen, I'd say you're the most generous man I know, Mr. McCraig.
Just this afternoon alone you've insisted on loaning me sixpence,
your coat, and your horse, and I know you gave that old woman
back there at least a sovereign."

Mr. McCraig looked embarrassed at being taxed with his good
deeds, but he soon recovered himself. "Ah, there's no denying
the Scotch can be a bit close with their money," he said, with a
shake of his head. "If you want to see a stingy Scotchman, Miss
Hartman, you ought to make the acquaintance of my Uncle Jock.
He's so close that a ha'penny candle lasts him near a twelve-
month, and he swears he hasn't got the good out of a soup bone
until he's used it at least twa or three times!"

Melanie laughed. "Your uncle sounds like quite a character,
Mr. McCraig," she said. "Almost I would be tempted to say a
fictional character!"

"Och, nay, he's real enough, Miss Hartman," said Mr.
McCraig, resuming the hurt expression he had used earlier to
such great effect. "Ask anyone around Aberdeen if you dinna
believe me. There's none to match Jock McCraig when it comes
to squeezing a shilling's worth out of every penny."

In support of this statement, Mr. McCraig went on to relate sundry other incidents of his uncle's stinginess. Melanie suspected most of them of being apocryphal, but she could not help being entertained by them all the same. Beneath his stern and sober exterior, Mr. McCraig appeared to possess a lively sense of humor and could recount the most outrageous incidents with a solemnity that reduced her to giggles.

"And then there'll be the time my uncle thought of marrying," said Mr. McCraig, embarking with relish upon yet another story. They were almost to the gates of Hartman Hall by this time. Melanie was astonished to see how quickly the journey had gone. "Jock'd been a bachelor for near three score years, but there was a widow lately moved to the neighborhood who'd greatly taken his fancy," continued Mr. McCraig. "A handsome woman she was, no mair than just middle-aged, with a fine dark head of hair. It was rumored that she'd been left verra well off by her late husband. I willna say that was the reason my uncle was so taken with the idea of marrying her, but I willna say it wasna, either. At all events, he decided to try his luck with the widow, and one fine evening he got himself up to go a-courting. I was staying with him at the time, you ken, and I saw him off in fine style, wearing his one auld coat that'd been brushed within an inch of its life and a shine to his boots that would've put Brummel to shame.

"Well, he hadna been gone but a few minutes when there came a knock at the door. I went to answer it and found it was Jock himself, in a great taking. 'Why, Jock, what's the matter?' I asked. 'Didna she want to hear you, man?'

" 'I didna see her,' he replied. 'When I got there, I went oop t' the door, intending to knock, as ye may suppose. But it happened that the curtains wasna yet drawn for the night, and I happened to catch a glimpse inside the parlor as I was standing upon the stoop. And what d'ye think I saw?' " Mr. McCraig lowered his voice to a sepulchral whisper, in imitation of his uncle's tone.

" 'A fire burning in the parlor, Will, m'boy. A fire, and never a soul in the room at the time!'

" 'But that's nae so shocking a thing, Jock,' said I. 'She'll maybe have been expecting company.'

" 'Well, and what if she was?' he retorted. 'Time enough to be lighting fires when her company got there. 'Tis extravagance, Will, that's what it is—and I'll be having none o' it.' And from that time on, Jock made up his mind to remain a bachelor, and a bachelor he's been ever since!"

Melanie laughed at this story as at the others, but her laughter died abruptly a few seconds later. A curricle had just come into view at the far end of the lane and was coming toward them at a spanking pace.

Melanie looked toward it with painful anxiety. The horses were a familiar team of match bays, and a moment later she was able to recognize Lord Colby's elegant figure on the box. But instead of feeling delighted by the appearance of her beloved, as she usually was, Melanie felt only the deepest chagrin.

A sense of the improprieties of her situation swept over her with damning force. Here she was with the acknowledged enemy of the Colby family, wearing his coat, mounted on his horse, and laughing at his jokes! What would Lord Colby think, to see her on such seemingly intimate terms with Mr. McCraig? Was it possible that he might *not* see her? Ajax was almost into the drive now, and dusk was falling fast around them. Melanie began to pray frantically that some miracle might occur—a temporary blindness on Lord Colby's part, perhaps—which would prevent him from seeing her with Mr. McCraig and save her from making explanations which, under the circumstances, could only sound lame.

All Melanie's prayers were in vain, however, or perhaps they only came too late. It was obvious that Lord Colby had already seen her. His curricle slowed as he came up beside her and Mr. McCraig, and he lifted his hat with a smile, preparing to greet her. Then he caught sight of her companion, and the smile on his face changed to a look of astonishment. He looked from her to Mr. McCraig and back again, and his expression hardened into one of distaste. He gave a terse nod to each of them, whipped up his horses, and drove on without saying a word.

Five

After Lord Colby had driven off, Melanie's feelings were in such a state of turmoil that she was unable to speak another word the rest of the way home. Mr. McCraig, too, seemed to have been affected by the encounter. He was silent and thoughtful as they went up the drive together, and when he helped her dismount from Ajax at Hartman Hall's front entrance, his manner was noticeably more formal than it had been earlier. Melanie thanked him coldly for the loan of his horse and coat, promised to send one of the servants to his room that evening with the sixpence she owed him, and lost no time in repairing to the house.

In her room, she was able to give way to the feelings of vexation that she had been holding in check ever since her meeting with Lord Colby. It seemed to her that fate had been extraordinarily unkind to allow of such a meeting. If only she and Mr. McCraig had reached the gates five minutes earlier! Lord Colby never would have seen them then, and the whole foolish misunderstanding might have been avoided. For misunderstanding it was, Melanie felt grimly certain. She could not forget Lord Colby's expression as he had looked from her to Mr. McCraig. It was obvious that he was disgusted to find her on such intimate terms with the Scotchman. What if he had been so disgusted that he decided she was unworthy of the honor of being Lady Colby?

This idea made all Melanie's old resentment of Mr. McCraig rise to the fore again. If it had not been for him, there never would have been any misunderstanding between her and Lord Colby in the first place, and she would not be sitting here now, wondering miserably whether her longed-for proposal would ever come to pass. Taking out her diary, Melanie proceeded to pour out an impassioned account of this latest blow to her hopes. She concluded by renewing her resolution to avoid Mr. McCraig's company in the days ahead. If by some miracle Lord Colby was willing to overlook her indiscretion that afternoon, she was determined that he should have no grounds to reproach her for similar indiscretions in the future.

She was just putting away her diary when Nina came into the room.

"Why, you're not dressed yet, Mellie," said Nina, stopping short and regarding her with surprise. "I thought I heard you come upstairs half an hour ago. Did you just get back from the village?"

"No, I've been back for some time, Kitten. But I've been so busy up here I haven't had a chance to dress for dinner yet. Heavens, I'm going to be late, aren't I? Would you be an angel and get out my blue muslin for me?"

Nina went obediently to the wardrobe. While she was getting out her sister's dinner dress, Melanie stripped off her walking dress, splashed a little water on her face, and dragged a comb hastily through her curls.

"Here, I can do the buttons for you," said Nina, as Melanie struggled with the fasteners on her dress. Melanie gratefully abandoned her struggle and stood still as her sister quickly did up the row of buttons down her back.

"Now my slippers, and I'll be all ready. Gracious, what a vexatious day. I wonder what will happen next."

"Has it been a vexatious day for you? It's been very quiet here, except we had some people from the village come Thomasing a little earlier."

"Did you?" Melanie bent down to put on her slippers. In a slightly muffled voice, she added, "There must be more Thomasers than usual out this year. Mr. McCraig and I saw some, too, when we were on our way back from the village." Having tied the ribbons of her slippers with a jerk, she stood up again. "There, I'm all done. If we hurry, I think we can just make it downstairs by the time the bell rings."

Nina kept pace beside Melanie as she hurried out of her bedroom and down the hall. "I had forgotten it was St. Thomas's Day until the Thomasers came by. Do you know, Mellie, Rebecca says that if you sleep with an onion under your pillow on St. Thomas's Day, you'll dream of your future husband?"

"That sounds just the sort of silly thing Rebecca *would* say," said Melanie, briskly descending the staircase. "You ought to know better than to take your ideas from the maidservants, Kitten. How in the world would an onion be able to tell you whom you're going to marry?"

"Oh, but it's not the onion that tells you. The thing is, you see, that just before you go to bed you peel a layer off the onion and say a prayer to St. Thomas—"

"Which sounds even sillier than the other. We're not papists like Bridget, to go making our prayers to saints!"

"Bridget says Catholics don't make their prayers *to* saints," said Nina seriously. "They just ask the saints to pass on their prayers to God. It's rather like asking somebody who's close to a very important person to use their influence with that person to obtain a favor. I must say, it sounded rather sensible the way Bridget explained it. She says there's even something in the Bible about it."

Melanie was not sufficiently well versed in Biblical lore to be able to refute these arguments with any certainty. She contented herself with saying, in a faintly sneering voice, "I suppose Bridget plans to sleep with an onion under her pillow tonight, too?"

"No, she thought it sounded too much like witchcraft. She's the only one of the maids who isn't going to. But she said she would copy out a prayer to St. Thomas for me if I wanted to try it. Don't you think it sounds like fun, Mellie? I don't see that there would be any harm in it really, do you?"

Nina's voice was wistful as she asked this question. The two girls had reached the bottom of the stairs by this time and were approaching the drawing room door. "Oh, I don't see that there's any *harm* in it," said Melanie, pausing to consider the idea. "But

I should think you would know better than to put your faith in a piece of superstitious foolishness, Kitten."

"Oh, I know it is foolishness," said Nina eagerly. "And of course I would not really put my faith in it. But I did think it sounded rather fun. Don't you think it sounds like fun, too, Mellie? Wouldn't you like to try it with me? We could easily get some onions from Cook."

"Oh, I don't think I care to try it for myself, Kitten. You go ahead and do it without me," said Melanie, in a voice of studied amusement.

Inwardly, however, Melanie had already resolved to obtain an onion and see what St. Thomas might have to show her that night. Of course she knew perfectly well that there was nothing in it. Lord Colby would propose to her or not, exactly as he chose, and an onion under her pillow could not possibly influence his decision either way. But if she dreamed of him that night, it would seem to be some confirmation of her hopes, and with things in their present state of uncertainty, Melanie felt her hopes could use all the reassurance they could get.

Mrs. Hartman, Charles, and Mr. McCraig were already in the drawing room when she and Nina came in. Melanie was aware that Mr. McCraig looked up quickly at their entrance, but she would not allow herself to meet his eyes. Even when he came over to take her arm and lead her into dinner, she refused to look at him. And when they were seated at the table, she continued to steadfastly avoid his gaze and to respond as dampeningly as possible to his conversational overtures.

"May I help you to some mutton, Miss Hartman? It's a verra fine joint, upon my word. My Uncle Jock would call it a sair extravagance. He never buys any but the scrag end himself, you ken, and then only as a special treat at Christmastide!"

"Thank you, no mutton," said Melanie, resolutely keeping her eyes on her plate. Mr. McCraig persevered, however, even in the face of this palpable discouragement.

"You must tell me something of your Christmas customs hereabouts, Miss Hartman. You ken that in Scotland we dinna make so much of the day as you Southrons do."

"I wouldn't know about that," said Melanie, continuing to keep her eyes on her plate. "In any case, if you want to learn more about the local customs, you should consult our housekeeper, Mrs. Lowry. She can tell you a great deal more about them than I could."

This was an ungracious speech, and Melanie knew it. Even with her eyes on her plate, she could tell that Mr. McCraig had been hurt by it. Nina and her mother were both regarding her with surprise, and Charles's face wore a look of downright disapproval. Melanie continued to keep her eyes on her plate, however. She felt guilty about snubbing Mr. McCraig's friendly overtures, but she was determined to put their relations back on a formal footing. It had been a great mistake to ever admit him to a more intimate one. He was a very pleasant man in his way, and she had enjoyed talking to him that afternoon; but she could not allow all her matrimonial hopes to be destroyed by a mistaken soft-heartedness for a stranger.

Mrs. Hartman managed to smooth over the awkwardness of the moment by asking Mr. McCraig a question about the holiday customs of Scotland. He responded willingly with descriptions of Hogmanay, black bun, and first footings, but he did not address any more remarks to Melanie. Melanie told herself that this was as it should be, but still she could not free herself from a niggling sense of guilt as she listened to Mr. McCraig's low, pleasantly burred voice describe his country's holiday customs. She was glad when dinner was over and she was able to escape to the drawing room with her mother and sister.

Nina, although allowed to dine with her elders on informal occasions, was never permitted to stay long in the drawing room after dinner. Soon after the tea tray was brought in, Mrs. Hartman dismissed her with a kiss and a gentle "Good night." Once Nina was gone she then turned to Melanie.

"My dear, I did not like to hear you speak so rudely to Mr. McCraig at dinner," she said sternly. "He is a guest in our house, you know. We would owe him our best courtesy for that reason alone, even if our own sense of decency did not prompt us to it."

It had been a long time since Mrs. Hartman had addressed her elder daughter in this style. Melanie had the uncomfortable feeling that she was back in the schoolroom, being scolded for some girlish piece of misconduct.

"I'm sorry, Mama," she said with downcast eyes. "I did not mean to be rude to him. But indeed, after the way he behaved last night—"

"No matter how he behaved, it would be no excuse for rudeness on your part now," said Mrs. Hartman firmly. "Certainly that was an awkward business at the party last night, and I could wish he had settled his quarrel with Mr. Colby in some other manner. But it does seem as though he had strong provocation. You must know that he came to me this morning and told me the whole story, begging pardon for his part in the affair very properly. After that, you know, we could hardly hold it against him—"

"Perhaps *we* couldn't, but *I* could," said Melanie in a rebellious undertone.

"I beg your pardon, my dear?"

"Nothing, Mama. I believe I have a touch of the headache this evening. May I go upstairs now?"

"Certainly, my dear, if you do not feel equal to behaving with ordinary propriety," said Mrs. Hartman. Her voice was as calm and matter-of-fact as it had been throughout the conversation, but Melanie left the room feeling as though she had received a scolding of unusual severity.

She had just reached the top of the stairs when Nina popped out from behind the banister railing.

"Oh, there you are, Mellie! I didn't expect you for hours and hours yet. Look, I got us some onions for tonight." Nina held out her hand to disclose a couple of these homely objects. "You will try it with me, won't you, Mellie?"

"Oh, very well," said Melanie, who was in a mood to be grateful for kindness in any form. "What is it I'm supposed to do again?"

"Just before you go to bed, peel a layer off the onion, and then say a prayer to St. Thomas. Then put the onion under your pillow and go to sleep. Here's a copy of the prayer Bridget gave me." Nina put a slip of paper into her sister's hand along with one of the onions. "I wrote one out for you, too, just in case you wanted to try it."

"Thank you, Kitten. If I must do it at bedtime, I expect I'll be doing it soon, for I was planning to go to bed early tonight. I feel as though I've got a headache coming on."

Nina followed Melanie into her room and seated herself at the foot of the bed while her sister began to make her preparations for the night. "Do you want me to ring for Rebecca?" she asked, as Melanie began to struggle once more with the buttons on her dress.

"No, if you'll help me with these buttons as you did earlier, I'll put myself to bed. I don't feel in the mood to listen to Rebecca's chatter tonight."

Melanie spoke thus in hopes of discouraging her sister from talking, but Nina did not appear to take the hint. "Yes, Rebecca does talk a lot," she agreed, as she began to unbutton her sister's dress. "Bridget is much better, *I* think, but I know you don't care for her."

"I like Bridget perfectly well, just not so much as you do, Kitten. I'll admit that for an Irish girl she is very intelligent and capable."

"Yes, she is, and I feel so sorry for her, Mellie. Most of the other maids won't have anything to do with her because she's Irish and a Roman Catholic. It seems funny, doesn't it, that Ireland should be part of the kingdom and yet a foreign country! Just like Scotland. I expect Mr. McCraig runs into people now and then who don't like him simply because he's Scottish, don't you think?"

"Yes . . . yes, I expect so," said Melanie, in whom this idea aroused some uncomfortable reflections. Pushing them aside, she went on with asperity. "But in Mr. McCraig's case, it's more likely the way he behaves that prejudices people against him, rather than the fact that he's Scottish."

"You don't like him, do you?" Nina looked at her sister curiously. "Why not, Mellie? He seems very nice to me."

Melanie gave an exasperated sigh. "Do you have to ask why not?" she said. "After the way he behaved last night, I should think it was perfectly obvious."

Nina giggled. "It *was* rather shocking of him to put the Honorable John's head in the punch bowl, wasn't it? But I don't know that I like him any the worse for that. And I don't see why you should, either, Mellie. After all, you're the one who's always calling the Honorable John an odious little toad, and you were mad enough to spit last year when he kissed you at the Christmas party."

"Yes, but—oh, well, there's no use talking about it." Melanie turned away from her sister and began to pull her dress over her head. "All I can say is that it was inexcusably rude of Mr. McCraig to behave as he did last night, and I'm afraid it will be a long time before I can forgive him for it. Would you mind going to your own room now, Kitten? I really do have a wretched headache coming on."

Nina headed obediently for the door. "Don't forget your onion," she reminded her sister.

"I won't, Kitten. Good night, and sweet dreams." Melanie gave her sister a meaningful smile.

"Sweet dreams to you, too," said Nina, with an understanding grin. She saluted her sister with a flourish of her onion as she went out the door.

When she was gone, Melanie did not go immediately to bed. Instead, she went to her desk and got out her diary. She spent a considerable time recording the evening's events in meticulous detail.

"At Nina's urging, I am going to sleep with an onion beneath my pillow tonight," she wrote. "This is a charm which the maids believe will induce one to dream of one's future husband. Of course it is nonsense, but Nina would be disappointed if I did not try. I shall record the results of this experiment tomorrow morning, assuming there are any."

This seemed just the proper, lighthearted note to end on, but as Melanie was putting away her diary, she caught sight of the prayer her sister had given her lying on the blotter of her desk. Picking it up, she read through it pensively After a moment's thought, she reopened her diary and wrote, "Resolved: that I shall be kinder to Bridget in the future." And having recorded this resolution, she put away her writing materials, picked up the paper and onion, and went to bed.

Six

In the end, Melanie decided against using the prayer Nina had given her. She was uncomfortable with the idea of using a serious set prayer for such a purpose and even more uncomfortable about using one that had been intended for Roman Catholics. On the whole she felt she would prefer to address St. Thomas in her own words, so as to mitigate any possible sacrilege. So after she had peeled a layer of skin from the onion, she bowed her head and whispered, "Dear St. Thomas, if it isn't asking wrong, please send me a vision of my future husband tonight. And if you can, please make it a vision of Lord Colby. And if it's wrong or improper of me to be asking any of this, then please just forget the whole thing. Amen."

Melanie felt very foolish as she halted out this petition. She was glad there was no one else about to hear her. Bowing her head again, she quickly rattled off her usual nighttime prayers, then thrust the onion under her pillow, jumped into bed, and pulled the covers up to her chin.

Once in bed, however, she found sleep was a long time coming to her. In part this might have been due to the unusually early hour at which she had retired. But more likely it had something to do with the strong smell of onion that assaulted her nostrils as soon as she had lain down. Still, this proved only a temporary irritation, for after half an hour or so she became more or less inured to the odor. A worse irritation was the discomfort of sleeping with a hard, round object beneath her pillow. Nina in her enthusiasm had selected fine, large onions that did not accommodate themselves to being slept on, and Melanie tossed and turned for a considerable time before drifting at last into a shallow, troubled sleep.

When morning dawned, Melanie awoke with smarting eyes, a stiff neck, and a bad temper. Her first act on arising was to take the onion from beneath her pillow and hurl it into her bedroom fireplace. Since no fire was burning there at the time, this gesture was largely symbolic, but at least it served to relieve her feelings somewhat. Her hair, her nightdress, her bed linens, her whole room, in fact: all seemed to be permeated with the scent of onions.

"I shall have to wash my hair to get the smell out," said Melanie, crossly reaching for the bell rope. "Bother St. Thomas's onion!" While she waited for the maid to arrive in answer to her ring, she went to her desk, got out her diary, and wrote savagely, "December 22, 7:00 A.M. It was all nonsense, just as I thought."

She felt a little better after this, and better still after she had bathed and washed her hair and the maids had made up her bed with fresh linens. As she sat in front of the fire, drying her hair and drinking her morning chocolate, Nina came bouncing into the room.

"Good morning, Mellie! Did you dream about your future husband last night?"

These words revived Melanies sense of grievance. "No, I did not," she said crossly, setting down her chocolate cup with a rattle. "In fact, I hardly slept at all with that wretched onion under my pillow. And when I did finally fall asleep, the only thing I could dream about was Mr. McCraig putting the Honorable John's head in the punch bowl. And I hope I am not to marry the Honorable John!"

Melanie paused. She thought Nina was looking at her rather

oddly, but all her sister said was, "No, I should hope not indeed, Mellie!"

"But I don't mean to blame you, Kitten," said Melanie, in a milder voice. "It was a fun idea, only there must be easier ways of telling one's fortune than sleeping on onions. Did *you* dream of anybody in particular last night?"

Nina nodded. "Yes, I dreamed about Giles. I thought I would," she added matter-of-factly.

Giles was Giles Meredith, the eldest son of a neighboring squire. He and Nina had been friends since infancy, and for nearly as long had been declaring to all and sundry their intention of marrying each other when they grew up. Melanie had often been amused by her sister's perfect assurance in this childish betrothal, but now she felt a twinge of envy. At the moment, her own hopes of betrothal did not seem half so assured.

"So St. Thomas predicts that you and Giles will marry, does he?" said Melanie, with a rather false gaiety. "I cannot say I think much of his acumen. Why, we have all of us known these twelve years that the two of you were destined for the altar!"

"Yes," said Nina, accepting her sister's jest as a simple statement of fact. "Giles means to formally ask Charles for my hand as soon as he turns eighteen. We settled it all the last time he was down from Eton."

"Gracious, I had no idea it was as settled as that! I'm sure I wish you very happy, Kitten."

Nina accepted her congratulations with a becoming gravity and then left the room, leaving Melanie with the depressed feeling that her fourteen-year-old sister was likely to be settled in life sooner than she was.

It was nearly noon before Melanie's hair was dry enough for her to venture downstairs. She consoled herself with the reflection that though she would have preferred not to wash her hair that morning, the necessity of doing so had at least saved her from meeting with Mr. McCraig at the breakfast table. And since

Charles had spoken of taking his friend out hunting again that day, there was every possibility that she would not see him again until dinnertime. After partaking of a light luncheon of fruit, cheese, and cold meat in the breakfast room with her mother and sister, Melanie went to the library to continue her study of Italy, which had been rather neglected during the excitement of the past two days.

She soon found she was in no mood for serious study, however. Memorizing long lists of irregular verbs had seemed a worthwhile labor when she had felt a reasonable prospect of going to Italy, but now, when that prospect seemed to be growing daily more remote, she could not apply herself to her labor with the same enthusiasm. After twenty minutes' struggle, Melanie put aside her Italian grammar and took up *Childe Harold's Pilgrimage,* salving her conscience with the reflection that though not itself Italian, it did at least deal largely with the subject of Italy. She was just reading over Lord Byron's well-known stanzas on Venice when Mr. McCraig walked into the library.

"I thought you were out hunting with Charles!" was Melanie's first, involuntary exclamation. Realizing belatedly how rude it sounded, she tried to soften her words. "Is it possible you are not so enthusiastic a sportsman as Charles, Mr. McCraig? You must know my brother never comes home this early from a meet unless absolutely obliged to, by reasons beyond his control. A broken leg, for instance, or the foxes refusing to draw, as they did yesterday!"

Mr. McCraig smiled a little at this, but the grave expression her first words had produced remained in his eyes as he replied, "Nay, we found foxes aplenty today, and I didna damage my leg. It's Ajax's legs that have me fashed, as it happens. He took a bit of a stumble over a fence yesterday, and I didna think it well to press him too hard today."

"I can quite understand your prudence, Mr. McCraig. It would be a shame to damage a lovely horse like your Ajax. But could not Charles loan you a mount, so you could continue your day's sport?"

"Aye, your brother offered me one of his animals, but I didna like to take it. I'd had enough of sport today for myself, and I wouldna do anything to spoil his, you ken. So I just excused myself after the first twa fields and came back early. But I'm afraid I'm spoiling sport just the same, Miss Hartman. I didna mean to intrude on your studies. I just came in to get something to read—"

Melanie protested at the idea of his intruding, as in duty bound. "No, you're not disturbing me, Mr. McCraig. I was studying earlier, but now I'm just reading. Can I help you find a book? The novels are on those shelves over there. Or there's some sporting papers in the corner cabinet if you prefer."

Mr. McCraig did not show much interest in novels or sporting papers. Instead, he remained standing beside the table where Melanie was working. "What are you reading, Miss Hartman?" he asked, looking curiously at her book.

"Poetry, Mr. McCraig," said Melanie, rather shortly. She had no desire to discuss her own reading with him; she wished only to help him find a book and go. The resolution she had made earlier was still strong in her mind, and she was determined that he should not linger in the library on her account. Yet linger he did, looking down at her with an expression that was noticeably wistful.

"Miss Hartman, have I done aught else to offend you?" he ventured at last, in a humble voice. "Or is it that you're still fashed with me over the dust-up the other night? Whatever it is, I hope you'll tell me and give me a chance to make it right, if I can. It pains me to be at outs with you."

Melanie knew she ought to make a cool reply to this speech, but she could not bring herself to do it. Mr. McCraig was looking so extremely unhappy that in spite of her resolution, she found herself softening toward him. She did of course still rue the incident of the punch bowl and probably always would; but she had told him he was forgiven for it, and her mother was quite right in saying that it would be wrong for her to cherish a grudge against him on that account. Still more would it be wrong to

cherish a grudge against him for his behavior the previous afternoon. Although she might regret that Lord Colby had seen her
in Mr. McCraig's company, she could scarcely hold Mr. McCraig
responsible for Lord Colby's mistaken conclusions. He had
merely been being friendly. It was inexcusable for her not to be
friendly in return. After all, he would undoubtedly be leaving
Hartman Hall within the next week or two. Once he was gone,
Lord Colby would see that there had been nothing between her
and Mr. McCraig after all, and the whole misunderstanding
would probably straighten itself out quite painlessly.

Having reached this conclusion in the space of a few seconds'
cogitation, Melanie smiled and shook her head. "Indeed, no, Mr.
McCraig," she said. "You must not apologize again, for it is I
who was at fault this time. I was dreadfully cross and stupid at
dinner last night, I'm afraid, but it had nothing to do with you.
Indeed, I have been reproaching myself for it ever since," she
added, with some truth.

The warm, engaging smile that she remembered from the day
before spread across Mr. McCraig's face. He took her hand between his own in a grip that was almost painful.

"Nay, you've nothing to reproach yourself for, Miss Hartman," he said. "I ken well enough it must try you sairly to have
such a great, blundering gowk as I am about the house. The fact
is that I'm not much used to being in ladies' company, and I
dinna always just ken when I'm putting my foot in it. If you'd be
so good as to drop a word in my lug when I do something amiss,
I'll be much obliged to you."

"Indeed, I would not presume to do such a thing, Mr. McCraig.
Your behavior has been very much better than mine—except
perhaps for your behavior toward Mr. Colby the other night!"

This teasing reference to his earlier offense seemed to set Mr.
McCraig entirely at his ease. "Ah, well, if I dinna do anything
worse than that in the time I'm here, I'll be doing well, I trow,"
he said, dropping down into the chair next to Melanie's and folding his hands comfortably across his knee. "You've a bieldy

place here for your reading, Miss Hartman. I hope you dinna mind if I join you in it?"

"No, not at all. As I said before, I'm not doing any serious studying, just reading some poetry."

"Aye, I remember your brother saying at school you were a great one for poetry. What poet is it you're reading?"

"Byron," said Melanie, showing him the book's cover. *"Childe Harold's Pilgrimage."*

He nodded, but she noted that there was a faint curl to his lip as he regarded the book. "Byron, is it? Ah, I should have guessed as muckle. The young ladies in London are all mad for his lordship's verse, they say, and in the country it'll be the same, I trow."

He spoke humorously, but to Melanie's ears there was a definite note of disparagement in his voice. For a moment she felt almost inclined to apologize for her choice of literature. But that was ridiculous, of course. There was no reason why she need justify herself to a simple Scotchman who had probably never even read one of Byron's poems.

"Yes, I enjoy Lord Byron's poetry very much," she said, putting up her chin. And I cannot imagine anyone reading it and failing to be impressed by it. But of course, tastes do vary in these matters. I suppose you prefer Burns's poetry yourself, Mr. McCraig?"

Melanie intended this question as a jab, but its force appeared lost on Mr. McCraig. He considered her words gravely a moment, then nodded. "Aye, given a choice between the twa, I'd take Burns every time."

"As a Scotchman, you would naturally say so!"

"Ah, but you're forgetting Byron was half a Scotchman, too, Miss Hartman. He spent all his early life there and only went to England when he came into the title."

Melanie *had* forgotten this fact and was obliged to pause a moment to reconsider her position. "Yes, but Byron doesn't write in the dialect as Burns does," was the objection she produced at last. "Indeed, I think that is the reason I have never been able to admire Burns's poems. I have no doubt they seem very fine to you, Mr. McCraig, but I personally find it off-putting to have to stop every line or two to puzzle out some word or expression that might as well be Greek for all I can make of it. It's as bad as those tiresome novels where the characters talk French half the time and I have to keep my French lexicon beside me to make out what they're saying!"

Mr. McCraig let out a low, rumbling chuckle. "Ah, I can see how that might put you off, Miss Hartman," he said, with a shake of his head. "But still I think that if you made a fair trial of it, you'd come to agree that Burns was the better poet. Byron has his points, I dinna deny it, but to me most of his work seems blow and bluster. Not that Burns was without his faults—"

"His faults are pretty well known, to be sure," said Melanie, with a significant arch of her eyebrows.

"I wasna talking about the faults of his private life," said Mr. McCraig mildly. "He wasna what you could call a moral man, to be sure, but for all that I dinna think he was any worse sinner than your Lord Byron. Indeed, it might be held he was a lesser one, for from aught I've been given to understand, Burns's sins were at least natural ones."

Melanie, not being exactly sure what was meant by this statement, thought it better to let it pass without remark. "In any event, I fail to see how you can consider Burns the greater poet," she said, taking up the book in front of her. "Listen to this, for instance," and she read aloud several stanzas from *Childe Harold.* "You cannot—indeed, you cannot deny the beauty of that, Mr. McCraig!"

Mr. McCraig did not deny it, but took the book from her hand, flipped over a couple of pages, and proceeded to read aloud one or two stanzas that Melanie could not but own were rather inferior. "I dinna deny the fellow has a talent for rhyming, but he takes himself a deal too seriously for my taste. It's my contention that a man's worth nothing wha canna laugh at himself. In Burns's poetry—his best poetry, you ken—there's humor, and color, and expression, all such as poor Byron canna hope to match. You wouldna have a book of Burns's verse in your library by chance, would you, Miss Hartman?"

Melanie, by now quite interested in the matter, made a search of the shelves and at length turned up a dusty volume of Burns's verse. She and Mr. McCraig then settled down to argue the cause of their favorites with great enthusiasm. Melanie read aloud her favorite passages from Byron, while Mr. McCraig countered with passages of Burns. He read with so much ease and expression and showed such a thorough familiarity with the work of both poets as to rather astonish Melanie, who from his appearance would never have supposed him to be at all bookish.

"I must say, I can appreciate Burns much more now that I've heard *you* read him, Mr. McCraig," she owned, at the conclusion of a stirring reading of "The Holy Fair." "Perhaps it takes a Scotchman to give Scotch things their proper value. There is certainly a beauty to some of Burns's verse—a rough, wild beauty, to be sure, but a beauty nonetheless. It is rather like the beauty of Scotland itself, I suppose. I have often heard that it is a very picturesque country."

"Aye, that it is, Miss Hartman." Both Burns and Byron were swept aside as Mr. McCraig leaned forward in his chair, his eyes aglow with enthusiasm. "I would that you could see it, Miss Hartman. There's no beauty like it, to my mind."

For the next twenty minutes, the astonished Melanie found herself dragged from lochs deep in trackless forests to the peaks of craggy mountaintops, as Mr. McCraig proceeded to expound upon the beauties of his native land. He did this so well and with so much real eloquence that Melanie could hardly believe he was the same tongue-tied gentleman who had sat across from her at the dinner table two nights before.

"Why, you are a poet yourself, Mr. McCraig," she said, when he had given her a fairly comprehensive description of all that lay between Gretna and John o' Groat's. "I'm sure I wish I *could* see Scotland, if it is all you describe."

"Ah, would you?" A new light suddenly kindled in Mr. McCraig's dark eyes. Before Melanie could grasp his intention, he had reached out and captured her hand between his own. "For my part, I would like nothing better than to show it to you," he said, with great solemnity. "Miss Hartman, I ken well enough I've nae business to be speaking so soon, but I doubtna you've guessed how matters stand with me. I think I lost my heart to you the first minute I laid eyes on you. If you could see your way clear to marrying me, it would make me the happiest man on earth."

"*Marry* you?" Melanie was so astonished she could hardly believe her ears. "You want to marry me, Mr. McCraig?"

"Aye," he said, with a fervor that left no room for doubt. Melanie attempted a little laugh.

"But this is all so sudden! You do have an impulsive temper, don't you, Mr. McCraig?"

He looked at her reproachfully. "As to that, I canna deny it," he said. "But my worst enemy's never called me fickle, Miss Hartman. Ask your brother if it isna so."

The last thing Melanie wanted to do was to bring Charles into the matter. She attempted another laugh. "But you only met me two days ago, Mr. McCraig! You hardly know me. And I hardly know you, either. Indeed, you must see it's impossible."

The grasp on her hand tightened. "Dinna say impossible, Miss Hartman," he begged. "I doubtna you're a bit taken back by my declaring myself so sudden-like, but when you've had a bit of time to consider it, you'll see it's not impossible at all. I've considered it, you ken—trowth, I've been considering it ever since I met you. And from aught I've seen of you, I'm sure I couldna do better for a wife."

"Oh! Well, I'm sure that's very flattering, Mr. McCraig. But really, I don't think—"

"You mustna think I'm expecting an answer immediately, Miss Hartman," said Mr. McCraig, overriding these protests with anxious solicitude. "It's only that I wanted to put my cards on the table, so to speak, just so you'd ken where I stand. I perfectly understand that you wouldna want to enter into an engagement with a man who's scarcely known to you. Your brother can tell you something of my character, but I'm thinking the best way for us to become acquainted would be if you came and visited me at Craigmoor after the holidays. Craigmoor is my family home, you ken, up in the Highlands near Glen Roy."

"I'm sure it's a very nice place, Mr. McCraig, but—"

"Aye, I hope you'll find it so. You may be sure I'll do all in my power to make you comfortable there, Miss Hartman. I willna badger you about marrying me while you're a guest at Craigmoor, you ken: only let you take your time and look about and see if the place might suit you. And then, once you've made up your mind, you can give me your final answer."

"Oh," said Melanie weakly. She knew it behooved her to refuse this proposal without equivocation, but so mesmerizing was the force of Mr. McCraig's personality that she had trouble finding words to do it. "But this is all so sudden, Mr. McCraig," she managed at last, with a shaky laugh. "I don't think you've given full consideration to what you are doing."

"Nay, Miss Hartman, I've considered it verra well, I assure you. The fact of the matter is that once I'd made up my mind, I didna dare dally over the business. Maybe it's not just the convention to propose to young ladies you've only known twa days, but you ken most young ladies aren't as exceptional as you are, Miss Hartman." Mr. McCraig's expression softened as he looked down at Melanie. "I felt that if I waited I might miss my chance altogether, you ken."

"I see," said Melanie. It was really all she could think to say. Mr. McCraig's words, together with the way he was looking at her, seemed to have robbed her of all presence of mind.

He tightened his hold on her hand, and a faint smile broke across his craggy face. "It's the same as you might feel if you saw an especially bonny hat in a shop window, Miss Hartman. You wouldna hang back for weeks before going into the shop and making an offer for it, would you? Nay, for if you did, you might expect to see your friend Miss Smith wearing your hat at kirk the next Sunday. That's how it was with me. I kenned full well it wasna quite the thing to ask you so soon, but I'd rather risk your thinking me daft than miss my chance altogether."

Melanie could not help smiling at this analogy, though she felt obliged to protest its relevance. "Yes, but proposing marriage is a great deal more serious than buying hats, Mr. McCraig!" she said.

"Aye, to be sure it is. I'd expect you to give it at least as much consideration as you would in buying a new muslin!" Mr. McCraig was smiling as he made this statement, but his expression grew serious as he went on. "Indeed, I dinna mean to make you think I'm not in earnest about this business, Miss Hartman. I want to marry you with all my heart. And you mustna be thinking it's only because of your bonny face. You've such a pretty laughing way with you, and such a kind heart, too. I'll never forget how you gave that old woman the shawl off your back when we were out walking yesterday."

"Oh, that! But that was nothing, Mr. McCraig. A foolish impulse on my part."

"Ah, but that only shows how well suited we are to each other. You ken I'm inclined to be just a wee bit impulsive myself." A smile both mischievous and tender touched Mr. McCraig's lips as he looked down at Melanie. "In trowth, I think we might suit verra well, Miss Hartman. You're fond of books and poetry like I am—not the same books and poetry, perhaps, but we've that taste in common, and I've nae doubt we could discover many more if we came to know each other better. Willna you come up and visit me at Craigmoor next month and see for yourself?"

"Oh, but I couldn't, Mr. McCraig," protested Melanie. It took all the strength of will she possessed to make the protest. Mr. McCraig made the idea of visiting him sound so simple and natural—so inevitable, almost—that it seemed irrational to oppose it. "I really couldn't, upon my word," said Melanie again, lamely.

Mr. McCraig shook his head. "Ah, I dinna doubt you misunderstand me, Miss Hartman," he said. "You mustna think I'm asking you to come up to Craigmoor alone. That would look a bit particular, I wis, but if you and your family came up together and made me a visit in the regular way, there wouldna be anything in it to set people's tongues wagging. We needna say a word about marriage or even an engagement until you'd had a chance to think on the idea a bit."

"That's very kind of you, but still I don't think—and of course, Mama would never agree to it." With a sense of relief, Melanie seized on this excuse, knowing it to be both viable and convincing. "Indeed, Mr. McCraig, my mother dislikes travel of all things. And she would think it so very peculiar of you to speak of marrying me on such short acquaintance—"

"I'll talk to your mother," said Mr. McCraig firmly. "It's high time I did that any gate, now I've asked for your hand. She'll want to know how I'm circumstanced and what I would be able to do for you in the way of settlements if you were to accept my suit. I'll talk to her tonight after dinner."

"I really don't think—" began Melanie, and then gave up. Nothing she could say seemed likely to halt Mr. McCraig, who once set in motion appeared to be a well-nigh irresistible force. Already he had risen to his feet and was starting for the door. At her words, however, he came back and took her hand in his once more.

"Dinna fash yourself, Miss Hartman," he said earnestly. "I'll make it all right with your mother, you'll see." Carrying her hand to his lips, he kissed it fervently, then released it and started for the door once more with an air of purposeful determination.

Seven

After Mr. McCraig had left, Melanie remained sitting where she was at the library table. She felt dazed by the interview just past. Who, she asked herself, who could have supposed that Mr. McCraig would have conceived an attachment for her in such a short time? And who could have supposed he would actually propose to her on the strength of it—and propose, too, with so much eloquence and warmth and sincerity? It was impossible not to be flattered by it all.

Flattered Melanie was, and for a considerable time, too. Gradually, however, her feeling of gratified amazement began to fade and was replaced by a very different feeling. While Mr. McCraig had been actually with her, it was as though she had been transfixed by the force of his personality. Now that he was gone, the force had been withdrawn, and she began first to wonder at herself and then to blame herself for having listened to his proposal.

Of course it was impossible that she could ever marry Mr. McCraig. Even if she had been free to accept his offer, she could never marry an odd, half-civilized Scotchman who went around putting people's heads in punch bowls. And the fact was that she was not free to accept his offer. She was as good as engaged to Lord Colby—at least, she hoped she was—and she certainly ought to have told Mr. McCraig about that engagement and put an end to his hopes in no uncertain terms.

The more she thought about it, the more appalled Melanie became by her own behavior. How could she have so far forgotten Lord Colby's claims upon her as to listen to another man's proposal? And not only to listen to it, but to seem to accede to it by her silence? Most dreadful of all was the way she had allowed him to kiss her hand without making the least demur. Melanie gripped the offending hand in her other one and told herself that she was not worthy to be Lord Colby's wife. If he were ever to learn what had taken place that afternoon, he would be perfectly justified in washing his hands of her.

Having reproached herself for her weakness in the past, Melanie began to turn her thoughts toward the future. Obviously she must lose no time in putting down this new threat to her happiness as quickly and decisively as possible. It was Mr. McCraig's intention to speak to her mother that night after dinner. The thing to do would be to speak to her mother first and enlist her help in putting an end to the Scotchman's suit.

Rising swiftly to her feet, Melanie left the library and went down the hall to her mother's room. "Mama," she called, tapping on the door. "Mama, are you there? I need to speak to you."

"Come in, my dear," came her mother's voice. Melanie went in and found her mother in the process of having her hair dressed by the indomitable Temple.

"Why, my dear, you are not dressed yet," said Mrs. Hartman, regarding Melanie with mild concern. "Did you not hear the bell? You will be late for dinner if you don't hurry."

"It doesn't matter, Mama. It won't take me a minute to throw on a different dress. But I really do need to talk to you right away."

Temple looked scandalized by this speech, but Mrs. Hartman nodded. "Very well, my dear. Let Temple finish with my hair, and then we can talk."

After Temple had completed her mistress's coiffure and taken herself off with a disapproving sniff, Melanie sat down on the edge of Mrs. Hartman's bed and delivered herself of a brief but pithy account of all that had taken place between her and Mr. McCraig in the library. "And he wants us to go visit him in Scotland, Mama, after the holidays! Of course I told him it was impossible, but he simply would not listen to me. When he speaks to you this evening, will you please explain it all to him and make him understand I can't possibly marry him?"

"Why, certainly, my dear, if that is what you wish me to do. You *are* a bit young to be thinking of marrying, to be sure. It does not do to be in too much of a hurry about these things. I'm sure I had a dozen beaux when I was your age, but it was not until I met your father that I knew I had found the one I wanted to marry."

"I don't want a dozen beaux," said Melanie, a little nettled by a speech that seemed to imply she was too young to know her own mind. "All I want is one beau, Mama—the *right* beau, that is. Which Mr. McCraig is not! You will tell him, won't you, Mama? You must make him understand that I will not marry him under any circumstances."

This Mrs. Hartman promised to do, and Melanie went to her

room somewhat assuaged in her feelings. She knew that once her mother had committed herself to a course of action, she would follow it through even in the face of the most determined opposition. With luck, the whole unfortunate business of Mr. McCraig's proposal might be nipped in the bud before it could grow to any inconvenient proportions.

Dinner that night was an awkward sort of meal. Melanie had made a point of coming downstairs with her mother and of remaining at her side in the drawing room, so that Mr. McCraig would have no opportunity to address her alone. To do him justice, he made no effort to do this, although Melanie was aware that he looked at her a great deal. But she kept her eyes rigidly downcast as on the previous evening and refused to meet his gaze.

Yet she was very aware of him all the same. He made a striking figure standing there in front of the drawing room fireplace, tall and dark and if not precisely handsome, at least very distinguished-looking in his black and white evening clothes. It gave her a strange feeling to think that this same distinguished-looking gentleman had been figuratively on his knees to her that afternoon, offering her his heart and hand. When he came over to take her arm and lead her into dinner, she could not repress a small, involuntary shiver at the touch of his hand.

Melanie was very annoyed at this demonstration of sensibility on her part. In his absence she was able to demean herself in a perfectly sane, sensible manner. Why could it not be the same in his presence? As soon as they were within the dining room, she drew her arm away from him and seated herself in the chair he held for her with a single brusque word of thanks.

The soup arrived soon after, and Melanie devoted herself to consuming it in silence. Mr. McCraig did the same, and neither Nina nor Mrs. Hartman was much more talkative. Conversation would have languished had it not been for Charles, who had just returned from hunting a short time ago and who was full of indignation about some fancied mismanagement on the part of the huntmaster.

"By God, I've half a mind to take over the job myself and put an end to old Dodgson's blundering. It wouldn't cost me above a hundred a year to have the hounds here, I daresay. Should you mind if I did, Mama?"

"No, certainly not, my dear," said Mrs. Hartman, placidly consuming her soup. "You must do just as you think best."

Charles continued to debate the pros and cons of this issue throughout dinner. He was still debating them when the ladies left the dining room. Melanie was glad of this, reckoning that his volubility would likely detain Mr. McCraig at the table for some time. But she proved out in her reckoning, for she and Mrs. Hartman had scarcely bidden Nina good night and taken their seats in the drawing room when Mr. McCraig came in.

"I wonder, ma'am, if you would be good enough to grant me a few minutes' private conversation?" he said, addressing Mrs. Hartman with a courteous bow.

"Certainly, Mr.—Mr.—"

"McCraig, ma'am."

"Yes, to be sure. I am afraid I am very stupid with names, Mr. McCraig. But I would be happy to give you a few minutes alone." With the utmost placidity, Mrs. Hartman rose to her feet and accepted the arm Mr. McCraig offered her. As he turned away, Melanie made an urgent face at her mother behind his back. Mrs. Hartman acknowledged it with a nod before accompanying the Scotchman out of the room.

Alone in the drawing room, Melanie paced nervously back and forth in front of the fire. She had been at this occupation about ten minutes when Charles came into the room.

"I say, give me a cup of tea, won't you, Mellie?" he said, throwing himself down upon the sofa. As Melanie went to fetch the tea, he raked his fingers through his hair with a heavy frown. "I don't know what's the matter with Will this evening," he complained. "He didn't drink but half a glass of port when we was at the table just now. And when I was trying to tell him some of what Dodgson said to me this afternoon, he cut me off with hardly a word and walked out of the room."

Melanie said nothing, but handed Charles his teacup. He drank off its contents in a single gulp and looked around the room. "I say, where is Will?" he said with surprise. "I thought he was coming in here."

"He is with Mama," said Melanie briefly, and resumed her pacing in front of the fireplace. She had completed half a dozen more passes when the drawing room door opened and Mrs. Hartman came in. Her color was rather high, and she was fanning herself with unwonted energy. Melanie immediately left off her pacing and flew to her mother's side.

"Did you tell him, Mama?" she said eagerly.

"Tell him what?" said Charles, regarding them both with an uncomprehending frown.

Mrs. Hartman sank down on the sofa beside him and rearranged the shawl over her shoulders before replying. It seemed to take her a very long time to do this to her satisfaction. "Well, to be sure, my dear, I did *try* to tell him," she said, stealing a guilty look at her daughter. "But he is a most determined young man, I find—really very determined indeed. And then, he seemed so set on the notion of our visiting him. I could see it would hurt his feelings very much if I refused, and of course I could not like to do that. There could be no harm in all of us going to Scotland for a *short* visit, you know. He quite understands that there could be no question of an engagement on such short acquaintance."

"Mama! You did not agree that we should go *visit* him? After all I said?"

Mrs. Hartman's guilty expression became more pronounced. "Well, yes, I believe I did agree, my dear," she said, plucking nervously at her shawl. "Upon my word, I hardly know how it was. As I said, he is a most determined young man—he was so insistent on returning our hospitality that I felt I could hardly say no. It would not be until after the holidays, of course. Sometime about the middle of January, I told him it would probably be."

Melanie was so exasperated that she could have stamped her foot. Mingled with her exasperation, however, was a kind of grudging admiration for Mr. McCraig. It was difficult to pry Mrs. Hartman away from her own fireside at any time and nearly impossible during the winter months. To persuade her to undertake a journey to Scotland in January was no inconsiderable feat.

"Well, you and Nina and Charles may go to Scotland if you like, Mama," said Melanie, speaking through tight lips. "All I can say is that *I'm* not going."

"But that would be very awkward, my dear. It is you he wishes to marry, after all."

"Mama, I thought I made it clear to you when I spoke with you before dinner. I cannot marry that wild Scotchman!"

Charles had been listening to this exchange in dumfounded silence. Now he looked at his sister in sudden suspicion. "What wild Scotchman are you talking about, Mell?"

"What wild Scotchman do you think? Your friend Mr. McCraig, to be sure! He has actually asked me to marry him, if you can credit it."

"No, has he? What's in that to make you hysterical? I'd say myself he could do a deal better than marry a ninnyhammer like you, but that's his lookout, not mine."

Melanie's temper was already running high, and this provoking address made it boil over altogether. "Upon my word, Charles, you are very obliging! I suppose you think I should accept his offer? It's kind of you, but I think I could do better than marry a rude, half-bred Scotchman who probably lives in a hovel with dirt floors—"

"Oh, I would not call him rude, my dear," protested Mrs. Hartman from the sofa. "His manners are not polished, to be sure, but when I spoke with him earlier he expressed himself very properly and seemed to feel just as he ought."

"To me, he seems very rude. And I cannot possibly marry him. Lord Colby—" Melanie brought herself up short. She had not intended to bring Lord Colby's name into the argument while her engagement to him remained unofficial, but having gone this far she felt obliged to continue. "You must know that Lord Colby intends to offer for me, Mama," she went on resolutely. "I did not like to say anything before it is quite settled, but he told me the other night at the party that he has spoken to his mother about it and believes she will give her consent."

"You surprise me, my dear," said Mrs. Hartman, looking as though this was no exaggeration. "You and Lord Colby to marry! I did not realize matters had gone so far as that between you."

"Yes, they have," said Melanie. With a defiant look at her brother, she added, "So you see why I cannot possibly marry Mr. McCraig, Charles. I think even you must admit that Colby Castle would be a more agreeable residence than a Scottish hovel with dirt floors!"

Charles was looking grim. "It beats me how you can be such a fool, Mellie," he said. "Craigmoor may not be a castle like your friend Colby's place, but it's nothing to sneer at. I'd trade it for this place straight across and think I'd done well out of the bargain. And when you talk of Will being rude and half-bred— well, I suppose it all depends on your point of view. His title may not be as high as Colby's, but it's a deal older—aye, and a deal more respectably come by, too, if it comes to that. Everybody knows the first Lord Colby only got the title because he wasn't particular about sharing his wife with his king—"

"Charles, really," protested Mrs. Hartman faintly from the sofa.

Melanie overlooked this provocative statement, for her attention had been captured by Charles's earlier one. "Title?" she said. "What are you talking about, Charles? You don't mean Mr. McCraig has a title, do you?"

"Aye, to be sure he does," said Charles impatiently. "He's Sir William McCraig of Craigmoor—a baronet, y'know. I told you so when I introduced you."

"You did not, Charles! You introduced him as 'my friend Will McCraig, from University'! And I have been calling him Mr. McCraig for the past two days, and he has never once corrected me."

"Well, maybe I did neglect to mention it," said Charles, look-ing a little conscious. "But that just shows you the difference between him and your friends at the castle. Not *everybody* feels it's necessary to go around boasting about their position. But there, it's nothing to me who you marry. From what I can see, you and Colby ought to do very well together."

The tone of this statement was not agreeable to Melanie, but she let it pass. Her brother's revelation had come as a shock to her, and although the knowledge that her suitor was a wealthy Sir William rather than an impoverished Mr. McCraig did not in the least sway her determination to refuse him, she was conscious that she had been unjust in the way she had spoken of him earlier.

"Indeed, Charles, I should not have spoken as I did of your friend," she said, in a milder tone. "He is a very pleasant gentle-man in his own way, I will admit. But you must see that I can't possibly marry him, Charles. Our tastes—our backgrounds—our educations have all been so different. I doubt we have two ideas in common."

"Aye, there's no question about that. Will was Senior Wrangler at University, after all. It's doubtful he'd have much in common with a girl who couldn't stick out two terms at Miss Pearson's Academy for Young Ladies!"

"You know I left Miss Pearson's because the situation was unhealthy, Charles. If I had stayed, I am sure I would have ended up with perpetual catarrh like the other girls. But do you mean to say that Mr. McCraig—Sir William, I mean—was Senior Wrangler at Cambridge?"

"Aye, and that's no easy title to come by, I can tell you that. Especially for a Scotchman. A couple of the dons were pretty sore to see the prize go to him, but he was so far and away above the other candidates that they couldn't in conscience give it to anybody else."

"Indeed, I thought he seemed quite an intelligent, well-spoken young gentleman," observed Mrs. Hartman with mild pleasure. "And you say he is actually a baronet, Charles? That is very gratifying. Sir William will be a much easier name for me to remember than the other."

Melanie said nothing in reply to either of these statements, and Charles pressed ruthlessly on. "Upon my word, Mell, I can't admire your taste in bridegrooms. You may not have much in common with Will, as you say, but it seems to me you'd do better to marry him than a fellow who got thrown out of Oxford after half a term for—I'd better not say for what," said Charles, with a glance at his mother. "Will's twice the man Colby is: a very decent fellow and tolerably well blunted, too, if he isn't a lord. But being a lord ain't everything, you know. At least if you took Will, you wouldn't have to wait for him to get his mama's permission to have the banns posted. However, it's your decision, and you must do as you please."

Melanie was in truth profoundly shaken by her brother's words, but there was no enduring such a gibe as this. "Yes, that's just what I intend to do, Charles," she said, raising her chin defiantly. "And I would appreciate it if you would tell your friend that it is quite impossible that I visit him in Scotland. I intend to marry Lord Colby, or no one."

"Aye, I'll tell him," said Charles grimly, and put an end to the interview by stalking out of the drawing room.

Eight

Melanie never knew exactly what Charles told his friend that evening, but his words must have been effective. In the days that followed, Sir William made no repetition of his offer of marriage, and the subject of the Hartmans' visit to Scotland was quietly allowed to drop. Melanie felt she should be grateful that the matter had been settled so quickly and definitively. In actual fact, however, she felt not grateful but guilty, especially when she was in Sir William's company. Although he did not reproach her in any way, he treated her with a grave courtesy that seemed worse than a reproach to Melanie's guilty conscience, and she had also to endure the rather less courteous behavior of Charles, who clearly still resented the slight she had dealt his friend and showed it by treating her with an air of stiff disapproval.

Mrs. Hartman, less partial than her son, continued to treat Melanie exactly as she had previous to Sir William's proposal. This was a relief to Melanie, who would sooner have endured twenty open snubs from her brother than a single look of reproach from her mother. But though Mrs. Hartman did not reproach her daughter either by look or word, her behavior toward Sir William was so much warmer than it had been before that Melanie felt this in itself to be a kind of reproach. If it had not been for Nina, she felt she would have had no sympathizer in the house at all. Nina was very ready to sympathize, but when the situation had been explained to her, she annoyed her sister very much by dividing her sympathies between the two principals of the drama.

"Imagine how badly Sir William must feel if he really cares for you, Mellie," she said solemnly. "Indeed, it must be very difficult for him, knowing you are to marry someone else."

"Not half so difficult as it is for me! And I don't suppose he cares a fig about me," said Melanie crossly. She felt a pang of conscience as she spoke, for she could not forget the way Sir William had looked at her that day in the library. But it made her more uncomfortable still to suppose his emotion had been sincere. "How could he care for me, when he had only known me for two days? I expect he had been drinking," she scoffed, driven by some perverse impulse to belittle her erstwhile suitor.

"Yes, perhaps that was it," agreed Nina, whereupon Melanie felt a contrary urge to deny that it had been any such thing. She fought down the urge, however, as her sister went on thoughtfully. "But I must say, Mellie, I have never seen any sign that Sir William habitually drinks to excess. Indeed, I do not think he does. If he was drunk the day he proposed to you, I daresay he is very ashamed of himself now and wants only to forget the whole thing."

These words, too, irritated Melanie, although she was unable to put her finger on the precise reason why. "You may be sure that *I* shall not remind him," she said curtly, and left her sister's room in a bad temper.

Christmas Eve was another occasion of strain. As in years past, the Hartmans celebrated the day quietly at home with an elaborate dinner in the evening followed by games in the drawing room. The dinner of roast beef, turkey, and mince pie was as good as it ever was, but Melanie could not enjoy it as she had in previous years. She had even less enjoyment in the rubber of whist that followed the dinner. Mr. McCraig deferred to her with the same air of grave courtesy she had found so trying during the past few days, while Charles, her partner, treated her with icy civility when he was not warmly reviling her lack of skill. Mrs. Hartman was her usual placid self, but she persisted in yawning over her cards in a way that was rather off-putting. Even Nina, who had prattled quite cheerfully during dinner, became silent and abstracted as she sat by the fireside, watching the others at their play.

The servants in the servants' hall below seemed to be having a much better time at their own Christmas Eve celebration, to judge by the sounds of revelry that came drifting up from below. Melanie, as she sat poring miserably over her cards, felt she would much rather have been taking part in the festivities below stairs. Her only consolation was the immense basket of flowers and hothouse fruit that stood upon the low table in front of the sofa and had been delivered to her earlier that evening along with Lord Colby's card.

It ought to have been a great consolation. Here was proof, if proof were needed, that Lord Colby still intended to offer for her. He would hardly have sent her so munificent a gift if he had intended to break off their relationship. Melanie felt it to be so and was thus unable to explain the lack of enthusiasm with which she received this token of her intended's continuing regard.

Perhaps it was Charles's scathing criticism of Lord Colby, which continued to linger in her thoughts even after she had resolved to banish it from mind. Or perhaps it was the fact that Lord Colby had included no personal message with his gift.

Melanie had searched the basket carefully to see if he had perhaps tucked a *billet-doux* among the fruit and flowers, but the only written matter contained therein was his card, on which he had not even bothered to score out the engraved name.

Melanie supposed she was being unreasonable to have expected anything more. She told herself she was being unreasonable, but still she felt disappointed, and it was an effort to behave with a decent pretense of Yuletide cheer throughout the evening's interminable dinner and still more interminable card game. Melanie was glad when both were over and she could go upstairs to bed.

She was awakened the next morning by the distant sound of the village church bells ringing out their Christmas peal. Arising from her bed with a shiver, Melanie observed with surprise that the fire had not been made up and that the water in her washstand was covered with a thin skin of ice. A glance at the clock showed her it was eight o'clock, full time for these tasks to have been attended to. She rang the bell and then wrapped herself in her dressing gown to await the arrival of the maidservants with fuel and hot water.

She waited some ten minutes without receiving any answer to her ring. Growing impatient at last, she rang the bell again, this time in a somewhat peremptory manner. This summons, too, went unanswered. Astonished and irritated, Melanie went to her bedroom door and peeped out into the hallway to see if she could espy any reason for this surprising lack of response.

There were no signs of unusual activity in the hallway. Indeed, Melanie could perceive no activity at all, either above or below stairs. The house seemed as silent as a tomb, and very nearly as cold. Shutting the door again, Melanie went to the washstand, made a hasty and shivering ablution, dressed herself in her warmest stuff gown and knitted shawl, and went downstairs to see what could be taking place.

By this time, she was beginning to feel a vague sense of alarm.

The feeling was intensified when she reached the house's main floor and found that here, too, fires remained unmade and rooms disordered and undusted. It was only when she reached the breakfast room that she found signs of life. A fire was burning in the grate, and there had been some attempt at breakfast laid out upon the sideboard. As Melanie stood regarding with surprise the thick slices of bread and butter that stood in place of the usual silver dishes of bacon and eggs, ham and sirloin, hot rolls, toast, and plum cake, the maidservant Bridget came bustling into the room carrying a steaming tea kettle on a tray.

"Oh, Miss Melanie, thanks be to heaven *you're* well," exclaimed Bridget, setting the tray upon the table. "Your brother came down just a few minutes ago, and I've sent him off for the doctor. Sure, and it's to be hoped he comes back with him soon. I'm that distracted, I don't know if I'm on my head or my heels."

At these words, the vague sense of alarm Melanie had been feeling sharpened into fear. "Charles gone for the doctor?" she repeated. "Who is sick, Bridget? And where are the other servants? I couldn't get anyone to answer my bell."

"Lord bless you, Miss Melanie, there's nobody to answer it but me, and I've had all I can do without answering bells this morning, I can tell you that. Every mortal soul of the staff is down sick except me. It's a wonder I've had time to light the fire in here and make you a bit of breakfast, what with running for basins and towels all morning."

"Good heavens," said Melanie blankly. Bridget, not waiting for any further comment, was already turning to leave the room. "Bridget, wait," said Melanie, rousing herself from her stupor. "Is there anything I can do to help?"

"Sure, and that's very kind of you, Miss Melanie. If you'd just go up and see to your mother and sister, I'd be much obliged to you. They haven't rung yet this morning; but I've no doubt they will soon, and it's better they should know what's going on before they come down. Unless, to be sure, they're sick themselves and *can't* ring. Saints preserve us, wouldn't that be a turn-out!"

Bridget looked appalled by this idea, and Melanie, who found it no less appalling, lost no time running upstairs to her mother's and sister's rooms. She found them both well, however, and just in the act of rising from their beds. Having informed them of what had happened and assisted them with those particulars of their toilette in which they required assistance, Melanie accompanied them downstairs to the breakfast room, where they all sat consuming tea and bread and butter while anxiously awaiting the arrival of Charles and the doctor.

The two arrived not long after. The doctor went immediately to his patients while Charles sat down with his mother and sisters in the breakfast room. They were joined a few minutes later by Sir William, wearing an expression even more grave than that which had been habitual to him of late.

"Aye, I've already heard the ill news, ma'am," he told Mrs. Hartman, when she endeavored to explain what had happened. "I've been with my valet most of the morning, poor carle. When he didna come in answer to the bell, I went to him and found he needed serving a deal worse than I did. He's in a bad way, and my groom isna much better. It seems to be an unco' virulent epidemic."

"No, not so bad as that, my good sir," said the doctor, entering the breakfast room in time to hear Sir William's last words. "I doubt myself that it's an epidemic illness." He accepted a cup of tea from Mrs. Hartman and stood before the fireplace, rocking back and forth on his heels as he drank it. When he had refreshed himself in this manner, he set the cup down upon the mantel and turned to address the others.

"I've seen your servants," he announced. "They're sick enough, but it's my opinion that the culprit in this case is a tainted joint or meat pie rather than a disease *per se.*"

There were surprised murmurs from everyone except Mrs. Hartman, who nodded wisely. "Ah, I daresay it was a meat pie," she said. "My own grandmother was nearly killed once by eating a bad meat pie. Although, to be sure, there were oysters at dinner last night, and it might equally well have been those. I have often heard of people falling ill from eating tainted shellfish."

The doctor shook his head with decision. "No, I think we can rule out shellfish in this case, Mrs. Hartman," he said. "I can't tell you exactly which dish did the damage, but on three points we can be tolerably certain." With a pedantic air that made Melanie want to laugh in spite of the gravity of the situation, he began to tick off these points on his fingers, looking sharply from one to the other of his audience to make sure they all followed his course of logic.

"One, we can be sure that the dish in question was served at last night's dinner," he said, wagging his first finger at them solemnly. "Two, we can be even more sure that it was a dish served only at the servants' table. And three, I would hazard almost any amount you like that the tainted dish was a meat dish, or at least a dish containing meat."

Here he paused, looking around at them all with an air at once suspenseful and triumphant. It was obvious that he was dying to be questioned about his conclusions, and Mrs. Hartman kindly obliged him.

"My, that is very clever, Dr. Bainbridge," she said. "However were you able to deduce all that?"

The doctor beamed and rocked twice or thrice on his heels in an access of gratification. "Ah, we doctors are forced to be detectives sometimes, Mrs. Hartman," he said, wagging his finger at her once more. "But I shall be very happy to explain the process by which I reached the conclusions I did. To begin with, I was fairly sure that the tainted dish was a dish served at dinner last night, simply by taking into consideration the time at which the symptoms began to appear. Food poisoning generally makes itself felt within a few hours after the tainted food is ingested, you know. And I was sure it was a dish served only at the servants' table because none of you appear to be suffering any ill effects." Once more he paused, looking around at them all with the same half-triumphant, half-suspenseful air.

Once more Mrs. Hartman obliged him. "And your third conclusion?" she prompted. "How did you conclude that it was a meat dish that caused the trouble, Doctor?"

"Ah, that was a more subtle point. You observe that the maid-servant Bridget, alone of all the servants, has escaped any symptoms of illness. She is a Roman Catholic, as you may probably know, and upon questioning her, I learned that she had abstained from meat dishes on Christmas Eve as is the custom among those of her religion. Therefore, we can be quite certain that it was a ham, or a meat pie or pudding, or some such thing that was at fault on this occasion. But I have ordered her to make a clean sweep of all the made dishes in the larder, just to be on the safe side. One cannot be too careful in these cases."

"Oh, dear, the Christmas pudding," said Nina, in a voice of distress.

Mrs. Hartman nodded with a melancholy air. "Yes, it is a great pity," she said. "But as Dr. Bainbridge says, one cannot be too careful where serious illness is concerned. Very well, Doctor. I trust all the servants will recover from their ills with proper care?"

"Oh, dear, yes. Indeed, very little care should be necessary. The symptoms are naturally distressing, but in cases such as this, I find it generally answers best to simply stand back and allow Nature to rid herself of the poison by her own—ahem—natural means. In the case of all except possibly your butler, whose great age renders him more vulnerable to illness than the others, I should not imagine the debility will last beyond a single day, or two at the utmost."

A gloomy silence greeted this statement. The doctor looked around at them all rather reprovingly. "Indeed, although it might be thought unfortunate that such a thing should happen at Christmas, in another sense it might be considered almost a blessing. Since the servants' dinner was an unusually festive one last night, there were a greater than usual number of dishes on the table, so that no one dish was indulged in to any great extent. If it had been an ordinary dinner, with the tainted dish served as the *pièce de résistance,* perhaps, their illness would probably have been much more severe. I'll drop by later this afternoon and have another look at them all, but I anticipate no difficulties."

The doctor departed soon after this, having taken his fee and wished them all a cordial Merry Christmas. Since he had brought his own gig with him, it was not necessary for Charles to accompany him out, and that young gentleman remained sitting morosely at the breakfast room table.

"A Merry Christmas," he said with a mirthless laugh. "It ain't likely to be much of a Christmas at all, at this rate. Who the deuce is going to take care of my cattle while all the grooms are out sick? I had to saddle Laertes myself just to ride for the doctor. And Ben and Barnabas need to be exercised if they're not to become as fat as flawns."

"I'll lend you a hand with the nags, Charles," said Sir William, rising to his feet with obliging promptness. "With the twa of us working, I doubtna we can manage the job well enough."

Charles gloomily accepted his friend's offer, and the two of them went out to the stables. They had been gone only a matter of minutes when a knock sounded on the front door.

"I suppose the doctor must have forgotten something," said Mrs. Hartman, getting up and going to the door. When she returned to the breakfast room a moment later, her face wore a dazed expression, and she was bearing in her hand a folded note sealed with a gold and crimson crest.

"What is it, Mama?" asked Nina. Melanie did not speak, but she had a presentiment as to the note's contents. Both she and Nina leaned forward to watch as Mrs. Hartman broke the seal and spread the note on the table to read it.

"Oh, dear," said Mrs. Hartman, and then again a moment later, "Oh, dear, whatever next? Of all the days to choose!"

"What is it, Mama?" asked Nina again. Mrs. Hartman did not answer, but mutely handed the note to her elder daughter. Melanie took it and read it through in silence. As she had expected, it came from Lady Colby. In the stateliest of third person periods, Lady Colby presented her compliments to Mrs. Hartman and her daughter and intimated her intention of calling upon them at four o'clock that afternoon.

This news produced much the same effect upon Melanie as it

had on her mother. "Oh, no," she said, letting the note slide nervelessly from her hand. "Oh, dear!" Nina picked up the note and read through it eagerly as Melanie turned to her mother. "Whatever shall we do, Mama? How shall we receive Lady Colby while the servants are ill?"

Mrs. Hartman shook her head. "It is very vexatious, is it not?" she said. "I suppose we shall have to write and put her off until another day."

"Oh, no! No, we must not put her off." Melanie grasped at this one point with the fervor of a drowning man clutching at a spar. The house might be cold and disordered, the entire staff sick in their beds, but there should be no more put-offs where her engagement to Lord Colby was concerned.

"But, my dear, how can we possibly receive Lady Colby when all the servants are ill?" said Mrs. Hartman, in the same reasonable voice she had used when Melanie was a child and had proposed some impractical course of action. "There will be no one to open the door to her, and no one to serve her tea—"

"I'll open the door to her. I'll serve her tea," said Melanie grimly.

"But what will you serve her, Mellie?" said Nina, looking up from the note. "You can't just give a lady like Lady Colby tea and nothing else. She will expect cakes or sandwiches or something with it. And you know Dr. Bainbridge had Bridget throw out all the made dishes. I expect that includes cakes and things as well as meat dishes, don't you think?"

"I don't know. But it doesn't matter. I'll find something to serve Lady Colby if I have to make it myself," said Melanie, more grimly still. She turned to her mother. "Will you please write to Lady Colby, Mama, and tell her four o'clock this afternoon will do very well?"

"Well . . . yes. Yes, I suppose I must, if you insist on it, my dear. Although I do not see that it is really necessary that I write Lady Colby. In her note to us, you know, she writes only to tell us she is coming, not to ask if it is convenient for us to receive her." Mrs. Hartman cast a disparaging look at the note in Nina's hand. "Then, too, there is no one to carry a note to Lady Colby even if I did write one. Her footman did not wait for an answer, and all ours are sick in bed. Although I suppose Charles or Sir William might be willing to ride over to the castle if we explained the matter to them—"

"No, there's no need for that," said Melanie, with some haste. "As you say, Lady Colby only writes to notify us she is coming. There would be no need to answer her unless for some reason we were unable to receive her."

Mrs. Hartman sighed. "Upon my word, I think we do have reason," she said ruefully. "But if you are set on seeing her today, my dear, I suppose we shall simply have to make the best of it."

"*I* intend to, at least," said Melanie, rising determinedly to her feet. "Now if you'll excuse me, Mama, I must go down to the kitchen and see what I can find to give Lady Colby with her tea."

Nine

Nina trailed after Melanie as she went downstairs to the kitchen.

"We are having quite the day, aren't we?" she said. "First the servants falling ill, and now Lady Colby coming to tea. Is there something I can do to help, Melanie? I could slice bread for bread and butter, if you like. Or I could make some toast, perhaps. I am very good at making toast."

"Thank you, Kitten, but I'll have to see what's in the larder before I decide what to make," said Melanie evasively. She was grateful for her sister's offer of help, but the idea of Lady Colby coming for tea had fired her with ambitions beyond toast or bread and butter. Following this line of thought, she added hopefully, "Surely Bridget cannot have thrown out *everything*."

But an examination of the larder proved that Bridget had been depressingly thorough. She had not thrown out milk, butter, eggs, or cheese, or any of the dry ingredients in the pantry, but she had spared nothing resembling a made dish save the loaf of bread from which she had cut the breakfast bread and butter. Even this was so much diminished in size as to be useless for Melanie's purposes.

"Very well, then," said Melanie, having taken stock of this depressing state of affairs. "I'll just have to make something myself to serve Lady Colby. A cake, I think. At least there's plenty of eggs and butter and flour."

Nina at once volunteered her assistance in this project. "Although I don't know much about making cakes," she added dubiously. "But I daresay there's something I could do to help, if you want me."

"That's very kind of you, Kitten," said Melanie, giving her sister an impetuous hug. "I could certainly use some help, for I'm afraid I don't know much about making cakes, either. But if we can find Cook's receipt book, it ought to be a simple enough matter. All we will have to do is follow the instructions."

She and Nina were searching the kitchen for the receipt book when there was a sound of brisk footsteps in the corridor outside. A moment later Bridget passed by the doorway, headed down the corridor toward the laundry room.

"Oh, there's Bridget," said Nina, hastily descending the steps she had mounted to search the kitchen cupboards. "Perhaps she knows where Mrs. Everett keeps her receipt book."

"Yes, of course," said Melanie, turning eagerly toward the door. "Why, I forgot all about Bridget. I expect she can help us with making the cake, too. Bridget, would you come here for a minute, please?" she called.

There was a moment's pause, and then Bridget reappeared in the kitchen doorway. She was carrying in her arms a basket of dubious-looking linens, and her normally rosy face was wan and weary-looking. "Yes, Miss Melanie?" she said, dropping an abbreviated curtsy.

"Do you know where Mrs. Everett keeps her receipt book, Bridget? Nina and I can't find it."

The maid paused and shifted the basket to her hip as she considered the question. "Sure, and it must be somewhere close about," she said, frowning with concentration. "Over on the dresser, I think. I've an idea I've seen it there when I was in to fetch the breakfast trays."

"Yes, here it is," said Nina, triumphantly pulling the book from the top shelf of the dresser. "Thank you, Bridget."

"Yes, thank you, Bridget," said Melanie. "Nina and I were wanting to make a cake, you see, but since neither of us has ever made one before, we needed a receipt book to tell us how."

"Ah, did you?" said Bridget politely. "Sure, and that'll be a grand treat." She shifted the basket to her other hip and stood waiting patiently to be dismissed.

Melanie knew she must speak now if she wanted to enlist the maidservant's help in her cake-making enterprise. But somehow, when it came to the point, her courage failed her. Bridget looked so utterly weary as she stood there, drooping beneath her unspeakable burden, that Melanie could not find it in her heart to burden her with any more.

"That's all, Bridget," she said. "You may go now." As Bridget shouldered her basket and prepared to go, Melanie added awkwardly, "And perhaps if things have quieted down a bit in the servants' wing, you can lie down for an hour or two. I'm sure you've been on your feet all morning."

Bridget shook her head resolutely. "No, I can't be spared as yet, Miss Melanie. Things have quieted down a bit since this morning, the saints be praised, but there's still a deal to do and nobody but me to do it. I must put these towels to soak in the laundry and get back to the servants' wing before I'm missed." With another abbreviated curtsy, she set off down the hall once more.

After she had gone, Melanie made no remark, but accepted the receipt book from Nina with a rather shamefaced air. Encouraged by the book's title, which promised to make the art of cookery plain and easy, she turned to the pages on cake making.

"Goodness, this doesn't sound so easy, does it? And four hours to bake! I think I had better make little cakes rather than a great one," said Melanie, gazing in dismay at a receipt for this last-named dish.

"Little ones will taste just as good," said Nina consolingly. "And they would look nicer on the tea tray anyway."

"Yes, that's so. Ah, here's a receipt that sound fairly simple—or comparatively so, at any rate. 'Queen cakes.' But oh, dear, it calls for 'half a pound of currants washed and picked.' That sounds very tedious." Melanie flipped through several more pages of the receipt book. "I can't make Bath cakes, because I haven't the time to let them rise—and I'm not exactly sure how to manage all that business about barm and yeast anyway. And if I make ratafia cakes, I'll have to scald and blanch almonds, and that sounds worse than picking currants. Queen cakes it will have to be." Melanie flipped back to the appropriate page of the recipe book. "Here's the recipe. Let's see, I'll need butter and eggs from the larder, a pound of sugar—"

"First you need to start the fire," said Nina knowledgeably. "Cook always lights the fire in the oven before she starts baking."

"Oh, yes, of course." Melanie was annoyed with herself for having forgotten this obvious first step. "Yes, I'll light the fire right now. But first I'd better put on an apron, so I don't spoil my dress. Here, Kitten, you'd better have one, too. We look very professional, don't we?" She laughed as she surveyed herself and her sister swathed in the cook's voluminous white muslin aprons. "Now perhaps you can have a look around for the baking tins while I start the fire."

Unfortunately, *The Art of Cookery Made Plain and Easy* had no word to say about starting fires, doubtless assuming that even the most inexperienced cook would have a grasp of this basic skill. Melanie was on her knees, struggling vainly with the damper, when Sir William came through the back door into the kitchen.

At the sight of her, he stopped short with a look of surprise. Melanie was annoyed to be caught in such an undignified position, and annoyed, too, at Sir William's reaction. He did not speak, but merely stood there watching as she wrestled with the damper.

"I thought you were helping Charles in the stables," she said, giving the damper a vicious yank.

He nodded. "Aye, but we're in the way of being done there, Miss Hartman. Your brother's taken his grays out for a bit of exercise; but I didna see that he needed help for that, so I came back to the house." For a moment or two he watched Melanie struggle with the damper. At last, clearing his throat, he spoke again in a diffident voice. "Canna I help you with that, Miss Hartman?"

"Oh, no," said Melanie. "At least—yes, if you know anything about ovens, I would appreciate your help very much. I can't seem to get this one lighted."

"Well, I dinna ken that I'm just an expert at it, but I daresay I can puzzle it out," said Sir William, squatting down beside her. "Whisht, you'd best stand back and let me do that, Miss Hartman. You'll get yourself all over coal dust."

Melanie gladly relinquished the damper to him, and in a matter of minutes he had a fire blazing gaily within the grate. "Thank you," said Melanie in real gratitude. "I couldn't seem to get the wretched thing to light. Thank you very much, Sir William."

It was the first time she had called him by his real name and title, having carefully avoided calling him anything at all during the past few days. Sir William accepted her thanks with modest demur and stood up, absently wiping his hands on his breeches.

"Oh, you've got your hands dusty," said Melanie, observing the gesture. "Here, you'd better come into the scullery and wash." She led Sir William into the scullery and ran the pump for him while he washed his hands. While they were thus occupied, Nina came into the scullery carrying a stack of baking tins.

"See, I found them, Mellie! Oh, hullo, Sir William. We are baking cakes, Mellie and I."

"Ah, that's what you're doing, is it?" said Sir William, smiling down at her. "Is it Christmas cakes you're making?"

"No, tea cakes. Lady Colby is coming for tea, you see, and Melanie wanted to have something nice to serve her."

Melanie blushed at this disastrous frankness and stole an embarrassed look at Sir William. His expression was grave, but when he spoke again it was in a noncommittal voice. "Ah, the great lady at the castle," he said. "That will put you lasses on your mettle, I dinna doubt."

"Yes, and we would be nervous enough even without her coming," continued Nina, with the same disastrous frankness. "Mellie and I have never done any baking before, you see."

"Aye, I had rather wondered if that might not be the case," said Sir William. He spoke seriously enough, but there was something almost mischievous in the look he gave Melanie. "Perhaps I could help the twa of you a bit? I dinna set up to be anything great in the pastrycook line, you ken, but when I was a lad I used to lend a hand now and then when my auld nurse was making scones or oatcake. I doubtna I still remember the way of it."

Nina opened her mouth to speak, but Melanie forestalled her. "That's very kind of you, Sir William, but we won't trespass on your good nature as much as that. You've already spent all morning helping Charles with the horses."

"All the more reason I should bide here awhile," he returned, unbuttoning his greatcoat. "It'll serve to warm me up a bit."

"Really, Sir William, you mustn't think of it. It's not at all necessary, upon my word."

"Oh, let him stay, Mellie," objected Nina. "It *is* warmer in here than anywhere else. And if he has helped his nurse make scones and oatcakes, he probably knows more about baking than we do."

Sir William said nothing, but stood with his greatcoat half off, looking at Melanie hopefully. She was unable to withstand the mute appeal in his eyes.

"Oh, very well," she said crossly. He looked so pleased that she relented further and went on in a lighter tone. "But I must warn you, Sir William. If you intend to help us, you must put on one of Cook's aprons like the rest of us. I am head cook today, you know, and it is one of the rules of my kitchen that my assistants be properly attired!"

Sir William submitted to this dictum without a murmur. "Just like Hercules amang the Amazons," he said cheerfully as he knotted an apron about his waist. "What next, Miss Hartman? I'm ready for my orders."

"Well, I don't know." Melanie bent over the recipe book. "You help us wash and pick currants, I suppose. No, I tell you what, Sir William: Nina and I shall pick currants, and you shall beat eggs. It says here you must beat the whites 'near half an hour,' and then the yolks the same. You will be sorry you insisted on helping us," she said, flashing him an uncertain smile. He smiled back reassuringly and seated himself at the kitchen table.

"Och, nay, Miss Hartman, that's child play," he said. "Bring on your eggs and 'let us do or die,' as the poet says!"

The eggs were brought out and at length separated, though this operation in itself proved to be something of a challenge. When at last eight unsullied whites had been successfully separated from their accompanying yolks and contained within a copper bowl, Sir William settled down to beat them with a ferocity that boded well for their speedy transformation. While he was busy doing this, Nina and Melanie labored over the currants.

"Well, now, that wasn't so bad, was it? With two of us working it didn't take so very long," said Nina happily, when this tedious job was finally completed. "Mellie, I've been thinking. Now that the cakes are started, perhaps I could make something else while you and Sir William finish them up. I am quite sure I could make tarts. I've seen Cook do it a hundred times, and it looks very easy."

"Do you think so, Kitten?" Melanie paused in the midst of grating a nutmeg and considered the idea with interest. "It would be lovely to have some nice little tarts to serve along with the cakes. But isn't pastry rather difficult to make?"

"No, there's a receipt in the receipt book for it, and it's really very simple—just butter and flour mixed together. I'm sure I could do it. And there's nothing to making the tarts themselves. Once you've lined the tart tins with pastry, all you do is fill them with preserves and bake them. I expect really it's easier than baking cakes when you come right down to it."

"Very well, Kitten. It won't hurt for you to try, I suppose. And if they do turn out, it will be nice to have tarts as well as cakes on the tea tray."

With this matter decided, the three cooks settled down to work with a will. Sir William finished with the egg whites and moved on to the yolks while Melanie grated spices, measured sugar and flour, and buttered the baking tins. Nina fetched more flour and butter from pantry and larder and began to mix her pastry. She encountered some initial difficulty in rolling it out, but after she had fussed with it for some time, rolling it and rerolling it and working in a quantity of additional flour, she announced jubilantly that it was beginning to hold together very nicely.

The hours passed quickly while they were all so busily employed. Melanie found them remarkably pleasant hours, upon the whole. She was at first rather stiff with Sir William, for she could not forget their last interview together and imagined that he must be remembering it, too. But Sir William gave no sign that this was so. He was altogether such a comfortable companion, laughing and joking and deferring to her instructions with so much mock humility that she could not long maintain the stiffness of her original demeanor.

"Now you must stir in the flour, currants, and spices, Sir William, and then your work will be done. And very nobly done, too," she told him, looking up from the receipt book with a smile. "I expect your arm must be nearly ready to fall off, as much as you've had to use it today. No wonder Mrs. Everett has arms like a blacksmith! I never realized before how much work it was to make cakes."

"Neither did I," said Sir William, surreptitiously flexing his fingers before taking up the whisk once more. "And I dinna mind telling you that the first thing I intend to do when I get back to Scotland is raise my poor cook's salary. Now that I ken firsthand what goes into the business, it's a wonder to me anybody would want to earn their living in such a way. The work itself is bad enough, without which you've got to make sense of a set of instructions that might have been written on purpose to confound a body." Sir William looked darkly at the receipt book, the vagueness of whose directions had cost him and Melanie no small perplexity that morning. "It's worse than the trigonometry problems they used to set us at Cambridge."

Nina, who with her tongue between her teeth was painstakingly filling tarts with apricot preserves, looked up to smile at him. "But in that case it ought not to have given you much difficulty, Sir William," she said. "Melanie tells me you were Senior Wrangler for your year at Cambridge."

"Charles told us," said Melanie quickly. "Told Mama and me, that is, and I happened to mention it to Nina the other day. Indeed, that is a very impressive accomplishment, Sir William."

"Och, nae so impressive as all that, Miss Hartman. The dons had but a poor lot to choose from that year," said Sir William, looking modest. "They were obliged to give it to me, dinna you ken, for want of anybody better."

"Don't believe him, Nina! I am convinced he habitually understates the case—or overstates it, as the case may be. He told me the most unconscionable stories the other day about his Uncle Jock."

" 'Twas gospel, every word," said Sir William solemnly, and went on to regale both girls with several more stories about his miserly uncle. This occupied the time very agreeably while the cake batter was transferred to the tins and put to bake and the last tarts were filled with preserves. So agreeably did the time pass, in fact, that it was not until a strong smell of burning began to fill the kitchen that Melanie remembered her cakes and flew to the oven to rescue them.

"Oh, dear, oh, dear," she said, looking with dismay at the tin of blackened cakes. "Now who would have supposed they would be done so soon? If a 'great cake' takes four hours to bake, you would think small ones would take at least one hour, wouldn't you?"

"I don't think they are really burned," said Nina soothingly. "Just a little dark around the edges."

Sir William took up a fork, prized a cake from the tin, and bit into it experimentally. "Aye, they dinna taste ill," he said, chewing meditatively. "Quite toothsome, in fact. We're braw bakers and no mistake, Miss Hartman." He smiled encouragingly into Melanie's downcast face. "Nay, dinna let it fash you, lass. There must be some way to rescue your bit cakes. Mayhap we could trim them a bit around the edges, just to take off the parts that are over-brown. Or stay, here's another idea. Could we not put an icing on them? That would dress them up finely, I trow."

"That's an excellent idea, Sir William," said Melanie, brightening. "But I'm afraid it will mean more work for your poor arm."

"My arm's quite recovered itself, Miss Hartman," said Sir William gallantly, and undertook to prove it by beating up another lot of egg whites and sugar. While he was busy with this task, Melanie and Nina removed the rest of the cakes from the tins and then put the tarts in the oven. Determined not to let a second disaster of the same kind take place, the two girls hovered nervously over the oven, peeking inside every few minutes while the tarts were baking. This naturally retarded the process a good deal, but in due time they were done and set to cool on a wire rack beside the cakes.

"They look lovely, Kitten," said Melanie, surveying with pleasure the rows of nicely browned tarts. "At least the tarts came out well, even if the cakes didn't."

"They did turn out nicely, didn't they? I made half apricot and half strawberry," said Nina, regarding her work proudly. "I hope Lady Colby will like them."

"Gracious, yes, Lady Colby!" So engrossed had Melanie been in her labors that she had almost forgotten the object toward which they were directed. She looked hastily at the kitchen clock. "Three o'clock. I have just time to ice the cakes, I think, and then I must run and change my dress. Oh, dear, and there's no fire in the drawing room, either. And I really ought to dust, and put some fresh flowers in the vases—"

"I'll make up the fire, if you like," said Sir William, setting down bowl and whisk. "This icing's thick enough to spread now, I trow."

"That's very good of you, Sir William." For the first time in more than two hours, Melanie felt a touch of constraint in addressing him. They had been upon such terms of easy camaraderie throughout the afternoon that she had nearly forgotten the circumstance of his earlier proposal. It came home to her now, however, and with a pang of something like contrition she realized that the object toward which he had been working so cheerfully was nothing more or less than an alliance between her and Lord Colby. As she watched Sir William depart for the drawing room with an armful of kindling, it struck her that he was behaving rather nobly.

The cakes were soon iced, though all Melanie's best efforts with feather and broad board could not give them quite the professional appearance she had hoped for. "But I suppose they will have to do as they are," she said, laying down the feather with a sigh. "I don't dare waste any more time on them. I'll just pick out the bestlooking ones for the tea tray and fill out the rest of the tray with your tarts, Nina."

"I'll do that," said Nina, coming over to assist her. "You go on and change, Mellie. Sir William and I will have everything ready for you when you need it."

Sir William, returning from his errand, corroborated this statement good-naturedly, so that Melanie had no choice but to take off her apron and leave the kitchen. She did so with a distinct feeling of reluctance. The afternoon had been very enjoyable up till now—really surprisingly enjoyable, Melanie discovered, in looking back on it. And though she was of course eager to have her engagement to Lord Colby made official, she was not much looking forward to the interview with his mother which faced her in the immediate future. On the whole, she felt she would rather have stayed in the kitchen.

Ten

It took Melanie longer than she expected to make her toilette. She had to struggle out of her morning dress and into an afternoon one with no maid or Nina to help her with the buttons, and she had also to remove a quantity of flour that had found its way upon her person even in spite of her apron. Her hair, too, proved to be in need of extensive repair, so that it was some minutes after four o'clock when at last she left her bedroom and ran downstairs to the drawing room.

As she went, she rejoiced within herself that on this occasion Lady Colby had been less than punctual. How dreadful it would have been if Lady Colby had arrived exactly at four and sought in vain for admittance because there was no servant to admit her! How even more dreadful if she, Melanie, had been forced to run downstairs in a state of *déshabillé* to perform this menial task! Melanie had kept an ear anxiously cocked while she was dressing in expectation of just such an occurrence.

But there had been no summons while she was in her bedroom. As Melanie went downstairs now, she congratulated herself that she would be able to meet her noble guest with her hair tidily arranged, her complexion free from flour, and her blue sprig muslin afternoon dress in neat and irreproachable order. With luck, she might even have time to give a quick dusting to the drawing room before Lady Colby should arrive. Hastening to that chamber, Melanie flung open the door and found herself confronted by the unexpected sight of Lady Colby, bonneted, mittened, and mantled in lurid purple and seated bolt upright on the sofa.

The vision in purple rose stiffly to its feet at her entrance.

"Good afternoon, Miss Hartman," it said, nodding cordially and extending a couple of fingers for Melanie to shake.

Melanie shook the fingers, but was quite unable to return Lady Colby's greeting. Fortunately, her mother arrived on the scene just at this awkward juncture. Mrs. Hartman was looking a little more flurried than usual, but she still managed to carry off the situation with tolerable aplomb.

"Good afternoon, Lady Colby," she said, curtsying with just the right degree of deference. "It is very good of you to call on us this way." With a touch of anxiety, she added, "I hope you were not kept waiting at the door? I'm afraid that most of our servants are—"

"No, not kept waiting a bit," said Lady Colby, overriding her hostess's explanation with good-humored condescension. "One of your footmen let me in. And *he* didn't keep me waiting, I warrant you. Why, he had the door open for me before ever my man had a chance to knock."

Mrs. Hartman looked bewildered. "One of the footmen?" she repeated. "I hardly see how that is possible, Lady Colby. You must know that all of our footmen are unfortunately—"

"Aye, one of the footmen it was," said Lady Colby, cutting in upon her hostess's second speech with as little compunction as the first. "You know the one I mean, I daresay—a big, dark fellow with a handsome leg. By the by, I notice you've adopted this new-fangled fashion of letting your menservants go without powder since the last time I was here. I still hold with the old ways myself, but there are times when I've been tempted to do the same, I don't mind telling you. Why, I spent upward of fifty pounds on hair powder last year, if you can believe it."

"Indeed," said Mrs. Hartman, looking more bewildered than ever. "I believe a great many people do allow their servants to go without powder in the country." Pulling herself together, she added politely, "Won't you please be seated, Lady Colby? The sofa is the most comfortable place, I think. I'll draw up the fire-screen so you won't feel the heat too much."

While Mrs. Hartman was attending to her guest's comfort,

Melanie seated herself in a straight chair nearby, arranging her skirts neatly around her. Lady Colby's speech about the footman had puzzled her nearly as much as it had her mother, but she had dismissed it without too much thought, supposing vaguely that James or Edward or one of the other footmen had disobeyed the doctor's orders and risen heroically from his sickbed to perform some part of his regular duties. Her thoughts at the moment were chiefly concerned with the tea tray. She was wondering if Nina would remember to fill the milk pitcher and sugar bowl and put napkins on the tray along with the tea service.

Lady Colby, once established on the sofa, came directly to the point of her call. "You know why I'm here, I expect," she said, nodding kindly to Melanie. "To be sure, I was in the way of owing you a call anyway after your party the other night, but I thought I might as well kill two birds with one stone and get this business of Colby's settled at the same time. He is twenty-five, you know, and I've been telling him for the past year or two it's high time he was marrying and setting up his nursery."

She paused here, apparently looking for some word of commendation from Melanie and her mother. "Just so," said Mrs. Hartman, who had regained her usual tranquillity of manner. "Although I don't think it does for young men to be in too great a hurry to settle. Or young women either, for that matter. I am always telling my children that they should—"

"Bless you, ma'am, would you have 'em wait until they're as old as you or I?" Lady Colby let out a cackle of laughter. "Stuff and nonsense! I often tell my sons that the sooner they're married, the better I'll be pleased. Young men must sow their wild oats, of course—I don't dispute that—but as soon as they've reached their majority, it's time they was looking around for a wife." Leaning closer to Mrs. Hartman, Lady Colby addressed her in a confidential tone. "Just between you and me, Mrs. H., I did hope to make a match between Colby and Lady Madeleine Seale, old Rundell's daughter. You know the family, I suppose?"

"Oh, yes," said Mrs. Hartman, a trifle stiffly. "But I have never had the fortune to make Lady Madeleine's acquaintance."

"Forty thousand pounds," said Lady Colby, still in the same confidential voice. "Not a penny less than forty thousand pounds. I had it from Lady Rundell herself. And Lady Madeleine's not a bad-looking gel, either. A bit on the scrawny side, perhaps, and of course she's got that ginger hair, same as her father. But not a bad-looking gel, take it all and all. Colby couldn't abide her, however, and so the whole business went off. I suppose he prefers *fair* hair." Lady Colby accompanied these words with a friendly leer in Melanie's direction.

Melanie blushed and looked down at her feet. Lady Colby apparently adjudged this an appropriately modest response for a young lady to make, for there was an approving note in her voice as she went on.

"When Colby told me he had his eye on Miss Hartman here, I was that surprised, you might have knocked me over with a feather. You won't either of you be offended, I hope, if I say I did think he might have looked higher for a bride? But of course it's not a bad match as such things go, and he talked me round to it in the end. It was your being a Milford that reconciled me to the business," she informed Mrs. Hartman with a condescending air. "That's a connection nobody need blush for, and so I shall tell anyone who asks about it. I daresay there'll be plenty of people who'll raise their eyebrows when they hear Colby's marrying a country miss with no fortune to speak of. Er—as to that, Mrs. H., I suppose Melanie will have at least ten thousand when she marries?"

"I really could not say," said Mrs. Hartman coldly. In spite of Lady Colby's hopes, she had looked notably offended throughout most of this speech, and her voice grew chillier as she continued. "I am afraid I am very stupid about money matters, Lady Colby. If you are concerned about Melanie's marriage portion, you will have to wait and speak to my son Charles. In the meantime, can I offer you some tea?" Not waiting for an answer, she grasped the bell rope and pulled it twice, forgetting in her dudgeon that there was no one to answer the summons.

Melanie rose hastily to her feet. "I'll fetch the tea tray, Mama," she said. "You forget that the servants are—oh!"

This last exclamation was quite involuntary. While she had been speaking, the drawing room door had opened, and Sir William came in, solemnly bearing the tea tray in his hands. He was still in his breeches but had changed his riding boots for shoes and his apron for one of the footmen's livery jackets, which garment was strained to the utmost to contain his brawny figure. His hair was drawn back and neatly tied at the nape of his neck, although, as Lady Colby had observed, he had not gone so far as to powder it. Behind him walked Nina, demure in a maid's cap and apron and carrying the platter of cakes and tarts.

Mrs. Hartman watched spellbound as the two "servants" arranged the tea things on the table in front of her. "Thank you," she managed to say when they were done. In reply, Nina dropped her a curtsy and Sir William bowed. As he turned away, he caught sight of Melanie, and a hint of a smile appeared on his face, which had been perfectly solemn and impassive up till then.

"Can I get you aught else, miss?" he inquired politely.

"Nothing, thank you," said Melanie weakly. He bowed again, and together he and Nina left the room, closing the door behind them. Just before the door swung closed, however, Melanie heard him say something to Nina in a low voice, to which Nina responded with an audible giggle.

Lady Colby had not heard the giggle, but she had watched the ersatz servants' performance with a critical eye. "That's the fellow I was talking about earlier," she told Mrs. Hartman, as soon as the door had closed behind Nina and Sir William. "That footman there, who was serving tea—he was the one who opened the door to me. A fine, strapping fellow, ain't he? Looks to be at least six-foot-three or -four. Got a nice leg on him for a stocking, too. I take it he's a Scotchman from the way he spoke just now?"

Mrs. Hartman opened her mouth and shut it again. It was evident that she was still overcome by the sight of a baronet serving tea in her drawing room. Melanie thought it well to come to her mother's aid. "Yes, he is Scotch, my lady," she told Lady Colby.

"That's what I thought," said Lady Colby, nodding with a self-satisfied air. "I've got a good ear for an accent, though my hearing's not what it used to be. Neither's my eyesight, worse luck. Still, I'm not so blind that I can't tell a good servant when I see one, and I tell you, Miss H., I like the look of that man of yours who was in here a minute ago. He wouldn't be looking for a new situation by any chance, would he? I wouldn't mind having such a fellow as that up at the castle—him, and a couple more like him. Has he got any brothers, do you know?"

"I'm afraid not," said Melanie, in a not quite steady voice. "And I am certain he has no desire to change his situation."

Lady Colby shook her head sadly. "Pity," she said. "It'd be something to have a couple of fellows like that sitting up behind your carriage. If he ever wants to change his place, you tell him to come on up to the castle, and I'll give him a trial. I wouldn't mind having your maid there, either. Pretty little thing, ain't she? Seems to know her business pretty well, too. But of course *she* would never do at the castle."

Lady Colby lowered her voice to a discreet murmur. "With John and Colby in the house, you know—well! I find it serves best to hire plain maidservants, if you understand my meaning. The last girl I hired was positively pudding-faced, I vow and declare. And even then Colby—but of course, young men will be young men, and I don't doubt she was no better than she should have been from the beginning."

Neither Melanie nor her mother made any response to this statement. After a moment's pause, Lady Colby went on, a bit defensively. "Mind you, I don't think that Colby's a bit worse than most young men—no, nor John, either, if it comes to that. Once they're married, I have no doubt the two of them'll settle down nicely. But with Colby being the elder and having the title and estate to think of, I'm anxious that he shouldn't waste any more time about the business. I told him just a few months ago that if he married within the year, I'd put him in full control of his inheritance instead of making him wait until he was thirty."

Here Mrs. Hartman found her voice, if only to avert another vulgar discussion of money. "May I offer you a cup of tea, Lady Colby?" she asked.

"Yes, thank you, Mrs. H. Just sugar, if you please: no milk."

"Do have a cake, too," said Melanie, anxious that her work should not go unappreciated. "They taste better than they look, I assure you."

Even in spite of this assurance, Lady Colby was resolute in declining the cakes. "I'll have one of these, I think," she said, regarding the tarts with a greedy eye. Having selected a particularly fine strawberry-filled one, she raised it to her lips and bit into it. A peculiar expression overspread her face. Melanie saw that she seemed to be experiencing difficulties of some sort. Alarmed, she took a tart of her own and bit into it, whereupon the source of Lady Colby's difficulties immediately became clear to her. Nina's pastry, although tempting to the eye, proved quite impervious to the tooth, and after a prolonged struggle the only thing Melanie got for her trouble was a mouthful of apricot preserves.

Lady Colby, having likewise struggled in vain, set down her tart and teacup with extreme precision and rose to her feet. "Dear me, look at the time," she said. Both Mrs. Hartman and Melanie looked obediently at the drawing room clock and saw that its hands stood at a quarter of twelve, through the circumstance of its not having been wound that morning. Neither of them said anything, however, and Lady Colby went on, squinting nearsightedly at the timepiece. "I really must be going now. Thank you very much for the tea, Mrs. H. And I'm very glad to have had this chance to talk to you, my dear," she continued, shifting her gaze to Melanie. "You're a pretty girl with very pretty manners, and I don't doubt you'll do very well at the castle. Colby and I'll expect to see you there for our New Year's Eve party next week. Perhaps by then we'll have an announcement to make, hey?" She gave Melanie a nudge in the ribs and a knowing smile.

Melanie managed a weak smile in return and dropped a polite curtsy. Lady Colby acknowledged it with a nod, then started for the door. Midway there, she paused to address Mrs. Hartman.

"Just a word of advice, Mrs. H.," she said. "If I were you, I would sack that cook of yours. I daresay she has her points, but pastry making ain't one of them." Nodding portentously, Lady Colby drew her purple robes close around her and sailed out of the drawing room.

Eleven

When Lady Colby had gone, Melanie looked apprehensively at her mother. She expected Mrs. Hartman would have some cogent remark to make about Lady Colby's manners or behavior, but all she said was, "Do you know, Melanie, I rather think that when the footmen are well again, I will tell them they no longer need wear powder. As Lady Colby says, a great many people do dispense with it nowadays, and I'm sure it must be a great nuisance for them to have to wear it, poor things."

"Yes, Mama," said Melanie. In a hesitating voice, she added, "I think I will go down to the kitchen now and see what Nina and Sir William are doing, if you don't need me for anything."

"No, to be sure I do not, my dear. Run along if you like."

In the kitchen, Melanie found her former associates once again elbow deep in culinary endeavors. Sir William had resumed his apron and was vigorously stirring a large pot at one end of the stove while Nina, at the other end, was gingerly prodding the contents of a kettle with a long fork. As Melanie came in, Sir William was admonishing Nina in a stern but friendly voice.

"Nay, lass, you'd best be moving that kettle a bit off the fire. Those poor chuckies'll be tough as boot leather if you boil them as hard as that."

"No, will they?" said Nina with interest. "I thought that the harder I boiled them, the sooner they would be done."

"Aye, but whether they'll be worth eating when they're done's another matter," said Sir William, moving the kettle off the fire for her. Melanie observed that the two of them seemed on very good terms with each other, and a pang of something like jealousy went through her. Damping it down with a ruthless hand, she forced a smile to her face and went over to join them.

"Oh, Mellie, wasn't that a famous joke?" cried Nina, turning to her with a face bright with laughter. "Didn't you just die when William and I came into the drawing room with the tea tray? It was all I could do to keep from laughing at the look on your face. And Mama! She looked as though she couldn't believe her eyes. But I don't think Lady Colby suspected anything, do you?"

"No, not a thing, Kitten. In fact, she was so impressed with Sir—with William here, that she wanted to hire him herself."

Defiantly, Melanie told herself that if her sister could call him William without the "Sir," then so could she. She stole a quick look at him to see his reaction. He was regarding her with an arrested expression, but whether it was caused by her words or the informality of her address, she could not tell. "Yes, indeed, William," she told him, assuming a boldly playful air to mask her trepidation. "If ever you lose your fortune, you are sure of finding employment with Lady Colby. But I'm afraid *you* must not think of applying to her, Nina. She says you are much too pretty to work at the castle!"

"Did she say that?" said Nina delightedly. "Truly, Mellie? Lady Colby said I was pretty?"

"Yes, indeed she did, Kitten. And she says William is a fine, strapping fellow with a good leg." Melanie shot him a quick smile, then went on quickly, conscious that she was blushing. "But I'm afraid Lady Colby didn't have anything good to say about our cooking. She wouldn't even try the cakes, after all our hard work! And I hate to say this, Kitten, but I think there was something wrong with the pastry you made for those tarts. Lady Colby nearly pulled her teeth out trying to take a bite out of one of them."

Nina burst out laughing. "No, did she? Oh, dear! You must be very angry with me, Mellie, but indeed, I didn't know anything

was wrong with them until just a few minutes ago. William tried
to eat one when we got back to the kitchen, and he said it was
like pasteboard with jam on it. But by then, of course, it was too
late to do anything about it."

"I hope it didna spoil your tea party," said Sir William, addressing Melanie for the first time since she had reentered the
kitchen. "That would be a great shame after all your hard work—
Melanie?"

He spoke the name questioningly, almost timidly. "Yes," said
Melanie, smiling and answering his unspoken question rather
than his spoken one. "But you needn't worry, William. The party
went off well enough, thanks to your and Nina's help. Lady Colby
was quite satisfied with her reception, I think."

The mention of Lady Colby struck Melanie as a jarring note
in the conversation. For some reason or other, she felt disinclined
to dwell on the interview that had just taken place between her
and that lady. In an effort to change the subject, she walked over
to the stove and peered into Nina's kettle. "What are you cooking
now?" she asked. "It smells good, Kitten."

"I'm boiling some chickens," said Nina, giving the contents
of her kettle another poke with her fork. "And William is making
water gruel. I let him cook the gruel because it has oatmeal in
it, and being a Scotchman, he would naturally have more of an
acquaintance with oatmeal than I do!" She threw Sir William a
laughing look.

Melanie gave him a look, too, but it was a look of surprised
approval. "Boiled chicken and water gruel," she repeated. "But
that is invalids' food. Are you cooking for the servants, then?"

"Yes, the doctor was just here, and he said they would probably
be ready for some very light, plain food later this evening," explained Nina. "Chicken and water gruel was what he suggested.
Bridget said she would fix it, but you know she has nearly been
run off her legs today, trying to take care of everything else. It
seemed a bit much to make her do all the cooking as well as all
the nursing. So William and I decided we would help her out a
little, seeing that we are now experienced cooks!"

"That was very generous of you," said Melanie in a low voice. She felt suddenly very small and mean. Of course she had offered to help Bridget earlier in the day and had perhaps rendered her some small service by helping her mother and sister dress. But it had never occurred to her to offer Bridget any assistance beyond that. Indeed, she had been within a hairsbreadth of asking Bridget to abandon her nursing and assist her in her own selfish concerns. It seemed to Melanie that the scales had fallen from her eyes and she saw herself as she really was: thoughtless, self-absorbed, and sadly lacking in Christian charity.

With a sense of mortification, Melanie looked at Sir William. She felt he, too, must see and be repelled by this new vision of herself. He was looking at her searchingly, but there was no disgust in his eyes. It seemed rather as though he were trying to make up his mind about something. At last he cleared his throat and spoke, with a diffident air. "Your sister and I have been doing our poor best, I ken," he said. "But we sairly miss our head cook. You dinna care to take the job on once more, do you, Melanie?"

"There is nothing I would like more," said Melanie fervently. Taking up her discarded apron, she began to tie it round her waist once more. In a humble voice, she added, "But I think I should resign the job of head cook to you, William. You seemed to be doing very well at it when I came in just now. Tell me what I can do to help, and I will do it."

The next hour passed as quickly and enjoyably as the hours that had preceded Lady Colby's call. While Nina arranged trays with bowls and cutlery, Melanie and Sir William strained gruel, minced chicken, and argued amicably about whether milk or barley water was the most soothing beverage for an upset stomach. They had just compromised on milk, slightly warmed, when Charles came into the kitchen.

"What the deuce?" he said, looking with astonishment from his sisters to Sir William.

"We are cooking," explained Nina. "William is helping us."

"I can see that," said Charles, surveying his friend's costume with a grin. "Hi, Will, looks like they was one too many for you, old man. Got you properly pressed into service, didn't they? You ought to have come out driving with me while you had the chance!"

"Indeed, we are very glad he did *not* go with you, Charles," said Nina sternly. "William has been a real help to us today. You can't think how hard we have all been working. But we have been having fun, too. Oh, Charles, you will never guess what we did! Lady Colby came to tea, and William and I dressed up as servants and served it to her and Mama and Mellie! And Mellie said Lady Colby was so impressed, she wanted to hire William away from us and would have hired me, too, only she said I was too pretty to work at the castle. Didn't she say so, Mellie?"

"By Jove, you don't mean it," said Charles, with a shout of laughter. "What a lark! I wish I'd been there to see it. But there, it's a good enough joke just seeing you in an apron, Will, old man. If the fellows back at school could see you now!"

Sir William refused to be embarrassed by his apron, however. Assuming a lofty air, he pointed out that the best-known and most celebrated cooks throughout history had invariably been male, and that an apron in this context was an honorable badge of office. "Aye, and that gives me a braw idea. If ever my fortunes should fail me, I'll just swap my Scotch accent for a French one and hire myself out as one of your fancy chefs for four or five hundred a year."

With such raillery as this, Charles was gradually drawn into their circle. He did not do much in the way of cooking, it was true, or indeed of any actual work, but he added greatly to the atmosphere of fun and frolic. And when at last the frugal repast was ready to be served to the invalid servants, it was Charles who suggested that they themselves do the serving rather than leaving it to Bridget.

"We can do as you did with old Lady Colby and dress up like servants to deliver it, don't you know," said Charles, on whom the story of Nina and Sir William's exploit had clearly made a great impression. "I'll be a coachman, I think. I can wear my own greatcoat, and I know where John keeps his hat and wig.

And Will and Nina can be a maid and a footman like they was before—and Mellie can be a cook or a housekeeper or some such thing."

Everybody entered into this scheme with enthusiasm, and there was a mad scramble for mobcaps and livery jackets. When at last they were all costumed and ready to start on their rounds, however, Nina developed an attack of last-minute qualms.

"Don't you think perhaps the servants will think we are making fun of them if we go to them like this, Charles?" she asked, looking down at her apron. "I would not like to hurt their feelings."

"Dash it all, who wants to hurt their feelings? I expect they'll think it a very good joke," said Charles indignantly.

Nina's conscience could not be so easily satisfied, however. She was still arguing the matter with her brother when Bridget, worn and weary-looking, came into the kitchen carrying a stack of basins. She took one look at the four of them and burst out laughing so heartily that Charles declared himself vindicated.

"There, you see, Kitten? Bridget thinks it's funny, and so will the rest of 'em, I daresay. They could probably use a laugh after spending the day sick in bed."

Bridget endorsed this proposition so whole-heartedly that Nina had no further objection to make, and together the four of them set off to deliver the servants' suppers. Charles was a coachman with a wig and striped waistcoat, Sir William was a footman and Nina a maid, as before, and Melanie was a cook with a be-ribboned mobcap and a wooden spoon tucked into her apron pocket to show her calling.

"We might as well give 'em their Christmas presents at the same time," said Charles, whose natural high spirits seemed to be soaring higher by the minute. "I almost forgot about its being Christmas, what with all the trouble and all. There's gloves for the men, handkerchiefs for the women, and half crowns for everybody, man and woman alike."

It was Charles, too, who had the idea of singing while they delivered the gifts. He had a fine tenor voice of which he was rather proud, and as they approached the servants' wing, he spontaneously burst into song.

"God rest ye merry gentlemen, let nothing you dismay," caroled Charles gaily, throwing open the door of the first servants' room. Nina and Melanie immediately joined in, and after a momentary hesitation Sir William took up the chorus with a deep bass growl. From room to room they went, singing Christmas carols and distributing Christmas gifts and trays of food to the invalid servants, all of whom were now well enough to appreciate the spectacle they presented.

"Lud, sir, you didn't ought to have," protested Mrs. Everett the cook, chuckling weakly nonetheless. "I never heard of such a thing being done, not in all my born days." In the footmen's rooms they were received with roars of laughter, in the maidservants' by blushes and giggles, and Mrs. Lowry the housekeeper blessed herself countless times and said she didn't know when she'd been so diverted. Even Abbott the butler, who had been among the worst sufferers and who was in any case a high stickler for propriety, could not keep from smiling.

"But indeed, it's not at all fitting that you should come here, Master Charles," he said, reverting to this childhood form of address in an effort to daunt his master's exuberance. "And in such a dress, too! I don't know what your father would have said about it all."

"Father would have laughed and said it was just the sort of rig he would have run in his own youth," responded Charles, pressing a pair of gloves and a half crown into the butler's hand and depositing a tray on his bedside table. "Merry Christmas, Abbott, old man. I hope by tomorrow you'll be feeling more the thing."

The doctor came in just as they were finishing their rounds of the servants' rooms. "What's this, what's this?" he exclaimed, looking around at them with a smile. "Ah, I see you've been getting up a masque in honor of the day!"

"Something like that," admitted Charles with a grin. "We've been giving the servants their supper."

"Have you indeed? But that's another good old Christmas custom, you know. Indeed, I ought rather to say that it is a custom a good deal *older* than Christmas." The doctor beamed and rocked back and forth on his heels as he expounded on this statement. "Although we are most likely to think of the custom in connection with such medieval institutions as the Boy Bishop and Feast of Fools, it is in fact of much more ancient derivation. As far back as Roman times, it has been traditional at this time of year to reverse the natural order between inferior and superior, or servant and master. So you young people may congratulate yourselves on keeping up a custom some thousands of years old!"

The last person on whom the four choristers paid a call that evening was Mrs. Hartman. After seeing the doctor off the premises, they went back to the kitchen and filled a tray with cheese, fruit, nuts, and the leftover teacakes. This they carried to the drawing room and burst in upon Mrs. Hartman with their voices upraised in song.

"It's not much of a Christmas dinner, Mama, but it's the best we can do," said Melanie, laughing and presenting the tray to her mother at the end of their impromptu concert. "I hope you don't mind that we didn't dress for the occasion?"

Mrs. Hartman looked around at the four of them and shook her head slowly, more as an expression of disbelief than in answer to Melanie's question. There was a hint of a smile tugging at her lips, however, and when they had recounted to her the story of their evening's activities she actually nodded approval.

"That was very considerate of you, my dears. My own mother used to say that a wise mistress will treat her servants as she would treat honored guests in her home. On this occasion, we may truly say that both guests and servants received exactly equal treatment!"

So it was that the Christmas that had begun so inauspiciously ended up being very merry after all. Everyone ate largely of the makeshift Christmas dinner, and it was agreed that Lady Colby had been foolish in spurning the cakes.

"You don't mean to say you made these, do you, Mellie? Why, they ain't half bad," said Charles, finishing off his fourth cake and reaching for a fifth.

"Thank you, Charles. But you ought really to compliment William. It was he who did most of the work." Melanie looked at Sir William, who was seated beside her on the sofa. He shook his head with a smile.

"Nay, I didna do anything to speak of," he said.

"Oh, but you did, William." Impulsively Melanie laid her hand on his arm. "Indeed, I don't know how we would have managed without you."

Sir William glanced down at the hand on his arm, then lifted his eyes to Melanie's face. His color had risen slightly but when he spoke his voice was as light and self-deprecating as before. "Ah, I daresay you'd have managed," he said, and turned the conversation with a jest about his experiences in livery that afternoon.

Melanie was not satisfied, however. There was a growing determination in her heart as she watched Sir William crack filberts and walnuts for Nina, then turn courteously to assist her mother in peeling an orange. Her determination had hardened into a resolve by the time he and Charles left the drawing room to shut up the stables for the night. Melanie assisted her mother and Nina in carrying the dishes down to the scullery and putting the kitchen in something resembling its usual order. When they were done, however, she did not accompany them upstairs, but lingered below in the hall, waiting.

Presently she heard a door open and shut and the sound of voices in the corridor leading from the kitchen. Charles came into the hall a moment later. He was in his shirtsleeves with his greatcoat slung over one arm and the coachman's wig and cocked hat tucked casually beneath the other.

" 'Night, Will," he called over his shoulder. "See you at eight tomorrow, then."

Melanie shrank back into the shadows so that he would not see her. A minute or two went by, and then Sir William came into the hall. Like Charles, he was in his shirtsleeves, carrying his coat over his arm and a candlestick in his hand.

As he neared the stairs, Melanie came out from her place of concealment. "William," she said timidly, "I wanted to talk to you."

At her voice he started slightly and turned around with a look of surprise. Now he came toward her, an imposing and rather intimidating figure in the shadowy hall. The candle in his hand threw a flickering light over his features, giving them a saturnine cast. Beneath the shadow of his brows his deep-set eyes appeared deeper and darker than ever as he looked down at Melanie.

"Ah, it's you," he said. "I didna ken for a minute but it was some ghoul or ghaistie calling my name."

"Oh, but it's Christmas, remember?" said Melanie, striving without success to sound gay and at her ease. "As Shakespeare says, in that season, 'no spirit dare stir abroad; the nights are wholesome; then no planets strike—' "

" '—no fairy takes, nor witch hath power to charm, so hallow'd and so gracious is that time,' " said Sir William, finishing the quote. "To be sure, I ought to have remembered." He continued to stand, looking down at Melanie.

"I wanted to talk to you," she said again, feeling desperately ill-at-ease. "To thank you, rather. It was quite true, you know, what I said this evening in the drawing room. I don't know how we—how *I* would have managed without you today."

He smiled a little and shook his head. "And what I said was true, too. I dinna know that I did so verra muckle, but what I did was all a pleasure. You needna thank me."

"But I do need to thank you. What I mean is, it was very good of you to help me when I—when you—" Melanie faltered for a moment, then went on resolutely. "What I mean is, I'm afraid I haven't been very deserving of your kindness, William. I've treated you abominably these past few days. And yet you've been so good, so generous . . . so forgiving about it all. I wish there was something I could do to make it up to you."

"Do you?" said Sir William. There was a peculiar expression

on his face. He glanced upward, and Melanie, following his gaze, saw that they were standing beneath the hall chandelier, among whose branches had been entwined a few sprigs of mistletoe. Sir William put down his coat and candlestick upon the stairs and took a step toward Melanie. She realized what he was going to do an instant before he did it, but somehow her mind failed to act in that instant to prevent it. Putting his hands on her shoulders, he bent down and kissed her gently, a mere brushing of his lips on hers. He then lifted his head to regard her searchingly.

Melanie looked back at him, her eyes wide and troubled. He reached out to stroke her cheek with one finger. "Why so tragic, love?" he said softly.

Melanie felt strongly that she ought to object: to the kiss, the caress, and the endearment all three. But she could not find the words to do it while he was looking down at her with so much tenderness.

"William—Sir William—I don't know if Charles has told you, but Lord Colby and I—" she began, but found herself unable to go on. Sir William's eyes, dark and serious, continued to gaze steadily into her own.

"Charles told me something about you and the young laird at the castle," he said, after a moment's silence. "You are betrothed to him, then?"

"No," said Melanie doubtfully. "No, not betrothed to him. Not yet, anyway. . . ."

Sir William smiled. "Then he must look out for himself, I wis," he said, and proceeded to kiss Melanie again with much greater enthusiasm. Again she felt she ought to object, but the fact was that she had no particular desire to. Sir William's arms around her felt very pleasant, and Sir William's lips on hers more pleasant still, and what with one thing and another, she found she lacked the necessary strength of will to extricate herself from his embrace. When at last he released her and she opened her eyes, she felt weak and disoriented, like a swimmer who had just struggled her way up from some unimaginable depth.

"Oh," she said, raising a trembling hand to her lips. "Oh,

William! I can't believe I did that, William. I don't think I ought to have done that. . . ."

Sir William regarded her intently a moment, then smiled a rather twisted smile. "Well, if ever you want to do it again, I'm your lad," he said. "Merry Christmas, my love." Stooping, he pressed a kiss on Melanie's brow, then took up his coat and candlestick once more and started up the stairs.

Twelve

When Melanie got to her room that night, she followed her usual routine of getting out her diary and sitting down at her desk to record the day's events. After painstakingly inscribing the date in her best handwriting, she sat for a long time looking down at the empty page in front of her. At last she wrote tersely, "Christmas Day—servants ill—Lady Colby to tea," put the book away, blew out the candles, and went to bed.

In the days that followed, Melanie found herself in a strange, unsettled state of mind. She was unable to apply herself to any regular activity and drifted from room to room, picking up and discarding books, needlework, and drawing pad. During her driftings she made no effort to avoid Sir William, though if that had been her intention, she could hardly have seen less of him. There were constant hunting and shooting parties in the neighborhood during the week between Christmas and New Year's. Charles, as an enthusiastic sportsman, made it a point to be present at every one of them, and he generally saw to it that his friend was present, too.

In the evening, of course, it was a different matter. Sir William was part of the family circle then and was treated as such by the rest of the Hartman family, who had gathered him to their collective bosom after his heroic service on Christmas Day. Melanie could not treat him so easily and informally as the others, but she was very polite to him. Sir William in return treated her with the same grave courtesy he had used toward her during the previous week. He made no effort to presume upon what had taken place between them in the hall on Christmas night.

Now and then, as they sat at the dinner table or around the fire in the drawing room, Melanie could not help looking at him, wondering if she had dreamed that episode beneath the mistletoe. He generally seemed oblivious to her gaze on these occasions, but once, when they happened to be left alone for a few minutes, he had raised his own eyes and looked at her gravely, as though waiting for some word or sign from her. Melanie could not long endure that steady questioning gaze and looked away, feeling more confused in mind than ever.

Hunting and shooting parties were not the only activities taking place in the neighborhood during this period. Every day brought visits from friends, neighbors, and relatives, and nearly every evening there was a dinner or dancing party at some local home or hostelry. Melanie had always enjoyed these diversions in years past, but this year she was unable to enter into them with her former whole-hearted enjoyment. On one occasion she even went so far as to plead an imaginary indisposition and stay home rather than attend.

This was on the occasion of the Madisons' rout party, an annual event which was one of the most lavish and looked-forward-to parties of the season. Lord Colby was to be there, Melanie knew: he had sent her a bouquet the day of the party, along with a formal note expressing the hope of dancing the first two sets with her. Melanie almost smiled as she read it, for it was clear what had prompted him to take such a precaution. But she did not answer the note. Instead, she sent word to her mother that she had a headache, asked her to make her apologies to Lord Colby and the Madisons, and spent the evening by the fire, contemplating the bouquet on her dressing table. Although her head was not actually aching, Melanie felt its condition was sufficiently disordered to make such an excuse justifiable.

So the days passed, and then at last it was New Year's Eve, the day of the Colbys' grand ball. Another bouquet was dispatched to Melanie from the castle, and with it another note requesting her hand for the first two dances. To this note Melanie returned a brief note of thanks and acceptance before turning her attention to her toilette for the evening.

It had been only a week and a half since she had made her toilette under very similar circumstances, on the evening of her own family's holiday party. Yet how different had been her feelings on that occasion! Then her heart had been all aflutter with a mixture of anxiety, excitement, and anticipation. Now, as the maid arranged Melanie's hair and helped her into her ball dress of pale blue silk, her heart was anxious enough, but it also felt oppressed by an emotion not far removed from dread.

As usual, Nina was an admiring spectator during the dressing process. "My, that's a pretty dress, Mellie," she said, watching as the maid deftly adjusted the lace around Melanie's corsage. "I think I like it even better than your white one. How I wish I was old enough to wear a real ball dress and go with you to the castle tonight. But perhaps it's as well that I'm not. Lady Colby might recognize me!" Nina giggled and lowered her voice to a theatrical whisper. "I wonder if she will recognize Sir William?"

"Probably not," said Melanie, turning away from her sister under pretext of examining her profile in the glass. "I understand she is rather short-sighted."

"Well, thank goodness for that! It would be too embarrassing for poor William if Lady Colby recognized him. But it was a famous joke, wasn't it, him dressing up and waiting on her like that? And then, the way he helped us in the kitchen! He is so good-natured . . . the best-natured gentleman in the world, I think."

"Yes, he is very good-natured," said Melanie shortly. She continued to feign great interest in her profile, but she was aware that Nina was looking at her thoughtfully.

"I don't see why you don't like him, Mellie," was her sister's next remark, spoken in a reproachful voice. "He really is very nice."

"I don't not like him," said Melanie, not very coherently. Turning away from the mirror, she picked up her fan and evening cloak. "I'd better be getting downstairs now," she said, avoiding her sister's eye. "I expect everyone is waiting for me."

"Don't forget your bouquet," said Nina helpfully. Melanie, who was already halfway to the door, came back to the dressing table, snatched up the bouquet, and left the room without a word.

As she had prophesied, the rest of the party was waiting for her downstairs in the drawing room. Like her, they were all in formal dress: Mrs. Hartman in white velvet and diamonds, Charles in a blue topcoat and buff pantaloons, and Sir William in the austere black and white evening clothes he had worn the night of the Hartmans' party.

When Melanie came in, Sir William was standing beside the drawing room window with the curtain drawn back, looking out into the darkness in which a few flakes of snow swirled and danced. He let go of the curtain and turned around quickly as Melanie came into the room. Charles turned, too, and let out an admiring whistle. "By Jove, you look fine as fivepence, Mellie," he said with a grin.

Involuntarily Melanie's eyes went to Sir William, as though to seek confirmation of her brother's words. Sir William nodded gravely. "Aye, she does, Charles," he said. "But I'd say your estimate's a deal too low. Fivepence wouldna begin to cover it."

It was Sir William who escorted Melanie out to the waiting carriage. He did not speak as he helped her up the steps, and Melanie did not speak, either, apart from an almost inaudible "Thank you" when she was seated. When Charles had performed the same office for his mother, he gave the order to the coachman, and the carriage set off for Colby Castle.

The castle lay about five miles from Hartman Hall, along the same lane that led into the village. Every inch of the way was familiar territory to Melanie, but tonight, as she watched landmark after landmark come into view of the coach lamps and then recede into darkness once more, she was seized by a strange feeling of unfamiliarity.

The sensation did not diminish as they neared the castle. The heavy iron gates set in twin obelisks of stone, the long drive with its avenue of over-arching elms, the house itself, stern, gray, and uncompromising as the ice in the ornamental lake that surrounded it: all had for her an air of the alien and inhospitable. It was grand as ever to look at, of course, but when Melanie reflected that she was likely to receive an invitation that evening to make it her permanent home, she could not make the idea seem real to her.

When the carriage reached the castle's imposing front entrance, Sir William helped Melanie from her seat and down the carriage steps. As the two of them followed Charles and Mrs. Hartman up the front steps of the castle, Melanie clutched convulsively at Sir William's arm. It felt strong and dependable and so warm to the touch that she knew her hands must be icy cold. Just outside the door he paused, looking down at her searchingly.

"I would consider it a great honor if you would dance with me this evening. Not the first dance, you ken," he added hastily, seeing the doubt in her eyes. "Any dance you like—in fact, the later, the better. I'd sooner dance with you last than first, Melanie."

"All right," said Melanie. She had no time to say more, for the castle doors had been flung open by a pair of footmen resplendent in gold and crimson livery. An instant later she and Sir William were being ushered into the castle's great hall, where Lady Colby was receiving her guests.

The interior of the castle was no less imposing than its exterior and hardly less grim, although attempts had been made to give it a festive air through the lavish use of flowers and greenery. The hall where the ball was taking place was vast, dark, and bitterly cold in spite of the great oaken log that blazed in its cavernous fireplace. Lady Colby, too, was ablaze, in a figurative sense at least: she wore a full-skirted dress of scarlet brocade, a towering turban of gold tissue, and an impressive set of rubies.

"My dear, I am very glad to see you," she told Melanie, extending the usual two fingers for her to salute. "Missed you the other night at the Madisons'. Sorry to hear you wasn't feeling well. You didn't miss much, at least. It was a vulgar squeeze, as it always is, but Colby was sorry you wasn't there to stand up with him, weren't you, Colby?"

These last words were addressed to her son, who had come up to join them at the door. "To be sure, ma'am," said Lord Colby, gracefully saluting Melanie's hand. To Sir William he tendered a brief nod and dark look, before turning again to Melanie. "Glad you're here, Melanie. The fiddlers are about ready to start, and if we're to lead the dancing, it's time we took our places, what?"

Melanie passively allowed herself to be led onto the dance floor. Sir William made no demur at being left to himself. When Melanie looked back at him, she saw him deep in conversation with Lady Colby. She wondered what he was saying and if Lady Colby suspected under what circumstances she had met him last. On the whole she thought not, for the expression on Lady Colby's face was gracious rather than otherwise. When she summoned the Honorable John to her side a moment later and watched approvingly as he exchanged a stiff handshake with Sir William, Melanie concluded that Sir William had been apologizing for his earlier misdemeanor and had succeeded in placating at least one member of the Colby family.

The dancing began soon after, with Melanie and Lord Colby leading off. Melanie felt as though every eye in the room was fixed upon her and her partner. If this was not quite the case, it was undoubtedly true that the sight of her standing opposite Lord Colby had given rise to a fair amount of speculation among their neighbors. Miss Madison, farther down the set, gave Melanie a nod and a smile replete with significance, while Charles, Miss Madison's partner, merely looked grave. Still farther down the line, Melanie heard someone say to someone else in an avid whisper, "Is it true, then, that he means to offer for her?" To which the someone else replied, "To be sure, my dear. I had it from Sophy Potter, who had it from Jane March, and *she* says that the matter is quite settled."

Lord Colby did not appear conscious of his neighbors' scrutiny. He seemed uncomfortable and ill-at-ease, tugging at the intricately tied cravat at his throat as though it were too tight for him. Several times he complained of the heat, a remarkable circumstance considering that he and Melanie could see their breath in puffs of vapor as they advanced and retreated, bowed and turned.

"I say, I can't take much more of this," he muttered in Melanie's ear at the conclusion of the dance. "Would you mind if we took a turn in the gallery instead of dancing this next set? There's something I need to—that's to say, I wanted to have a word with you in private, don't you know."

Melanie's every nerve sprang to the alert at this speech. She had known such a summons must be coming at some time during the evening, but now that it had come, she felt suddenly unprepared for it. In silence she took Lord Colby's arm and let him lead her out of the hall. As they passed through the doorway, she caught a glimpse of Sir William standing at the far end of the hall, watching her. His expression was even more than usually stern and sober. The recollection of it stayed with Melanie as she accompanied Lord Colby down a drafty passage and through several deserted parlors to the gallery.

The gallery was a long, narrow room, windowed on one side to give a view of the castle courtyard. On the opposite wall, portraits of various dead Colbys stared coldly down at Melanie as though she were an interloper of the worst sort. It seemed a chill room in spite of the fires that burned in the elegant marble fireplaces distributed at intervals down the gallery's length.

Once inside the gallery, Lord Colby turned to Melanie with an air of relief. "That's better," he said, tugging at his neckcloth once more. "Glad to get away from the crowd. So here we are, then, and now I suppose it's time we got down to business. You know why I brought you here, I expect."

Melanie said nothing, but waited for the proposal that she knew must follow. She was astonished to see how nervous Lord Colby seemed about making it. Now that the critical moment had come, she herself felt not nervous at all, but rather icy and detached. Watching Lord Colby finger his neckcloth, it struck her that she had never seen him so utterly deserted by his usual savoir faire.

Her silence seemed to make Lord Colby more nervous than ever. "I suppose you know why I brought you here," he repeated, taking her hand in his and squeezing it awkwardly. "Because of that, don't you know." He nodded toward an engraving of Venice which decorated the wall of the gallery alongside the portraits. "What I mean is, I told you once before I'd like to show you Italy and Venice and all that, and now—well, dash it all, now I'm asking if you'd like me to. Melanie—Miss Hartman—will you do me the honor of becoming my wife?"

Melanie still said nothing but merely looked at him. In an odd way, she felt as though she were only seeing him for the first time. His hair was still as golden and his face as handsome as ever, but it struck her suddenly that it was an essentially humorless face. It was impossible to imagine the owner of such a face ever forgetting his own rank and dignity. Melanie felt sure he would sooner die than don livery to assist in a crisis, or put on an apron and beat egg whites. She had never supposed such things could be criteria for one's future husband, but now, as she considered the matter, she realized they might be as important in their way as a handsome face or the ability to cut a dash in a curricle-and-four.

"Well?" said Lord Colby, a trifle impatiently.

Melanie looked at him in fascination. In the speaking of that syllable something in his demeanor had shifted, so that she had caught a glimpse of a Lord Colby who was neither the nervous gentleman who had just proposed to her, nor yet the urbane one who had courted her, but rather the essential man beneath. It had only been a glimpse, but it had seemed to Melanie that the man beneath bore more than a passing resemblance to the Honorable John.

Could such a thing be possible? She had always stoutly denied there being any resemblance between the brothers, but now, as she studied Lord Colby's handsome face, she was able to trace a faint but unmistakable resemblance. It was about the mouth that it was most noticable, a certain turn of lip that was not so much sensual as selfish.

"Well?" said Lord Colby, sounding almost cross.

In that moment, Melanie was overcome by a feeling of pity for him. He was obviously no more in love with her than she was with him and thus was unlikely to suffer much heartache from the rejection she was about to give him, but his pride undoubtedly would suffer, and suffer profoundly. She divined clearly that for such a man, a blow to his pride would be more painful than any other blow that could befall him.

"I'm sorry," she said softly, looking down at her feet.

It was as well that she did, for had she been looking at Lord Colby's face, his expression might have prompted her to an inappropriate laughter. "I *beg* your pardon?" he said incredulously.

"I'm sorry," said Melanie again, giving him a brief apologetic glance and then looking down at her feet again. "I can't marry you, my lord. You do me great honor by asking me, but I'm afraid I can't."

"You can't marry me," said Lord Colby blankly. "But why not, in God's name? I thought—and you said—and when my mother called on you the other day—well, dash it all! I thought it was all but settled."

Melanie flushed and hung her head lower. "I know, my lord. It must seem as though I've been leading you on all this time. But indeed, that was not the case." Raising her head, she looked earnestly at Lord Colby. "You must believe me, my lord. I only came to a decision about it this evening—and I'm afraid the decision was that I cannot marry you. I don't think we should suit, my lord. I don't think I'm the woman to make you happy, and I'm quite sure you're not the—well, I'm quite sure we shouldn't suit, that's all."

This attempt at tact did not deceive Lord Colby. "You don't think *I* am the man to make *you* happy," he said bitterly. "Very good, ma'am. Very good. And may I ask if—" With an effort, he stopped himself. "Well, never mind. If you won't, you won't, and there's an end of it."

"I'm sorry," said Melanie again, meekly. She watched with sympathy as Lord Colby took a couple of turns up and down the gallery, trying to compose himself.

"Well, never mind," he said at last. "You couldn't help it, I suppose, although I can tell you it puts me in a dashed awkward spot. However, that's neither here nor there. You've given me my answer, and now I suppose there's nothing to do but go on back to the party."

Offering Melanie his arm, he led her back through the parlors and passage in offended silence. When they reached the doors that led into the hall, however, Melanie hung back.

"You go on without me, my lord," she told him. "Given the circumstances, I think it would be better—less embarrassing, you know—if we entered separately."

Lord Colby made no argument to this, but merely bowed and continued on into the hall. Melanie watched his progress a moment, then turned her attention to the crowd of merrymakers on and around the dance floor. She soon found the particular merrymaker she was looking for, although it could not be said that he looked especially merry. Sir William was still standing against the wall where she had last seen him, morosely watching the dancers going through the steps of a country dance. Making her way through the ranks of chaperons that stood on either side of him, Melanie came up and touched him on the sleeve.

"I will collect that dance now, William, if you please," she told him with a smiling curtsy.

He did not return her smile, but gave her his arm and silently accompanied her onto the floor. As they began to go through the figures, he looked down at her gravely. "I suppose—I suppose I am to wish you happy?" he said at last, with an obvious effort.

"Yes," said Melanie, smiling as though entertained by some secret reflection. "Yes, I trust I shall be very happy." But the expression on Sir William's face struck her so painfully that she could not continue the jest. In a serious voice, she continued, "You may certainly wish me happy, William, but not as Lord

Colby's wife. It is a melancholy fact that everything is over between us—everything but friendship, that is. We have decided
we would not suit after all."

"Not suit?" echoed Sir William. There was a dawning light
of hope in his eyes, yet he looked as though he could not bring
himself to believe the truth of Melanie's words. She shook her
head firmly.

"No," she said. "I will tell you the truth, William, for I know
I can trust you not to let it go any further. Lord Colby was good
enough to make me an offer of marriage, and I'll admit I was
tempted to accept it. Why, he even offered to take me to Italy
next month for our wedding trip. But after thinking it over, I find
I would rather go to Scotland than Italy this winter. Is not that a
queer thing?"

A slow smile spread across Sir William's face. "A verra queer
thing," he agreed gravely. "There's no accounting for tastes, however."

The tranquillity of his response surprised Melanie, who had
expected he would show more emotion on hearing her decision.
She looked at him closely and a little worriedly.

"And so your invitation is still open, William?" she asked.
"Perhaps I am being presumptuous to suppose that it is—"

Sir William assured her she was not being presumptuous in a
manner that caused a number of their fellow dancers to turn and
stare at them. "Will, really," protested Melanie, blushing and
laughing at the same time. "If you're going to kiss me, you really
must wait until we're by ourselves. Or at least until there's a
mistletoe bough about to excuse you." In a conspiratorial voice,
she added, "There's a branch just outside the door over there. I
noticed it most particularly coming in."

"Did you now?" was all Sir William said, but his voice held
great promise.

Later that evening, Melanie sat at the desk in her room, writing
in her diary.

"January 1, 2:30 A.M.," she wrote. "Just returned home from the Colbys' ball. Orchestra excellent and supper first-rate; we saw out the old year and saw in the new in prodigious style. One awkward moment early in the evening when I was obliged to turn down an offer of marriage from Lord Colby. Saw him flirting with his cousin Lady Aurelia from London not half an hour later, so I don't think his heart was broken. Danced six dances altogether: one with Lord Colby, one with Jack Chambers, one with Richard Potter, one with Edgar March, and two with Sir William, whom I also kissed under the mistletoe. Promised to visit him later this year in Scotland. A very pleasant evening all told, and a fitting conclusion to this Year of Our Lord 1818. I wonder what the year ahead will hold for us all?"

For a moment, Melanie sat smiling to herself as she considered this question. Finally she picked up her pen and wrote, "Resolved: that in the year ahead, I shall make a thorough study of the language, geography, and customs of Scotland." And having put a period to the sentence and underscored it twice for greater emphasis, she put away pen, ink and diary, blew out the candles, and went to bed.

ZEBRA'S REGENCY ROMANCES DAZZLE AND DELIGHT

A BEGUILING INTRIGUE (4441, $3.99)

by Olivia Sumner

Pretty as a picture Justine Riggs cared nothing for propriety. She dressed as a boy, sat on her horse like a jockey, and pondered the stars like a scientist. But when she tried to best the handsome Quenton Fletcher, Marquess of Devon, by proving that she was the better equestrian, he would try to prove Justine's antics were pure folly. The game he had in mind was seduction—never imagining that he might lose his heart in the process!

AN INCONVENIENT ENGAGEMENT (4442, $3.99)

by Joy Reed

Rebecca Wentworth was furious when she saw her betrothed waltzing with another. So she decides to make him jealous by flirting with the handsomest man at the ball, John Collinwood, Earl of Stanford. The "wicked" nobleman knew exactly what the enticing miss was up to—and he was only too happy to play along. But as Rebecca gazed into his magnificent eyes, her errant fiancé was soon utterly forgotten.

SCANDAL'S LADY (4472, $3.99)

by Mary Kingsley

Cassandra was shocked to learn that the new Earl of Litton was her childhood friend, Nicholas St. John. After years at sea and mixed feelings Nicholas had come home to take the family title. And although Cassandra knew her place as a governess, she could not help the thrill that went through her each time he was near. Nicholas was pleased to find that his old friend Cassandra was his new next door neighbor, but after being near her, he wondered if mere friendship would be enough . . .

HIS LORDSHIP'S REWARD (4473, $3.99)

by Carola Dunn

As the daughter of a seasoned soldier, Fanny Ingram was accustomed to the vagaries of military life and cared not a whit about matters of rank and social standing. So she certainly never foresaw her *tendre* for handsome Viscount Roworth of Kent with whom she was forced to share lodgings, while he carried out his clandestine activities on behalf of the British Army. And though good sense told Roworth to keep his distance, he couldn't stop from taking Fanny in his arms for a kiss that made all hearts equal!

HISTORICAL ROMANCE FROM PINNACLE BOOKS

LOVE'S RAGING TIDE   (381, $4.50)
by Patricia Matthews
Melissa stood on the veranda and looked over the sweeping acres of Great Oaks that had been her family's home for two generations, and her eyes burned with anger and humiliation. Today her home would go beneath the auctioneer's hammer and be lost to her forever. Two men eagerly awaited the auction: Simon Crouse and Luke Devereaux. Both would try to have her, but they would have to contend with the anger and pride of girl turned woman . . .

CASTLE OF DREAMS   (334, $4.50)
by Flora M. Speer
Meredith would never forget the moment she first saw the baron of Afoncaer, with his armor glistening and blue eyes shining honest and true. Though she knew she should hate this Norman intruder, she could only admire the lean strength of his body, the golden hue of his face. And the innocent Welsh maiden realized that she had lost her heart to one she could only call enemy.

LOVE'S DARING DREAM   (372, $4.50)
by Patricia Matthews
Maggie's escape from the poverty of her family's bleak existence gives fire to her dream of happiness in the arms of a true, loving man. But the men she encounters on her tempestuous journey are men of wealth, greed, and lust. To survive in their world she must control her newly awakened desires, as her beautiful body threatens to betray her at every turn.

Available wherever paperbacks are sold, or order direct from the Publisher. Send cover price plus 50¢ per copy for mailing and handling to Penguin USA, P.O. Box 999, c/o Dept. 17109, Bergenfield, NJ 07621. Residents of New York and Tennessee must include sales tax. DO NOT SEND CASH.

About the Author

Joy Reed lives with her family in the Cincinnati area. She is the author of three Zebra regency romances: AN INCONVENIENT ENGAGEMENT, TWELFTH NIGHT and THE SEDUCTION OF LADY CARROLL. Joy's newest regency romance, MIDSUMMER MOON, will be published in February 1997. Joy loves to hear from her readers and you may write to her c/o Zebra Books. Please include a self-addressed stamped envelope if you wish a response.